"So, it was about m(
Southern Cross, th
people off the scent?"

"And to make it easier to get rid of you, said _____ _____ _____ since we can't wait for the mercury to kill you, we'll have to do it the old-fashioned way.'

As he lay on the floor, Jon could feel the outline of O'Brien's small automatic in his pants pocket.

"What's going to be your explanation for killing me?"

"That's just it—we're not the ones who are going to kill you. Dr. Townsend here is going to kill you. The poor man just couldn't take the resentment that built up over thirty years. He drove all the way up here to give you a personal New Year's greeting. First, he killed the guard at the main gate—"

God in heaven, thought Jon.

"—and then he caved in Agent Lewis' face on his way up to get you."

"Nobody's going to believe that."

"When all three of us say the same thing?" Doria continued. "That when we went out for a walk, we saw Townsend shoot the cabin guard? That poor Agent Saunders rushed back a fraction late to save you? Come on, they'll believe it just fine."

Jon needed an opening. Lying there, beneath a man holding a submachine gun, he knew he didn't stand a chance. But since they planned to kill him anyway, he was going to seize the slightest opportunity.

"I had no idea how much you hated my guts, Tony."

"I don't hate you, Mr. President. I hate what you're doing to this country. Your stupid softness on abortion. Your bullshit economic globalization. Your troops in the Middle East, gimme a break. The country deserves better."

"Put down the gun, Mr. Saunders!"

Out of the corner of his eye, Jon saw a blur of movement...

THE PRESIDENT'S DOCTOR

BY DAVID SHOBIN

2005

PROLOGUE

Baltimore, Maryland
October, 2005, 5:30 P.M.

The frigid late-October rain sprayed sideways in torrential, wind-driven sheets that flayed everything they struck. It was a hard, dirty rain that carried the city's airborne filth in opaque gray droplets. Drumming fiercely on the car's metal frame, the downpour caused a roaring din that made hearing difficult. The men inside had to shout, which emphasized their decidedly Southern accents.

"That him?" said one.

The man sitting beside him, wearing a dark ski jacket and a black baseball cap, held up binoculars that aimed through the rain-streaked windshield. "Sure looks like him."

"Don't look like shit to me. Yes or no."

"Yeah, that's him."

"Then let's go." He put the rental van into gear and slowly drove beside the curb.

The time change from Daylight Savings to Eastern Standard Time had occurred two days before, and it was already dark. The van's headlamps created twin cones of ivory light in which the driving raindrops were incandescent jewels. The vehicle had been parked on North Caroline Street, facing uptown. Thirty yards away, Dr. Jeremy Raskin turned on foot from McElderry onto North Caroline, heading for the parking garage. He'd just finished work at the Outpatient Center of what was now known as the Johns Hopkins Medical Institutions.

Forty-year-old Dr. Raskin, an obstetrician-gynecologist,

was a specialist in the Institution's Division of Reproductive Endocrinology and Infertility. A champion of women's issues and reproductive rights, he was a maverick infertility expert who also performed abortions. His outspoken persona gained him national prominence. He was also a brilliant, if controversial, researcher, a pioneer in stem cell research who also supported human cloning. His viewpoints often differed from Hopkins' stated policy. Recently, Dr. Raskin had improved on groundbreaking Israeli experiments by successfully growing mature cardiac tissue out of human fetal stem cells. This contentious research earned him both praise and infamy.

Head down, Raskin scurried toward the garage, protecting himself from the intense rain. No other passersby braved the storm. Hatless, he clutched the collar of his winter coat with one hand. Looking down at the pavement, he was so intent on his footwork that he didn't spot the approaching vehicle. The van stopped just before him and both passengers jumped out. They moved swiftly, oblivious to the biting rain. While the driver jogged curbside and opened the van's side cargo doors, the other man leapt in front of the physician. He was holding a sturdy leather sap crammed with BB-size lead shot.

"Dr. Raskin?" he called.

Already drenched, Raskin barely looked up. But the confirmatory glance was enough for the man to verify the doctor's identity. Without uttering another word, the man ferociously swung the sap toward Raskin's head. The heavy instrument made a sickening wet smack as it struck the doctor at the base of his forehead, just above the nose. Raskin's legs gave way, and he collapsed in a heap.

"Get his legs," said the attacker.

As the driver grabbed the legs, the other man pocketed the sap and lifted the unconscious researcher under the armpits. The rain pelted them mercilessly. Together, grunting as they worked, the men dragged the doctor inside the van.

"This is one fuckin' fat Jewboy," the driver grumbled.

Tossing Raskin's limp body onto the metal floor, they quickly slammed the van's doors. Blood streamed down the physician's face. The men were in a hurry now. Jumping into his seat, the driver gunned the engine and they sped away, up North Caroline to East Madison, then across town, past the Inner Harbor. Skirting Camden Yards, they took I-395 to I-95, following the signs for the Baltimore Washington International Airport. The rain turned to sleet. In the glowing swath of the van's headlights, the beads of frozen rain resembled iridescent buttons.

Despite the rush hour, traffic was sparse and had been slowed by the inclement weather. Nevertheless, they moved at a steady pace, making desultory conversation as they drove. The van had a window between the passenger compartment and the cargo bay. From time to time the men would peer into the back, checking on their captive. Raskin remained unconscious. The sap had broken his nose, and clotted blood congealed around his nose and upper lip. At length, the van left the highway and entered the airport complex.

BWI was a growing airport in the midst of an expansion. The shell of a ninth cargo terminal had been erected, though its interior remained unfinished. Owing to the day-long storm that had diverted most flights, ground traffic was light. The van wound its way along the surface roads toward the cargo complex. Eventually it reached the uncompleted cargo building, where it backed up to a service ramp. Despite the rain, the air had the unmistakable kerosene smell of aircraft fuel. In the background, an occasional whine of jet engines rose and fell. The van's driver honked the horn three quick times. In the new building, a retractable metal door began to rise.

A workman emerged, shielded by an overhang. With no letup in the storm, sleet and rain continued to hammer the van. Seeing what they wanted, the two passengers jumped out and ran up the ramp's steps, where they were approached by the man in coveralls.

"What the hell took so long?" he asked.

"In case you ain't noticed," said the driver, "this weather's for shit."

"The hell with that. You got our boy?"

"We got him, all right," said the second man, opening the van's doors. "Give us a hand, huh? He's a fat fuck."

Working together, the trio entered the van, lifting Raskin by his soaked clothing and carrying him into the terminal. The vacant building was huge, smelling of fresh concrete and paint and damp timber. It was cold and largely unlit, save for one spotlight that shined down from above. In the center of its beam, roughly in the middle of the terminal, was a Hawker 700, an eight-passenger corporate aircraft. The men deposited Raskin beside the jet's nose wheel, propping him up in a sitting position against the strut. Working with rehearsed smoothness, one of them readied a Polaroid camera while another placed a newspaper in the doctor's lap. It was that day's copy of *The Sun*, Baltimore's leading newspaper.

The photographer snapped the picture. He wore latex surgical gloves to prevent fingerprints. Carefully removing the print, he showed it to the others.

"Pretty, huh? That could win me a Pulitzer Prize."

"I don't care about no prizes," said the driver. "Long as they print it. Now let's take care of this tub of shit."

They dragged Raskin over to the port wing, where the photographer steadied him while the first two climbed atop the wing. Pushing from below and lifting from above, the trio hauled the physician up with the gentleness of butchers moving a beef carcass. It was an effort, but they finally laid him on his back, beside the fuselage. Although Raskin was still unconscious, they took the precaution of binding his legs and cuffing his hands behind him.

A wide piece of tubing lay on the aft portion of the wing. The transparent polypropylene conduit was eighteen inches in diameter. It extended back to the cowling of the port engine, which was situated just behind the wing. The words "Abortionist Special" were hand-painted on the tubing in large block letters. The men on the wing swung Raskin's bound feet into the tube's opening. Meanwhile, at the wing tip, the man in coveralls looked through a video camera's viewfinder, composing a shot.

"How's it look?" called one of the men on the wing.

"Damn good, yes sir. Ready when you are. Make sure you stay outa the shot."

The driver nodded and turned toward the second man. "Start 'er up."

The Hawker's open cabin door was just in front of the wing. The second man walked to the wing's forward edge and, steadying himself, swung his left leg over into the aircraft entrance. Closing the door and entering the cockpit, he sat down and worked several switches. Seconds later, the Garrett TFE jet engine started up with a distinctive whine. Due to the jet's increasing roar, hearing was now impossible. The two men outside donned ear protectors. Looking out of his window, the pilot gave a thumbs-up to the driver, who nodded back. Then the driver looked at the cameraman at the wing tip.

Arching his eyebrows, the driver mimed the word, "Okay?" Satisfied with his camera image, the man in coveralls gave a return thumbs-up. On the wing, the driver reached into his pocket and removed an ampoule of smelling salts. Crushing it between his fingertips, he held it to the unconscious man's nose. The volatile spirits of ammonia wafted into the doctor's nasal passages. With a forceful blink and a cough, Raskin jolted into wakefulness.

He had no idea where he was. Parts of his body were in intense pain. There was a steady, merciless ache inside his head, his upper nose was swollen and clogged, and his ears were filled with a shrieking whine that grew by the second. When he tried to move his hands, he found that they were wedged behind his back, painfully joined together. His head was being buffeted by howling wind that raced down his body. Craning his neck, looking toward his feet, he saw that his wet shoes had been placed inside a transparent tube that was slightly wider than his body.

Suddenly identifying the origin of the roar, Raskin's eyes went wide. There, not more than six feet away, was the intake of a jet engine. Its whirling blades were unmistakable. As the now-shrieking wind began pulling at his torso, he gaped in fearful disbelief. He tried to jackknife his legs out of the tube, but there was a rope around his ankles, and the suction was too great. Heart pounding wildly, Raskin thrashed madly from side to side, desperate to escape the force that was steadily pulling him into the tube. Looking frantically to his right, he spotted two men at the wing tip.

"Please!" he screamed, his voice indistinguishable over the roar. "Help me!"

One of the men was holding a camera. The other, who was grinning, waved a hand in sadistic goodbye. Then the smiling man looked toward the cockpit, raised his hand, and made circles in the air. The already deafening noise increased, along with the deadly pull. All at once, Dr. Raskin understood.

"No!" he pleaded. "You can't do this!"

But they could. With the camera rolling, the man inside the cockpit advanced the throttle. As the monstrous suction strengthened its tug, Raskin's body was drawn steadily, inexorably into the tube—slowly, at first, but then with mounting speed, until his terrified shrieks were obliterated by the machine that consumed him.

CHAPTER 1

Washington, D.C.

"Noted Researcher Presumed Murdered," read the title of the page one article in The Washington Post.

"Shortly prior to our publication deadline," the article began, "a videotape was anonymously delivered to this news organization. The tape reveals the apparent murder of Dr. Jeremy Raskin, a Baltimore-based physician, women's rights advocate, and stem cell researcher at the Johns Hopkins Medical Institutions. Sources verify the tape as authentic. In a handwritten note that accompanied the videotape, the words 'Abortionists Must Die' were printed above the signature, 'The Southern Cross.' A Polaroid print allegedly showing the victim holding yesterday's The Sun was also enclosed.

"As we went to press, the Baltimore City Police confirm that Dr. Raskin cannot be located and is presumed missing. Raskin, a forty-year-old obstetrician-gynecologist, came to prominence last March with the successful growth of adult cardiac cells from fetal stem cells. Locally, he has been a vocal abortion rights advocate.

"Neither The Washington Post nor the combined news media are familiar with an individual or group that calls itself The Southern Cross. The videotape and photograph have been turned over to the FBI for evaluation."

The White House

"Jesus, turn that thing off," insisted the chief of staff.

"Mr. President?" asked the Secret Service agent at the VCR's controls.

"That's enough," said President Meredith. "I think we get the point."

They met in the White House Situation Room, shortly after the president's daily briefing. The Situation Room, the executive branch's twenty-four-hour watch and alert center, was intended to provide intelligence and information that could assist in the implementation of national security policy. Occasionally, however, the underground room—also known as WHSR, or the "Sit Room"—was used for urgent domestic matters. That was the circumstance today, after the *Post* forwarded the videotape to the FBI early that morning. In addition to the chief of staff, who doubled as the president's national security advisor, also in attendance were the Deputy Director of the FBI, the Attorney General, the chief of security of BWI, and the CIA's Director of Counterintelligence.

The president rubbed his chin. "This has been verified as authentic?"

"Yes, sir," said the FBI man. "No question about it. Our lab is trying to get some evidence off the tape and the print, but they look clean. There are traces of talc, which suggests the photographer used latex gloves. Certainly not an amateur."

"What about the doctor?"

"As of an hour ago, Dr. Raskin was still missing. There's also a preliminary match on the victim's blood remains with the Hopkins database. All employee health data is on file."

"No DNA yet?" the president asked.

"Too early for that, sir. That'll take days, maybe a week."

The president looked across the table. "What happened at the airport, Chief?" he asked the security man.

"It was pretty ugly, Mr. President. We're expanding our cargo facilities, and it happened in one of the new, unoccupied buildings."

"I can deal with ugly, Chief. God knows I saw my share of it in Vietnam. I just want to know how something like this could occur in a busy major airport. When did it happen?"

"Early evening, probably. I don't mean to make excuses, but the building's still under construction. The workmen left at four. The building's locked, or it's supposed to be, until a security team comes by at midnight. When they got there, the lock was broken, and the aircraft was inside."

"Whose plane is it?"

"It belongs to Mid-Atlantic Aviation, a charter company in Delaware. They reported it stolen two weeks ago. There's no record of it flying into BWI. We figure it must have been trucked in today and put in the building after the workmen left."

Meredith looked dubious. "And nobody saw it?"

"There's a lot of unregulated ground traffic, sir. We also had a pretty strong storm."

"So, this plane just shows up, gets put in an empty building, and is used to chop someone into hamburger?"

The security man lowered his chin sheepishly. "Looks that way, sir."

Shaking his head, the president looked at the Deputy Director of the FBI. "What about this Southern Cross outfit? What's their background?"

"They're a new group to us, Mr. President. But they're obviously not crackpot novices. An operation like this took a lot of planning. From the anti-abortion rhetoric and the word Cross in their name, we presume they're a conservative religious organization. Or the activist arm of a very deadly one."

"No relationship to Islamic terrorists or international groups?"

"None that we can see."

"A new hate group, then?"

"Maybe. The Anti-Defamation League monitors these groups closely, but they haven't heard of them either."

"What about the Southern part?" asked Meredith, himself a Southerner.

"Too soon to talk geopolitics, Mr. President. It might mean something, or it could be a feint. We're looking at all angles, but we just don't know yet."

Meredith eyed the Attorney General. "Is there anything I should know on the abortion front? I haven't heard of any clinic problems. I thought it was pretty quiet."

"It is," the AG agreed. "Abortion-related violence is at its lowest level in years. Part of that's because abortions are way down. We have no indication this is part of a new trend. Not yet, anyway."

"Seems to be a hell of a lot we don't know," the president said, slowly filling his pipe and deliberately tamping down the tobacco. "What about Raskin himself? Isn't he a stem cell expert?"

"Yes, sir. Dr. Raskin is—or was—someone who did abortions, but he was also a well-known cell biologist. He did a lot of his work with private funding, which let him get around Federal guidelines. He was outspoken and very controversial. That may have made him a target."

"Something certainly did. I may not agree with his line of work, but no one deserves to get chopped up like that."

"The tubing, the jet engine," the chief of staff observed. "That's supposed to represent an abortion machine, right? Jesus, talk about making a statement. The ultimate eye-for-an-eye-message. Keep aborting pregnancies, and we'll abort you."

"Thank you for that insight," said the president. He sighed wearily. "I can't say I like hearing how depressingly little we sometimes know. One thing is sure. With CNN already onto the *Post* story, the whole country will get wind of it by noon."

"A very important consideration," agreed the chief of staff. "You can't have your fellow citizens thinking they can knock off whoever they disagree with."

"What do you suggest?"

"Beat 'em to the punch, Mr. President. Preempt the media."

Press conferences could be arranged at a moment's notice, but the eleven-a.m. appearance by the president surprised even veteran White House correspondents. As the reporters hurriedly took their seats, Meredith stepped up to the podium that bore the Presidential Seal.

"By now," he began, reading from prepared remarks, "many of you have heard of the tragic death of Dr. Jeremy Raskin last night. Dr. Raskin was a dedicated researcher and physician whose life was brutally ended by enemies of tolerance and dissent. He leaves behind a widow, two children, many grateful patients, and a country dedicated to stamping out mindless violence."

The journalists took hurried notes, wondering where the president was headed. Meredith was a skilled orator whose words were easy on the ear. It was unusual, however, for him to give an unscheduled press conference, except in cases of dire national emergency. For something akin to a eulogy, why not let a staff member handle it? They wondered about the intent of his remarks.

"This administration's policies differed from the views espoused by Dr. Raskin. While he favored abortion on demand, we consider it an option only in dire circumstances; and while he did pioneering work with fetal stem cells, we favor research on embryonic stem cells only. But whatever our differences, there can be no discounting the dedication Dr. Raskin gave to his patients. For that reason alone, we mourn his death. But beyond the loss of a skilled caregiver, there is the larger question of why certain extremists feel that radical means are the only avenue of legitimate dissent. We cannot, and will not, let that view prevail. As Americans, we cherish our differences, not try to limit them.

"Federal, state, and local law enforcement agencies are working together to solve this cowardly crime. We will spare no effort to bring the perpetrators to justice. Freedom of speech and expression are among our most cherished principles. In our country no man may abridge the freedom of another, nor succeed by force in imposing his will. Those who try will learn that justice can be both swift and harsh." Ending the brief address, the president folded his remarks.

"Mr. President," shouted one of the journalists, "are you saying that Dr. Raskin was murdered because of political views in the areas you mentioned?"

"It seems that way to us. Out of respect to the family, we've asked that copies of the *Post* videotape not be made public. But those of us who have seen the tape are convinced it was intended to make a statement."

"A follow-up, sir, if I could. Do you think this signals a

return of abortion-related violence?"

"First of all," said the president, "I've been informed that events like this are at an all-time low, and we don't think it's the start of a pattern. Second, Dr. Raskin was a champion of many causes, some of them controversial. He was outspoken about his views. In addition to abortion, he was a supporter of fetal stem cell research and human cloning. At this point, we're not sure which issue his killers may have been reacting to." He pointed at another reporter.

"What about the group that claims responsibility, Mr. President? The Southern Cross?"

"We're looking into that. It's not an organization that the FBI or domestic counter-terrorism experts are familiar with. We're asking anyone who can provide information to contact their local police department or the toll-free number we've established."

"Sir," said another correspondent, "aren't you concerned that your remarks might alienate your core constituency? After all, most of the people who supported you didn't share Dr. Raskin's views."

Meredith's gaze drifted across the pressroom, and for several seconds he seemed to stare blankly at the wall.

"Sir?" prompted the questioner.

"Sorry. Mind was elsewhere. Could you repeat that, please?"

"I asked if you were worried about offending party conservatives with your remarks about abortion and fetal research."

"No, John, I'm not. My views remain the same and haven't changed one bit. But this is not an issue that people of conscience should keep quiet about. When an innocent man is sacrificed because of his beliefs, a serious injustice is committed. It doesn't matter that his views may have differed from mine. If voters disagree with what Dr. Raskin stood for, the place to make their feelings known is at the ballot box. We are a nation of laws. I am here today to emphasize that this administration will pursue those laws with vigor. If some of my supporters differ with me on this, so be it. Reasonable men may disagree on important issues, but in the end, justice will prevail." Waving to the reporters, he walked from the podium, ignoring the continued chorus of questions.

"Core constituency," said Smith, slowly elongating each syllable. "That supposed to be us? Sumbitch don't have much gratitude, does he?"

"What happened to dancin' with the girl that brung ya'?" said the second man. "Seems to me the man has himself a memory problem, right, Sean?"

The man called Sean concentrated on the ash of his lit cigarette. He rolled the Marlboro between his nicotine-stained fingers, staring thoughtfully at the wisp of smoke that curled from its tip. "He's a politician, C.J." Placing the filter in his lips, he took a deep drag. "That means he's a professional liar. Memory and gratitude have nothing to do with it. It doesn't matter what platform the man ran on. You've heard of politically correct? He'll say whatever the money and the polls tell him to say."

They were drinking been at a corner table of the Dew Drop Inn, a claustrophobically small tavern on the outskirts of Lynchburg, Virginia. Finishing their previous night's work at the airport, they left the videotape at the entrance to the newspaper's editorial offices. Using a voice scrambler, Sean had phoned the city desk to check outside for a special package. Then the men immediately drove south in the stolen van. The rain provided excellent cover. Never exceeding the speed limit, they attracted no suspicion and had no interruptions. The storm tapered off around Charlottesville, and by the time they reached the motel, there was only inconsequential drizzle. After dumping the van and changing cars, they turned in for the night.

They were an unlikely trio. Long and lanky, a tall farmer's boy, C.J. Walker's scarecrow façade concealed the strength in his sinewy muscles. He was the one who had wielded the sap. The man called Smith, the van driver who was twice C.J.'s age, had a sandpaper voice roughened by years of cheap whiskey and unfiltered cigarettes. His unshaven cheeks bore visible white stubble. The third man, the photographer, was unlike the others. Shorter, more visibly compact, he had a leader's sureness of movement and a no-nonsense demeanor. His name was Sean

O'Brien, and he was the obvious man in charge.

"You know what they can do with their goddamn politics," said the gravelly-voiced Smith.

"It's politics done got him elected," observed C.J. "We voted him in, we can vote him out."

Sean smiled. "That's the American way, C.J. The power of the polling place. Very democratic."

"I ain't no Democrat."

"No, you're not," said Sean. "And you're also not the kind of guy who has the patience to wait for an election. Besides, it looks like he's going to get re-elected. You think most people think the way we do? Hell, they love ol' Bobby Meredith."

"I was just sayin', it ain't right."

"No, it's not. People should have a little more integrity and stick to their word. They should remember their principles a little better. But once they're in Washington, you can't depend on them anymore. You've got to depend on yourself."

"Amen to that," croaked Smith, taking a swig of his Bud.

"Question is," Sean continued, "what are we going to do about it? We know what *we* believe in. Taking care of the doctor showed 'em we're serious. We just won't put up with that kind of shit. But if we thought we were sending a message they'd understand, forget it. You heard what the man said. We might have to think again. Maybe take matters into our own hands."

C.J. stared at Sean several seconds before a smile slowly spread across his face. "Don't be shittin' me, man. What're you sayin', Sean?"

"I'm saying there are times you give up, and times you circle the wagons and fight. I don't think there are quitters in the Southern Cross. When you know what you want, sometimes you have to go out and get it. Remember, we're just an instrument. In the end, God speaks through us. His will be done."

"You got somethin' specific in mind, don't ya?" C.J. said, his excited eyes aglow. "I jes know it!"

"That's a fact," said Smith. "I can see them wheels turnin'."

"Here's the thing, boys," Sean said, stubbing out his Marlboro and placing his palms on the table. "Sometimes when it's hard for a man to learn, he has to be taught a different lesson. Something he'll understand."

"Like what?" C.J. asked.

"Like something that hurts. Losing something important, for instance."

C.J.'s eyes narrowed. "I don't get it."

"What he's sayin'," Smith said, gesturing with his beer can, "is that if you want to run with the big dogs, you gotta get off the porch. Time to move up to the big leagues. Right, Sean?"

Sean smiled at the aphorism. "Something like that. Maybe our last statement wasn't impressive enough for the folks in Washington. Maybe it's time for some serious loss."

"I'm with you, Sean," C.J. nodded. "Just point the way."

"Remember, gentlemen. Life is precious. All life. And sometimes you have to lose life to appreciate that. It's the Lord's way."

Smith's expression grew solemn. "Thy will be done."

Bethesda, Maryland

To her, he looked like a shorter version of NSYNC's Justin. Michael's straw-colored blond hair was a little longer, perhaps, and a little straighter, falling with horsehair flatness to the mid-point of his head, where it abruptly ended in a fade. Also, his chin might have been a bit more prominent. No matter. To twelve-year-old Tommie, he was the most gorgeous male she'd seen in her young life.

Not that she'd seen all that many. There was her father, naturally, who she thought was probably handsome, in a father's kind of way. Recently, she'd begun noticing the way older women glanced at him, sidelong glances that lingered when he wasn't looking. Then there were all the entertainers on TV and in magazines, but seen from a distance, they were plastic people. There was a neighborhood boy Tommie liked when she was five, but she was just a kid then. Anyway, it was before she'd been injured. Now that she was older, she had different feelings—new, confusing emotions that both buoyed and battered her.

The strangest part was, Michael hardly even talked to her before they became cast members in the school play. They were rehearsing *The Tempest*, a production that some might consider advanced for the sixth grade in a public school, but one that was considered appropriate for the bright, well-heeled youngsters in the private schools of Washington's suburbs, where the children of diplomats, politicians, and upper-echelon government employees were educated. The project was begun last May, toward the end of the fifth grade, when the Shakespearean work was read aloud in class and parts assigned. Tommie was given the role of Ariel, while Michael played the charming young Ferdinand. They'd had all summer to learn their lines.

Tommie liked the fact that Ariel's character—a fairy spirit—was supposed to be invisible. Somehow that made it a lot more believable for her to zip about the stage in her wheelchair without feeling ridiculous. Before the school year began, Tommie had gotten together with her best friend, Heather, to go over their lines. Heather had been assigned the part of Miranda, the play's fifteen-year-old heroine. From the start, there was no question that Tommie was the better actress. Despite her handicap, she had a keen memory and delivered her lines well. This was a great help to Heather, whose power of recall was suspect, at best. By the time school began after Labor Day, Tommie was polished and poised, while Heather, with Tommie's assistance, had improved to the point of adequacy.

Once fall rehearsals began in earnest, however, everything changed. It was because of Michael's presence. During the summer, he had grown and filled out. Similarly, Heather, who was already tall and attractive, had begun to become a woman. During the summer when Tommie had rehearsed with Heather, she'd joked about her friend's increasingly noticeable curves, development that Tommie lacked. But once the semester began and Tommie saw the way Michael and Heather were looking at one another, all joking stopped. Tommie suddenly felt self-conscious and inadequate. Her former theatrical confidence fled like a startled deer. Not only did she blank out her lines, but she lapsed into tongue-tied inarticulation. She grew to hate the play, just like she hated her looks.

Who would look at her, anyway? Everyone kept telling her she was pretty, but Michael and the other boys never once looked her way. Even if they did, she doubted they would see beyond her wheelchair. She'd give anything to be normal, or at the very least, to be able to walk again.

"Tommie?" prompted the drama coach. "Earth to Tommie, you're on."

"What?" She'd been looking at Heather, whose beaming smile, even across the stage, was fixed on Michael, who'd just perfectly delivered her lines. "Oh, sorry."

"Full fathom five thy father lies,
Of his bones are coral made,"

"Come on, Tommie," interrupted the coach, "get with it. This isn't a funeral. You're supposed to be singing, right? Start again, and show a little life, okay?"

To her credit, Tommie tried. But her heart just wasn't in it. It couldn't be. Now that she'd given her heart away, it would take a while to reclaim it.

CHAPTER 2

Washington, D.C.

"In a moment, we'll have the privilege of being addressed by someone who is undeniably the world's most influential woman," said the speaker, glancing at the guest. "She's certainly the most controversial. Among her many accomplishments...."

On the dais, the woman seated next to the first lady leaned over to whisper in her ear. "Are you sure you're up to this? There's blood in the water, and the sharks are circling."

"That makes the timing perfect," said the first lady. "It'll give me a chance to test my shark repellent."

"—without further ado, The First Lady of the United States, Roxanne Meredith." Clapping enthusiastically, the crowd got to its feet. Roxanne stood up, acknowledging the ovation with a convivial wave as she strode to the podium. This was her first opportunity to address the Gay Women's Alliance. The GWA, the nation's most outspoken lesbian organization, was also the most contentious, owing to its endorsement of almost any liberal women's cause. Mrs. Meredith's mere presence was enough to ensure more than adequate publicity; and as she was the wife of a conservative president, whatever she said was certain to create a political firestorm.

Roxanne, known to family and friends as Rocky, was no stranger to publicity. Virtually everything she said or did was thoroughly covered by the press. This was only partly due to the fact that she was a presidential wife. Extremely popular in her own right, she was the most photographed White House occupant since the days of Jacqueline Kennedy. The paparazzi adored her. Trim and athletic, she made a killer photographic subject. No matter what she wore, her perfectly coordinated fashions were appropriate for either the cover of *Vanity Fair* or a ten-thousand-dollars-per-plate fundraiser. Her eclectic mix of Versace, Christian Dior, and Anna Sui inspired countless knockoffs. But perhaps her most endearing quality was that, in addition to a heart and a brain, she had a voice of her own.

"Thank you all very much," she began. "It's a privilege to be invited to speak to such an influential organization. To be honest, I wasn't sure what to say when I agreed to address the GWA. I usually strive for originality, but this time I was at a loss. So last week, when I finally wrote my speech," she said, holding up several typed pages, "I put together the usual things. Things like the courage and the leadership of your group.

Things about responsibility and self-respect, and about the role of government in guaranteeing workplace and marital equality. I realized you'd heard it all before. Maybe I thought, coming from me, my remarks might carry a certain importance and respectability. As you may know, I've never been a big fan of humility."

From the audience, laughter and applause.

"But today, I'm going to dispense with my prepared remarks," she said, putting the pages aside, "to talk about something that concerns me greatly. It is very much a women's issue, and to that extent it is entirely appropriate for our gathering today.

"Most of you have heard by now that last night, one of our country's leading researchers was killed in cold blood. Dr. Jeremy Raskin, a physician and one of our country's leading stem cell researchers, was kidnapped and murdered in an indescribably horrible fashion. This occurred when he left work after caring for dozens of patients. The president addressed that outrage this morning. I know I won't be compromising the investigation of this crime by revealing that little is known at this point about the perpetrators. But I have every reason to believe that the men who did this are a disgusting bunch of ultra-right-wing reactionaries. They may call themselves patriots, but they are terrorist scum. They are lowlife. They threaten, corrupt, and pollute everything our nation stands for."

There was a burst of applause, and a cry of "Go get 'em, Rocky!"

"Dr. Raskin did abortions. That's no secret, and he was proud of the service he performed for his patients. But he was also a leading researcher into the use and application of fetal stem cells. I use the word 'fetal' advisedly, and please believe me when I say I'm aware of the different types of human stem cells. Use of fetal stem cells is not federally funded, and Dr. Raskin bore much of the financial burden himself. He was quite open and honest about it because that's what he believed in. He had few professional secrets. He talked the talk and walked the walk of a man who, to be blunt, put his money where his mouth was.

"Would that more health care providers, regardless of their politics, were so dedicated. This country thrives on effort and enterprise and self-expression, and Dr. Raskin combined them all. Yet no matter how many people he helped, there were those who are unaccountably threatened by what he stood for. This, some say, is both the message and the price of a free society. The right to be different—to feel differently, to speak and act differently. Our courts have always protected that right, so long as it doesn't impinge on the rights of others.

"What they have *never* protected, and what I find so cowardly and reprehensible, is the so-called right some groups give themselves to correct society's wrongs. Never mind that these are wrongs in their eyes only. Sometimes they call these acts sins. Sometimes they label these events as contrary to God's will. Whatever. The bottom line is, they alone are the arbiters of improper conduct. They alone decide what's right and wrong, good and evil. But they have sanctimoniously moved beyond simple moral condemnation. When they took matters into their own hands, those who murdered Dr. Raskin gave themselves the right to be judge, jury, and executioner."

Nods and whispered murmurs flowed through the crowd.

"As my former therapists told me, I have issues," Rocky said with a half-smile that drew a knowing laugh. "I have conflicts with some of those about me. It will come as no surprise to those who've heard me before that I have differences with my political party. In fact, I don't always see eye to eye with my husband. Who knows, maybe that's one of the reasons we've stayed together. But whatever our disparities, we manage to resolve them without violence. We don't always succeed, but we get an A for effort. So, we talk. Sometimes we argue, or bully, or tease. In private, we don't always act as adult as we do in public. Your president is a strong and capable man, but I'm proud to say he has never raised a hand to me. Which is good, because I wouldn't want to hurt him.

"Like most Americans, where we differ, we try to persuade, not impose. The fundamentally wonderful thing about our society is that we prosper without fundamentalism. Absolutes may be useful to some, but they're the curse of a free nation. As this organization well knows, real Americans will not tolerate intolerance. We celebrate our right to be different without fearing the consequences. This is why Dr. Raskin's murder diminishes us all. His death is everyone's loss.

"Haven't we had enough of this? Haven't the narrow-minded purveyors of hate spread enough of their poison? Those of you who really know me know I support everything your organization stands for. You of all people appreciate the tragedies brought on by bigotry and prejudice. So, rather than for me to once more get behind you, this time I call for you to stand behind *me*. Collectively, we must say, enough! Enough hate, enough violence

The seated woman who'd whispered to the first lady now turned to the person on her other side. "She really put her foot into it this time?"

"Really? I think she's marvelous. It takes so much courage to go out on a limb like that."

"I'm talking about with her husband."

Indeed, Rocky's comments, so clearly at odds with the administration's policies, were a recipe for matrimonial conflict. But Rocky was no stranger to controversy. She could give as well as take, and she held her own in political debates. Some thought it a wonder that she and the president got along as well as they did. But these were the same people who didn't understand that Rocky was her own person, one who combined femininity with intelligence and charisma.

Where it came to women in politics, Roxanne Meredith was the complete package.

Having sent Smith and Walker on prearranged duties, O'Brien got down to more important business. From an encrypted phone in a secure location, he contacted his boss. This was a need-to-know call, and neither Smith nor C.J. had that need. Nor, for that matter, did any other members of the Southern Cross. They were all cogs in a wheel, means to an end, an end about which they knew nothing. The line came alive.

"Yes, sir, we're all set. Walker got the weapon and it'll be tested soon. No problems that I can see. Is the target's schedule still the same...? Yes, sir, I understand that. Nothing's final until it actually goes down."

O'Brien succinctly answered several questions from the man to whom he owed everything. They were questions about timing, finances, possible security leaks. Each of O'Brien's replies was precise and well thought out. Yet intent though he was, he was distracted, as happened on occasion, by thoughts of who he was and what he stood for. Sometimes he himself wasn't sure. All he *did* know was that, contrary to what he'd told his men, God's will had nothing to do with it. The concept that all life was precious was merely one of Lenin's opiates, fodder for the masses, the frontline sacrificial troops without whom nothing could be accomplished. Certainly, there were far more important things in life—things like loyalty, and direction, and accomplishment.

"He certainly does, sir," O'Brien concluded. "He's primed and ready. Everything will be done in the name of Allah. Religion's a beautiful thing, isn't it? I'll keep you informed of his progress. But right now, it's looking good."

CHAPTER 3

"You just couldn't resist, could you?" said the president. "You just had to get your two cents in, to hell with other people! Why is every issue about you—what you think, how you feel? Where are other people in this equation? What about what the party thinks?"

"To hell with the party!" Rocky shot back. "For God's sake, Raskin had a wife and kids! Don't tell me the party condones what happened to him!"

"Of course they don't. But that's not the point, and you know it. Why do you constantly twist things around?" He sighed. "Jesus, Rocky, why are we always having this same argument? I keep telling you, it's your method, not your message. And where you deliver it. It's not what you say, but how you say it. There's..."

"I know, I know," she interrupted. "'There's a time and a place for everything.' And good wittle woman that I am," she said, lapsing into baby talk, "I should wisten to what Daddy says."

He shook his head. "Come on, Rocky."

"Look, Bob, I am what I am. This is the real me. You know I'm not trying to embarrass you, the administration, or the party. But I do have to be true to what I believe in."

They were in the White House private residence, an entire floor with a palpable sense of power and history. The president took off his suit jacket and shrugged out of his suspenders. "Even when I wind up looking like a fool?"

Rocky walked over and kissed him on the cheek. "You don't look like a fool, darling."

"All right, what would you call it?"

"I call it doing what you have to do as president. I wasn't elected like you, but we both have jobs." She softened. "Look, you know that most of the country supports you on this."

"Meaning what?"

"They may be sorry Dr. Raskin was killed, but he *did* do abortions. There's no getting around that fact. I also don't doubt that a lot of your supporters won't lose any sleep over his death. And Raskin also worked with fetal stem cells derived from abortions, and most people don't like that either, no sir. So, they're sorry, but they're not *that* sorry. You know what that's called?"

"I'm sure you're going to tell me," said Meredith.

"It's called hypocrisy."

"Oh, please."

"And it's the *worst* kind of hypocrisy, because it involves someone's death.

That's all I'm saying. I know you condemned what happened, but I felt I had to go a little further. I did it for myself."

"My point precisely. It's always about you, isn't it?" said the president. "What *you* feel and think. But what about us? Where do we fit in your crusade?"

When she saw how wounded he was, she chose her words carefully. "It's not just about me, Bob. Or about us. It's about what's right. You've always stood for fairness and decency, and I know that deep down, you're just as sickened by what happened as I am."

She had him there, and he had to smile. For all his real indignation, and despite his wife's insufferable preaching, he had indeed been revolted by what he'd seen on the videotape. And there was no evading the fact that his wife was skilled at manipulating him. He walked over and put his arms around her. "You're right, I am. I guess I'm still teachable, huh?"

"Stick with me, big boy," she said, kissing him lightly on the lips. "The school year's just starting."

"Just remember one thing. These hate groups you're complaining about really do hate. They're dangerous, Rocky. They're fearless when it comes to making their point. Look at what they did to Dr. Raskin."

"Don't worry, darling, I'll be careful. With you and the Secret Service to protect me, why should I worry?"

The school play had begun at six P.M. to accommodate parents on their way home from work. The turnout was larger than anticipated, and there were few available seats. From the stage, Tommie kept looking expectantly at the audience. Her mother was there, looking prim and in control, occasionally venturing a modest wave. But where was her father? She was sure he knew what time the play began. Not only had she told him several times, but also he'd repeated it. He said he was looking forward to it and had set aside time on his calendar.

Tommie realized her father was very busy. After all, he was the president's doctor—something she was very proud of—and he had many demands on his time. But he was also her biggest fan. He applauded everything she did, supporting her through good times and bad. She dearly wanted him to see her on stage, especially now that she'd regained her confidence. Her father was a man of his word; and if he said he'd attend, he'd make every effort to show up. So why, she wondered, wasn't he there? Was something wrong?

The play was in the fourth of its five acts, with not much time remaining. Across stage, Michael and Heather exchanged lines. Tommie wondered what her father would have thought of the young man who so completely filled her thoughts. Then again, she wasn't sure she could trust his opinion, for her father rarely had an unkind word to say about anyone. Still, maybe she could tell from his expression. If he showed up. Tommie cast one last wistful look at the auditorium entrance and sighed. Alas. She rolled her wheelchair up to her next stage mark.

The show must go on.

There was an ageless quality to cell reproduction—so inexorable, so like the constant tides. It had been thus since time immemorial. Life went on without regard for the conditions around it. Filled with promise, the immutable process had the richness of a tropical sea.

Inside the incubator, all was quiet. Noise could not penetrate the heat-and-sound-impeding baffles. Insulated from their surroundings, the culture plates were evenly stacked, row on row. In the petri dishes, the cells formed a single layer on the jelled media. Ever so slowly, hour after hour, the chromosomes emerged from their resting phase to line up on their spindles. There they replicated, then separated, pulling apart evenly at the equatorial plane to form identical daughter cells.

The atmosphere was warm, dark, and fertile, perfect for growth. The oxygen and carbon dioxide levels were kept constant, as was the humidity. In this lush, primordial stew, the basic units of human life slowly simmered.

CHAPTER 4

Bethesda, Maryland
October, 2005

He saw the blood even before he heard the noise.

By seven p.m., Dr. Jon Townsend had left the medical center and was heading north on the Rockville Pike toward the Capitol Beltway. It was already dark, although rush hour traffic had considerably subsided. Townsend had worked late that day, but he thought he'd still be able to make it to his daughter's school play, which began at seven-thirty.

Rockville Pike was a three-lane highway. He was in the center lane when it happened, twenty feet behind and to the right of a Chevy Suburban.

Everything occurred in a split second. The Suburban was a large, heavy vehicle, but it abruptly spun at a right angle in the road, turning directly in front of him.

Townsend reacted reflexively, wrenching his wheel to the right and veering out of the way. As he careened past the Chevy, a heavy crimson stain splattered his windshield. It was then that his mind registered the horrifying screech of twisting metal. At the same instant, a large, blurry object rocketed over his hood and shot off to the right.

His mind couldn't absorb everything at once. He understood that there had been a severe collision, a there-but-for-the-grace-of-God impact that narrowly missed him. Heart pounding, he steered his vehicle to the far side of the intersection, stopped, and got out. He never considered himself particularly skilled in medical crises, whose frantic, urgent nature could overwhelm him. He preferred to leave emergency medicine to those more emotionally equipped to deal with it. So, for a moment, he simply stood and looked back at the accident scene, trying to comprehend what had just happened.

It looked like a small sedan had, for some reason, gone through a red light at the Pike's intersection with West Cedar Lane. It broadsided the Suburban. The outcome was as predictable as the devastation. The huge Suburban was more than twice the weight of the sedan, which had been accordioned. Despite the darkness, Dr. Townsend had the impression that the sedan's driver was pinned behind its twisted steering wheel. As Jon's trained mind clicked into gear, he somehow overcame his fears and began jogging toward the wreck.

He hadn't seen this degree of mayhem since Vietnam. Yet however frightened he might be, he would never forget the ABCs of emergency management—airway, breathing, and circulation. He knew there would be several people injured, perhaps seriously. It would boil down to a question of triage, of assisting the critically injured first. But as he dashed ahead, something caught his eye at the side of the road. Something moving.

More precisely, it was twitching. It vaguely occurred to him that this was the object that had hurtled past his windshield. His pace lessened, and he turned in that direction. As he did, a passing vehicle slowed, and its passenger window opened. The teenage boy sitting there took one look at what lay beside the road and started to vomit. The woman driving never stopped completely. As she continued past Townsend, she simply looked at him, open-mouthed and ashen.

"Call 911!" he shouted as he ran past.

The car sped away without reply.

Other vehicles drew near and stopped. Their nervous drivers were mere spectators who offered no assistance. Reaching the curb, Townsend gazed downward. One look convinced him that he wouldn't need help anyway.

Lying there was a man, or what was left of a man. The twitching had ceased. The man had gone through the sedan's windshield, which he now wore like a grotesque collar. He couldn't have been wearing his seatbelt. When the collision occurred, he must have been ejected from his seat and thrown headfirst into the windshield. Upon impact, the sedan's entire windshield had come loose, but only once the man's head was impaled.

Now, the fractured windshield was down around the victim's shoulders like macabre epaulets. Where his skull penetrated, the glass had been jagged enough to sever the head down to the vertebrae. Both carotid arteries were cut in half. It was no wonder Townsend's car had been splattered with blood when the man flew past. Undoubtedly unconscious right after the collision, the victim had quickly succumbed to massive hemorrhage and traumatic impact. He died rather quickly. Realizing this, Townsend turned around and ran back across the Pike.

The sturdy Suburban had survived the crash well. The impact was forward of the passenger compartment, and although the front end was caved in, the occupants appeared to have escaped severe injury. The airbags had deployed, leaving them shaken. Townsend continued toward the sedan.

The small car was crushed like a pack of cigarettes. The buckled frame had collapsed on itself, front to back. The mangled destruction was so complete that Townsend was amazed anyone had survived. But as he reached the car, he could clearly see the driver through the void of the former windshield. Unlike his passenger, the olive-skinned driver had been wearing his seatbelt. He was conscious, gazing ahead through dull, dazed eyes. He didn't seem able to move. The remnants of the dashboard were snugged-up about him like a mangled vest. The steering column protruded over his right shoulder, barely missing his chest. The steering wheel itself had broken into several ragged shards.

As Townsend approached, his eyes took everything in. Caucasian, late twenties, in shock. The victim was very pale, and his lower jaw sagged. His breathing was shallow.

"Take it easy, pal," Townsend softly reassured. "Help's on the way. What bothers you most?"

The driver didn't answer. Townsend couldn't tell if the man

heard him or not. The car had the pungent, metallic odor of spilt blood. He reached through the windshield-that-wasn't and felt for the man's carotid pulse. It was very rapid, very weak. It occurred to Townsend that the shock might be of the hemorrhagic variety. The man's head bobbed.

"Don't go out on me, man. Can you hear me?"

The driver's bloodless lips pursed. "Can't...my legs," he managed, in heavily accented English.

"Can't what? Can't feel 'em, can't move 'em?"

"Can't."

The man's legs were trapped, pinned under the buckled dashboard. His shock might be explained by the fact that his legs were crushed. Alternatively, if the driver couldn't move them, it could be because of the way they were held down. But if he couldn't *feel* them, there might be a spinal cord injury. Another vehicle pulled up and illuminated the sedan. And then, in the headlights' glare, Townsend noticed the spurting blood.

It was a steady crimson jet that shot sideways in a gentle arc. Backlit by the headlamps, a fine steam wafted upward from the spray, curling ghostlike toward the roof. The blood squirted like dark oil, splattering the passenger seat. At first, Townsend couldn't tell where it was coming from; but as he peered closer, he found its source in the man's upper arm.

One of the steering wheel's sharp edges had lacerated the biceps. The torn belly of the muscle bared the humerus, and the bone glistened with an otherworldly whiteness. Above it, a severed branch of the brachial artery pumped blood toward oblivion.

"Need a hand?" said the driver of the car that had pulled up.

"He needs an ambulance," Townsend replied, quickly removing his belt. "Do you know if anyone called for help?"

"I did, and I think other people did, too." He looked into the wreck. "Jesus, this looks like a butcher shop. Can we get *him* out of there?"

"Not yet." Townsend reached through and wrapped his belt around the driver's upper arm. When he cinched it tight, the bleeding immediately ceased.

"I hope you know what you're doing."

"I'm a doctor. I can't tell if he has a neck or back injury, so unless you see something else that needs fixing, we'd better let the paramedics move him. It looks like they'll need the Jaws of Life anyway."

"You're the boss, Doc—oh, boy, there he goes."

Townsend saw the driver's chin sag to his chest. "No sir, can't have you doing that!" he shouted. The man didn't stir. Townsend slapped his cheeks, and when that failed, he pinched the skin on the side of the man's neck. The driver didn't stir.

Townsend again felt for the carotid pulse, which was still present. But when he put his hand under the man's mouth and nose, he felt no respirations.

"Wonderful, he just stopped breathing," he said to no one in particular. He immediately jumped onto what was left of the hood and wormed his way through the windshield opening. Half on his side, he carefully tilted back the patient's head. Squeezing the man's nostrils with his fingertips, Townsend placed his mouth over the victim's and began artificial respiration. But it was soon apparent that the driver's lungs wouldn't expand.

"Christ, he's obstructed," Townsend said, backing off. "Quick, see if anyone's got a penknife. A flashlight would help, too."

His assistant backed off and spoke rapid-fire to the small but growing crowd. In the distance came the first, faint wail of a siren. Keeping the man's head back, Townsend explored the man's neck, touching, probing. Soon a light shined on the driver's anatomy, and Townsend located the crucial depression beneath the thyroid cartilage. Someone passed him a knife, handle first. Townsend steadied its point on a spot on the skin and then deftly pierced the cricothyroid membrane. The victim's chest heaved, and there was a whistling sound as air rushed through the newly created opening.

"I need a pen," he said, "the fatter the better." Within seconds, he inserted a fat ballpoint through the incision to keep its edges open. Satisfied, he wriggled out of the wreck just as the ambulance pulled up.

The paramedics rushed over and brushed Townsend aside. "Outa the way, folks, let us in. We're the good guys."

"This good guy's a doctor," someone called, "and he just saved that man's life."

There is an unspoken pecking order in emergency healthcare, and no matter how skilled the EMS personnel, they give deference to physicians. "Sorry, Doc," said the lead paramedic. "What can you tell us?"

"Something's obstructing his airway," said Dr. Townsend, an object that later proved to be a large was of chewing gum. "You've got a Nu-Trake, right?" he said, referring to a temporary tracheotomy tube that would go through the incision.

"You bet." The paramedic motioned for his assistant to get it.

"He's also in shock, probably hypovolemic. There's a lacerated brachial artery, and he needs volume fast. His passenger's across the street, dead. The people in the Suburban are probably just shaken up."

"Okay, Doc. We'll take it from here."

Soon three ambulance crews were on site attending to the victims. When Townsend returned to his car, he realized he was shaking. His white Naval uniform was bloodstained and smudged with grease. There was no way he could go to his daughter's play like that; he'd embarrass her if he tried. But if he hurried home and changed, he might be able to catch the tail end of the event.

Failing that, there was one other place he just might visit.

CHAPTER 5

The White House

He was late.

In fact, fifty-year-old Jon Townsend, M.D., wasn't even supposed to be there. When the invitations to the White House dinner had been mailed four weeks ago, he'd declined because his daughter's play posed a scheduling conflict. But then his schedule was unexpectedly freed up. Although he couldn't arrive at the start of festivities, Jon might get there in time for the main meal. Ever since the White House got a new chef, Townsend never missed an opportunity to dine. As the president's personal physician, he was a frequent White House visitor, and he could show up virtually whenever he wanted.

Having changed from his soiled whites, he was still adjusting the tie to his dress blue uniform when he drove through the Northwest Gate. His hands still shook slightly. Although his heart rate had slowed, he felt emotionally drained from the recent accident. The guard waved him past, and he headed for his reserved space in the back. Although he was known to the Secret Service, he still had to pass through a metal detector and be officially checked in before he could gain entrance to the mansion proper.

Once inside, he made his way through the Cross Hall and past The Parlors to the State Dining Room. He paused at the doorway, taking in the scene. Tonight, the president and first lady were hosting the Israeli Prime Minister at a formal dinner. The room's one-hundred-thirty-person capacity was limited to a modest seventy invitees, all of whom were seated, looking at the dais. The president stood before the famous George Healy portrait of Abraham Lincoln as he finished his prepared remarks.

Townsend always considered it a pleasure to be an official White House guest. Though it was the First Family's abode, it was still the people's house, with an ongoing, pervasive sense of history. Yet despite its being owned by the common man, it had a sense of majesty most exquisite in its artwork and ornate furnishings. On the mantle above the dining room's central fireplace was the John Adams quotation that Townsend found inspiring: "I Pray Heaven To Bestow The Best Of Blessings On This House And All that shall hereafter Inhabit it. May none but Honest and Wise Men ever rule under This Roof." Noble words, he thought.

He watched the president receive polite applause and return to the head table. The staggered seating included the president's wife Roxanne, the Prime Minister and his wife, and the vice president's wife, Amanda, with whom Roxanne was animatedly talking. Jon had known the president for several decades. President Robert Meredith had aged well.

At sixty-five, he was still vigorous and trim. His white hair, combed straight back, remained long and full. A charismatic speaker, most people considered Meredith an attractive man in the prime of adult life. When he took his seat, the first course was served.

Still in the doorway, Townsend searched for a place at one of the tables. Although attendance at state dinners was a high honor, there were invariably a handful of no-shows. Tonight, however, he couldn't spot any available seats. He'd have to wait for the dinner staff to find him a place. Standing on his right was a uniformed official of the National Park Service. Nominally in charge of the park that comprised White House grounds, Park Service employees were rarely seen at official functions, and Townsend didn't recognize this one. On his left, however, was a female Secret Service agent he'd known for several years. He whispered what was on his mind, and she called over one of the staff. Moments later, he was shown to a place hidden from view.

The guests on either side of him had already begun to eat. Their appetizer was some sort of dumpling in a green herb sauce—very colorful, very appealing. The guest on his left was Mitchell Forbes, the president's chief of staff. He didn't recognize the woman on his right. Townsend clasped Forbes on the shoulder and held out his hand.

"Hello, Mitch. What'd I miss so far?"

Forbes looked up, wiped his mouth with his napkin, and shook hands. "Hi, Jon. I didn't know you were coming tonight. Everything okay? You look a little pale."

"I'm fine. I wasn't going to come, but I finished up early," he said simply. He didn't want to talk about the crash or about missing his daughter's play. "I like to be here whenever this chef's working."

"She's something, isn't she? I don't think you missed much. The president was waxing poetic on the long years of American-Israeli friendship."

"Ah," said Townsend, leaning closer. "I think I heard that one already." He turned to his right and smiled. "Hi, my name's Jon Townsend. I see you saved me a seat."

"Yael Meyer," she said with a pinched expression. "I'm the Prime Minister's press secretary. Actually, that seat wasn't for you, General—"

The smile never left his face. "Admiral."

"Yes, of course. My husband was supposed to sit there, but he's ill."

"He's missing a great meal," Townsend said, studying the woman. She was fortyish and moderately attractive, but severe-looking, with a sabra's humorless intensity. Her voice had only a trace of Israeli accent, more Netanyahu than Barak. "I hope it's nothing serious."

"His asthma acts up in weather this humid. We live in Jerusalem, where it's always dry. Are you in the administration?"

"I'm the president's doctor. I can usually weasel my way into a state dinner if it's not too crowded."

"And here I'd taken you for a military man. So, you're not going to command the ship that brings your troops to Israel?"

"No, ma'am, I'm not."

"And what do you think of the president's proposal, in general?"

The proposal she referred to was Bob Meredith's suggested way out of the Syrian-Israeli logjam. After the framework of an Israeli-Palestinian peace was erected, the last regional obstacle was Syria. The president modernized the old idea of sending American troops to the Golan Heights as a way of finalizing peace in the area. Not surprisingly, right-wing militant Arab groups like Hamas and Hezbollah strongly opposed the suggestion, as did some Americans. Tonight's dinner was a way of showing unified support for the proposal.

"Frankly, Mrs. Meyer, politics are not my strong suit. I'd rather talk about the food. How are the dumplings?"

"You're more of a diplomat than you admit, Doctor. The 'dumplings' are actually salmon and mango ravioli, and they are superb. Kosher, too, I'm told."

As she resumed eating, Townsend turned back to Forbes. "How's the old man doing tonight?"

"Pretty damn good. Relaxed and funny. The Israelis are enjoying it. Well, most of them, anyway."

One of the servers brought his appetizer, and Townsend quickly ate a bite-size piece. It was astonishingly good, with a rich flavor that made him want to close his eyes and sigh. The flavors were textured, and he could taste the sweetness of coconut, the tartness of lemongrass, and, in the background, the hearty fullness of basil. Heaven had descended upon the dinner table.

There was a sudden commotion from the direction of the dais. It began as intense murmuring, increased to shrilly raised voices, and was soon punctuated by a scream. Startled, Townsend listened for a moment. He suspected there was another emergency, and he worried that he might be expected to perform feats of medical magic once again—here, on stage, in front of an international audience. His eyes widened and his heart began to pound, nearly paralyzing him with fear. All heads turned in the direction of the excitement, and most expressions had the uncertain, momentary paralysis that accompanies confusion. It was the alert, wide-eyed look of startled deer. But as the others stared, Townsend suddenly got hold of himself. He leapt from his seat, galvanized into action, running toward the source of the noise.

Bob Meredith had risen from his seat, leaning slightly forward, hunched over at the waist. His mouth was slightly open, and although he didn't make a sound, he appeared to be struggling. His open hand trembled claw-like at his neck. The expression on his face mixed panic with terror, and his color was fast going from pale to gray. He was clearly in dire straits.

The first lady remained in her seat, both her fluttering hands about her mouth as she helplessly, repeatedly mumbled, "Oh my God." Two Secret Service agents came up behind the stricken president. While one scanned the room for danger, the other took Meredith under the armpits and was trying to lower him to the floor.

Townsend knew many of the agents, but he'd never met these two. They both wore necklace IDs. The name of the African-American agent nearest Townsend began with capital letter L, but before he could decipher it, he heard people whisper, "CPR." He was aghast. His trained mind quickly processed the visible clues: the patient was conscious, had obvious anxiety, couldn't talk, and was struggling to breathe. He'd been stricken in the middle of a meal. Much as those around him wanted to help, CPR was the *last* thing they should try. Dr. Henry Heimlich had described what to do years before.

"Oxygen!" he shouted. Emergency medical equipment was strategically placed throughout the White House, and Townsend knew one such location was just beyond the dining room. "Get that oxygen out here!"

Seeing someone race toward the president, a third agent materialized and was moving in to intercept. But the second agent raised an arm to stop him.

"Let him go, that's Dr. Townsend."

By now the other Secret Service man had lowered the president to a sitting position. Meredith's eyes were starting to glaze over.

"Let me in, he's choking!" Townsend shouted.

The president was dead weight. As Meredith's eyes started to close, Townsend pulled him up by one arm while the agent lifted by the other. Once the president was up and leaning toward the dinner table, Townsend went behind him and circled the president's midsection. Meredith was heavy, and he slumped forward in Townsend's grasp. Townsend quickly clenched his right fist and placed it midway between the president's umbilicus and lower sternum. Then, grasping the fist with his left hand, he delivered a sharp upward thrust to Meredith's abdomen.

While this was happening, the president sensed everything from afar, in a daze. He was in a nether state—not quite unconscious, but not awake, either. He didn't realize the sensation came from oxygen deprivation; the only thing he was aware of was someone's arms hugging him from behind. There was something familiar about those arms, something reassuring. They were the same arms that had held him thirty years before, on a bloody morning on a hillside thousands of miles away. He felt safe.

With Townsend's forceful thrust, a large piece of food was dislodged from the president's throat onto the table. The moment it did, Meredith audibly gasped. His color quickly became pink. As he hungrily sucked in air, his strength began to return. He leaned forward onto the table, wheezing, resting on his palms. His eyes moistened with tears of exertion.

Too frightened to speak, the first lady, still shaken, got up and took her husband's arm. All she could do was hold on.

The assisting Secret Service agent thumped Meredith's back. "It's okay, Mr. President. You feel all right?"

A growing crowd of concerned guests formed a tightening circle. "Step back, everyone," said Townsend. "Give him some room." He saw the small green tank of oxygen being wheeled over. "I'll take that. Help him into a chair."

As he cranked open the tank and unwrapped the plastic tubing, the agent and first lady helped Meredith into a chair. Townsend lowered the tubing over the president's head and fit the prongs into his nostrils.

"Try to relax, Mr. President," he said. "It's all over now. You probably weren't that hungry anyway."

With a shaking hand, Meredith lifted a napkin and wiped his face and eyes. The raspiness in his chest soon cleared as he rinsed his lungs with fresh air. His breathing returned to normal, and he pushed himself upright. "That was close," he finally said. "Thanks, Jon. Just like old times, huh?"

"Yes, sir. Like old times."

The Secret Service agent leaned toward Townsend. "The ambulance is outside, Doctor," he whispered. "Should they bring in the stretcher?"

"I heard that," Meredith said. "This is a state dinner, for God's sake. I'm not going anywhere, especially horizontal."

"Mr. President...." the agent insisted.

"He's probably right," Townsend said. "The worst is over. Give us five minutes. Come on, Bob. Let's take a walk."

As he helped the president across the floor, everyone in the room rose to their feet. They began to clap. Meredith smiled gamely and waved at them.

"Can you believe it?" he said through clenched teeth. "I nearly fall on my face, and they give me a standing ovation."

"You're their man, Bob."

Secret Service agents in tow, they entered the kitchen. Inside, the kitchen staff hung back, giving them space. Townsend wasn't sure how much they'd seen.

"He's all right, folks," he said. "Just let him catch his breath." He turned to one of the agents. "See if you can find me a stethoscope. It should be in the emergency supplies, where the oxygen was."

"I'm fine, Jon. Really."

"Well, you certainly look better. Let me check your lungs, and in a minute or two, I'll send you out there to dazzle 'em."

The agent returned with the stethoscope. With everyone watching, the president opened his shirt, and Townsend listened to his chest. Soon he took the earpieces out of his ears.

"Lungs are clear," he said. "What happened, Bob? Did you notice other symptoms, anything unusual? Or are you just getting clumsy in your old age?"

"That's your diagnosis, senility? According to the latest Gallup Poll, most of your countrymen think I'm in pretty good shape."

"So you are, Mr. President. But that doesn't answer my question."

"Well, all I know is that I was eating one of those raviolis, and it was fantastic. Spicy, but fantastic. The next thing I know, I was choking."

"Okay. You're good to go, Mr. President. Just remember to chew your food before you swallow it."

The president smiled and clasped Townsend's shoulder. Then he straightened his tux, squared his shoulders, and returned to the dining room. After watching Meredith's departure, Townsend called over an agent.

"Maybe I'm being paranoid, but the appetizer didn't taste spicy to me. It wouldn't hurt to check out his food, would it?"

"Yes, sir. I was thinking the same thing."

Deep in thought, Townsend sat there amidst the kitchen's bustle. The president was right: that had been close indeed. He didn't want to sound his own horn, but if he hadn't come to dinner tonight, the president would now be dead. He was a little surprised by the feeble emergency efforts others made before he came over. Surely they'd heard of the Heimlich maneuver. He'd have to talk with everyone about that.

Like old times, the president said. Townsend gave an amused snort, shaking his head. He reflected on that. When he closed his eyes, the sights and sounds of those days were as starkly vivid in his memory as they'd been thirty years before. He was young, then.

But in the naked harshness of battle, one grew up very quickly.

CHAPTER 6

Petra, Jordan

O'Brien disliked flying. But as there was no way to finalize the plan without a face-to-face meeting, and as it was impossible these days for an Islamic Arab to be assured of safe travel to the United States, Sean was forced to meet his Middle Eastern contact on the man's home turf. In fact, the man was not Jordanian at all, but a heavyset Yemeni who usually resided in Ramallah, on Israel's West Bank. Israeli security was so tight that it was more prudent to meet in a nearby Arab country. O'Brien suggested the capitol of Amman, but his contact pointed out that the Jordanian secret police was notoriously anti-Palestinian. They agreed on the ancient city of Petra, south of Amman, a site that would be filled with travelers, even at that time of year.

O'Brien took the red-eye on Austrian Airlines from Dulles Airport to Vienna, connecting the following morning to a Royal Jordanian flight that flew to Amman. He arrived in midafternoon. He was not due to meet his contact until noon the following day. This would give him ample time recover from the flight. Taking a cab into town, he registered at the new Hyatt. The concierge arranged a rental car for early the next morning. With no desire to see the local sights, O'Brien bathed, settled in for the night, and went to sleep.

He was up at six and out by seven. Although he didn't look forward to the car ride, the two-and-a-half-hour drive south from Amman to Petra was remarkable for its beauty. The ancient city was located on an old crossroads for a caravan route, strategically situated on a pass through the Shara Mountains that divided ancient Arabia and Syria from Palestine and Egypt. As it came into view in the mid-morning sun, the canyon city looked vast, mysteriously alluring. The concierge had told him that this had once been the realm of the Nabateans. Even from a distance, Petra still seemed to echo with mysteries of the past. Its ancient buildings, forgotten for centuries, were anchored into the cliffs from which they were carved.

To O'Brien's relief, there were countless tourists milling around when he pulled up, with their requisite vans and buses. He was early and still had two hours to kill. He parked his car, opened his map, and slowly made for a place called *Al Deir.* Once an immense monastery, the site was thought to have been a Nabatean shrine. En route, he could not help being dazzled by the rich structures and subtle palette of colors around him. Following the *Wadi Musa,* he took in the Winged Lions Temple and the Byzantine Church before reaching the *Wadi al Deir,* the path that led to the monastery.

He checked his watch. It was precisely twelve. Up ahead, he couldn't spot anyone who seemed to be his contact. O'Brien was gazing up at the quiet grandeur of the immense stone building when there was a tap on his shoulder.

"Remarkable, isn't it?" asked a heavily accented man's voice.

Startled, O'Brien whirled. The man before him was dark and mustachioed, with intense black eyes. Although only slightly taller than O'Brien, he was thick and heavyset, which was no doubt why he was called The Bear. He certainly resembled the photo O'Brien has studied. "And who might you be?" he asked. There was only one acceptable reply. His hand settled around a knife in his pocket.

"A friend in need," said the Arab, using the code phrase.

"Is a friend indeed," O'Brien replied in kind. "Now—"

"One minute, my newfound friend," said the man. He grasped O'Brien by the elbow and casually steered him away from the crowd. "Do not look up. There are security men up there. They are dressed like Bedouins. Walk with me, smile a little, and pretend we are very old friends."

The Middle Easterner was obviously an old hand at inter-Arab surveillance. As he slowly led O'Brien back toward the *wadi*, he offhandedly pointed at various rock formations, as if he were a tour guide.

"Two thousand years have passed since this was the Nabatean capital. Now it is a living antiquity. This was once a natural fortress, rich and alive, but now...." He reached into his pocket and withdrew a small slab, handing it to O'Brien. "I was told that to fully identify myself, I must give you something that shows I know you."

Sean looked obliquely at the plastic-slabbed item before his eyes widened and he inspected it more closely. "This is a Carl Yastrzemski rookie card. Is it real?"

The man shrugged. "So I have been told. It has meaning for you?"

O'Brien's eyes went far away and his thoughts thousands of miles distant, to hot summer afternoons at Fenway Park. "You might say that."

"Good. Then you may have something for me."

O'Brien took the thick envelope containing fifty thousand dollars from his inside windbreaker pocket. The Arab took it with the casual ease of someone accustomed to accepting large cash transactions and slid it into his pants without checking the amount. "Thank you. Do you know the most precious thing to the Nabateans?"

"Haven't a clue."

"Water. This is a desert, but they somehow managed to harvest water like the Egyptians did grain."

They walked and talked, easily and with apparent good nature, so that anyone paying them unusual interest would spot nothing out of the ordinary. Yet most of what they discussed was far from ordinary. It involved complicated plans and scheduling and timing in a distant land far from the carefully carved cliffs at Petra. And finally, it involved accuracy, the sort of accuracy only a well-tuned rifle could bring.

Without naming names, O'Brien described C.J. Walker, the person who would serve as a cut-out for his side. "And your man?" he asked.

"Oh, he is good. Very dedicated to the cause. He considers himself a martyr."

"Does he have a name, this martyr?"

The big man fixed O'Brien with a piercing stare. "He is called Mahmoud."

Quang Nam Province, South Vietnam
February, 1971

"Just grit your teeth, corpsman," the crew chief shouted over the noise of the rotors. "Don't even *think* about puking on this slick."

Jon Townsend, a pasty-faced twenty-year-old Marine corpsman, simply nodded his head, wondering what in the world had possessed him to down the greasy rations before boarding the helicopter. Around him, twenty other Marines—half of 4th platoon, Company M, 2 Battalion, Fifth Marines—seemed to be faring much better. No one else had a complexion so green that it matched his fatigues. But then, most of them had been in country much longer than he had. Perhaps they'd become used to dawn helicopter insertions near an enemy determined to kill them.

"Five more minutes, son," shouted Captain Meredith, seated diagonally across from Townsend. His voice could barely be heard over the din of the twin rotors. "You'll feel better once we're on the deck. Check your gear and tighten your straps."

Like the others, Corpsman Townsend was seated in a web seat against the helicopter's fuselage. His M-16 was between his knees, stock down, barrel straight up, with mag in, a round in the chamber, and safety on. His rucksack was full, and the wide pockets on the front of his web gear carried the first-aid items he might need quickest.

Townsend had met the captain only once before, when he was cherry in the platoon ten days before. Word had it that Meredith was liked and respected by the men under his command. Part of the reason was that, like most of his men, Meredith was not a Marine lifer. He'd been a young officer stateside right out of college, remaining in the Marine Reserves. When the captain's unit was mobilized a year ago, he was sent to Vietnam.

Stomach swimming, Townsend gazed through the porthole windows of the CH 4D Boeing Sea Knight. It was similar in appearance to the CH-47 Chinook helicopter, which was often referred to by the troops as Shithook, or simply Hook. Townsend noticed that up ahead, the Que Son Mountains were wreathed in rain clouds, and the weather looked dismal. It seemed a particularly treacherous time to seek out the enemy; but then, no weather was ever ideal for the grunts humping the mountains and rice paddies of Quang Nam Province. According to recon, their quarry was a band of VC spotted on one of the mountain infiltration routes.

For the Marines in I Corps, the war in Vietnam was fast drawing to a close. The large, major battles of three years before were a thing of the past. There were no more regimental size conflicts. By mid-1970, NVA and VC units were infrequently encountered in more than platoon strength. The level of enemy activity continued to decline in early 1971. Rarely did the Marines encounter the enemy in groups larger than six men. Today's patrol was a continuation of what was called Operation Imperial Lake.

Imperial Lake began five months before in the eastern Que Son Mountains, twenty-five miles southwest of Da Nang. The enemy had never been completely flushed from the area, for the lowlands of Quang Nam Province were rich in rice, and the mountains beyond provided excellent trails for infiltration of men and supplies. Typical of field battalion operations, Imperial Lake consisted of one or more companies conducting snoop 'n' poop operations—cordon and search efforts against areas suspected of harboring enemy soldiers. The goal was to keep pressure on the enemy in the Fifth Marines tactical area of operations.

1st Platoon was divided among two Sea Knights, both of which began their descent as they neared the LZ. The LZ was not supposed to be hot, and the elephant grass at the base of the mountain had already been flattened by fifteen-thousand-pound Daisy Cutters. Captain Meredith got up and shouted words of encouragement to each Marine. Behind him, the crew chief spoke to the pilot through a headset. Townsend was surprised Meredith knew everyone's name. As CO, he had four platoons and one hundred fifty men under his command. Meredith was tall, about six-two, and he had a lanky muscularity.

His short, jet-black hair had a touch of gray at the temples. Soon he stood over Townsend.

"You're going to be okay, Doc," Meredith said. He had a rich, kind voice.

"If you say so, sir."

"This your first patrol?"

"Yes, sir. I'm a field hospital kind of guy."

"So I heard. Just stick with me, and I'll keep you out of trouble. I know how you feel about combat, but keep your weapon ready, hear?"

"Yes, sir."

He wasn't surprised the captain knew his views on the necessity of war; few people didn't. They were probably written on the jacket of his personnel file. Until a year ago, those feelings were the cornerstone of his young existence. Those who knew him thought of Jon as a young man with a social conscience. He'd been against the war in Vietnam for years. When he turned eighteen, he was registered 1-0 with the Selective Service Administration as a conscientious objector; and that summer, he demonstrated at the Democratic National Convention in his hometown of Chicago.

Northwestern University had an active antiwar movement, and when Jon registered for classes in the fall, he participated in campus protests. It was a heady time of activism liberally mixed with marijuana. And then, in the late spring of 1970, Jon's world fell apart. Word came that his best friend had been killed in combat.

Jon was devastated. He and Randy had been closer than brothers since kindergarten. They agreed on virtually everything except the war. The saddest moment of Jon's life was when Randy joined the service. But on the eve of Randy's departure, they celebrated old times together, kidding one another good-naturedly, promising to get together as soon as Randy returned home. But then....

When he heard the news, Jon went into an emotional tailspin. He couldn't eat or sleep for days. The pointlessness of Randy's death was precisely the sort of thing over which the two of them often quarreled. But in the wake of his friend's death, something strange happened to Jon. Given the circumstances, any other person would have redoubled his antiwar efforts. Yet Jon couldn't. He felt profound guilt, and a part of him died along with his friend. The other part would not, or could not, keep demonstrating. The day the spring semester ended, he enlisted in the Navy.

He didn't want to fight. He had no interest in pay back, no desire to hurt the enemy as they'd done to him. Rather, he wanted to serve. To help. To be there for others the way he hoped someone would have been there for Randy. To that end, he hoped to become a Marine corpsman. If he couldn't stop the fighting, at least he could come to the aid of those wounded by it.

The Navy agreed—but first he had to become a soldier. After basic training in San Diego, they sent him to Camp Pendleton, where they taught him to shoot and fight like any other grunt. Only once he qualified with his weapon did they teach him about battle dressings and plasma expanders and sucking chest wounds. They taught him quickly, and they taught him well. By New Year's Eve, 1970, Jon Townsend was a Marine corpsman.

His platoon, however, was not sent to Vietnam. With peace negotiations underway, Marine units were returning home. Still, there was a need for individual soldiers, and Jon was ordered to Vietnam as a replacement. Once in country, he was first assigned to an evacuation hospital, which was temporarily shorthanded. Shortly thereafter, he was sent to 1st Platoon, M Company, as a replacement corpsman.

The men in his platoon were distant, noncommittal. They had little inclination to socialize. Redeployment was in the air, and they'd heard that the Marines would soon cease combat operations. Staying alive and unhurt was paramount in their minds, but they still had to do an occasional patrol. Their last one had been scrubbed; but now, as the Sea Knight descended toward the LZ four klicks from Fire Support Base Ross, they were once again in the thick of it.

As they came in for a landing, Jon saw the base of the mountain before them. Up in the hills, the clouds had opened up. In the distance, he could see rippling sheets of gray rain sliding down the mountain in ghostly waves. The crew chief was shouting, readying everyone; but as Jon had become lost in his own fear, he scarcely heard what the man was saying. His knees shook, his bowels tightened, and he was experiencing maximum pucker factor. The chopper wheels hit the ground with a thump.

Then the men were rushing outside through the rear ramp, M-16s at the ready.

The next thing Jon knew, someone had seized his arm and propelled him forward. It was Captain Meredith.

"Let's go, Doc. Stick with me!"

Jon followed blindly. Running behind the captain, he charged out of the helicopter into the rotor wash and onto the flattened grass. Nearby, the platoon's second helicopter was coming in for a landing. All at once, they were struck by the rain. Instead of advancing slowly, the storm came on like a descending curtain, a sudden wall of hammering water. Enormous raindrops pelted them like hail. The rotor-whipped deluge made a thunderous sound as it splattered their helmets and splashed through the grass.

Within seconds, visibility was nonexistent. The men hunkered down, open and vulnerable, not sure what to do. The sergeant rushed up.

"The tree line, Captain?"

"Right. On the double."

"All right, let's go, *di di mau!*" the sergeant shouted to the men. "Form up and follow me!"

Within seconds, Jon was once more running in Captain Meredith's footsteps. Beneath the grass, the soft earth was quickly turning to mud. Jon's boots made huge splashes where his pounding feet struck the ground. He couldn't see more than ten feet in front of him. Heart in his mouth, Jon followed the other men toward the forest refuge, terrified that they'd be hit by gunfire at any minute.

But they reached the woods unscathed. The men huddled together in small groups behind tree trunks, weapons up and ready. Diverted by the foliage overhead, the rain seemed to lessen. Frightened and soaked, Jon didn't know what to do.

"Should I put on my poncho?" he asked the man beside him.

"Fuck that. It'll clear up soon."

As predicted, the rain stopped within minutes. The storm departed as fast as it arrived, sweeping east over the lowlands toward the South China Sea. Jon counted the men around him and reckoned the entire platoon was present. A mile away, the departing choppers became disappearing specks.

The patrol's destination was an infiltration trail halfway up the mountain. Intelligence said the enemy was there, and it was 1st platoon's job to intercept and destroy them. Soon the men split up into squads and cautiously advanced up the hillside.

The change in weather was abrupt. Within minutes the storm was gone as quickly as it had struck, and bright morning light filtered through the jungle canopy. Hidden forest creatures began to trill. Where the light touched damp foliage, the sunbeams created clouds of steamy vapor. Within minutes the jungle air became sweltering. Here and there, the rays of sun penetrating the overhead boughs shined like spotlights on the emerald objects below.

Jon was in the captain's squad, along with six other Marines. The point man, a corporal, led the way, with Meredith second, and Jon behind him. They moved slowly, cautiously. The trail was only a fifteen-degree incline, but the sudden heat, and the weight of what he was carrying, made Jon sweat profusely. The field pack on his shoulders weighed twenty-five pounds.

To provide treatment, Fleet Marine Force Field Medical Service Corpsmen relied on a rucksack of supplies called a "Unit One," officially termed the Surgical Instrument and Supply Set. It contained combat dressings and bandages of various sizes, a suture set, scissors, airways, intracaths, syringes, and a gas mask bag. Diagnostic equipment was limited to a stethoscope, a blood pressure cuff, and a flashlight. The corpsman's primary mission was to render emergency first aid: hit 'em with volume, patch 'em, give them morphine, and prepare them for medevac.

To that end, the corpsman usually carried several containers of IV solutions, IV tubing, auto-injectable morphine, and epinephrine. There were also oral drugs—vials of Darvon, Benadryl, Compazine, injectable penicillin, and penicillin and erythromycin in tablet form. In addition, Jon's pack contained two pounds of C-4 explosive, a few poncho liners, personal items like extra socks, and a five-pound spare radio battery.

As if that weight were not enough, he also carried his personal weapon, several knives, and two bandoleers of twenty-round M-16 magazines. Other corpsmen carried .45s as sidearms, but Jon thought that was overdoing it. As it was, he doubted he'd ever use his weapon. He knew *how*, but that wasn't why he joined the Marines.

Fortunately, he was in good shape. He was five-eleven and one hundred seventy-five pounds, and he'd always been athletic. After the squad advanced a hundred yards, his breath came easier. Walking more comfortably, he slowly took in his surroundings. He'd been told these mountains were typical Southeast Asian rainforest, something the density and dampness attested to. He recognized pine, ferns, and immense thickets of bamboo. There were numerous species of tropical broadleaf trees, but the most striking feature was the vines— curled, gnarled masses that attached to everything.

Leaves dripped all over. And coming from everywhere were the audible cries, shrieks, and whoops of forest creatures, a cacophony of mammal, bird, and insect. There was an occasional screech, followed by a frantic, maniacal chattering, interrupted by the riffling of branch and bough. The most noticeable sound, coming from on high, was the incessant, high-pitched frenzy of insects at work, a noise reminiscent of locust, or cicada.

For Jon, the sensory stimulation by sight and sound was both overwhelming and otherworldly. There was madness here, but also great beauty. At any other time, he might have thought he was in a magical place, but now his overriding emotion was fear. He tread lightly, and his palms were so damp they felt oily. His eyes darted about as he nervously scanned the trail. Suddenly, he saw two eyes staring at him from the middle of a tree trunk. He was terrified.

"Holy shit," he mumbled.

Meredith whirled, bringing his rifle to bear. He squinted at what Jon was looking at. Then he lowered his M-16's barrel and approached the tree. "Come here, Doc."

Jon ambled closer, never taking his eyes off of what was staring at him. Soon, he saw that they weren't eyes at all. "Is that a butterfly?"

"Yes, it is," Meredith said softly. "Looks human, from a distance. Those blobs are a defense mechanism. They're called pseudo-eyes."

On the tips of the lower wings were quarter-size, orange globules that resembled perfect irises. In their centers were elliptical ebony slits, like the irises of a cat. The overall impression was that of a dangerous feline, but it was offset by the beautiful wings above them—chocolate brown in color, with delicate turquoise streaking.

"That's amazing," Jon said. "I never would've guessed."

"Keep your voice down, son. There are lots of beautiful things in this hell hole." He turned and looked overhead, pointing up at the jungle canopy.

Jon gazed up at the curious creatures forty feet away. "Wow, are those monkeys?"

"Macaques. They're all over the place. Also, rhesus monkeys, langurs, and a dozen other species I can't identify. But look, Doc. I know this is your first patrol, but we have a job to do here, and there's not much time for sightseeing. You'll pick up on that, in time. So, look sharp and keep your eyes peeled for bad guys, okay?"

"Yes, sir."

The patrol resumed. There came the metallic snick of safeties being thumbed from safe to fire. Spaced five yards apart, the men moved cautiously but steadily and were soon five hundred yards up the mountainside. There was no sign of the enemy. This was fine with Jon, who pointed his M-16 down at a forty-five-degree angle, with his right index finger outside the trigger guard. His initial terror had lessened to a state of continuous anxiety. As he walked, he had to concentrate on keeping the damp vines off him. He was truly a stranger in a strange land, bewildered, frightened, and yet fascinated.

The squad moved on. Suddenly the corporal stopped and raised his hand. The men halted, and everyone took a knee. The air grew tense, and Jon held his breath. Then the man on point signaled for them to stay put while he went ahead, approaching something in the bush. Soon, he waved the squad forward.

Following the captain, Jon came up behind the point man, who gestured toward a nearby tree. Turning in that direction, Jon immediately noticed the snake. The wriggling reptile was five feet long and hung by its tail from a tree branch. It vaguely resembled a rattler, but Jon thought it far more beautiful, with evenly spaced brown bands around a white body. It writhed because it was in the process of devouring something.

Protruding from the snake's jaws were a green torso attached to a pair of legs. At first, Jon thought it was a frog. The legs jerked spasmodically as it struggled to free itself. But its head and forelegs were well inside the snake's gullet, and there was no escape. Every few seconds the snake would twist as it widened its jaws for another swallow. Branch, snake, and prey swayed together in a macabre ballet of death. Captain Meredith spoke in a whisper.

"Bamboo snake," he told Townsend. "Probably his breakfast."

"It that a frog?"

"No, a green gecko. That snake loves lizards. They're all part of the master food chain." Nodding toward the point man, Meredith signaled the squad to resume patrol. The men silently paraded past the reptilian struggle.

The trail narrowed, walled in by dense hanging vines. A little farther up, the corporal again signaled a halt, this time more urgently. Once more, the squad took a knee. The point man slowly crawled ahead in a tight crouch, eyes on something around the trail's bend. He pointed at the captain and waved him up alone. Jon's pounding heart wanted to erupt from his chest. Not wanting to leave his commander, he followed at a safe distance.

The two men up front communicated by hand signals. Jon gathered that the corporal might have spotted the enemy and wanted to know how to proceed. Meredith indicated that the two of them would check it out, with the rest of the men staying put until indicated. Signaling his intentions to the men in the rear, Meredith inched ahead.

Corporal and captain moved stealthily toward the trail bend, M-16s at the ready. Overhead, the relentless insect chatter continued, oblivious to the movement below. Jon's eyes bulged as he watched them advance. He wasn't ready for this. Deep down, he hoped the point man was mistaken, that his eyes were playing tricks on him. Beads of sweat rolled down Jon's cheeks. Well trained though he was, he felt emotionally unequipped for combat. Perhaps he might be, after a few more patrols. But now....

All of a sudden, the corporal straightened up and charged ahead, firing a deafening burst from his weapon. Jon's jaw dropped, completely unprepared for what he was seeing. The captain immediately followed, rounding the bend. Jon's heart was in his throat. Behind him, the rest of the squad rushed forward for support. But they'd just begun to move when the air was ripped by an ear-splitting explosion that shook the ground.

What happened after that seemed to occur in slow motion. The next thing Jon knew, Captain Meredith was flying backward like a rag doll. His spine struck a massive pine, and then his torso slumped over, supported by a bamboo thicket. For some reason, the thing Jon noticed most was the abrupt cessation of insect noise.

"Corpsman!" someone shouted. "Corpsman up!"

Suddenly energized, Jon leapt ahead, oblivious to danger. His hollow legs felt brittle, but he had to reach the captain. His gaze never left Captain Meredith, who appeared unconscious. His senseless body tilted into the bamboo at a peculiar angle. Jon spotted a widening bloodstain on the front of the captain's shirt. Reaching his CO, Jon tugged off Meredith's rucksack and web gear and dropped them on the ground.

"Captain!" he said. "Can you hear me, Captain Meredith?"

Meredith didn't reply. His eyes were narrowed to slits, and he was clearly stunned into unconsciousness, or worse. The blood was a problem that needed immediate attention. Jon tried to ease the captain to the jungle floor. Yet when he touched the captain's shoulder, Meredith's weight shifted. He leaned heavily into the bamboo, which started to give way.

Looking at the spot where the captain was going to fall, something caught Jon's eye. A strand of what looked like horizontal fishing line was stretched taut, a foot off the ground. Jon's eyes widened in horror. He instantly recognized it as the trip wire for a booby trap. If the captain's toppling continued, they'd both be blown to bits. Jon lunged and grabbed Meredith from behind.

Dazed and glassy-eyed, Meredith saw everything in a blur. His ears were ringing, and green forest foliage danced before him. He felt arms encircling him—strong, steady arms, pulling him up and away. Then they pulled him free from the bamboo and laid him back down on the trail.

The voices up ahead were shrill.

"Oh Jesus, Jesus," one said.

"Fuckin' booby trap," said another. "Blew the shit out of him."

And then a sound like bees zinged through the air, followed by the distinctive crack of AK-47s.

"We're taking fire!" someone shouted. "Fall back!"

The men retreated into defensive positions. Almost immediately, the ambush gunfire ceased. Jon grabbed Meredith under the armpits and dragged him to the rear. Another man retrieved their packs. The defensive perimeter stabilized enough for them to tend to the wounded. Jon quickly knelt beside the captain and ripped open his blouse. Meredith blinked his eyes, struggling to focus.

"Take it easy, Captain," Jon said. "You're going to be okay."

Meredith's upper abdomen was soaked in blood. Just beneath the left rib cage, a tiny puncture oozed briskly. Jon retrieved a large field dressing from his pack and ripped open its wrapper. Though labeled camouflage, the dressing was pink. He pressed it firmly to the wound to stanch the flow of blood. Several Marines looked on.

"Did he take a round, Doc?" one asked.

"Something hit him, but I don't know if it's a bullet. Looks more like shrapnel. Give me a hand and press on this."

They switched places. Jon removed a two-hundred-fifty cc container of albumin from his aid kit and attached IV tubing. After draining the infusion through the tubing, he rolled up the captain's sleeve and wrapped a latex tourniquet around the biceps. Opening an intracath, he found a vein, plunged the catheter home, and attached the IV tubing.

Once he adjusted the flow, Jon looked up and found Meredith watching him.

"Don't worry, sir, they radioed for a dust-off. We'll have you out of here pronto."

Just then, the Marine helping him with the dressing shouted incomprehensibly and reached for his rifle. But before he could level it, Jon was nearly deafened by a sudden burst of AK-47 fire. His face was stung by muzzle blast, and as he reflexively averted his head, he saw the Marine go down with a shoulder wound. Turning back, Jon's eyes went wide at the sight of a black-pyjamaed Viet Cong rising from the bush two meters away.

In that instant, Jon was certain he was dead. His entire life had come down to this, and he felt utterly helpless. Events once again moved with infinite slowness. He felt peculiarly paralyzed as he reached for the M-16 the wounded Marine had dropped at Jon's feet. His hand closed around its black stock just as the VC raised his AK and fired toward Jon's midsection.

The searing pain in his left hip coincided with another deafening roar. Jon looked in his enemy's dark eyes, and the man stared back at him. Then the AK's muzzle rose to Jon's chest. He watched with a strangely detached curiosity as the VC's finger tightened on the trigger. But nothing happened. Both soldiers looked down at the rifle. A shell casing was stuck in the ejection port, and the weapon was jammed.

"Shoot him!" shouted Meredith, now awake. "For Christ sake, shoot him!"

As Jon leveled his M-16, the black-clad enemy looked up, his eyes gone round with terror. Jon's finger slipped past the trigger guard. But for some reason, he hesitated.

He was in a kill or be killed situation, preparing to take the life of a man who'd just shot him—yet he could not.

A second later, a fusillade of gunfire erupted from the men behind him. Jon heard the whizzing rounds zing past. The impact of a dozen rounds on the enemy's chest was ferocious. The VC's head snapped back, and he collapsed in a lifeless heap. Then the shooters rushed over, kicking the man to make sure he was dead.

Rifles at their shoulders, the rest of the squad gathered round, forming a protective semicircle for aid and cover. Jon snapped out of the doldrums and knelt beside the wounded Marine. The 7.62-millimeter bullet had struck him just above the clavicle and torn through the upper border of his trapezius muscle. Although the grunt was moaning, it wasn't a life-threatening injury. In less than a minute, Jon had him patched and injected with morphine.

"Bird's up," called the radioman. "They'll be at the LZ in ten minutes."

By this time, the sergeant in the squad nearest Jon's arrived and assumed charge. Whatever enemy there was seemed to have melted away. Four men not providing cover made a litter from a poncho liner and lifted Meredith onto it. Although pale, Meredith was now fully alert. He and the sergeant discussed the withdrawal.

"They're also sending a gunship, Sarge," the radioman said. "I told 'em we're in deep serious, and they want us down the hill, hotel alpha."

"All right, move out!" the sergeant called. "My squad's on the drag while you guys get down there with the wounded."

Holding the four ends of the poncho liner, the men lifted Meredith up. He glanced at the other wounded man, then at Townsend.

"How's he doing, Doc?"

"A clean hole in the muscle, he'll be okay. He can hump it down the hill. It'll be a few minutes before the morphine turns him stupid."

Meredith looked at Jon's hip. "Looks like you got dinged yourself."

In the frenzied aftermath of battle, Jon had forgotten his

own wound. The momentary flash of pain was gone, and now it was numb. Looking below his left hip, a large crimson stain moistened his fatigues down to the middle of his thigh. Using one of his knives, he made a slit in the fatigues. The .30-caliber bullet had gouged an inch-deep crease on the outside of his quadriceps, barely missing bone.

"Jesus, will you look at that. I can hardly feel it." He took a heavy pad from his pack and pressed it to the wound.

The sergeant had enough of the delaying chitchat. "Goddammit, let's get this litter down the hill!"

"We had a KIA, Sarge," one of the men said, handing over the dead man's dog tags. "The corporal took a Bouncing Betty right in the nuts."

"Shit! Are you bringing him down?"

"No can do. He's in pieces."

"Then what are you waiting for? Move out!"

Both squads began a defensive retreat down the mountainside, with riflemen covering the front and rear. Jon's wound started to ache dully, and he knew it wouldn't be long before it began throbbing. He couldn't believe the day had turned to shit so quickly. Between the rain, the steamy sun, and the forest creatures, the patrol had begun with a kind of exotic beauty; but in an astonishingly short time, violence and death stood enchantment on its head. At war, Vietnam was an intense land of extremes.

Walking alongside the makeshift litter, Jon changed and reinforced the captain's quickly saturated dressing. The brisk bleeding had slowed. Captain Meredith was going to need exploratory surgery to learn what damage had been done. It didn't appear that anything life-threatening had been injured; his groin pulses were full and regular, and he could move his legs. Still, even a tiny piece of shrapnel could have torn through a piece of bowel, or lacerated the spleen or kidney. They were all significant injuries, but unless an artery had been severed, they shouldn't prove mortal.

"You're doing fine, sir," Jon said. "How's the pain?"

"Tolerable. Maybe you can hit me with some of that morphine at the LZ."

"No problem, Captain."

Meredith looked him in the eye. "Tell me something, Doc. Why did you hesitate back there?"

"Sir?"

"Why didn't you shoot?"

Jon felt his face redden. He looked away, unable to maintain eye contact. He felt an overpowering sense of shame, of having disappointed those who depended on him. With comrades killed and wounded, how could he explain to Captain Meredith that what happened to him was the truest test of his convictions, of the fabric of his person, of what he really felt about war? At least, that was his rationalization. The strangest thing was, now that he was a member of the platoon, he wasn't sure he still felt that way. When it came right down to it, maybe he just choked.

"I...I don't know, sir."

"I'm going to say this just once, son," Meredith continued. "Sometimes life has a way of forcing a man to see what he's made of. And you never realize it until that moment arrives. But if you're ever forced to make that decision again, don't dwell on it. Just pull the damn trigger."

CHAPTER 7

Great Smoky Mountains

An unusually cold fall wind ripped across the Appalachian hilltops, sending scores of yellow and gold leaves fluttering skyward. Seen from the ridgeline, the valley that stretched toward Asheville was a quilted patchwork of farmland that neared the end of harvest season. To O'Brien, the mountains were a sanctuary of solitude in a frenzied world, a placid retreat where wilderness met rural countryside. So different from Boston, he thought. The mountains, called balds, had densely-timbered forests that suddenly gave way to open panoramas of wild, unforgettable vegetation—toothwort, mountain laurel, and Michaux's saxifrage. There were acres of tall grasses and purple sedges that rippled in the wind. On the wooded hillsides of the Great Smoky Mountains, where the Appalachian Trail rides the border between Tennessee and North Carolina, one could easily become lost in the natural beauty. Or one could hide. It was for precisely this reason that the Southern Cross used the area as a refuge.

There were times, though, that he longed for the bustle and crowds of Beantown, his birthplace. Southern whiskey was a frequent comfort, but it wasn't the same as the saloon-based sociability of Charlestown and South Boston, where one could drift from one hallowed Hibernian bar to the next, where one's loyalty was forged in a heady mixture of dark stout and chowder and daily Mass, and where the sense of history was thick in the air, like fog. What had happened to the place? His onetime cronies claimed that the city's slide began in the early

Sixties, when the town fathers ran bulldozers through Scollay Square to make room for Government Center and City Hall. Nothing, they said, had been the same since. As time went by, stately old brick houses on cobblestone streets became townhouses, which were turned into condominiums. The Irish left their neighborhoods, ceding the streets and the schools to minorities, to the Haitians and Lebanese and blacks who now accounted for half of the city's population. With the infusion of immigrants, an elegant brogue yielded to the lilting sounds of foreign tongues. An exotic grocery store was on every street corner, and smells of mango and goat and curry hung in the air.

But there was no going back now. He might travel to the Middle or Far East in search of men named Mahmoud, or to anywhere in the world for that matter, but never to his hometown. Returning to Boston would be suicidal. The door to that part of his life was closed forever, not because of his Irish heritage, but due to events in his line of work. It wasn't simply that he had run afoul of the law; that's what criminals did. Rather, he had crossed too many people, and he owed too many personal debts. There was one he could never repay. He owed his life to someone, and that debt bound him as inextricably to another man as if they shared the same organs. It was because of that debt that Sean O'Brien had left Boston and joined—and in many ways founded—the Southern Cross. And it was in service of that gratitude that he now followed what he considered a higher calling.

The Gaza Strip

From the Shati refugee camp, the tranquil westward view across the blue Mediterranean was a stark contrast to the steady undercurrent of tension within the camp.

The camp had eighty thousand residents, and most had lived in turmoil and discomfort for years. This was especially true for the children, who made up more than half of Gaza's population. They had to play near open sewers during the day, and they slept eight to a room at night.

Twenty-eight-year-old Mahmoud al-Abed no longer

crowded into a bedroom, for he had his own place in Gaza City with two other Palestinians. All were members of Hamas, the militant Islamic resistance movement dedicated to the destruction of Israel. Growing up a directionless, poorly educated child, Mahmoud grew into manhood during the *intifada*, the Palestinian uprising against Israeli occupation. It was then that he uncovered his sense of self. In Hamas he found a purpose, a goal that transcended the days of his life or the small space of his existence. His duty lay in waging jihad to liberate Palestine. Martyrdom, if it came to that, would be an honor.

For months, Mahmoud had lived in a state of heightened anxiety. It was the sort of emotional dissatisfaction that could only be relieved by firm, determined action. The possibility of American troops in the Middle East was intolerable to Hamas— and, by extension, to Mahmoud—for Americans had long proved themselves to be Zionist lackeys. Not that those in the struggle hadn't experienced similar moments before. The Oslo peace accords between Israel and the PLO were demoralizing, but Hamas had regrouped and intensified its campaign of terror. Now, too, Hamas knew what had to be done.

As the Americans had not yet arrived, Mahmoud had no finite plans. Mahmoud did not know his part, but he knew it would be big. Over the past fifteen years, he had proven his loyalty many times, most recently in a devastating Tel Aviv bombing. Long before that, he'd spent five years in southern Lebanon, harassing Israeli troops until they finally withdrew. This time, both the Israelis and the Americans would be taught a lesson.

Until then, however, he was tightly wound. Mahmoud was a slender, dark-haired, black-eyed man whom women found attractive. He spent the bulk of his down time—which, at present, was all the time—in cafes, trying to lessen the tension. It didn't help that he drank coffee by the liter and smoked a carton of cigarettes every three days. His mind was constantly active. The times he needed to get away from his thoughts were becoming more and more frequent.

When he did, his proven release was the same it had been

since he was a child. He would walk directly toward the sea—away from the Shati camp, across the asphalt highway, and down the barren, sandy slope toward the beach. He once walked barefoot, but now he wore designer sneakers. The slopes were littered with dangerous rubble, the detritus of a people that was losing hope.

On the coarse brown sand, Mahmoud walked out into the gentle surf and rolled up his pants legs. He was standing in the same location that, over three thousand years before, had been invaded by the Philistines, a seafaring people that eventually overran the Eastern Mediterranean. The Philistines were direct ancestors of all Palestinians.

After several minutes of gazing out to sea, Mahmoud repeated the ritual that always soothed him as much as his mother's breast. He felt in the moment, in the midst of an eternity that was his fate. With a long, wistful look at the watery horizon, he turned around and gazed back over the camp, across the city, and toward Israel. One part belonged to his people, the other part to their sworn enemy. *Insh-Allah*, one day soon the Israelis would be driven away, and all the land would be theirs.

The thought calmed him. Restored, filled with resolve, he slowly left the water and returned to the beach. A successful jihad was both God's will and his own destiny.

The White House

First Lady Roxanne Meredith slipped out of the donated black Versace dress and hung it on the valet in the bedroom. At fifty-five, ten years younger than her husband, she still had the good looks that had initially attracted him years before. At five-five and one hundred thirty pounds, her trim body was toned by daily workouts in the White House gym. Undoing the French bun in her hair, she began to brush her long blond tresses.

Across the room, President Meredith lay on the bed in his white shirt and tuxedo pants. His arm rested across his face, its crook shielding his eyes from the light. Every so often, he coughed.

"How're you feeling, Bob? Any after-effects?"

"Nothing but embarrassment. I'm just tired. Those damn Israelis are the most stubborn people I've ever dealt with. Getting them to go along with something is like pulling teeth."

"Do you think they'll come around?"

"They can't afford not to. There's too much riding on this. After the progress they made with the Palestinians, the whole world expects them make peace with the Syrians. Asad's kid," he said, referring to the Syrian president, "is on board with the idea of our troops, but the Israelis, God almighty."

"They didn't sound opposed to it tonight."

"Fundamentally they're not. They *want* us there. It was as much their idea as ours. It's just the crazy kind of government they have, the coalition business. They have to kiss the butt of all their coalition partners to get the deal done, and from what I gather, their fundamentalists are just as extreme as some of the nuts we have down where I come from. So, we're back to arm-twisting and ass-kissing."

"At that, you have no equal."

"Which?"

"The arm-twisting, of course." She put down the brush, walked over, and sat on the bed beside him, stroking his nearly white hair. "Are you sure you're okay, Bob? When I saw you standing over the dinner table gasping for air, I thought I was going to die. I haven't been that frightened in years."

"Me either. Not being able to breathe has got to be the world's most helpless feeling. I couldn't move any air at all." He looked across the room, reflecting. "Actually, it happened to me once before."

"Recently?"

"No, I was a kid. I think I was about ten. I was up in Asheville, on vacation with my folks. I was canoeing with a friend of mine on a lake around there. For some reason the damn canoe tipped over, and the next thing I knew, I took in a lung full of water. I couldn't breathe, and I was choking. But all I remember was the other kid yelling at me to stop making noise and to help him right the canoe."

"Not very sympathetic of him."

"At that age, who is?"

She leaned over and kissed his forehead. "So, you're really okay now?"

"Yes, my dear, I am. Sometimes I might be at a loss for words, but I can't afford to be at a loss for breath."

In reality, the president was rarely at a loss for words. Not only a gifted speaker, some considered him an orator, the most dynamic Oval Office conversationalist since John Kennedy. But his greater gift was more for people than words. Both leader and charmer, his natural charisma made Americans rally to his side and support his programs, including the Israeli-Syrian military peacekeeper proposal. The president's approval ratings were consistently high.

Part of his charm owed to his appearance. Bob Meredith had the look of a statesman. His once-black hair was now a distinguished white, which he kept long and combed straight back. He was tall and fit. His long, angular face was sharp-featured, and in diplomatic discussions he had a no-nonsense, serious expression. But in casual speech, his austere appearance was transformed by a joking wit and a disarming smile that put everyone at ease.

Now nearing the end of the third year of his first term in office, there was little doubt in anyone's mind that President Meredith would seek re-election. The country demanded it. The economy remained robust, unemployment was low, and there was nationwide prosperity. Other than some unrest on the Pacific Rim and the Middle East, no major conflicts loomed. There was little reason for the American people to want a different leader, especially when the one they had was revered by nearly everyone.

Meredith got off the bed and stripped down to his shorts. Rocky watched him. For a man his age, he still had a remarkably good physique. He was only ten pounds heavier than when they first met. He had a personal trainer and worked out every other day.

If I get in five hours of sleep tonight, Meredith thought, *I'll be lucky.* He was a country boy at heart, and country boys needed their slumber, working hard during the day before sleeping soundly at night. But long, undisturbed nights were now a rarity. He sometimes longed for the cool, quilt-covered nights of his youth, when the stars filled the skies over Sumter National Forest.

Although he'd lost his Southern drawl, Robert Meredith was still very much a South Carolinian who loved his burley tobacco and bourbon whiskey. Raised in Columbia, he'd spent his pre-Washington years in Charleston. He'd been a modestly successful lawyer before Vietnam, but several years after he was discharged from the Marine Corps, he was elected to Congress. Four years later he was in the Senate, and once there, he never looked back.

Roxanne resumed brushing her hair. "I worry about you, darling. I don't want anything to happen to you."

"I'm too old and too stubborn for that, Rocky,"

"Sixty-five doesn't qualify as old these days. Ask anyone who wants you re-elected."

"I have. Mitch told me CNN will broadcast the results of a poll tomorrow that has me forty percentage points above any possible challenger."

"Forty?" she said with a smile. "That must be some kind of a record."

"It is."

"That's wonderful, darling. But most people your age retire, you know. Are you still certain this is what you want? No second thoughts?"

"None whatsoever," he said. "But even if I did, the people wouldn't let me. They're pretty satisfied with what I've done so far."

"So am I."

He reached out and squeezed her arm. His wife was the most adored first lady since Jackie Kennedy. "I don't suppose you'd have a problem living here another four years, would you?"

"Oh, I think I could manage it."

In truth, Roxanne Meredith loved being first lady. It was as if she'd been made for the job. Rocky reveled in public life the same way others cherished their privacy. She never dabbled in policy, but she was up front and outspoken on things Americans cherished most—family, health, and education. If she acted like she cared, it was because she did. She genuinely liked her fellow citizens as much as they seemed to adore her. It didn't hurt that she was photogenic. Rocky had bright, flashing eyes and an effervescent smile that radiated enthusiasm. Although she dressed very well, she was never ostentatious. Even her critics conceded her understated elegance. What was most appealing, however, was her sincerity. Rocky meant what she said, and her genuine honesty was deeply appreciated by a grateful public. By almost any definition, Roxanne Meredith was the real deal, the perfect complement to an equally adored husband.

Roxanne was the new definition of celebrity, and the press had an ongoing love affair with her. She'd been on the cover of every major newsmagazine at least once.

There was an article, large or small, about Rocky in every issue of *People*, and she graced its cover an average of once every seven months. Journalists frequently purported to know "what Roxanne Meredith's *really* like," but what they generally revealed was that Rocky was an intelligent, attractive woman from Atlanta who was devoted to her husband and her country.

In short, she looked forward to another four years as first lady as much as the voters looked forward to her being there. And why not? She represented the office with charm, wit, style, and grace.

"Have you decided on the date of the re-election announcement yet?" she asked.

"Probably the week before Thanksgiving. It'll make the Sunday morning talk shows and still be on people's minds when they get together for the holiday."

That was news to her. "A month from now? I thought you didn't want to wait that long."

"What makes you say that?"

"You did. You said yesterday that you were thinking of announcing your run a year to the day before the vote."

For several seconds, the president stared at his wife oddly. Then he slowly lapsed into a skeptical smile. "Come on, Rock. You funnin' this old boy? I never said that."

She was equally serious. "Bob, I am not making this up. Don't you remember, at breakfast yesterday morning? We had a long talk about it."

"I think you're dreaming."

She took a deep breath. "Darling, I am not imagining this. You said it plain as day." She paused. "It doesn't matter though. A month from now is fine with me."

There was a flash of annoyance in Meredith's eyes, and he turned around to face her. "So, what're you saying, that I don't remember what we talked about twenty-four hours ago?"

She returned to the valet and put on her robe. "Of course not. But maybe you should tell me. What *did* we talk about at yesterday's breakfast?"

Brow knitted, he looked toward the floor, concentrating. Then he paced across the floor until he put on his own robe. He wouldn't look at her. "This is silly. Let's change the subject."

Roxanne tied her robe and looked away, saying nothing. She knew her husband's physical health was good. According to Dr. Townsend, smoking and drinking were the only things Bob had to work on. But it was suddenly clear to Roxanne that her husband truly didn't recall their breakfast table conversation. Ordinarily, this wouldn't concern her. Any exceptionally busy person could be under enough stress to have an occasional memory lapse.

The problem was, this wasn't the first time it happened. Bob's forgetfulness was becoming increasingly noticeable. Rocky could recall three instances this month when he couldn't remember something they'd discussed. The first time she'd pointed it out to him, he'd been so embarrassed that she didn't point it out to him when it happened again—until tonight.

But he'd also been a little annoyed, something she noticed again this evening. When provoked in matters of state or politics, her husband could have a temper. Yet lately, he'd been growing terse with her, something decidedly out of character for him. Whatever strains their marriage had endured over the years, he'd never snapped at her. Now he'd begun acting peevish, crotchety, cranky as a baby.

Or was he at the other end of the spectrum? When Rocky's

mother had died two years ago, it had been from dementia. Even before the memory loss, the first symptom had been irritability. It had been an agonizingly cruel way to expire, and Rocky couldn't imagine going through it again. But she was letting her mind run away with her. Doubtless there were other more plausible explanations for her husband's behavior.

Although she might worry, she never thought it her role to be critical. Rather, her job was to be caring and supportive. Roxanne untied her robe and slipped out of it. Bob had just removed his shorts. She came up behind him, put her arms around him, and pressed her body into his.

"Changing the subject," she said into his ear, "is just what I had in mind."

San Diego, California

While the president was attending to matters in Washington, Vice President Anthony Doria got out of bed, unable to sleep. It was four a.m. He'd always been an early riser, and this was particularly true when he traveled. He switched on the bedside lamp and got out of bed. Putting on the hotel's complimentary robe, he walked to the heavy shades and pulled them open. His room had a terrace that looked out onto the Pacific. He unlatched the sliding glass doors and walked out into the early-morning air.

The temperature was in the seventies, and a steady westerly wind blew warmly onshore, ruffling the vice president's hair. He'd always loved an ocean breeze. When he was a child growing up in Quincy, he frequented the beaches at Cape Cod, where his brothers taught him to fly kites that soared aloft like sparkling prisms. There was something magical in the wind and the sky. He retained that fascination into adulthood and frequently referred to the elements in his speeches before the House of Representatives. He was an outspoken critic of pollution, and when Senator Meredith tapped him as his running mate, it went without saying that Doria would be the administration's point man on environmental issues.

He'd only been out of politics for four of the last twenty-six years. Doria's return to private life coincided with the oil crisis of the late 1970s. Applying his fondness of nature to business, he became president and later CEO of fledgling Trinity Energy Systems, a firm that specialized in alternative energy sources. Under his leadership, Trinity became a major manufacturer in wind and hydropower. When he returned to Congress, Doria remained a major Trinity board member.

Over the years, Trinity grew and expanded. They were now the national leader in providing clean, uninterrupted sources of energy and power. Trinity, always environmentally friendly, was opposed to the use of fossil fuels and combustion for generation of electricity. In addition to wind and waterpower, it had branched out into areas like proton-exchange membrane fuel cell development, fly wheels, and electrochemical technologies. If Trinity could have its way, it would pioneer the development of combustion-free vehicles and utility plants for the remainder of the century. Once he was elected to the vice presidency, Doria left Trinity's board but was frequently contacted as an unpaid consultant.

That was something he'd do today, in fact. And after breakfasting with Trinity executives, he was off to tour the Anza-Borrego Desert State Park before returning to La Jolla for a dinnertime fundraiser. It was common knowledge that the president would announce his re-election bid soon, and the party's coffers needed replenishing. When that was concluded, Air Force Two would fly him back to Washington.

Anthony Doria smiled at the prospect of re-election. Although he once had aspirations of the presidency himself, he enjoyed being vice president. Bob Meredith was both a capable national leader and a longtime friend. The president liked trinkets, and as Doria stood there savoring the pre-dawn breeze, he knew precisely what he'd bring to the White House this time.

CHAPTER 8

South China Sea
1971

The U.S.S. *Sanctuary*, an old, converted cargo ship, was one of seventeen U.S. Naval hospital ships assigned to the Seventh Fleet during the Vietnam War. Anchored three miles off Da Nang, the seven-hundred-fifty-bed *Sanctuary* often cruised the coastal waters of the southern Gulf of Tonkin abreast of the TAOR of I Corps, between Chu Lai and Hue. For patients, the ship's most conspicuous feature was a sign near the helicopter landing area that read, "You find 'em, we bind 'em. Open 24 hours." The *Sanctuary* often received casualties right out of the field. After Jon, Captain Meredith, and the other Marine were medevacked to the *Sanctuary*'s flight deck, they were rushed to triage. It had been a scant fifteen minutes since they left the field.

The ship's triage area, four main ORs, X-ray, and recovery room were amidships on the main deck, forward of the landing pads. The ship had two crews—one naval, one medical. When casualties were flown in, the deck was a frantically busy place. The wounded were often in such critical condition that they couldn't wait to be sent to the OR. Rather, they received urgent, lifesaving care right in X-ray or triage. Intubations were performed, blood was hung, and arterial bleeders clamped; chest tubes were inserted, urinary catheters were placed, and, time permitting, the patient was completely shaved and prepped for the OR.

Patients not quite so grievously wounded were assigned to surgical teams, such as general surgery, orthopedics, or urology, depending on their injuries. Captain Meredith was in that category, for although seriously injured, his life did not, at that point, hang in the balance. In triage he was stabilized and evaluated, where it was determined that the organs most likely damaged were the abdominal viscera, which was the domain of the general surgeons. The surgeons quickly readied him for the OR. At 0830, he went under the knife, and by 1000, he was in recovery. Everything considered, he was a lucky man. His spleen had to be removed, but aside from moderate blood loss, nothing else was seriously injured.

Patients not requiring exploratory surgery were treated in minor procedure rooms near the main ORs. Jon and the other Marine were in this category. Jon's gunshot wound was scrubbed, thoroughly debrided, and loosely closed with sutures. He'd be left with a noticeable scar, but no major deficits. By early afternoon, everyone, including the captain, was sent from recovery down to A Deck to convalesce.

The wards were unbelievably crowded. On occasion, those patients with minor wounds who awaited discharge were stacked six high in cramped bunks. Immediately post-op, however, patients had separate beds within an arm's reach of one another. Jon and Captain Meredith found themselves side by side on A Deck. When he awoke the day after surgery, Jon looked over at the captain, who was still asleep. An IV dripped into Meredith's arm. And his abdomen was dressed with gauze bandages that were held down with adhesive tape. A faint, watery bloodstain darkened the dressing under the tape.

"How're you feeling today, corpsman?"

A nurse at the foot of the bed had come to take his vital signs. She was young and pretty, with a pert, fresh-scrubbed look that seemed out of place among the wounded.

"Pretty good, ma'am."

"Do you have a lot of pain?"

His thigh wound throbbed continuously. But he was twenty years old, with a pretty girl in front of him. "Nothing I can't handle."

"Good. You're going to get out of bed today, and it might be a little uncomfortable at first. Don't be too proud to ask for a pain pill. Put this under your tongue."

After taking his temperature, pulse, and respirations, she wrote in her log and moved on to the next bed. By now, Meredith was awake.

"How was your night, Captain?" she asked. "Were you able to get any sleep?"

"Off and on. I'm thirsty as hell. Any chance I can get something to drink?"

"That's a good sign. The doctor will be by soon on rounds. He might start you on some liquids. Open up, and I'll take your temperature."

Soon she moved on. The patients didn't know it, but her bouncy, cheerful mood was as important to their recoveries as antibiotics. Meredith turned toward Jon.

"You have a girl back home, Doc?"

"'Morning, sir. No, no girl. I figure I've got plenty of time. Why, you think the nurse is available?"

"You never know. Of course, you'd have to fight off fifty other grunts, and probably a few dozen officers."

"You got that right," Jon said. "You sound pretty good, sir. But it must hurt like hell."

"It doesn't feel too bad. The doctor said most people don't need a spleen anyway. I'll tell you one thing, that Demerol is good stuff. I bet it'd go real well with some Kentucky sippin' whiskey."

Jon laughed. "Don't get *too* used to it, sir. It's addictive."

"I can understand why." He paused. "I want to thank you, Townsend, for what you did for me back there. The surgeon said your IV might've saved my life."

"Just doing my job, Captain. But...I want to apologize for what happened. I feel really bad about it. I think I let everyone down, including myself. It was on my mind all night. When I saw that guy in front of me, I just sort of froze, and—"

"Don't dwell on it, son," Meredith interrupted. "It's over and done with. As far as I'm concerned, I've already said all I want to about it."

Until then, Jon had been dreading this moment. Whatever his feelings were about the war, ever since he'd arrived at Camp Pendleton, he'd become a member of a team. Although he had a non-combat role, the men in his platoon had depended on him if things got hairy. But because of his inaction—or worse, cowardice—a fellow Marine had been wounded. Why hadn't he been able to shoot? What did the word courage mean to him? Had the years of non-violent confrontation come back to haunt him? As much as he thought about it, he didn't know. He fully expected to be reamed out for what happened, yet here, his CO had been unusually understanding. Had the roles been reversed, Jon didn't know if he could have done the same.

"Thank you, sir. I don't know what to say."

"Jesus, didn't I just tell you to forget about it?"

"Yes, sir. Are you really thirsty, Captain? I don't know if they can give you anything to drink after a bowel injury."

"They said my guts are fine," Meredith said. "The only thing that little piece of shrapnel just tore up was my spleen. What about you?"

"Just a deep gash. They told me I'm lucky. They debrided it and stitched it up. A month from now, I'll be back on patrol."

"Don't count on it, Doc. That might've been true a year ago, but I just heard it's DEROS for the entire MAF by May. Everyone's going home. Once that happens, the whole Corps will probably downsize. They don't need us any more, Townsend. We'll probably both get medical discharges."

"I don't get it, sir. Why would we be discharged?"

"Because it's too expensive to keep us in. We aren't going back into the field because there's not going to be any field, except for some Army units. So why pay us? I was a reservist who got called up, and you didn't want to be here anyway."

"Wow." Jon couldn't believe it. The war in Vietnam was finally drawing to a close, like he'd always wanted. It seemed so long in coming. But now that the end was in sight, it was rather unexpected, especially since he'd been in the thick of it. "That's great news."

"What are you going to do?"

"To be honest, Captain, I hadn't thought that far ahead. I expected to be here a while."

"You were in school, weren't you?"

"Yes, sir," Jon replied. "I finished two years at Northwestern."

"Seems like a perfect opportunity to go back. Who knows, if all your papers come through, you might even make it for the fall semester."

"I suppose. What about you, Captain Meredith? Aren't you a lawyer?"

"In fact, I am. I had a nice little country practice in Charleston. I doubt there's much left of it now."

"People always need the law, sir."

"Yes, but I wonder if I need it as much as they do. To tell you the truth, after what I've seen over here, I don't know if I have the heart for the law any more. You know, speeding tickets, drunk driving, petty larceny. I'm thinking of an entirely different direction."

"Like what?"

"Ten years ago, when I finished my first hitch and went to law school, I wanted to be a public defender, believe it or not. Instead, I wound up working for the DA's office just before I opened my own practice. But I still like the idea of public service. Next year's an election year, and I've been toying with the idea of running for Congress."

"For what it's worth, sir, you'd get my vote," Jon said. "You're a natural leader, and all the men look up to you."

"Thanks. My country's been good to me, Townsend. I think it's time I gave something back."

CHAPTER 9

Northern Israel

They picked up the van in Acre, an old Arab city to the north of Haifa. On its cargo panel, the van bore the Hebrew inscription, King David Plumbing. King David Plumbing was a legitimate, Israeli-registered business. What the Israelis did *not* know was that its Arab owners had strong sympathies with both Hamas and the Palestinians.

The van wound its way up Mt. Carmel toward the neighborhood of Nave Sha'anan. The mountain overlooked the picture-postcard city of Haifa, whose neat white-roofed buildings unrolled carpet-like toward the Mediterranean. The striking views from Mt. Carmel were often compared with San Francisco. The van slowed and parked in an inconspicuous spot.

Mahmoud got out of the passenger seat and waited in front of the van for the driver, Ibrahim Abu-Khalil. Both men wore plumber's overalls and work caps. A heavyset man in his thirties, Abu-Khalil had intense dark eyes and a thick, full mustache. Intimates called him The Bear. And a bear he was— deliberate, slow moving, yet extremely strong.

"What do you see, Mahmoud?" he said in a resonant voice.

"I see a view of Haifa Bay."

"Is that all?"

Mahmoud was puzzled. "What do you mean?"

"I mean, you should also see opportunity. All of this," he said, gesturing expansively, "is the Haifa Bay Industrial Zone. The complex there is the Lev HaMifratz Shopping Mall. Beyond it, across the Histadrut Road, are the oil refineries. You see the space between them?"

"I do. What of it?"

"That is where the Americans will build their headquarters."

A sly smile spread across Mahmoud's face. So, *this* is what the leaders had been planning. It was perfect. For weeks now lower-echelon Hamas members had been speculating on the likely target for a rumored strike. As Mahmoud recently learned, it was no rumor; once the Americans landed, Hamas would strike hard, delivering a decisive blow to anyone who dared interfere with their jihad.

There was never any doubt that American intervention would imperil their cause. The bully Americans were everywhere: the Balkans, Afghanistan, Somalia, and throughout the Middle East. But once the Americans had an Israeli presence, they— along with the Israelis—would use any pretext to expand their "peacekeeping" efforts. The term was synonymous with a crackdown on Hamas and Palestinian freedom fighters. But Hamas believed that the American public had no stomach for the shedding of American blood. If, once American troops arrived, they suffered a catastrophe far greater than the botched attempt on the destroyer *Cole* in Aden, the American people would insist on canceling the operation. Such had been the case in Beirut in 1983, in Saudi Arabia in 1991, and in Mogadishu in 1993.

"I like it, Ibrahim. I like it a lot."

"Very appropriate, don't you think?"

"Yes, I do. All along we have been speculating on the target. When we first learned their troops would arrive by ship, we first thought of dealing a blow to one of their warships."

"Impossible," said Ibrahim. "It was hard enough in Aden, but this port is too well guarded. Only Americans and Israelis can go in by land or sea. We considered an underwater approach, to the ship's keel, but their underwater surveillance cannot be defeated."

"Perhaps once they've established their base in the Golan, we could attack with rockets."

"Too puny. No real damage."

"Or with explosives, delivered by truck."

"Impossible," Ibrahim said, shaking his head. "Wherever they build that base, it will have only one, well-guarded access road. No, we will cripple them here. We are still working on the details."

"But whatever it is, I will play a role, won't I?"

Ibrahim smiled. He momentarily thought back to the recent car crash near Washington, D.C., in which one of their operatives had been killed, and the other maimed for life. It was because of that fiasco that they were here now. Not to mention the not-insubstantial sums certain Americans were giving to him alone. "I brought you here, *habibi*, to show you my complete trust in you. You are our best marksman. Others will carry out our plans here. But you, ah. For you, I have even greater plans."

Washington, 2005

The original Naval Medical Center, built with 1200 beds—whose size expanded or contracted over the years depending on the state of American military conflict—was consolidated into one command in 1973. A new state-of-the-art hospital was constructed in 1980 directly across the street from the National Institutes of Health. The center contained a five-hundred-bed inpatient building and a spacious, adjoining outpatient facility. Jon Townsend was a highly regarded internist on staff who performed both research and direct patient care.

His first-floor office in Building 9 of the National Naval Medical Center, still referred to locally as Bethesda Naval Hospital, had seen its share of celebrities, mainly politicians. Although his primary responsibility was the care of Naval personnel and their beneficiaries from military commands around the world, his civilian patient base had grown in tandem with his notoriety.

Harriet Friedman was a new patient of Dr. Townsend. The sixty-year-old, two-term senator had made an appointment for a general physical exam. Jon, who'd met her several times before at the White House, knew her to be an articulate, well-liked politician. Friedman was a modestly attractive woman with dark eyes and stylish graying hair. Although Jon's cramped office was intended for administrative duties, he used it as a pre-examination consultation area for the VIPs, who sometimes resented being crowded into a clinic. Soon Jon finished with his history.

"You sound pretty healthy, Senator. You're basically a low-risk individual from a genetically good background who's up to date with her immunizations and tests," he said, putting down his pen. "A corpsman will take you to the exam room to get changed."

"All right," she said pleasantly. "Are you going to do a pap smear?"

"If you'd like. Or you can see your own gynecologist."

"A little problem there, Admiral," looking sheepishly at Jon, who was dressed in his everyday whites. "One of the reasons I'm here is because my old gynecologist, who I knew and loved for twenty years, retired. He was my doctor for everything. To be honest, I might not even be here if I didn't need my prescription for hormones."

"I know how you feel, Senator. I hate going to the doctor myself."

She laughed. "You're very charming, Doctor. I feel comfortable with you, and that's important to me. It's no wonder Bob Meredith recommended you."

"That's very kind of him. How many other doctors can count on the president of the United States for referrals?"

"None I can think of. How long have you been his doctor, anyway?"

"About ten years," he replied. "The president and I go back a long way, thirty years or so."

"Really? You couldn't have been more than a boy then."

Coming from a patient, especially one he barely knew, such personal inquiries were irrelevant, and perhaps inappropriate. But Jon was aware that their interchange was part of an intricate ballet performed by the two of them. Not only was Harriet Friedman a patient looking for a doctor, but she was also a U.S. senator checking out information on another public servant.

"Actually, I was twenty. The president and I were in the

Marine Corps together in Vietnam. He was a captain, and I was a platoon corpsman. After he got elected to Congress, he helped me get a Navy scholarship to med school."

"You went into internal medicine when you graduated?"

"That's right. And once I finished up, I had to give time back to the Navy. I got stationed here, liked it, and stayed ever since."

"It's obviously agreed with you," she noted. "You're an admiral."

"That comes with time in uniform. When you've been a naval officer as long as I have, getting promoted is inevitable."

"You're married, I presume?"

He continued smiling to avoid showing how intensely wounded he was by the question. The last thing he needed was some well-intentioned public servant snooping into his private life, especially when that life had been as painful as his was. The scar left by his former marriage had never completely healed. Whenever someone brought it up, it felt like an open wound. He thought about his ex-wife often, although not as much as he thought about his daughter.

Ah, Tommie. Ten-year-old Thomasina was the light of his life. She'd been born a year before his separation from Victoria. He regretted not having fought harder for custody during the settlement, but it would have been an impossible battle. Victoria had few flaws and no vices, unless being a gold-digger was considered a character defect.

At the time of their divorce, they'd been married eleven years. Jon met Victoria during his last year of residency, and they were married shortly after he finished his training. Victoria was five years his junior—a stunningly attractive woman with golden hair and azure eyes. Jon initially considered her to be out of his league, but he was soon captivated by her. Victoria was an artist, a promising oil painter who'd already had one successful show in Manhattan.

Jon thought she was the perfect foil to his personality. On the occasions he might be withdrawn, she was a social butterfly, outgoing and upbeat. Where he thought he lacked guts, she was assertive. She was laid back when he was intense. It was the attraction of opposites, a complementary match. She even seemed to understand his need to repay the military for what the Navy had given him.

With Congressman Meredith's help, Jon had been one of the first students to enter the medical program of the newly formed Uniformed Services University Health Service in Bethesda, Maryland. The fact that he was a Vietnam vet hadn't hurt. Like many of his classmates, Jon incurred significant debt—in his case, the need to give the Navy four years of service for the schooling they'd given him. Such payback could be deferred until after the completion of specialty training. Yet although, while they were courting, Victoria seemed to accept the necessity of repayment, it was all lip service. Once they were married, it was an entirely different matter.

Victoria came from a family of means and prestige. She told him she'd been speaking with her parents, and with an attorney. They were convinced they could find a loophole—such as post-traumatic stress disorder, from his days in Vietnam—that would keep him from having to remain in the Navy. Other people did it all the time. Once freed from his obligations, Jon and she could go to New York, where the action was. Jon patiently explained that he wasn't other people. He was not the kind of person who'd use some lame excuse to dodge a debt. Besides, he'd only been in country for a month when he was wounded and in the Marines all of one year before being medically discharged.

It was then that Victoria's baser motives emerged. Jon slowly realized that all along, she'd been using him as a steppingstone toward success in her own career. As an artist, she believed that no mate could legitimatize her work more than a prestigious physician. Her prenuptial career fantasy consisted of one successful showing after another, a high-profile husband with a Park Avenue medical office, and perhaps a child or two. Her dreams could never come true if Jon remained in the Navy as an underpaid government employee. Once she understood that he had no intention of leaving the service, their marriage began to fall apart.

To Victoria's credit, there was a brief period when she seemed to try to make things work. Telling Jon she was certain they could iron out the kinks in their relationship, she came on to him like a tigress. There were several months of delirious, passion-filled nights during which Jon was convinced they'd put their differences aside. But it was not to be. It turned out that Victoria had been the consummate schemer. All along she'd wanted to get pregnant, hoping that Jon's honorable stance would soften once he became a father. In this, she was completely mistaken. Not long after Thomasina was born, they went their separate ways.

Naturally, Jon still saw his daughter every weekend. Victoria never did move to Manhattan, and Jon was grateful for that. Tommie was the light of his life. Rarely did a day go by that he didn't speak with her on the phone. And try though he did to keep his ex-wife out of his mind, he never fully succeeded. Even though they lived apart, thoughts of Victoria haunted him like a reappearing ghost.

The senator's exam took twenty minutes. If Jon had a hallmark as a physician, it was his thoroughness. Some colleagues kidded him that their five-minute exams looked bad in comparison. But Jon was compulsive, and he evaluated every organ system in detail. He spent extra time on the neurological exam, carefully evaluating all twelve cranial nerves. Over the years he'd developed a special interest in neurology, and for an internist, he was unusually competent. When the exam was complete and the senator had dressed, she returned to his office.

"So," the senator said brightly, "I take it I'm going to live?"

"No doubt about it. Your best years are ahead of you. But there is one thing I'd like to talk about. I'm sure you noticed the way your hand shakes a little."

Friedman raised her right hand, which had a fine, resting tremor. "This? That's just nerves."

"Maybe. But I noticed one or two other things, all very subtle. Your posture shows what's called instability, and your movements are slightly slow, at least clinically."

"Meaning what?"

"I think you may be in the early stages of Parkinson's disease."

She was stunned. "Are you sure?"

"Reasonably sure. There are other possibilities, like an

old stroke, an infection, or drug side effects, but they're pretty unlikely."

The senator seemed shell-shocked. "I... What does this all mean? I want to keep working. This is my life. I can do that, can't I? There's so much I have to do!"

"And you will, believe me." He leaned forward at his desk, effecting his most reassuring posture. "Look, Senator. I know this is upsetting, but it's not the end of the world. I won't bore you with statistics, but most people with Parkinson's have a normal life span and lead full and useful lives. I'm going to send you for some blood tests, and I'm going to send you for an MRI, so I don't overlook anything. Radiology and the lab are just down the hall, and I've already called them. Then, I want to start you on levodopa."

"L-dopa?"

"Exactly. The key to managing this condition is early diagnosis and treatment. It's a harmless enough medication. The results are very gratifying. Your symptoms are minor now, and they may even disappear. So, why don't you take it for two months," he said, writing out a prescription, "and then I'll re-examine you. If, at any point, you'd feel more comfortable with a neurological consultation, or if I think you need one, I won't hesitate to refer you."

She tapped a finger on his desk. "What happens if it progresses? I've known people with Parkinson's who are completely debilitated by it."

"That's always a possibility, down the road. Levodopa is a first-line drug. There are plenty of fallback medications, and a number in the pipeline. Speaking of which, I don't know your position on stem cell research, but I hope I can count on your support on The Hill."

"Is that something you're working on? Does it have anything to do with Parkinson's?"

"Yes to both. There are some neurological problems I'm interested in. In fact, I testified before your committee on Creutzfeldt-Jakob disease."

"I recall. I was very impressed. You're some sort of expert on Mad Cow disease, aren't you?"

"I'm unofficial liaison to the Europeans, who had a much bigger problem than we did. But another of my projects is the use of fetal stem cells. I'm doing research in that area over at the NIH, and there's every indication that stem cell implantation in patients with Parkinson's has a dramatic effect."

"That's very interesting. To be honest, I'm not sure what my position is on stem cell research. But I'll try to keep an open mind, especially since it's now personal. Isn't this an unusual area for an internist to become involved in?"

He caught her eye, pursed his lips, and then looked away. It was not the time to reveal how he'd become involved largely because of Tommie. "Oh, it's just a pet project of mine. Now, about the L-dopa. Is it a deal?"

The senator found Dr. Townsend's confidence and manner reassuring. Although she still had many questions, she admired decisiveness in her physician. "It's a deal. I can see why the president recommended you."

They rose and shook hands.

"You know what I like most about you, Dr. Townsend?" she continued. "You seem to care. I don't know if you really do, or if that's just the way you come across. But it's important these days, because so few doctors do."

"I appreciate that."

"And you've got guts. It takes a lot of courage to come right out and say what you think, especially when the news is not the greatest. I admire that."

"Thank you, Senator. I'll talk with you soon."

After Senator Friedman was gone, Jon gazed out his window. He thought about what she'd said, for her comment about caring was right on the mark. Over the years, he'd known a number of colleagues who'd burned out for various reasons: overwork, disenchantment, or just plain boredom. For them, medicine no longer held the interest or intrigue it did when they started their careers. But in reality, Jon thought, many who burned out simply ceased to care.

Not that they always had. When Jon entered med school, he'd been struck by how few students were motivated by altruism. There was the occasional classmate who wanted to do primary research, who wanted to become a missionary, or who hoped to become a small-town family doctor. There were no Albert Schweitzers or Marcus Welbys. After repaying the military, most of his fellow students aspired toward a thriving civilian practice with the attendant material rewards. In short, med students hoped for the good life like anyone else, and it was the rare student who really cared, in an idealized sense.

Did *he* care, as Senator Friedman implied? Jon wasn't sure. Certainly, he always tried to provide the best possible medical care. In his compulsivity, he was very thorough, overlooking nothing. Whenever a patient had a problem, at the end of the day he would ask himself, have I done everything I possibly can? Is there another test, or a different medication that I forgot about? Yet Jon was astute enough to realize that part of that thinking was a cover-your-ass mindset, a fear of blame that was not the same as the deep empathy necessary for real caring. So in the end, he still wondered: did he, or didn't he?

As for courage, well, of that he had no doubt. He possessed none of it. What the senator mistook for courage was little more than his diagnosis. He'd discovered a problem and told her about it—period. It was simple professional honesty. True, he knew other physicians who beat around the bush. Or who played things down, patronizing the patient. But that paternalistic approach always struck him as a lot of work, something easily avoided by being straightforward. It was the sort of role-playing for which he had no patience. The fact was, the only real courage he might have had vanished on a mountainside a generation ago.

The very word, he thought, was tossed around so loosely, so glibly. It was a romantic term, the stuff of poets. But had they personally experienced it? Plato, he recalled, claimed courage was knowing what to fear, while Mark Twain held that courage was resistance to fear, not mastery of it. Jon thought the person who defined it best was Harper Lee, who wrote that courage is when you know you're licked before you begin, but you begin anyway. Gazing outside, Jon sighed. Whatever courage was, he didn't have it. Anyway, courage was the province of patients, not physicians.

He'd best stick to medicine and leave something as illusory as courage to patriots.

CHAPTER 10

By Halloween, autumn in Washington was well underway. Due to an exceptionally damp summer, tree foliage had been unusually verdant; and as night temperatures fell into the forties, metabolized leaf sugars brought forth dazzling colors in flaming displays of red and gold. The city was at a latitude where sunny days retained their warmth. It was fifty-nine degrees this morning, with a blue sky overhead and a fair-weather pattern that would drive temperatures well into the seventies.

The president's day began at eight a.m. with a national security briefing over coffee and croissants in the Oval Office. The National Security Adviser was none other than Mitchell Forbes, the White House chief of staff. Both positions were full-time jobs. It was unusual, although not unheard of, for one man to serve in both capacities. Wearing two hats called for someone whose stamina matched his intelligence. Forbes had those qualities in abundance.

The fifty-two-year-old Forbes began his career as a Stanford-trained computer engineer. Twenty years ago, by marketing his company's software, he'd become a millionaire. He was a gregarious, hard-working, designer/engineer with considerable people skills. Forbes dealt with personalities and persuasion as well as he did with bits and bytes, perhaps better. He was called to Capitol Hill several times to testify on behalf of the computer industry. He proved a stellar witness. Finding the Washington political scene to his liking, he embarked on a career change. In his early thirties, with his financial future secure, he cashed in on his holdings and went to work as a lobbyist.

Here, too, he was a standout. There was something about

wheeling and dealing, wining and dining, which appealed to his extroverted personality. A standout in a crowded field of men and women with similar skills, Forbes excelled at genteel arm-twisting and the tactful distribution of perks. By that time, Bob Meredith was already a U. S. senator. During their first lunch together, they realized they were kindred spirits. Both men were outgoing, sociable, and easy to talk to. As time went by, their professional relationship grew and prospered; and eventually, perhaps inevitably, Forbes became the most trusted adviser to the senator from South Carolina. Long before he was elected president, Meredith knew Mitchell Forbes would be the go-to guy in his administration.

"Good morning, Mitch. How was your night?"

"Not bad, Mr. President," said Forbes, walking in and shaking hands. "And yours?"

"Fine, just fine. Sit down, let's have some coffee."

The chief of staff had a little-discussed but extremely important position in the administration. Many considered it to be the second toughest job in Washington. The challenges facing the chief of staff were immense, as was the cost of failure. The person wearing the title had tremendous power, but it was that of a staffer, not a principal.

Essentially, the chief of staff's role was to concentrate on "the four Ps." The first stood for people. At the beginning, the chief had to identify and recruit his own White House team. Only then could he begin building professional working relationships, based on common goals and mutual trust, with senior policy makers. The second P stood for process, simply defined as running the place. He had to focus attention on the president's priorities, then effectively implement them. Since there were so many claimants on the president's time, the chief of staff had to protect the president by learning how to say no. He had to be an honest broker while simultaneously raising issues the president would rather not hear.

The third P stood for politics, which, in a democracy, was inseparable from policy. While striking a balance between the two, the chief had to be the president's primary political adviser, explaining issues, positions, and interpretations. Finally, only once the first three Ps were in place, could the chief of staff concentrate on the fourth P—formulating an effective foreign and domestic policy agenda. This was the criterion of any administration's ultimate success. The chief had to reinvent the policy process in a manner consistent with the president's priorities.

To his credit, Forbes understood the four Ps from the administration's first day. He knew what the president expected of him, and he appreciated everyone's role. Equally important, he was a shrewd man who knew where the land mines were.

Their morning began with an outstanding Hawaiian roast sipped from one-of-a-kind china cups that were a gift from the Irish prime minister. As they sat on the twin couches before the president's desk, both men gazed outside toward the nearby trees, whose dappled leaves, caught in the morning sunlight, seemed touched by fire.

"How's the world holding up today, Mitch?"

"Still revolving normally, sir." From his briefcase, Forbes took out a copy of the PDB, or President's Daily Brief, a highly classified document prepared by the CIA's Office of Current Production and Analytical Support. The brief was a twenty-four-hour summary of information that might affect the country's national security. Some presidents wanted to peruse the document themselves, but Meredith preferred to have his national security adviser summarize it for him. "Should be another peaceful day, Mr. President. There was the usual grumbling from Hamas after last night's dinner. Some rock-throwing, a few arrests in Hebron. Nothing unexpected. No direct threats against America."

"Not yet, anyway. But as soon as the *George Washington* pulls into Haifa, they'll be screaming for our throats."

"No question," Forbes agreed, closing the brief. "We're helping the Israelis keep a close eye on all the militant groups over there. Over here, they're helping us. Everyone's on board on this and if anyone makes a move. We'll know it."

"Good. What else?"

"That's about it, on security matters. The Earth is a garden spot today. Incidentally, how're you feeling this morning, Mr. President?"

"You mean, after my little chewing problem last night?"

"Yes, sir."

"I feel fine," Meredith said. "Any sequelae are of the emotional variety."

There came a knock at the door, and the president's secretary poked her head into the room. "The vice president's here, sir. He wonders if he could have a minute of your time."

"Of course. Send him in."

Doria breezed in, smiling and carrying a gift-wrapped box. "Good morning, Mr. President," he said. "Sorry to disturb you, but I come bearing gifts."

"You're incorrigible, Tony. But I'll never say no. How's Amanda?"

"Healthy and happy. Always involved with one thing or another. And Roxanne?"

"The same. How was the West Coast swing?"

"Good. Very productive. They want you for another four years, Bob." He placed the box on the president's desk.

"Along with you." He got off the couch, untied the bow, and removed the paper. Slipping off the cardboard cover, he removed the gift and placed it on the desk. It was a windmill. "Will you look at that," he said, spinning the arms with his finger. "It's beautiful. Doesn't your old firm make something like this?"

"Yes, but much more modern. This is nineteenth-century, Dutch. It's the perfect statement for your energy policy, don't you think?"

"I do indeed. Thanks. Sit down, have a cup of coffee."

"Wish I could, but I have a breakfast appointment. I just wanted to drop this off." He shook hands with the president and Forbes. "Catch you later, guys."

When he was gone, Meredith smiled and shook his head. "Tony's got this thing for trinkets. He's always bringing something back from wherever he goes. But he's got damn good taste, I'll say that for him."

"Yes, sir, he does. I don't think anyone could ask for a better vice president."

"Amen to that. But back to what we were talking about, my

only concern is over what people are going to say about me."

"Oh, they already are. You didn't happen to watch the morning news today?"

"Are you joking?"

"No, sir. You can't keep what happens at a state dinner secret. The newswires had the gory details at midnight."

Meredith was mortified. "Good Lord. How did they play it? Am I now some doddering old fool who can't keep his dentures in place?"

"Not at all!" Forbes said with a laugh. "They know you've got all your teeth."

"Mitch..."

"I know, I know. Generally, they were very charitable."

"Oh, Jesus. Now I need charity?"

"Let's put it this way: this morning, all the networks, Fox, and CNN reported the story straight," Forbes said. "You might even say they played it down. They said you choked on your food and Dr. Townsend was there for first aid. Period. Only ABC specifically used the term Heimlich maneuver. It's over and done with, Mr. President. Yesterday's news."

Reassured, Meredith slowly nodded. "That's a relief. Frankly, I would have thought showing that kind of weakness would hurt me politically."

"No, just the opposite. The way I read public opinion, it actually helped your ratings. Provided it doesn't affect how you think, the American people are very sympathetic to their president's minor physical problems."

"If you say so. Let's just hope it doesn't happen again before next year's election."

"Speaking of which, we're all set for next Tuesday."

Meredith looked puzzled. "Tuesday?"

"Yes, Bob, Tuesday. Your re-election announcement. Don't tell me you forgot."

Feeling his face redden, Meredith turned away, gazing in the direction of the South Lawn. Rocky's recent remark about his memory was fresh in his mind. "Of course not. Everything's ready to go?"

"That's right," Mitch said. He noticed a slight twitch in the president's hand, a movement that made his cup and saucer shake. "Noon, in the East Room. All the networks are on board. Most Cabinet members will be there. Your speech is written and ready for your proofreading."

"Good. What about the opposition, the guys who want my job?"

"Same list of wannabees sniffing around the edges. Nothing new there."

"I'm talking about issues. Are they scoring points anywhere?"

"The only areas you're a little weak, Mr. President," Forbes said, "are national defense and the reproduction arena."

"Well, that's to be expected. But I won't back down on the Raskin business. Anything new there?"

"No, this Southern Cross, if it exists, is lying low. The Bureau's working hard on it."

"And national defense?" Meredith asked.

"Diehard saber-rattlers were never your favorite people. There are still some folks out there who cling to the idea of a two-theater war."

For over sixty years, U.S. military strategy had been based on the concept of America's ability to simultaneously conduct full-scale conflicts on two fronts, or theaters. It didn't matter that the concept was now an unrealistic, impractical philosophy, and that future conflicts would most likely be regional. Military hard-liners simply had a traditional, albeit inflexible, approach. When he first ran for the presidency, Meredith campaigned for a modern military strategy than emphasized goals rather than theaters. His motto was Strike Fast, Strike Hard, Strike Anywhere. It was a concept that combined readiness, mobility, and technology.

The American people were ready for it. It was an approach that emphasized quality over quantity, which recognized the skill and preparedness of elite U.S. fighting forces over sheer numbers. The fact that the president was a decorated war veteran was a strong selling point, not to mention that his approach would save hundreds of billions of tax dollars. Yet despite the new plan's popularity, there were still those who criticized it.

"The Neanderthals won't quit, will they?" said Meredith.

"They know we're right on this, so why keep harping on it?"

"Because it's the only place they're making any headway. The polls still give us an edge, but you're always going to have some Americans who equate military strength with numbers. You can't please everyone, Mr. President."

"I suppose. Anything else?"

"No, sir, that's about it," said Forbes, getting up. "I'll see you and the first lady later."

"Later?"

"Lunch, Mr. President. In the study."

"Of course. See you then."

Coffee cup in hand, Meredith walked to the window behind his desk. Not only had he forgotten about lunch, he wasn't even sure he ever knew. His embarrassment was tempered by anger, and his hands were shaking. He'd always prided himself on his memory, but lately, his memory had been suspect. It was the little things, recent things. Certainly, Rocky had noticed, and he was beginning to wonder if Forbes suspected, too. It was infuriating.

But beyond the question of his memory, there was the question of his manner. President Meredith was aware that for the past month or two, he'd been losing his patience. He had enough self-control that he didn't always show it, but he felt it inside—irritability, tenseness. He felt like snipping at people. If he were a woman, he'd have thought his attitude was due to PMS. And as if that weren't enough, his whole body felt tense. His muscles had the stiff spasticity he associated with being in a plaster cast.

What was wrong with him? He'd gotten a clean bill of health by Dr. Townsend at the beginning of the summer. Was it possible he was actually getting senile? Could this be the onset of a lifelong process of mental deterioration? He hoped not. Emotionally, he felt he was in the prime of his life. Except for this, he was robust, fit, and in control.

The real issue, he knew, was that he was afraid. With his background in the Marine Corps, the law, and then politics, he'd spent his entire adult life micromanaging one problem after another. Yet this was a situation he simply could not get his hands around. Bob Meredith didn't like being out of control; and if his body was acting independent of his will, it was very frightening indeed.

Tunisia

The old bus carrying Mahmoud rumbled south through the rock-strewn hills. A harsh wind was blowing through the upcoming Kasserine Pass, a stony notch in West Central Tunisia where GIs once held off Rommel's Afrika Korps. Nearby, low clouds wreathed the five-thousand-foot Jebel Chambi, the country's highest mountain. It was a raw day. Water formed pools on the rutted ground, and the distant, hazy sun rarely penetrated the overcast.

Mahmoud had been here once before. Like every member of Fatah or Hamas, he knew how to pull a trigger. But he had first learned to *really* shoot at the Al-Maidah camp, a base still a hundred miles away. Among those who took up jihad, there were few skilled marksmen, particularly among the Palestinians, whose customary weapons of choice were rocks, bottles, and explosives.

But occasionally, someone like Mahmoud, whose eyesight and reflexes exceeded his courage, came to the instructors' attention. These people were singled out for special training. Unfortunately, the quality of their weapons rarely equaled their enthusiasm.

Most of their Kalashnikov-type firearms were Soviet-era surplus of dubious reliability. The rare exception was the .30-caliber Dragunov rifle, a shortened version of the Russian SVD sniper rifle. While these were no match for high-quality Western arms, they were rugged, dependable, and reasonably accurate.

In his earlier training at the base, Mahmoud was quickly shooting expertly at stationary three-hundred-yard targets. The rifle's attached four-power scope was primitive, especially at extreme distance; but if Mahmoud did his part, the results were generally good. He'd had modest success with it in Southern Lebanon against the Israelis, until a retaliatory rocket nearly killed him—impairing his hearing, giving him a concussion, and turning his Dragunov into shrapnel.

For this mission, Mahmoud had flown from Gaza to Cairo, and then on to Tunis.

It had been a long, exhausting drive from the capitol, and another three hours remained before he reached the camp. He would get off the bus at Gafsa, a sleepy town where the esparto grass finally gave way to the sand that stretched south to the Sahara. In Gafsa, he'd be picked up for the final twenty-kilometer drive to Al-Maidah. Mahmoud always considered the name fitting.

It was Arabic for The Avenger.

Later that day, the president, first lady, and chief of staff lunched in the study next to the Oval Office. It was an informal meal, and the main item on the agenda was the re-election announcement. Roxanne, as usual, looked radiant. Her suit was elegant, her skin flawless. Although she was in early menopause, she could easily have passed for someone ten years younger. As a woman of the people, she made no attempt to hide the fact that she'd had a facelift and laser skin resurfacing. The public appreciated her honesty, and her cosmetic surgeon became the second-most sought-after person in Washington, after the president.

They sat down to a salad of fresh greens with Asian vegetables, topped with a sesame vinaigrette.

"I sense Mireille's hand here," said the president, after the first bite. "Incredible. She can turn an ordinary salad into a work of art."

"She's a helluva find, Bob," Forbes said. "Have you looked over the speech?"

The president handed him a manila folder containing the rough draft. "Yes, and I like it. Short and to the point. I penciled in a few changes in the margins." He looked at his wife. "You'll be there, right, Rocky?"

"By your side, as always."

"By the way," Forbes said, "a final communique from the Arab summit just came in. It's pretty much what we expected, no major surprises."

"The usual grumbling from Iran and Iraq?"

"Yes, sir. Very predictable."

"And the Saudis?"

"Still some fence straddling," Forbes said, "but it's just posturing. Nothing should come of it, and we'll be able to count on them."

Their empty salad plates were removed by a server, and in came the chef herself, pushing a linen-covered serving cart. She was wearing a chef s jacket, a tall white chef's hat, and a smile.

"Bonjour, Monsieur President," she jauntily exclaimed. It was frowned upon for an employee of The House to address the chief executive in a foreign language, but Mireille did it with such panache that tradition was overlooked.

"Hello, Chef Courtois," Meredith replied. "You look lovely, as usual. What delights have you prepared today?"

Mireille, a beautiful woman in her early thirties, was a rising star in Nouvelle French cuisine. Paris-born and raised, she graduated from Le Cordon Blue before enrolling in its bachelor program in restaurant management in Adelaide. Armed with culinary skills and a degree, she began her career at The Oriental in Bangkok before returning to Alain Ducasse in Paris, where she perfected her technique. After a brief sojourn at Manhattan's Four Seasons, she became head chef at the new, prestigious Rafters in San Francisco before being tapped for the White House. Her specialty was Asian/French fusion cooking.

"Something very light today," she said. Despite her years in English-speaking countries, her French accent was still pronounced. "We begin with a crab and papaya roll, striped bass and glass noodles in a lemongrass sauce."

"Sounds marvelous," Roxanne said.

Mireille removed the sterling covers from the appetizer plates, and the server brought over their dishes. Each plate contained three pieces of a sushi-style roll, cut on a bias. There were separate saucers containing a syrupy dipping sauce, and the utensils were salad forks.

"No chopsticks?" Forbes asked.

"Actually, you should use your fingers," said the chef. "Just dip the roll into the sauce."

The president went first, generously moistening the edge of the roll and then taking a hearty bite. "Unbelievable," he said, with his mouth full. "Never tasted anything like it."

Mireille beamed. She wore her ash-blond hair up under her cap, and her hazel eyes, flecked with green, were warm and friendly. She had a wide, expressive smile and unusually white teeth. Between her eyes and her smile, she had an innately cheerful expression that put others at ease.

"You like it?" she said, her "it" like an "eet."

"Very much. Marvelous."

"Thank you. Enjoy your meal." With a little bow, she left the study.

"We really have to find someone for her," said Roxanne. "She's such a doll."

"How do you know she's not already taken?" Forbes asked.

"Oh, I have my ways. We live in a very small world here. Didn't Jon Townsend say something flattering about her, Bob?"

"Did he? When?"

"About a week ago. The three of us had cocktails."

"Not that I can remember."

But Rocky *did* remember. Dr. Townsend's interest had been rather obvious, but he'd been rather obtuse where it came to her oblique attempts at matchmaking. What was currently more important, however, was the re-emerging question of her husband's memory, an issue never far from the surface. Rather than embarrass him, Rocky said nothing.

Once the appetizer plates were cleared, the main course was served. Like the two dishes preceding it, it was an eye-pleasing concoction. Chef Courtois excelled at food presentation, and the way she married sights with aroma, taste, and texture was what set her apart from her predecessors. Until she came on the scene, White House fare had been traditionally American and traditionally unspectacular. Now White House guests came as much for the food as for the function.

Finally, when coffee was served, the president lit his pipe. He smoked a Dunhill Straight Grain, having abandoned his trademark corncob pipe shortly after being elected. Soon the air was filled with aromatic smoke. There was a knock at the door, and the president's secretary Marian poked her head into the room.

"Your one o'clock is here, Mr. President," she said. "The Senegalese ambassador."

"How long?"

"It's scheduled for twenty minutes. No photo op."

"Thanks. I'll be right there."

Meredith lingered a few minutes, savoring his tobacco. Roxanne noticed that his hand had a slight tremor. She touched his wrist.

"Something tells me you won't mind another four years of this food."

"It's not home cooking," he replied, "but I think I can manage."

"Bob, why did you change your mind about when you'd make the re-election announcement?"

He looked at her oddly. "What are you talking about?"

"Remember the other night, after the Israeli dinner, when..." Her voice trailed off, and she looked away. His annoyed expression told her he didn't remember at all. Roxanne instantly felt guilty. Here she'd embarrassed him again, this time in front of someone else. She tried changing the subject. "Actually, I never asked you what you thought about the dress I was wearing. I was thinking of getting a different—"

"Tell Mitch about it," the president snapped, inverting his Dunhill and knocking out the ash. He stood up. "Excuse me, I've got business to attend to." With that, he left the room.

Forbes put down his napkin, looking from the closing door to the first lady. "What was that all about?"

Roxanne slowly shook her head. "God, I wish I knew. I really think there's something wrong with him."

"Careful, Roxanne. You don't want to be saying that during an election year."

"I'm serious, Mitch. Bob's been, well, a little off for a few months. He hasn't been himself."

"What do you mean, off?"

"It's little things," she explained. "For instance, you saw how he stormed out of here."

"He just didn't want to have to pay for another dress."

"You're joking, but I'm not. It has nothing to do with the dress. It's about his memory."

"What makes you say that?"

"Because he's having trouble remembering what he said. I'll give you a for-instance: he's been very confused about the timing of the re-election announcement."

"He's not confused at all," Forbes said. "He's always known it would be Tuesday."

"I wish that was true. But the fact is, one day he wants to make the announcement around Thanksgiving, and the next he's doing it three weeks earlier." She sighed. "I'm worried, Mitch."

"Don't be. Your husband's Old Faithful, always there on schedule."

"He certainly used to be. But that's not the only thing," Roxanne said, sipping her coffee. "He's had a very short fuse lately. You saw it a little while ago. Bob's always had a temper, but he never let it get out of control. When he gets his dander up, he's like an ornery old man."

Forbes leaned forward on his elbows. "Madame First Lady, allow me to remind you what must be obvious. For all his strengths, the president is only human."

"Christ, Mitch, don't patronize me. What are you trying to say?"

"I'm saying that he's been under a lot of stress these days—the Israeli thing, the re-election, and a bunch of other problems."

"Come on, that goes with the territory. He's a politician. Bob's life has *always* been stressful, but he's dealt with it." She looked out the window. "No, this is different. I can feel it."

"All right, let's say you can. Exactly what are you afraid of? What's the worst-case scenario?"

"I'm not a doctor, Mitch."

"I know, but what do you think? Too much bourbon and tobacco? Hardening of the arteries?"

"I suppose what I'm really afraid of is Alzheimer's. It's a slow, Godawful process. I've already seen enough of it in my family."

"Okay," Forbes said, "stick with that. Let's say, for the sake of discussion, that it *is* Alzheimer's. You remember what happened with President Reagan?"

"Bob's no Ronnie Reagan. Reagan was older. Also, he always delegated things, while Bob makes his own decisions."

"Yes, but my point is, Reagan's disease was very gradual. By all accounts, he already had Alzheimer's in his first term. But he seemed to do just fine for another four years, and he had a lot of people helping him."

"I know it's not always that gradual," she said, shaking her head. "With all the new drugs out there, maybe he should already be taking medication. I won't sit around and watch him deteriorate, Mitch."

"None of us wants that, Roxanne."

"You don't understand. I'm saying I want him to get help."

"So do I, if and when it comes to that."

"What do you mean, if and when? He's my husband, and I think he should get help now!"

"Are you talking about seeing a doctor?"

"What is this, some kind of a riddle?" she said annoyedly. "Of course I'm talking about a doctor, *his* doctor!"

Forbes stared at her without any obvious emotion. Then he slowly pushed away from the table. "I know where you're coming from," he said, getting up and pacing. "We all want what's best for the president, and certainly no one wants it more than you. But there are other considerations."

"The only consideration, Mr. Forbes, is his health."

"Look, Roxanne, you may not want to hear this, but it's my job. When your husband hired me, I insisted that he tell me what he expected of me. Our relationship depends on mutual frankness. Bob made it absolutely clear that my role was to advance his policy agenda. It's his legacy, and I have to always keep my eye on that prize. So, in order to accomplish that, I have to look at both sides of an issue and tell it like it is."

"What are you talking about? When his health's paramount, what other side is there?"

"Well, there's the physical reality, which I've begun to see even before you pointed it out. No one can deny that. But there's also the political reality. If I didn't point that out, the president would have a fit."

"Go on."

"The president is about to announce his bid for re-election, right? No matter how popular he may be, he has to appear strong and decisive. The American people can tolerate a lot, but they will *not* tolerate a weak, indecisive, or frail leader. And if, at this point, Bob starts getting a whole battery of tests, that's tantamount to admitting a serious medical problem. That would be the kiss of death, Roxanne."

"I don't believe that. What would be the big deal if he had, say, diabetes, or high blood pressure?"

"But we're not talking about those conditions, are we? We're talking about a possible problem up here," he said, tapping his head. "People will forgive high blood sugar, but they won't overlook forgetting what day of the week it is." He paused. "And then there's the whole question of his doctor."

"Dr. Townsend? What's wrong with Jon Townsend?"

"Medically, not a thing. He's a top-notch internist, and he's a friend of mine. But philosophically, ah—that's a different story."

"I don't follow you."

"How much do you know about him, Roxanne?"

"I know that he's taken care of my husband for the past decade."

"Yes, but did you know he was a medical whistle blower fifteen years ago? When he found out some doctors he worked with were defrauding the government, he turned them in."

"So? That sounds pretty responsible to me."

"Maybe. But were you aware that your husband saved him from getting court-martialed for cowardice in Vietnam?"

She wasn't, but she didn't see the relevance. "What are you getting at?"

"My point is that for all of Dr. Townsend's good personality and medical acumen, he's not a team player. Like I said before, it's my job to examine people, warts and all, for their political ramifications. However competent he is, in something as important as this, we need someone who's on our side."

"But I always thought he was."

"He's a Boy Scout, Roxanne. If you went up to him and said you thought the president's memory might be slipping, he'd order a complete neurological workup, sure. But it's not his nature to keep it to himself. He'd feel compelled to fill out some public-minded piece of paper, and before you know it, the press would find out. And that, as they say, would be that."

She frowned, unconvinced. "I don't know. I've always considered Jon more reliable than that."

"In medical matters, yes. In politics, forget it. He's not a real *mensch*, and as nice as he is, he's got no guts."

She sat there, brooding in silence.

"Don't misunderstand what I'm saying," he continued. "I'm not suggesting we overlook what might be happening to your husband. This isn't the emperor's new clothes. All I'm saying is, why not hold off any medical evaluation for a month or two? Let's get him through the announcement and into the re-election campaign. At that point, or before then, if his symptoms progress, we'll get him checked out."

Roxanne had been a political spouse long enough to know he was right. Her husband's strength lay in the fact that he was a consummate politician, and he would never forgive her for doing something reckless that might cost him his job. "All right. But how flexible are you where it comes to Dr. Townsend?"

"Roxanne, I'd trust the man implicitly with my life. I just don't trust him with my vote. If it's all the same to you, I'd just as soon keep him out of this."

CHAPTER 11

Cherokee, North Carolina

Unlike other religious right-wing activist organizations, the Southern Cross had no official camp or meeting place. Its numbers were small. Its main rendezvous points, as organized by Sean O'Brien, were anywhere in the upper rural South, although they were most often in the vicinity of the Great Smoky Mountains. When it was necessary to meet in public, O'Brien preferred well-frequented tourist sites. The presence of crowds enhanced security and minimized the chance of electronic surveillance. Today O'Brien was meeting Walker at the Oconaluftee Indian Village on U.S. Highway 441 North. The Village had recently extended its season until mid-November.

As O'Brien stood outside the visitor center, ostensible reading a brochure, Walker sidled up to him. C.J. knew the drill. Avoid eye contact. Speak softly and casually. Pretend disinterest.

"Our boy will be here soon, C.J. I'll let you know just when and where. Be good to him. Treat him like a guest."

"He's a fuckin' A-rab, Sean," said C.J.

"Doesn't matter. These people are very big on respect. We've all got a job to do, including him. So, don't piss him off."

"Shit," C.J. softly protested, spitting a piece of tobacco from his teeth. "Can he shoot?"

"So I've been told. But that's for you to find out, isn't it? You'll put him through his paces, and when you're done, clean up the weapon, especially the serial number."

"You got it, Sean. But what happens if he can't shoot worth a damn?"

"You'll let me know. Don't do anything yourself. And one more thing, C.J. Don't screw with the man's religion. You think we're serious about God's will? You're gonna hear the word Allah so much it'll be comin' out of your ass, but keep your mouth shut. Let him think what he wants. And for Christ sake, don't let on what's really happening, okay?"

C.J. spit disgustedly. "What you think I am, Sean? Stupid?"

O'Brien kept his thoughts to himself.

Bethesda

They met, as usual, in the shopping center's parking lot, two blocks from the abortion clinic in Four Corners. It was noon. The clinic's hours ended at eleven that day, and most of the staff left an hour later. Townsend got out of his car and entered the one that pulled up beside him.

"Hello, Ellen. How're things?"

"Pretty good, Dr. Townsend. How's Tommie doing?"

"About the same. Loves school. I'm not sure I can handle her becoming a teenager. What's up with Michael?"

"I had to up his NPH three units," she said, referring to the amount of insulin required by her son. "He's such a brave kid. I don't know where he gets the strength."

"From you, obviously. What you're doing takes guts."

Ellen, the abortion clinic's lab technician, had met Dr. Townsend two years ago when he'd given a public lecture at the NIH about the future applications of human fetal stem cells. After the lecture, she'd pulled him aside and asked pointed questions about one of the uses he referred to—diabetes. Theoretically, the stem cells could differentiate into insulin-producing islet cells of the pancreas. Her son Michael, who was then six, seemed to be an ideal candidate for stem cell therapy, if and when it became available.

The problem, Dr. Townsend pointed out, was the scarcity of fetal tissue. Historically, the NIH had been limited in the types and amounts of tissue it approved for research. Then, in 1993, an absolute ban on fetal tissue research was softened. In 1998, biologists announced that they had discovered a way to isolate and preserve human stem cells. There were obvious ethical considerations, and the NIH initially deflected the controversy by using "cell lines" derived from fetal tissue rather than the tissue itself. Finally, in 2000, the ban was removed entirely.

This was an interim solution, he explained, and not quite as useful as fresh fetal tissue. There were three sources of fresh fetal cells: miscarriages, unwanted surplus embryos from in-vitro fertilizations, and induced abortions. Miscarriages, unfortunately, often contained degenerating tissue. The second category was good, but the number of in-vitro embryos was too small for broad future applications. The abortion source was nearly ideal, although the collection methodology hadn't yet been worked out. It was here that Ellen's ears perked up.

She revealed that she worked in an abortion clinic. The facility performed about seventy-five procedures per week, all first trimester. There was certainly no shortage of fetal tissue. In day-to-day practice, after she removed the products of conception from the aspiration bottle, she would add formaldehyde to the specimens, after which they were sent to the lab for pathological confirmation of pregnancy. If Jon wanted, she could offer him portions of the specimens.

Jon told her he'd let her know. It was an idea that deserved considerable thought. It could be a new, untapped, very promising area of research. It was also a proposition that could get him into considerable trouble. The NIH had recently published guidelines for stem cell research, and this method of obtaining the tissue was decidedly outside the guidelines. Also, all NIH research had to be approved. Approval depended not only on the study's design and utility, but also on political considerations. Given the prevailing anti-abortion sentiment in Congress, getting the approval he wanted was highly doubtful.

If he were going to do the research, he'd have to do it unofficially, and in secret. Fortunately, through his legitimate research, Jon already had access to space and equipment. He considered Ellen's offer very thoroughly, but not for very long. Whether or not he'd do it was never really in doubt. In the end, he knew he'd do almost anything that might help Tommie.

Ellen opened a briefcase and removed a shoebox-size

container. It was a portable, battery-operated incubator that kept specimens at a steady thirty-eight degrees centigrade. "There are six here," she said, handing him the container.

"All between six and seven weeks?"

"Of course. Rinsed, juiced, and ready to go."

The part played by Ellen was essential. She not only delivered the tissue but also prepared it. First, she selected only those specimens at an early stage of gestation, before the organs had completed differentiation. In the privacy of her lab, she removed tiny bits of fetal tissue from the more voluminous placenta, which would be sent to the pathologist. Next, she thoroughly washed the tissue in saline to remove contamination by maternal blood. After placing the tissue in a test tube filled with transfer medium, she added several drops of "juice," a new antibiotic Jon had given her. It had both antibacterial and virucidal activity, including HIV. Finally, the tubes went into the incubator.

"Thanks, Ellen," he said, taking it from her. "I'll get back to you in a day or two."

"Fine. How's it going, anyway? Making progress?"

"Definitely. Slow but steady. I should have more to tell you by the end of the year."

After returning to his car, it was a short drive back to the NIH. He had the use of a lab two afternoons per week. His research dovetailed with his interest in neurological diseases, along the lines he'd suggested to Senator Friedman. In addition, he and other scientists, when they legitimately followed the guidelines, were using discarded surplus human embryos as a tissue source for the stem cells. Until now, he'd been growing the tissue in cell culture.

Jon's ultimate goal was to induce the cells to differentiate into neural cells, which could one day be transplanted into patients with degenerative neurological problems. A similar process was involved in the making of pancreatic cells for diabetics like Ellen's son.

One of the many problems faced by the researchers was getting the stem cells to differentiate in the desired direction. The scientist's goal was to foster differentiation along particular lines until the more mature tissue developed. But stem cells might, for reasons not completely understood, divide to form tissue of any of the three basic cell layers: mesoderm, ectoderm, and endoderm. Ectoderm ultimately formed neural tissue, while endoderm gave rise to the pancreas. But having the cells divide as intended wasn't always easy.

Late embryonic or fetal tissue, as opposed to the discarded in-vitro tissue, got around many potential problems by using cells that had already begun to differentiate. This saved time and uncertainty. If a trained technician examined a fifteen-millimeter embryo under magnification, there was no question about which tissue was developing into which organ. Isolating and growing that tissue was a surer bet if one's goal was a particular type of mature tissue. It was here that Jon had decided to concentrate his clandestine efforts.

Once in the lab, he closed and locked the door to his private office, which contained a large workstation and microscope. Working with one test tube at a time, he removed the specimens Ellen had collected and thoroughly rinsed them again. Then he took the first specimen and placed it in a microscope tissue chamber. Looking through the lenses, he examined the specimen for adequacy.

Many human embryos would not survive the abortion process. With a powerful suction device extracting them from the uterus at a pressure of seventy millimeters of mercury, few were physically intact. But the ones that survived were a wonder to behold. Under low magnification, the fifteen-millimeter embryo floated in its warm, watery bath. Though it no longer had a blood supply, the embryo's tissues could survive several hours by the process of diffusion. But once individual tissues were removed and placed in the proper medium, they could grow indefinitely.

Jon was always fascinated by what lay in his field of view. The pink and shiny embryo showed clear signs of human development. Properly backlit, the pale, translucent skin already revealed a fine network of developing blood vessels. The tiny embryo bent forward on itself, as if its rudimentary chin were touching its developing chest. The developing head, with its easily identifiable eyes, was as large as the remainder of the body. Under the head was a prominent precordial bulge in what would later become heart. Four limb buds had the beginnings of obvious fingers and toes. The moving sight spoke to the miracle that was nature. While it inspired Jon, it also attested to the seriousness of what he was doing. One of the many reasons he did what he did was because he thought it a shame to discard something that held such promise for treating human disease. Now came what was, for Jon, the distasteful part.

There was no getting around the necessity of removing tissue from the embryo. Miniature instruments had been designed for the process—tiny forceps, scalpels, and scissors. Using forceps braces to steady his hands on each side of the microscope, Jon inserted a grasper and microscalpel into the tissue chamber.

Under magnification, the instruments looked enormous. Working the grasper with his left hand, he immobilized the embryo by its caudal end. With his right hand, he made an incision from the top of the cranial region down to the middle of what would form the spine. Then he traded the scalpel for a pointed bayonet forceps. With deft movements, he teased out the rudimentary neural tissue. It had the silvery-gray appearance of fish flesh.

Removing the tissue, Jon rinsed it once again. He'd already prepared a cell culture tube, which was in a rack beside the microscope. The tube contained modified Eagle's medium enriched with fetal serum albumin, to which Leukemia Inhibiting Factor had been added. The LIF would prevent cell division for several days while the tissue stabilized. On his next trip to the lab, Jon would remove the LIF, allowing the neural cells to multiply.

He'd been repeating the process for months and already had a good supply of fetal neural stem cells. The main problem he faced was that he didn't know how much was enough. There were several case reports of fetal neural tissue transplantation, generally into diseased adult nervous systems for treatment of disorders like Parkinson's disease. However, the amounts transplanted, and the method of transplantation, differed from one report to the other. Jon would have to figure this out for himself, for there was as yet no standardized dosage, or regimen. Too little might prove ineffective, while too much might potentially be harmful. Where it came to his daughter's health, no additional harm would be tolerated.

"Thanks for coming by, Jon. I know this exam is window dressing, but Mitch thought it'd look good to the voters."

They were in the president's bedroom of the private residence. Finished taking the president's blood pressure, Jon put away his sphygmomanometer and had Meredith lie down. Earlier that afternoon, Mitchell Forbes had called and requested that Jon perform a brief physical before Tuesday's re-election announcement.

"You're going to have to remove your shirt, Mr. President. And I need you to roll your pants legs up to your knees."

That done, Jon listened to the commander-in-chief's heart and lungs. The heart sounds were normal, and the breath sounds were those of a much younger man. Then Jon opened his portable EKG machine and plugged it into the wall socket. After securing the limb leads, he applied the precordial leads and turned on the machine. The EKG pen traced smooth, healthy patterns. Twenty seconds later, he was finished. Trying not to pull off too many chest hairs, Jon carefully removed the thoracic leads.

"This looks fine to me," he said, comparing the printout with a similar tracing performed several months earlier. "If they ask you, you can tell them your doctor's given you a clean bill of health. Would you like me to let Mitch Forbes know?"

"Thanks, but I'm meeting him in ten minutes. He'll probably want you to put something in writing, though, just in case.

There was a hurried knock at the door, and Secret Service Agent Dave Saunders poked his head in. "Excuse, me, gentlemen, but there's an emergency downstairs. Could you take a look, Doctor? We've sent for an ambulance."

The president waved his hand. "Go, go."

Jon grabbed his bag and dashed out of the room, following Saunders. He and the agent were personal friends, having met shortly after the last election. The nearby elevator was waiting. Once they were inside, Saunders pushed the button for the first floor.

"What's going on, Dave?"

"They say somebody had a heart attack in the kitchen."

"Who?"

"You know that old guy, Mr. Phillips? One of the ushers?"

Jon did. The white-haired African American had been a White House fixture for years. Although, physically, he was a caricature of a traditional black servant, he was an exceedingly warm man, with a reassuring basso voice.

"You bet I do. Any idea what he was doing when it happened?"

"Not a clue."

The doors opened and they raced toward the kitchen. Inside, Mr. Phillips was lying on his back on the floor. Two Secret Service agents were trying to resuscitate him, one doing external chest compressions while the other breathed mouth-to-mouth. Jon stopped beside them, checking the wall clock.

"How long have you been at it?"

One of the agents looked up. "About four minutes. No response."

"Dave, give us a hand. Let's get him onto this table. Then find the emergency cart we used the other night."

The four men lifted the stricken patient onto one of the stainless-steel food preparation tables. As Saunders went to retrieve the emergency equipment, Jon hurriedly removed Mr. Phillips' shirt and undershirt. Then he had the agents resume their CPR.

The old man looked moribund. His cheeks were sunken, and his eyes appeared lifeless. When Jon shined a penlight into Phillips' eyes, the already-dilated pupils didn't react. Further efforts were probably futile, but once begun, there was no turning back until the man recovered or was pronounced dead. Jon quickly looked around.

"Did anyone see what happened?"

Most of the kitchen staff shrugged, but several turned toward the chef. Mireille was standing against a wall, eyes red and hands balled in front of her mouth. Jon stared at her, and she nodded.

"He was helping me carry something," she said, her voice tremulous. "He didn't have to, but that's the way he is, and..."

"What happened?" he interrupted.

"He said he didn't feel well, and he went outside to smoke. He has been smoking a lot lately. When he came back, he looked worse than ever. Then he just..."

Saunders brought over the emergency supplies, which Jon wheeled toward the patient's head. He hurriedly removed a laryngoscope and cranked open the oxygen. "Dave, go up to the residence and see if you can get that portable EKG machine, okay?"

"No problem."

As the rhythmic CPR continued, Jon quickly located an endotracheal tube, tape, and an ambu bag. As he got everything ready, he continued talking.

"How's his health been, Miss Courtois? Do you see him often?"

"Every day. He comes down here for coffee."

Jon had the agents stop a moment as he tilted back the patient's chin and extended the neck. Mr. Phillips had full dentures, which he whisked away. Then he inserted the laryngoscope's blade over the patient's tongue. "How did he look today?"

"Not well," she replied. "He's been acting strangely for a few months."

Using the instrument's blade, Jon lifted the tongue and lower jaw until the larynx was exposed. The usual ivory color of the vocal cords was now an unhealthy gray.

Nevertheless, Jon took the endotracheal tube in his right hand and slid its tip past the cords into Mr. Phillips' trachea.

"Strange?" he said, removing the scope and taping the tube to the patient's cheeks. He quickly motioned for the agent to resume chest compressions. "Strange in what way?"

She shrugged. "He hasn't been himself. He's been very

irritable," she said in French. "What is the word? Cranky."

Jon quickly inserted the oxygen tubing to the ambu bag, which he attached to the ET tube. "What else?" he asked, as he rhythmically squeezed the bag.

"He has these little jerks—twitches? And his memory is not so good as it once was."

"Okay." Saunders dashed into the room with the small EKG machine, which Jon opened and turned on. He told the agent to stop working on the chest while he applied the limb leads and turned on the power.

"EMTs are here, Doc," someone said.

"Good. Send 'em in."

"Is he going to be okay, Doctor?" Mireille said.

The machine's pen traced the formless pattern of an agonal rhythm. "No, Mireille, I'm afraid not."

The paramedics wheeled over the stretcher. "Want us to take him, Doc?"

Jon looked at the wall clock. It was now ten minutes into the arrest. The patient's pupils were fixed and dilated, he wasn't breathing, and his EKG showed a dead heart. "I don't think so, guys. He's a little beyond our reach. Call the time, and then take him to the ME's office."

Thusly pronounced dead, the efforts on Mr. Phillips ended. It was pointless to keep trying once a person's brain and heart ceased to function. They might persevere with a child or someone in midlife, but not on a seventy-year-old whose best years were behind him. As the EMTs put the deceased on the stretcher for the trip to the morgue, Mireille began to cry.

Jon realized that the death was going to generate hours of paperwork for the Secret Service agents, the paramedics, and the kitchen staff. Also, since performing CPR on a food-preparation table was rather unusual, the kitchen would doubtless be temporarily closed down for sanitizing and employee downtime. But he also knew that such minutiae were not the reason for Mireille's tears.

She had retreated to a corner where, in the shadows, she hugged herself and cried unashamedly. It was a soft noise, the lost and poignant sound of an abandoned child. Jon slowly approached and placed a hand on her shoulder.

"I'm sorry, Miss Courtois. I won't ask if you're okay, because I can see you're not. He must have been pretty special."

"You have no idea," she said.

"You're absolutely right. I realize this isn't the best time, Miss Courtois—"

"Mireille. Call me Mireille."

"Sure," he said. "What I'm getting at, some of what you said doesn't fit, medically. I'm trying to make sense out of all of this."

Mireille knew who Dr. Townsend was, having seen him several times before. It was always from a distance, and they'd never had any conversation of substance. Now, she was starting to resent his interference. Yet when she looked his way, his expression was so sincere that she softened. She accepted his offered handkerchief.

"Sometimes, when someone dies, there is no sense," she said, sniffling. "But what do you want to know?"

"Just go over a few things with me. It looks to me that Mr. Phillips had a killer heart attack. His increased smoking played right into that."

She took a pack of Marlboros from her pocket. "Here, these were his. He won't need them anymore."

Jon lifted the box's lid and took one out. The cigarette resembled a joint. "He rolled his own?"

"Pardon?"

He lifted the cigarette to his nose. "This isn't marijuana, is it?"

That made her laugh. "No, those are the cigarettes he made!"

"Interesting. A real cowboy. I haven't seen one of these in years. But what else can you remember? You mentioned irritation, twitching, and forgetfulness. Those symptoms suggest a neurological problem more than a cardiac one."

"You're the doctor, not me. I'll take your word for it."

"Yes, but was there any pattern to his new habits? I'm not asking you to guess at a diagnosis. Just give me your impressions."

Lids narrowed, she gazed up at the ceiling in recollection. "All I can say is that everything happened together. It was around Father's Day. That was when I first noticed the changes in his behavior, the movements, the memory problem."

"Did he ever complain of heart trouble?"

"Not to me, no."

"What about the smoking? You said you thought he smoked more. Did he always smoke his own cigarettes?"

"Oh. No. He used to smoke regular Marlboros until... Now that I think about it, that is about the same time his other symptoms began. Does that mean something?"

He pocketed the box of smokes. "I don't know. I'll have to check the literature on roll-your-own cigarettes. Anything else?"

"No, I don't think so."

"Okay. Look, Miss...Mireille. I appreciate your help. I hope you didn't have a big dinner planned for tonight," he said, gesturing toward the rest of the kitchen, "because I think you're going to be shut down a few hours."

"Nothing big. The First Family's meal is already prepared. We were working on things for tomorrow."

"Perfect. I hope you don't think I'm out of line here, but when something like this happens, I usually tell my patients that they are their own worst enemy."

"I'm sorry?"

"They should avoid being alone. Seriously. When there's a tragedy like this and you're trapped inside your own head, you're behind enemy lines."

"I see. But I'm not your patient."

"True," he conceded, "but I also tell them to avoid depressing situations and try to relax. So, would you like to go out for a drink? It might be helpful. Medically speaking, of course."

For the first time, she had a smile. "Are you hitting on me, Doctor?"

"Perish the thought."

"Thank you for the offer, but I really need some time by myself."

"Okay. You're sure you'll be all right?"

She nodded. "I'm sure."

For several seconds Jon stood there in artless silence before he found his voice. "Give me a call if I can be of any help."

Mireille watched him walk away. She thought he was very professional, and he certainly meant well. Yet he seemed like a wounded little boy, crushed by her reply. His expression was somewhere between a pout and being shot at sunrise. In truth, she thought, she really didn't want to be alone right now. Perhaps his suggestion was a good one.

"Dr. Townsend?"

He turned. "What?"

"Maybe I *could* use that drink. Medically speaking, that is."

It was his turn to smile. "Of course."

Near Gafsa, Tunisia

The Al-Maidah camp was a base in name only. It was little more than a collection of tents and rickety wooden supply shacks. There was, however, a deep freshwater well, around which all camp life centered. Its water was slightly brackish, due to the salinity of the local water table. Indeed, there were large salt lakes just south of the camp.

The area around the camp was semi-desert. As far as the eye could see, there were only dunes, rocks, and low ridges. It was very arid, for only Tunisia's north was reliably watered. Yet amid the dunes, near the well, there were signs of life: a palm, a few twisted trees, patches of grass, and a half dozen sheep.

Despite the ostensibly hardscrabble existence, the camp had abundant technology that seemed strikingly out of place. A satellite dish was mounted to one of the shacks. Linked solar panels captured the sun's energy and delivered it to banks of storage batteries. In case of a sustained overcast, a powerful diesel generator stood ready to be cranked on. The camp could create more electrical energy than it could ever consume.

Certain creature comforts paralleled the glut of technology. One of the shacks had shelves brimming with foodstuffs. Although there was no fresh produce, tinned goods were plentiful. There were cases of canned meats, fruit, and vegetables, in addition to oddities like Italian olive oil, German sausage, and Iranian caviar, which no one ate. Another shack was filled with durable goods—Irish sweaters and sweatshirts, Moroccan tee shirts, and French fatigues. The most plentiful items were dozens of Adidas sneakers, lifted from a pier in Algeria, all new in the box. Lastly, there were huge quantities of bottled water. Exhausted from his journey, Mahmoud retired to his tent and went to bed early. The camp had no beds, only sleeping bags. At this time of year, nights could be cold. He built a fire of sticks and dried palm fronds, but it quickly burned out. Mahmoud wrapped himself in the down and was soon asleep. Sometime after midnight he was awakened by a cold, gusty wind. One of the tent flaps had loosened, and wind-driven sand was pelting his face, accumulating in his hair, teeth, and sleeping bag. He quickly sealed and tightened the flap, brushed himself off, and went back to sleep.

Al-Maidah was temporary home to twenty men. At sunrise, an electronic muezzin called everyone to morning prayer. Although the skies were clear, it was still cold, and Mahmoud put a sweatshirt over his fatigue top. One of the sheds contained prayer mats. Mahmoud placed his next to others outdoors in the sand, facing east-northeast toward Mecca. Soon, after a breakfast of dates, flatbread, and Pellegrino water, it was time to go to work.

Al-Maidah had been constructed for the sole purpose of training men to become proficient in the use of firearms and explosives. There were no novices, only experts in their craft seeking to finely hone their edge. Mahmoud approached the munitions storage area. The munitions shack had large quantities of plastic explosives—about fifty kilos of C-4, crates of Czech Semtex, and smaller quantities of newer American and Chinese compounds. In addition, there were hundreds of detonators, blasting caps, and remotely operated radio initiators. But what interested Mahmoud more were the firearms.

As a marksman, he specialized in midrange shots of extreme accuracy. Such shots were usually at a distance of one hundred to two hundred fifty meters. Under ideal conditions, he could place three shots into a one-inch circle at two hundred meters. But such precision called for state-of-the-art equipment. A bolt-action rifle, rather than the semi-automatic Dragunov, was required. The rifle's action, barrel, and scope had to be first-rate. Long before he left Gaza, Mahmoud was told that he'd be getting a gift from a firearms dealer in Southern California. American equipment was far and away the best for this situation. Mahmoud was assured the items required would arrive at Al-Maidah before he did.

Amid racks of AK-47s, what Mahmoud wanted was still in its shipping boxes. The rifle came in a molded Styrofoam case, which he opened with his knife. When he lifted the weapon and held it before him, he made a noise like a sigh. The rifle was made of a titanium alloy and was very lightweight. The receiver bore the name of Harris Gunworks. All metal surfaces were bead-blasted to reduce glare, then painted flat black. The ebony stock was graphite-reinforced fiberglass. A lightweight Swarovski scope topped the weapon off.

The entire package had an air of lethality. It was a sinister-looking weapon. Mahmoud worked the bolt, which moved crisply, smoothly. He carried the rifle into the bright sun outside and removed the scope covers. Putting his cheek to the stock, he sighted on a nearby dune. The optics were sharp and clear. When he lightly touched the trigger, it broke at a scant three ounces of pressure.

Soon he was out on the makeshift range, preparing to shoot from a weathered bench. Targets were stapled to wooden frames one hundred, two hundred, and three hundred meters away. The cartridges were in plastic cases holding fifty rounds each. Mahmoud took one out, lifted it, and examined it closely.

The round was a 6mm BR, standing for benchrest. BR implied an accurate round, and the caliber was used in precision, competitive benchrest shooting. Each round was hand loaded. It was an oddly shaped, stubby little cartridge. The bullet was an eighty-grain solid point projectile, rather than hollow point. That hardly mattered when one's target was most often the human head. Mahmoud chambered one of the rounds and peered through the scope. It was time to see how the rifle shot.

He had three hundred rounds to work with. He'd use however many were necessary to master the rifle and cartridge, though he had to keep twenty in reserve for an as-yet-undisclosed mission. One by one, he touched the rounds off,

leaving ample time between shots to let the barrel cool down.
After an hour of shooting, he knew he was dealing with a
remarkable weapon.

The rifle had minimal recoil and was a pleasure to shoot.
Beyond that, it was astonishingly accurate. His first five-shot
group measured a scant eleven millimeters across. He zeroed
the optics until he was dead-on point of aim at one hundred fifty
meters. He shot all morning, patiently and precisely, cleaning
the weapon after every twenty shots, until he'd expended one
hundred rounds. When he was finished, he knew he possessed
the most accurate rifle/cartridge combination he'd ever fired.

Although he needed only one more day of practice,
Mahmoud would stay at Al-Maidah until called. He didn't
know where he would be sent or what the target was. All he
knew was that it was vital to the Palestinian movement.

And, if it was Allah's will, he would give his life for it.

Patsy's was a cozy Georgetown pub popular with the military
and cops. It was largely unknown to politicians and the press
corps, which was one of the reasons Jon chose it. The last thing he
needed was for some hungry gossip columnist to link the White
House chef with the president's doctor. After she changed into
street clothes, Mireille followed Jon to his car. Fifteen minutes
later, they were inside the pub.

Heads turned. Jon found it oddly satisfying that nearly
everyone stopped to stare at his companion. Mireille wasn't
supermodel gorgeous, but she was very attractive, and she
had undeniable poise. Her body language was unmistakably
feminine, and she moved with charm and grace in the lithe
stride of a dancer. She glided, rather than stepped, across the
floor, delicate movements with a nuance of bounce.

"Let's sit here," he said.

A corner booth had just been vacated. If Mireille was aware
of the attention she was getting, she didn't show it. As she took
her seat, all of her attention was on Jon.

"It is very crowded here," she said, pronouncing "it" as
"eet."

"Do you come here often?"

"From time to time." He signaled a waitress, then turned to Mireille. "What would you like?"

"Just a Pernod, please."

"Excuse me?" asked the waitress.

"Pernod," said Jon, pronouncing the D Mireille had omitted. "And bring me a single malt scotch, neat."

As the waitress walked away, Mireille smiled. "I keep forgetting how to speak American."

"Don't worry, so do most Americans. How long have you been in the States?"

"Three years. I worked in San Francisco before I came here."

"Great town. Where in France do you come from?"

"Paris, originally. I was born there. But my family originates in Brittany."

"On the coast?" he asked.

"Yes. They were farmers for centuries."

While she spoke about the subject with animation, Jon studied her. Mireille had glossy, ash blond hair that fell below her shoulders. Her nose was long and slender, but not aquiline. With its alternate extremes of nonchalance and expressiveness, her face had the imprint of Gallic origins. There was an understated aloofness in her facial mannerisms, and when she spoke, she would dismiss something with a single cluck of her head, or, in disagreement, purse her lips and emit a nearly inaudible "pfff."

But when something pleased her, there was nothing French about her enthusiasm. Her eyes would go wide, and her broad, effervescent smile was all California. She punctuated her speech with her hands—slender-fingered, strong, yet undeniably feminine.

"Do other people in your family cook?" he asked.

"Yes, it is a family passion. I think it comes from generations of farming. Harvesting and cooking go together very naturally."

When the waitress returned with their drinks, Jon offered a toast. "To the memory of Mr. Phillips, a sweet man."

Mireille said nothing as she touched her glass to his. Her eyes clouded over, and she turned away. Not wanting sadness to overtake her, Jon quickly changed the subject. "In case I didn't mention it, your cooking is out of this world. What makes you so passionate about it?"

She took a long sip of her drink, closing her eyes as the fire stoked her gullet. "When you grow crops, you begin with something raw and unformed, like a seed. You plough the earth, plant the seed, and water it. Soon it sprouts, but you still have to weed around it, protect it. When it grows, you nurture it. Finally, it blossoms, and in the end you have this wonderful creation everyone can enjoy. Cooking is a lot like that. The recipe begins with raw ingredients, but you bring them together. Then you mix it, shape it, let it rise, and then heat it. If you have done your job well, it can become a masterpiece. So you see, cooking, like farming, is in my blood."

"It all sounds rather like life."

"I never thought of it that way," she said, "but it's true. If you want your life to prosper, you have to work at it. Sometimes you have to change it. Take dough, for instance. You have to knead it, shape it, roll it. It will only rise if you work it properly."

"You're quite the philosopher, you know that?"

With Mr. Phillips a warm, pleasant memory, they continued talking about farming, cooking, and life. Jon enjoyed watching her speak. Disarmed by her candor, fascinated by her mannerisms, he knew he was becoming enchanted with her.

CHAPTER 12

With precisely a year to go before Election Day, the president met the assembled press in the briefing room. In addition to Roxanne and the chief of staff, the vice president and his wife Amanda were there, along with the Secretaries of State, Defense, and Treasury. The press secretary had already briefed those in attendance that there would be no question-and-answer period. Without fanfare, Bob Meredith entered and walked up to the podium.

"Good morning, ladies and gentlemen. Three years ago, our fellow citizens bestowed a great honor on me, and an even greater responsibility. In a desire for change, the American people, in their collective wisdom, entrusted me with implementing policies and that best reflected their wishes. That has always been this administration's priority. I am happy to say that we are halfway there."

That brought polite laughter from the press corps, and Forbes smiled. Like a musician, the president knew how to play his audience—when to hit the high notes, and when to draw out his speech in a shimmering vibrato. Given his considerable skills, Mitch Forbes thought Meredith should have no problem getting re-elected. A greater challenge would be managing the year-long re-election process, a tangled maze dense as chaparral.

In an ideal world, Forbes thought, it would be best to insulate the executive branch from the mercenary nature of politics. But politics were never ideal. In the real world of a national political campaign for the country's highest office, it was simply impossible to keep re-election politics out of the White House. Yet Forbes would be very careful how they intertwined. It was a juggling act that would test his administrative skills to the utmost.

As some administrations had learned the hard way, it was imperative to keep fundraising out of the House. This was something Forbes was certain he could control. Yet for the next year, his non-financial responsibilities would assume a dual purpose: he had to assist the president in day-to-day governing while simultaneously helping run the re-election. There would now be two separate entities vying for the chief of staff's time— the White House and the campaign staff.

Forbes realized he was going to be a very busy man. He would earn his money during the year to come. He'd have to fit campaign time into the president's already-busy schedule. He would need to make key decisions about political strategy from his own office, where he'd be spending a great deal of time. And he would have to slow down political initiatives to give the president breathing room.

Most of all, he'd have to let the president do what the president did best, which was to lead the greatest nation on earth. If he did that, the rest should take care of itself; for in the end, the best politics was good governing.

"In the last three years," Meredith resumed, "we have accomplished a great deal. Our economy is robust and vital, and we as a nation are more prosperous than ever before. We have reshaped our military to meet the changing needs of a changing world, yet our military power and preparedness exceed what we once thought possible. In the areas of health, education, and equal opportunity, we are well on our way to meeting our admittedly ambitious goals. Yet for all our accomplishments, have we come far enough?

"I think not. The seeds that were planted have germinated, but they need more time to grow. When I assumed the presidency, I quickly realized that the American people would not accept half measures and partial solutions. They wanted progressive policies that would be carried to fruition. In order to fully realize the will of all Americans, we need more time.

"Therefore, I have decided to seek another term as your president. We have embarked on a journey that is at its midpoint.

The challenges before us are as great as the rewards, but with the help and support of you, my fellow Americans, I am confident I can safely guide the ship of state to its destination."

His prepared remarks complete, Meredith paused and looked out across the crowded room. Despite the press secretary's admonition about questions, reporters began loud, persistent inquiries. The president seemed confused. He turned and stared uncertainly at his wife. From the bewildered expression on his face, it was suddenly apparent to Roxanne that her husband didn't know what to do next. Before the situation could degenerate, she smiled broadly, walked over to him, and kissed him lovingly on the cheek. Her lips slid to his ear.

"Let's go, Bob."

"Did you see the announcement today?" Jon asked.

"Yes, I did," Mireille replied. "We have a TV in the kitchen. Do you think he will be re-elected?"

"He's what we call a shoo-in. That means a sure thing. Everybody loves him, and he's a great leader. But what did you think of that business at the end, when he looked a little lost?"

"He was just tired, no?"

"I don't know. I thought he was indecisive—about what, I'm not sure. But the journalists must have asked about it after he left, because an hour later, the press secretary was back there reassuring everyone. He said the president was thinking of adding to his prepared remarks but decided against it."

"That must be it, then. Are you worried about something? As his doctor, you're in a position to know."

It was almost seven p.m. Other than on the occasion of special dinners, Mireille's normal workday ended at five. After she'd gone home and changed, Jon picked her up at her Georgetown apartment and proceeded to his own home in Bethesda. The time he'd spent with her at Patsy's had been so enjoyable that he looked forward to seeing her again, and they set a date for Tuesday night.

The only distraction was Tommie. When Victoria made a last-minute call claiming to have urgent business in New York, Jon had gladly agreed—as usual—to having his daughter stay over. As soon as he picked Mireille up, he ran the complication by her. With endearing nonchalance, she dismissed it as a non-issue. She said she'd be delighted to have Tommie accompany them.

"When I examined the president last week," Jon said, "he was fine. I'll take the press secretary's word. The president's certainly got a lot on his mind."

"Are you a good doctor, Jon?"

"Now that's what I call being direct. No one's ever asked me that before."

The hint of a smile curled her lips. "Well, are you?"

"I suppose I am. Why?"

"When you saved the president's life last week, they said you were remarkable."

"They?" he asked. "That's nice to hear, but who's they?"

"Everyone. The kitchen staff, the servers, the Secret Service agents. They said that if you had not been there, President Meredith would be dead."

His mind flashed back to that night, to how he'd nearly been too paralyzed with fear to move. "That's nice to hear, but they're making a big deal out of basic first aid."

She made that poofing sound with her lips, dismissing his remark. "You can't take a compliment, can you?"

"It's not that, it's... Anyone with the least bit of medical knowledge could have done what I did."

"So why didn't they?"

It was a question that he, in fact, had wrestled with. The Secret Service agents who'd attended the president didn't seem to know what they were doing. "I'm not sure. Maybe they knew I was there. It's funny, though. I wasn't supposed to be."

"*Pardon?*" she said, in French.

"I got there at the last minute. I actually had something else to do that night."

"What a coincidence. I wasn't there either."

He hadn't been aware of it until she mentioned it. That night's dinner was certainly the sort of gala event she'd been hired for. Thinking back, he realized he hadn't seen her in the kitchen when he'd examined the president.

"Day off?"

"No, I was supposed to work. And I did, until the afternoon. Most of the dishes were already prepared. We do that in the morning, then cook it just before service. Then, around three, I was told to go home."

"You mean, just like that?"

"Just like that."

"Who told you?"

"Actually," she said, drawing out the word as she reflected, "no one told me. It was a note, on official stationery. White House chief of staff."

Jon fell silent, knitting his brow. That was strange indeed. Why would Mitch Forbes tell her to take off on the day of a state dinner? Mireille called it a coincidence that neither she nor Jon were supposed to be there that evening, but she didn't believe in coincidences.

"You didn't actually speak to Mr. Forbes?" he asked.

"No, I was too shocked. I just finished what I was doing, left instructions, and went home." She paused. "Do you think that I did something wrong?"

"Absolutely not. You did what you were told. Were you ever sent home before?"

"Never. That's what is so strange."

"Was there a reason given, an explanation?"

She shrugged. "Not at all."

"Hmmm. Why do you suppose he'd do that?"

"Oh, I don't know. In the back of my mind, I was afraid they were bringing in a big-name chef just for *la presentation*, but that didn't happen. What is it, Jon? You seem disturbed."

"Not really," he lied. "It's just a little weird. So, who was the big name?"

"Marcel Al-Hakeem. He's not a big name, really. A pastry chef."

"Is he French?"

"Algerian, I think. I'm not sure why they wanted him."

Soon his Audi turned onto a narrow lane lined by towering oaks. His home was one of the block's smaller dwellings, an older split-level fieldstone structure that spoke of warmth and

comfort. He parked in the driveway and escorted Mireille inside.
"Tommie, I'm home."

"In the living room, Daddy. Did she come with you?"

"Yes, she did." To Mireille, "I told her you were coming.
She's pretty excited. She never met a real chef before. This way."
The living room was done in wood, leather, and earth tones,
and an entire wall and fireplace were set in stone. It had a hearty,
lived-in look. Tommie was sitting on a long couch in front of
a TV, doing her homework. When they entered the room, she
looked up and beamed.

"Hi," she said cheerfully. "My dad said you're the White
House chef. Do you really cook for the president?"

"Yes, I do," Mireille said. Dr. Townsend's daughter, she
thought, was a lovely young woman. She had limpid blue eyes
and naturally curly brown hair that fell just below her shoulders.
Her most striking feature, however, was her expression. When
Tommie smiled, her lower face became all mouth. Her wide,
rising lips wanted to touch her cheekbones, and her eyelids
turned up gleefully. Her eyes shined mischievously, but they
also brimmed with joy—which was just as well, Mireille
thought, as for the first time she noticed the short metal crutches
propped up against the couch. She extended her arm. "Mireille
Courtois. *Enchantée.*"

"I'm Thomasina," she said, returning the handshake. "But
everyone calls me Tommie."

From the comer of his eye, Jon watched Mireille's reaction.
He hadn't mentioned Tommie's paraplegia because he wanted
to see what Mireille would do. If she was at all surprised by his
daughter's disability, she hid it well, seamlessly absorbing the
visual information and folding it into her database, just as she
might blend a cake.

"Yes, your father told me. It's a lovely name."

"That's so *cool*, cooking for the White House! Is it hard? Do
you have a lot of people to help you? I bet you make a lot of
money."

"Whoa, kiddo," said Jon. "Let her catch her breath, okay?
I'm sure Chef Courtois didn't expect to get grilled by Detective
Townsend tonight."

"That's all right," said Mireille, taking a seat on the couch next to Mireille. "Cooking is a lot of work, and it's very time consuming. It can take days to put a big meal together. You have to love what you're doing, and I do."

"Who taught you to cook?"

"Oh, my mother, my grandmother, my aunts. I learned a little from everyone. What about you? Do you enjoy cooking?'

"I probably would, but I don't know how."

Mireille clucked with her tongue and got to her feet. "Then this is the perfect time to learn. Come on, I'll show you."

"Mireille," Jon said, raising his hand, "that's very nice of you, but—"

"Come on, Dad," Tommie whined, grabbing her crutches. "She's the chef for the president!"

"Really, Jon, I would like to. Which way is the kitchen?"

Tommie slipped on her forearm crutches and pushed herself upright. "Follow me."

Mireille watched Tommie drag herself to the kitchen. For someone with paralyzed legs, the young woman moved surprisingly well, carrying herself like someone afflicted with polio or muscular dystrophy. The kitchen was just beyond the living room. Mireille followed at an appropriate distance, neither too close nor too far behind.

Tommie was soon behind the kitchen's central work area, a standalone countertop with a butcher-block surface. Several pots and pans hung country-style from overhead hooks. Mireille noticed that the kitchen had a large gas range, and the refrigerator was a newer Sub-Zero.

Tommie's eyes were bright with enthusiasm. "What're we going to make?"

"That depends on the ingredients. Let's see," Mireille said, opening the refrigerator door. "My goodness, this looks pretty basic."

"That's because I don't cook much," Jon said. "It's usually just me. That means carry-out or the microwave."

"Well, there are a *few* things," Mireille said, opening all the bins. "Scallions, cheese, sour cream, even some bacon. Didn't we pass a supermarket?"

"Very observant. Three minutes away."

"Would you mind going? We need an entrée, and that chain usually has fresh seafood."

"Sure, no problem. What do you need?"

"If they have sea bass, that would be nice. About two pounds. Also, fresh basil, and ...do you have wine?"

"In the living room," he said, "both red and white."

"Then that's it."

"Okay, it shouldn't take long. Tommie, listen to what she says and try not to pester her with too many questions."

As he left, he heard Mireille say something to Tommie about potatoes and bacon. Jon never expected Mireille and his daughter to be getting along as well as they seemed, so quickly. Tommie's charm notwithstanding, that hadn't always been the case with strange women. One female visitor had been so disconcerted that she'd actually screamed at the young woman. Perhaps Mireille's method lay in her manner. Her body language was non-confrontational, her movements languid, and her tone low-key.

When Jon returned twenty minutes later, packages in his arms, the two women were engrossed in food preparation. The potatoes had been microwaved and halved, with their centers scooped out. The skins were arranged on a baking dish. The cheese had been grated; the green onion chopped. On the range, the bacon was beginning to sizzle, its aroma filling the air. A bottle of wine was chilling in an ice-filled Tupperware container.

"That smells great," he said, eyeing the Tupperware. "Love your wine bucket."

Mireille shrugged good-naturedly. "When in Rome. Did they have the fish?"

"They did." He unwrapped the packages.

She plucked a basil leaf from the bunch and popped it into her mouth. "Perfect. We'll be ready to eat in twenty minutes. Can you open the wine, please, Jon?"

"And here I thought you were going to cook with it."

"I am, but I only need a little. This is such a good white Burgundy that I can't let it go to waste."

He found a corkscrew and eyed the label. "This has been lying around for years."

"That one gets better with age. Can you pour a glass for me?"

While he poured, he watched Mireille drain and crumble the bacon. She placed it in a bowl with the cheese and added seasonings. She took the wine, sipped it, and then showed Tommie how to stuff the potato skins with the bacon/cheese mixture. Tommie was having a ball.

"How's the wine?" Jon asked.

"Delicious. At its prime. You have a good selection in there."

"I'll take your word for it. I'm not much of a wine drinker."

Mireille went to work on the fish by first preparing its sauce. Jon was fascinated by her skill, which combined dexterity with economy of movement. Watching her nimble fingers was like watching a surgeon. She packed the basil leaves into a food processor, to which she added a little garlic, grated lemon peel, and the fresher parts of a wilting bunch of celery found in the vegetable crisper. After pureeing the ingredients, she brought bottled clam juice to a simmer, then added some wine, the puree, and salt and pepper.

With the potato skins in the lower oven, Mireille readied the upper broiler. She quartered the two-pound piece of bass into equal-size steaks, which she brushed with olive oil and arranged on a rimmed baking dish. The dish went under the upper oven. While the fish broiled, she added butter and evaporated milk to the basil sauce.

Eight minutes later, everything was ready. The tangy sauce was ladled across the sizzling steaks, and the aromatic potato skins slid onto a serving dish. After Mireille removed the pans and utensils, they all sat down to eat at the butcher block.

The savory smells of basil, cheese, and bacon were so mouth-watering that the meal demanded immediate consumption. Jon and Mireille continued with the wine, while Tommie drank Pepsi. They ate with gusto and speed. Ten minutes later, they were done. "That was fantastic, Mireille," Jon said. "Thanks."

"Mon *Plaisir.*"

"Tommie, now that you've been fed like royalty, I think you

better get back to your homework."

"Can I have ice cream first? We have some chocolate chip cookie dough left."

"When you finish your homework, you can have desert."

Tommie grumbled, put on her crutches, and slid off the stool. Once she was gone, Jon helped Mireille clean up.

"I'm amazed how easily you threw that together," he said.

"Of course, I'm sure it's just a walk in the park for you."

"A walk where?"

"That's an expression for easy, no big deal. You probably do it all the time."

"So," she said with a laugh, "you think I'm some sort of magician, no?"

"Looks that way to me. Most people would love to have a fraction of your talent."

"Thank you. To be honest, I enjoy this kind of cooking most, from scratch. Using what's available, for friends and family." She helped him rinse the plates and put them in the dishwasher.

After turning on the machine, he grasped her shoulders and kissed her softly on the cheek. "This was much more than I expected, Mireille. And I'm sorry if it put you on the spot. But Tommie's been through a lot, and I'll do everything I can for her. When she was helping you, the look on her face made it all worthwhile."

"This was some sort of test, *non*? Not telling me about her?"

"I never thought of it that way, but I suppose it was. You'd be surprised how cruel some people are when they learn a child's disabled. If it *was* a test, you passed with flying colors. With kids, you're a natural."

"That comes from growing up in a large family. I have many nieces and nephews at home." She wiped her hands, returned to the central work area, and poured the last of the wine. "What happened to Tommie? Was she born that way?"

"No, when she was born, Tommie was the perfect little baby. She was blessed with that wildly curly hair, and with those blue eyes, she looked like a child model. In fact, after my wife and I split up, there were a few offers, but I talked Victoria out of it."

"Why?"

"I didn't want that kind of life for her. Too much stress, too many spotlights. I figured she was under enough pressure as it was, dividing her time between two parents. Anyhow, she was physically well until her fifth birthday. She got hit by a truck."

Mireille's jaw dropped. "A *truck*? What happened?"

"Believe it or not, she was running after a ball into the street. Exactly what parents tell their kids never to do. But it was her birthday party, and she was excited. Kids forget what they're taught. So off into the street she went, and a garbage truck creamed her. Jesus, it was huge. I know, I know—she's lucky to be alive. But for a while there, it was touch and go."

"I'm so sorry, Jon. How long was she in the hospital?"

"Four months. She had a broken arm, a fractured skull, and a broken back. One of the vertebrae crushed her spinal cord, and even though they removed the bone, those things don't heal." He had a faraway look. "Usually."

"You mean, there are ways to fix it?"

"There are a few experimental things. I've got my fingers crossed. But back then, when I wasn't working, I spent day and night in the hospital. Believe me, it was a long four months. And on top of everything, Victoria blamed me for what happened."

Mireille saw the deep hurt in his expression. She shook her head and as her lips formed a little moue, she blew her breath out in a delicate poof. "I don't know you that well, but I don't think you were responsible."

"Sometimes I wonder. You see, I was watching the kids play on the lawn. 'Supervising,' according to Victoria, and not very well. Anyway, the ball goes into the street, and out of the corner of my eye, I saw Tommie dart out after it. The truck was hidden by a parked van, so she couldn't see it. But I did. I ran after her as fast as I could, but…"

"Not fast enough."

"That's the whole point, isn't it? You know how in the movies when the hero runs out into the street and snatches the victim from the jaws of death? For a fraction of a second, I had a feeling I could have done that. Maybe not pulled her out of the way, but *pushed* her out of the way. But I hesitated."

"What would have happened to you if you had pushed her?"

"That's not the point. I didn't do what a father's expected to do."

"Oh, I understand," Mireille said, her voice rising slightly. "So that makes you what, a coward?"

"Let's not talk cowardice. That's a sore subject with me."

"But what does it make you?"

"It makes me a father who put personal fear over the safety of his child. In a nutshell, I didn't have the guts."

Overtaken by a frown, Mireille nodded slowly. "Let me see if I understand. You saw the truck, and she didn't. You think you could have pushed her to safety but gotten squashed flat as a *crepe*. And because you didn't, you lack courage." She paused. "Did I get it right?"

"It's not that black and white, Mireille. It's an instantaneous thing. You either do, or you don't."

"Well, I have heard that the brain has little protective mechanisms built in. It doesn't want the organism to destroy itself. So, where you see cowardice, I see self-preservation."

"It's nice of you to say that," he said, "but I'm not convinced. Courage and cowardice aren't things I understand too well."

Mireille shrugged. "If you say so. But while you're feeling sorry for yourself, it is important not to forget that your daughter is a beautiful, intelligent young woman, *très charmante*, and totally in love with her father."

He put a grateful hand atop hers. It was sweet of her to say that, something he needed to remind himself from time to time. But as for what he worked on in secret, or for what the future might hold for Tommie, he didn't know Mireille well enough to share those things.

It was equally important that he remind himself he was determined that Tommie would walk again someday.

CHAPTER 13

Danville, Virginia

Before he washed out of the U.S. Marine Corps for chronic alcohol abuse, Charles Johnson Walker thought he had found his calling. A Southern Virginia farm boy accustomed to a marginal existence, he had learned to shoot at an early age, taking squirrels and rabbits with a vintage .22 pump gun. Everything he owned was threadbare and worn out. But in the Marines, he thought he'd died and gone to heaven. The food, clothing, and military supplies were so superior to anything to anything he'd ever come in contact with that he couldn't see ever leaving the Corps. This was particularly true of the weapons. To C.J., the M40A1 sniper rifle was to the rifleman what a crown was to a king.

It was indeed a remarkable weapon. First fielded in the 1970s, the Remington-based firearm fired the super-accurate 7.62 NATO round. Using 168-grain match-grade ammunition, it was incredibly accurate, with an error of less than ten inches at one thousand yards. Its only flaw was its weight. At fourteen pounds, it was difficult to lug around in the field; but then, snipers were generally stationary shooters.

C.J. was so smitten with the M40A1 that after his less-than-honorable discharge, he managed to scrounge one up on the surplus market. He spent countless hours tuning, polishing, and refurbishing it, so that when he finally put it through its paces, it could shoot as well as any weapon in the Corps' armory. When he wasn't doing God's work with the Southern Cross, he could usually be found on any of hundreds of impromptu rifle ranges scattered throughout Appalachia. C.J. scoffed at other weapons and calibers. With an arrogance only ignorance can muster, his disdain for different tools of the trade was profound. Thus, when O'Brien told him what their guest sniper would be shooting, C.J. was nearly apoplectic.

Now, as he lay prone on an Army surplus wool blanket, peering through his rifle scope in a deserted tobacco field, he tried to suppress his indignation. Shooting of any kind, even at paper targets as he did today, was a balm. As he smoothly worked the bolt of his rifle, ejecting a spent cartridge case and feeding in another, he also tried to work on his emotions. It wasn't easy. But O'Brien had given him a job, and like a good soldier, he would do it to the best of his ability.

"Fuckin' towelhead," he muttered under his breath.

A week after the re-election announcement, the president's indecisive appearance before the press corps was largely forgotten. On those rare occasions that the president's health was questioned during daily briefings, the press secretary casually reiterated Meredith's excellent physical condition, adding that the president had passed a thorough physical exam several days before the announcement. Few people gave it more thought, and no one delved into it any further. Except, that is, Vice President Anthony Doria.

Of the many people who were on a first-name basis with the president, Doria was perhaps his keenest observer. He'd known Bob Meredith for decades and had spent countless days and evenings with him. He was familiar with the president's passions, moods, and eccentricities. But beyond time spent in each other's company, there was the fact that Tony Doria was a shrewd judge of human behavior. He looked at things with a critical eye, perhaps due to his days with Trinity Power, where he'd learned to study the details. And now, when he looked closely at the president, something was not quite right.

For several days, Doria listened but said nothing. If anyone was concerned about the president, he didn't bring it up. But Doria continued his low-key observations. By the end of the week, he was convinced something was going on. There was an almost imperceptible tremor in Meredith's fingers and a nuance of spasticity to his muscles. Outwardly, the president's speech and manner seemed little changed, although there seemed to be the slightest hesitation in the way the president expressed himself. On Saturday morning, Doria dropped by Forbes' office.

Forbes looked up. "Good morning, Mr. Vice President. I didn't expect you to be in today. Campaigning doesn't start until next week. Aren't you taking the weekend off?"

"I've got a few things to catch up on before the whirlwind starts. But I want to run something about Bob past you."

Forbes silently raised his eyebrows.

"What do you think about the way he's acting lately? On Tuesday, I thought he faltered at the end of his remarks in the pressroom. I know what the press secretary said, but I trust my own eyes."

Forbes put his pencil down and sat up. "What can I say, Tony?"

"You can say I'm not imagining it. It's nice to blow off the press corps, but you're a sharp guy, Mitch. I know it wasn't just indecision."

"That's true," Forbes agreed with a nod. "And you're not the only one who noticed it. The first lady and I had a heart-to-heart about it."

"She's in a position to notice. What did she want?"

"She wanted to bring in Dr. Townsend."

"Ouch! If you want to keep things quiet, that's hardly the way to go about it."

"That's exactly what I told her," Forbes said. "The guy's a great doctor, but team player he's not."

"So, how did you leave it?"

"I told her to back off. At this point in the campaign, if the president had a lengthy work-up and was diagnosed with some minor problem, that'd be the end of his second term. And Roxanne could kiss being first lady goodbye."

"What did she say to that?"

"She's concerned," Forbes continued. "What wife wouldn't be? But I told her that if the situation got any worse, we'd call in a good doctor a couple of months down the road. Maybe. She's no dope, Roxanne. She understood what I was saying. She said she'd go along, but..."

"You're not sure."

"No, I'm not. I'm already thinking about damage control. But, hey—what's the worst that could happen? I'll always be the president's man, but if the situation really deteriorates, the people would have a damn good alternative. A very qualified man ready to step up to the plate and serve his country."

Doria smiled. "Anyone I know?"

Forbes quietly returned the smile. Then he picked up his pen and resumed work.

In the limo on the way back from taping *Meet the Press*, Bob Meredith loosened his tie and slouched back in the seat. Beside him, Rocky placed her hand atop his.

"You did great, darling. Everyone was impressed."

"You think so?" he said. "How'd I sound?"

"Strong. Determined. But always with that great Meredith charm."

"That's a relief. Because I have to tell you that for the first time in ages, I felt a little rattled in there."

"About what?"

"Oh, I don't know," he said, shaking his head. "He kept pressing me on the damn Golan Heights thing. That, and the Palestinians. Honest to God, I felt like smacking him He just wouldn't stop. Aren't there other important things to discuss in an election year?"

"If you *were* rattled, you didn't show it. I thought you handled the questioning really well."

"Oh, stop it!" he snapped. "I can't stand the way you patronize me!"

What hurt Roxanne wasn't so much what he said as how he said it. Over the years, Bob had been annoyed at her countless times, but he rarely exploded the way he did now. Yet, as wounded as she felt, she was also worried. Her husband's memory was suspect, and his recent irritability was going from bad to worse. In the past week alone, he'd continuously shouted at her, something that, two months earlier, she'd have sworn was impossible.

"I'm sorry if I sounded like that. I certainly didn't mean to."

"Like hell you didn't! What's wrong with you, anyway? I'm not some insecure little kid who needs someone to blow smoke up his ass every waking minute! Give it a rest already!"

He glared at her. There was spittle in the corners of his mouth, and his nostrils flared with anger. Roxanne struggled to find her voice.

"Bob, please. My hearing's fine, and you don't have to shout at me like that. If something's wrong, maybe we should..."

His suddenly upraised arm cut her short. In all their years of marriage, she'd never seen him in such a cold fury. His fingers were trembling, and his eyes had the look of a madman. For the first time since she'd known him, Roxanne felt afraid of him.

His head swiveled forward. "Stop the car!" he shouted to the Secret Service driver.

As he looked in the rearview mirror, the agent keyed his headphone mike, which had an open channel to the chase car.

"Sir, we're almost at the White—"

"I said stop the Goddamn car! I need some air, for Chrissake!"

"Yes, sir." Into the mike, "You heard it, chase. Pulling over now."

The motorcade smoothly neared the curb and stopped. The driver waited for the other agents to approach before unlocking the doors. The president leapt out of the vehicle, to the stunned amazement of the passersby across the street. Dave Saunders quickly drew abreast of POTUS, the president of the United States, and took hold of his elbow.

"Sir, this is not a very good idea."

Meredith tugged his arm free. He was shaking with thinly controlled rage. "Gimme a break, Dave. Haven't you ever needed a breather before?"

"Yes, sir, I have," he replied, carefully scanning the surroundings for threats. "But this stop wasn't on our schedule."

The deadpan remark struck the president as humorous, and he broke out laughing. "How do I look to you, Dave?"

"Sir?"

"Do I look like I need some hand-holding, or ass-kissing? How about a little false flattery to cheer me up?"

"Frankly, Mr. President, you look a little stressed out to me."
He again took the president's arm. "If you don't mind, sir, let's
get back into the vehicle."

Meredith took a deep breath. "Maybe I am a little stressed.
But, Christ—if you had a wife like mine on your case all the
time, wouldn't you be?"

"The car, sir. Please."

"Yeah, okay. Sorry, Dave. Not like me, is it? God, I need a
drink."

Fifteen minutes later, the agents in the president's detail were
summoned to the office of the chief of staff. Forbes looked up
from behind his desk and waited until the door was closed.

"Stand at ease, gentlemen. I'll make this very brief. I'm
aware of what happened with the president a little while ago.
Let me assure you that what you witnessed was nothing more
than re-election jitters. A lot of campaign events have collided
at the same time, and that causes some strain. Let's face it, the
man's only human. His behavior was unusual but temporary.
Once he's blown off some steam, Bob Meredith will be the same
president people have known and loved over the years. So, let's
not let this get out of hand, okay?"

"Sir," Saunders asked, "I know I may be a little out of line,
but I've never seen the president act like that before. Is it possible
there's something physically or emotionally wrong with him?"

"It's precisely comments like that which could blow things
out of proportion. I understand what you're asking, Dave. I know
your concern, and I also appreciate your loyalty. But believe me,
there's nothing happening to the president that couldn't happen
to any of us. Besides, he had a complete checkup last weekend,
and it was normal."

"Yes, sir, but the way he looked out on the street... Again, I
might be going out on a limb, but wouldn't it be a good idea to
let his doctor know what happened?"

"We already have. Dr. Townsend will take another look
and do whatever's necessary, which I don't think will be very
much. Gentlemen, I cannot stress enough how important it
is that whatever you saw remain with you. Even a *hint* that

something's happening to the president would derail the presidency and destroy everything Bob Meredith has worked for. So, remember your priorities. Do your job. And let what happened this morning end here."

It was one o'clock when the first lady asked the chief of staff to come over to the kitchen. Forbes wasn't looking forward to this. He knew what Roxanne was going to say, but there was no way he could diplomatically keep her from saying it.

In the kitchen, Roxanne was nibbling on a toasted bagel and sipping a cup of coffee. She looked haggard. She wasn't crying, but her eyes were red-rimmed and puffy.

Haphazard strands escaped her normally well-coifed hair, reaching out like golden tendrils. Her face was deeply lined, pummeled-looking, the appearance of the emotionally defeated. She barely looked up when Forbes approached.

"Well, Mitch? I know you heard what happened. You still think I should wait before getting him help?"

"I know it must have been very disturbing...."

"Actually," she interrupted, "you *don't* know. You weren't in the car with us, so you have absolutely no way of knowing the utter dread and humiliation I felt. And fear, too."

He tried a calming smile. "It was the interviewer, Roxanne. He's a damned relentless little bird, always pecking away to get under the president's skin."

"Did you know he actually raised his hand to me?" she said icily. "No matter what the provocation, he's never, ever, done that before. He didn't hit me, thank God. But he came damn close."

"I'm sorry to hear that, but look.... Obviously, I underestimated the strain he's under. I had some preliminary campaign events scheduled this week, but I think we'll back off a while, let everyone cool off a little."

She eyed him incredulously. "*Campaign?* I can't believe this! I'm talking about my husband flipping out, and you're talking about some Goddamn political event!"

Forbes walked closer and bent slightly toward her. Smile unbroken, he spoke very softly. "Madame First Lady, please try to keep your voice down. This is the job your husband hired me to do. He's the president of the United States, and I will do everything in my power to fulfill his needs and those of the office. That's not to say I don't feel for you. But the last thing he needs right now is to let hysteria determine what needs to be done."

Stung, she glared at him. "It's perfectly obvious what needs to be done. I know your priorities, but I'm his wife, and I have mine."

"Okay," he said, calmly lifting his hand, "Maybe we see things a little differently, but we both want what's best for him, right? I think he's under a strain, and you think it's a mental problem—"

"Don't put words in my mouth. People flip out for lots of different reasons."

"Agreed. That's something yet to be determined. But one of the things I learned in this job is the importance of timing and approach. It's important not to act out of desperation. So, let me talk to him, okay? I need to get a feel on how to go about this."

"Fine, talk to him. He's up in the bedroom into his second or third bourbon by now. And after you've gotten your 'feel,' whatever the hell that is, I'm calling Dr. Townsend."

"Please," Forbes implored, "try to hold off just a little. Believe me, I'm not going to turn my back on him. But I beg you to look at the big picture. At this point, the most critical thing is damage control."

"Damage control," she slowly said with a mirthless smile. "Suddenly you're the prince of one-liners. It all comes down to expedience to you, doesn't it, Mitch?"

"I'm not trying to be glib. I'm trying to do what's best for everyone. But I can guarantee you, bringing Dr. Townsend in prematurely is in nobody's best interest. So, I'm pleading with you, *please* try to hold off a little longer."

She stared at him with a determined, steely gaze. But if Roxanne expected his resolve to lessen, she didn't know Mitchell Forbes very well. His cast iron will was equal to hers, perhaps even stronger. At length, acknowledging the political animal within her, it was she who relented. Roxanne grudgingly nodded and left the kitchen.

That night, Bob Meredith apologized to his wife. He said he didn't know what had come over him. For some reason, he'd felt this inexplicable fury, and then he'd just exploded. He was sincerely sorry. As he rolled next to her in bed, cuddling up, he said he wanted to make it up to her. Roxanne pulled away. She said she accepted his apology, but right now, she was just too tired.

Five minutes later, the president was asleep.

For the next hour, Rocky lay there in the darkness, listening to her husband's rhythmic breathing, staring up at the ceiling. The entire day had been maddeningly confusing. The most mystifying aspect of her husband's quixotic moods was their unpredictability. He'd become an emotional chameleon— furious one minute, defensive the next, and then warm and loving. It was behavior far removed from the man she'd known and loved so long. If one characteristic had long defined Bob, it was his emotional steadiness. Although he had his ups and downs, his unruffled personality generally ran straight and smooth.

Now, Roxanne was perplexed. She was also worried, and more than a little frightened. Forbes *had* spoken with her husband, but as far as she could tell, nothing had come of it. He hadn't gotten back to her—as she'd hoped—with a therapeutic plan or strategy. It seemed to be business as usual. She thought Forbes had to be blind not to notice what, to her, was so obvious. Could it be that she was too close? Was it possible that she was so enmeshed in the fabric of Bob's life that she was overreacting?

That, she could not tell. Roxanne was astute enough to realize that she needed an outside opinion here, an objective observer. Ideally, that would be Dr. Townsend. It was Jon's job to evaluate and advise on medical matters. Yet, astute though she was, she was also politically shrewd. After all, she'd only seen one side of Jon Townsend. If there were any chance Forbes' concerns about the doctor were valid, she'd be taking a great risk.

But if not Dr. Townsend, then who? As Roxanne's eyes flitted around the darkened bedroom, dim fingers of city light skirted the heavy window curtains to ply at the room's shadows. Deep in thought, she lost herself in their playfulness.

There was one other person she could surely trust.

The sky had a yellow overcast, as if touched by sulfur. The November air was cool, but a steady northeast breeze raised the humidity and soothed an otherwise angry day. A storm approached. Roxanne and Amanda Doria slowly walked past the Rose Garden, discretely trailed by Secret Service agents.

"I just thought he was a little flustered," said Doria, flicking her cigarette ashes on the south lawn. She was a closet smoker in an era of anti-tobacco sentiment. "I doubt many people even noticed it."

"What about Tony? Did he say anything?"

"Tony was so busy smiling at the press corps that he wasn't even looking at Bob. Anyway, it's been over a week, and he's still a little dizzy from the re-election announcement. If he *did* say anything, it wasn't to me."

Both women were casually dressed in jeans and sweaters. Roxanne and Amanda had been socializing for a decade, and among the administration's top women, Amanda was Rocky's only confidante. That morning, when the first lady called and asked to get together, Mrs. Doria came right over from the U.S. Naval Observatory, site of the vice-presidential residence.

"Maybe it's not as obvious as I thought," Rocky said. "But I'm not imagining it."

"Did I say that? I never said that. You're the one who lives with him, not me. But believe me, all men have their moods. I can't tell you how many times Tony was so pissed he looked like he was going to strangle me, and the next minute, he's purring like a pussycat."

"Mandy, this is beyond moodiness. Bob's got the jitters, real, physical jitters. He has these annoying little jerks and twitches, and his memory, God…I'm just worried."

"I would hope so," Amanda said, exhaling a plume of smoke. "That's scary stuff."

"So, shouldn't I tell Bob's doctor? Why is Mitch making such a big deal out of it?"

Amanda stepped on her cigarette and stopped walking. She smiled and placed her hand reassuringly on her friend's wrist. "Tony always says a trusted political adviser is worth his weight in gold. I have no idea whether or not Mitch is right about Dr. Townsend. But I *do* know that Bob trusts Mitch and has always relied on his political judgment."

"You're saying I should follow his advice?"

"Within reason. Ask Forbes to commit to a timetable. I mean, if by such and such a time, you're still concerned, you'll talk to Dr. Townsend, okay?"

Despite his regal persona, in a bygone era, Bob Meredith would have made poor royalty. He was a hands-on person who disliked being doted upon. He was accustomed to doing for himself, a Protestant ethic mindset that reflected his working-class Southern roots. By extension, that viewpoint also led him to do for others, especially his own family, and particularly for Roxanne. During the first half of their marriage, he responded to her needs to the point where some considered him henpecked. It was a chivalry that bordered on being uxorious.

Meredith's upbringing made it hard for him to graciously accept the perks of the presidency. It wasn't that he thought such things beneath him, or that he wanted to be considered just one of the boys. If anything, he was a leader among men, more chief than Indian. Rather, he was one of those who truly believed that if you wanted something done, you did it yourself. Thus, early in his administration, he made it clear that he was uncomfortable with a staff that openly waited in the wings, ready to pounce at the bend of the presidential finger. While he didn't mind having ushers bring him things on occasion, he disliked any suggestion of hovering. This was especially true of food. He could pour his own bourbon, thank you, and fill his own pipe.

He had a refrigerator and microwave oven installed just off the bedroom. If he wanted a beer, he'd get it; if he wanted to rewarm his coffee, he'd nuke it. Much to Rocky's chagrin, he even prepared his own bedtime snacks. She wasn't keen on the nocturnal aroma of buttered popcorn or the cheesy scent or reheated burritos. He called her a traditionalist, and she called him a nut.

That night, a week after the re-election announcement, Meredith decided that his snack *de nuit* would be a sausage and egg sandwich. Damn the cholesterol, he told his wife. He was hungry. After putting it in the microwave, he took a quick shower. Five minutes later, he'd toweled off and was in bed, reading correspondence. Soon he put the papers down and wrinkled his nose. "What's that smell?"

"It's not health food, that's for sure," Roxanne said.

"I think something's burning."

"Maybe you cooked it too long."

He looked at her, his tone snippy. "Cooked *what* too long?"

"Look in the microwave, Bob. Your food's ready. I already heard the timer go off."

"Don't start with me, Roxanne!" He threw off the covers and stormed across the room. Seconds later, "Jesus Christ, Rocky! Get in here!"

Her heart sank. Steeling herself for a confrontation, she got out of bed and put on her slippers. The situation was quickly becoming intolerable. In the other room, Bob had opened the microwave door, and acrid smoke curled to the ceiling. He held the door handle and glared at her. Roxanne walked closer, perplexed. In the middle of the revolving dish, the sandwich had been cooked to the point of shriveling. But the stench was coming from its melted plastic wrapper, which hadn't been removed.

Roxanne smiled wanly. "I guess you didn't really want that sandwich anyway."

"Excuse me?" he said, voice rising. "Excuse *me*! Don't try to pin this on me! You've got some nerve. You know I just got out of the shower!"

Not knowing what to say, Roxanne stood there in battered silence. She was torn between feelings of humiliation and pity. The man she loved was going to pieces before her very eyes. There was a sharp knock on the door, and one of the Secret Service agents poked his head in.

"Sorry to bother you, sir. I heard shouts. Is everything all right?"

"No, it's not all right!" shot the president. "Some people can't do a Goddamn thing for themselves! Get somebody in here to clean up this mess!"

"Yes, sir." Watching the president walk away, he turned to Roxanne. "Ma'am, is there anything I can—"

She quickly shook her head, dismissing him with a wave of her hand. She knew her voice was so shaky that she didn't trust herself to speak. The fact was, there wasn't a thing the agent could do. She wasn't sure anyone could. Beyond that, she didn't want him to see her eyes filling up with tears, tears that were becoming a daily companion.

Okay, Roxanne said to herself, *I've tried it their way.* She'd listened to Mitch Forbes and Amanda Doria.

It was time to do what had to be done. She picked up the phone.

Toronto

From Tunisia, Mahmoud took a plane to Rome and then connected for a flight to Frankfurt. His passport, already stamped with a Tunisian visa, listed his name as Nabil Abu-Zeid, an Egyptian businessman. The Frankfurt flight connected to Dublin. From there, Mahmoud's Air Canada destination was Toronto.

Where it came to terrorists, particularly those of Middle Eastern extraction, Canadian immigration was very good. They had a comprehensive computer profile of likely suspects and routinely pulled travelers aside for questioning. Mr. Abu-Zeid, however, did not fit the profile. He was respectably dressed, well packed, and he spoke acceptable English.

"What's the nature of your visit here, sir?" asked the immigration officer.

"It's a business trip. Some sightseeing, perhaps."

"What sort of business would that be?"

"Microcircuits," Mahmoud said, handing the man a worn business card. "Our company makes components for motherboards."

"Motherboards, now?" the official said. "Can't say I'm

familiar with them."

"They run a computer's hard drive. They make the whole thing work."

"Right." He looked at the passport photo, then back at Mahmoud. "Great city, Cairo. Whereabouts do you live there?"

"The Garden City neighborhood, near the embassies. Do you know it?"

"No, sir, can't say that I do." He returned the passport. Had Mr. Abu-Zeid been unable to specify a location, he would have been detained. "Have a nice stay."

Mahmoud had no intention of staying in Canada. Canada was simply a way station that facilitated entry into the United States. When, in Tunisia, he learned that his target would be in the U.S., he was overjoyed. He got down on his knees and thanked Allah for this opportunity, even if it should end in martyrdom. What mattered was that he would be striking a blow at the great Satan right in the devil's own backyard.

Mahmoud rented a car and drove south, toward the American border. The tools he'd trained with had been shipped separately and would arrive later. Now, all he had to do was to safely reach his destination and make a phone call. He'd receive further instructions on where to go and what to do. He wasn't told how long he'd have to wait, but he'd been told it could be weeks. He still didn't know his target.

But then, there were a great many possible targets in Washington, D.C.

CHAPTER 14

Roxanne Meredith's semi-hysterical ramblings about her husband called her emotional stability into question. During the upcoming twelve months, it was crucial that she remain a reliable, levelheaded presence in the whirlwind that was the White House. She was counted upon to be a steadying influence on the most powerful man in the nation. But now, her recent behavior cast doubt on her supportive skills. As her reliability decreased, so did the need to watch her grow. A loose cannon could be catastrophic.

It was therefore imperative to keep an eye on her. In fact, the team was already at work. While it would be simple to watch her in and around the White House, surveillance in other areas was somewhat more difficult. She traveled everywhere in an official White House limousine, and her driver was too loyal to be approached. Yet there were other ways, like electronic bugs, to monitor her movements. But as important as knowing where she went was knowing whom she met, and more significantly, what was said. In the end, her cell phone proved very handy.

Cellular conversations weren't difficult to monitor. This was usually done through eavesdropping satellites that orbited the Earth. The government used a sophisticated listening-in software program called ECHELON to monitor cellular and fixed telephone conversations. This employed word-foraging technology that homed-in on key words or phrases for analysis and recording.

Roxanne used an advanced phone made by Qualcomm. Prototypes of new telecommunications equipment were often obtained by American security services. If approved, they were sometimes made available to White House staff or occupants. The first lady, who adored living on technology's cutting edge, acquired one of the new phones early and carried it with her everywhere. When she wasn't using it, she always kept it "on," in the standby mode. That made it relatively easy to track the phone's location. Unless she was actually using the phone, however, the conversation around her was a mystery.

But what their electronics expert did was install a tiny circuit that permitted the phone's microphone to be remotely turned on. The user could defeat this by using a microphone mute switch, but as Roxanne didn't suspect that anyone might want to monitor her conversations, she never put one in. Once the phone's electronics were rewired, both the first lady's location and her words could be monitored.

Keeping track of Dr. Townsend was much easier. Since he, too, went virtually everywhere by car, it was simple to follow the vehicle's travel activities. There were a number of sophisticated units that used a satellite-positioning network. Most were smaller than a paperback novel and could be magnet-mounted under the car within seconds. The GPS was cross-referenced with digital street maps of the entire United States.

Using proper software, the watcher could precisely monitor the car's time, speed, and precise location. Most of the units could be defeated by bug-sweepers, such as were used daily on the first lady's vehicle. But inspecting his vehicle for electronic surveillance was the last thought on Dr. Townsend's mind.

When and if Roxanne Meredith and Jon Townsend met, the watchers would know it. And they could hear every word that was being said.

"The president told me you'd called," Forbes said to Jon. "He said you wanted to examine him."

"That's right, Mitch. I didn't think it should wait that long."

"I can appreciate where you're coming from, but I'd also appreciate your trying to coordinate his activities with me. This is a helluva busy time of year."

"You're right," Jon nodded, "and I'm sorry about that. What I'd hoped to do was block out some time at the hospital for him before I called you."

"What's all this about, anyway?"

As succinctly as possible, Jon related what the first lady had described. He hadn't noticed anything himself, Jon added, but the patient's wife was certainly a qualified observer. He added that Roxanne mentioned the chief of staff's reluctance to contact the president's doctor.

For a moment, Forbes was silent. "Let me be clear on this," he finally said. "As a human being who likes and respects the man he works for, I want the very best for Bob Meredith. If he has a physical problem, no one—except the first lady—wants it taken care of more than me."

"So, what's the problem?"

"The problem is my job. Sure, I'm human, but I'm also chief of staff. Much as I'd sometimes like somebody else to do the job, I'm the man behind that desk. I'm expected to do what I was hired for. I have a very narrow mandate from the president to advance his policy agenda. Now that he wants a second term, I have to handle that, too. All of which means that I have to assess priorities, mete out time like it's gold, and do a heck of a lot of juggling."

"You don't think his health is a priority?" Jon asked.

"Please, Jon, don't put words in my mouth. Of *course* it's a priority. But whatever's going on here—*if* it's going on—is very subtle, right? I mean, we're not talking about a heart attack or cancer, right? So, what I said to Roxanne was, let's not go off half-cocked. If the symptoms she saw continued, okay, then it would be time to bring you in. All I asked her, which I'm also asking you, is to remember what's at stake here. We're talking about a man who lives and breathes politics, who expects the people who work for him to make the right decisions."

The tidal Potomac River begins at the fall line near Washington's western boundary and ends where the river empties into the Chesapeake Bay. The waters in and around the nation's capital are bass country, though the entire eighty-mile stretch of the lower Potomac offered exceptional all-around fishing. With nearly a dozen freshwater species and as many saltwater fish, anglers had a wealth of choices, from bass and catfish to bluefish and flounder.

Most fishermen were bait-casters who flung colorful rubber worms and glittering spinner baits from casting rods. Occasionally, fly fishermen took to the waters. If one understood the fundamentals of tidewater fishing, the results were quite rewarding. The species most sought was the largemouth bass, which were plentiful in the late spring and early summer, when the fish schooled in dense patches of submerged verdure. In the fall, when the aquatic grasses turned brown and lifeless, the bass converged on fallen trees and underwater rock structures.

Jon took up fly fishing at Dave Saunders' suggestion. Dave was an avid long-rodder eager to share his skill, a craft acquired through years of plying the trout-filled streams of Idaho and Wyoming. Once assigned to the president's detail, Dave's cross-country trips were curtailed. But the nearby Potomac provided an alternative. As soon as he was familiar with the river, Dave encouraged Jon to join him.

With clear skies overhead, Dave and Jon were a foursome with Tommie and Mireille. After a year of fishing the river, Tommie was a tidewater veteran. Dave drove south on U.S. 1 to Arkendale, where they would fish the Potomac's western bank at Aquia Creek. It was a cool, mid-autumn day in the upper fifties, with only a rare fair-weather cloud scudding across the sky. When Dave parked his van beside the creek, a rented bass boat awaited them. Compared with cramped tournament bass boats, their craft was a spacious, center console Boston Whaler. After they put Tommie and her wheelchair on board, Dave started the engine, untied the lines, and cast off.

Aquia, one of the Waterway's larger creeks, had ample stretches of fallen trees, gravel banks, and boat docks to shelter the autumn bass. The four of them would fish the shoreline. Dave gunned the Mercury outboard, and they were soon headed upstream. Mireille's hair was down. As the boat accelerated, the breeze caught her tresses, and their wind-driven strands fluttered like golden streamers.

During a summer squall, a massive oak had been knocked into the creek. It had fallen obliquely to the shoreline, and its sturdy branches extended thirty feet across the water's surface, and nearly as deep. At this time of year, with the waters cooling, the sunken boughs provided good cover for schooling largemouths. Dave prepared a flyrod for Mireille while Jon assembled Tommie's rig.

"Good thing you like to fish," Dave told Mireille, "because this'll be a good morning for it. What were your favorite fishing holes?"

"I loved Australia. San Francisco was fun, but I only went twice. I always used real bait, not those creatures," she said, pointing to the artificial flies on his vest.

"Then you haven't really fished. Bait fishing is for barefoot boys with cane poles and worms and more time than skill. This is science, artistry, and nature all rolled into one. How's your fly-fishing technique?"

"I wouldn't know. I've never done it."

"Okay, Chef Courtois, stand up and the master will begin the class."

While Dave showed Mireille the basics, Jon checked out the tackle box. "What do you think we should start with?"

"I'd try the wet flies, say a Zug Bug or a Coachman," Dave said. "Make sure your line sinks down there, and present the bug as slowly as possible."

The quantity and colors of flies available dazzled Mireille. "How do you know which one to use?"

"Hit and miss," Dave said. "Largemouths aren't very picky. A lot depends on the conditions and the tides. You keep switching patterns and colors until the bass tell you what they want."

Over the next few minutes, Dave worked on Mireille's fly-casting technique. She was an apt pupil. But when it was time for fine-tuned instruction that called for coming up behind her and putting his arms around hers, he deferred to Jon for the hands-on technique. Tommie, meanwhile, already had a nibble. Dave buddied up with her and began some serious fishing.

Jon snuggled up to Mireille and helped her cast. She had a knack for the rod and was soon casting the flies where intended.

"How's that?" she asked.

"Pretty darn good. Work the line slower and let it sink a little more. Don't worry about snagging the hook. They all have weed guards."

Mireille chatted enthusiastically, seeming to enjoy the close-quarters instruction as much as Jon. Just then the line went taut and the rod bent. Mireille let out an excited "Oh!" and Jon jerked the rod back.

"Set the hook!" he said. "Now reel it in—steady, steady." He backed away to give her space.

"Mireille," Tommie called, "you got one *already*?"

"I think so!" she burbled. *Dieu, c'est formidable?*"

"Keep reeling, Mireille," Dave said. "What're you using?"

"A Coach Dog," Jon said. "That's it, bring him alongside."

With the flyrod bent nearly in half, Jon got the net and scooped it underwater, lifting out a fat largemouth. "Now *that's* a keeper!"

"Whoa, check it out," Dave said. "We forgot to tell you, first fish buys the beers."

"Why not?" said Mireille, smiling broadly.

The day began brightly, with everyone whooping it up. For a while fishing was fast and furious, and everyone caught at least one good-size fish by nine a.m. Since the boat didn't have a live well, Dave gill-strung the keepers and towed them from the stern. Mireille paired up with Tommie on the starboard side, while Jon and Dave hung out to port.

By eleven, the action had slowed considerably. Mireille had brought a picnic basket stocked with French fare: pâté campagne, pommes de terre à la lyonnaise, and crusty French bread, which they liberally washed down with cider. It was a feast.

"Doesn't get better than this," Dave said. "Fish, food, and friends." He lowered his voice, leaning close to Jon. "She is just a friend, right?"

"Jeez, buddy, didn't your mother tell you there are some questions you never ask?"

"Can't say she did. How's she doing with the Phillips thing?"

"Pretty good, from what I can see. Not one to wallow in tragedy."

"You sure were Johnny-on-the-spot that day," Dave said. "Not to mention the night the president choked."

"I always said, I'd rather be lucky than smart. The fact is, I wasn't even supposed to be there that night."

"No?"

"No, sir. Funny thing was, neither was Mireille."

A frown slowly creased Saunders' forehead. "Better run that by me again."

Jon slowly related the curious tale of his late arrival and the equally peculiar instruction Mireille had received to take the day off. He watched Dave's frown deepen. "What's bugging you?"

"Every morning we get a briefing, and there are updates all day long," he said. "The idea is for everyone to know who's where and at what time, to ensure the president's safety. The kitchen staff is an integral part of goings-on in the House. And I can tell you that no one gave us a heads-up that the chef was taking off that day."

"Is that so unusual?"

"It's unheard of that she'd be absent during a state dinner. She's in charge of the meal, right? Having a substitute chef show up at the last minute…it's just not done."

"Maybe the guest chef was a special hot shot."

"I'd ask him, if I could find him."

"What do you mean?"

"His name's Marcel Al-Hakeem. Works at a place in Philly. The day after there's what we call an 'untoward event' involving the president, we always interview everyone around. It's standard procedure, even for a presidential hangnail. But this Al-Hakeem, he's disappeared. He wasn't at his usual job or where he's supposed to live."

"He probably just took some time off."

"Maybe, but something doesn't smell right. I want to hear this from Mireille." Dave put down his paper plate. "Let me have a word with her."

"I don't suppose this could wait until we get home?"

"This'll just take a second," Dave said. "I promise not to scare Tommie." Animated talking and giggling came from the other side of the boat. When the men turned, they saw Mireille on her hands and knees, eyes near the center keel as she searched for a wayward fly. Her compact derriere, snug against her jeans, was uplifted their way.

"Oh, my fucking word," Jon whispered.

"Like I said," Dave added, "it doesn't get any better than this."

Leaving Canada, Mahmoud was instructed to drive south on I-95 to the D.C. metro area, where he would get on the Capital Beltway. Once there, he would get off at the Oxon Hill, Maryland, exit and head for the nearby Burger King. He would wait in its parking lot until contacted.

Arriving after dark, he was relieved to find that he didn't have to wait long. Any swarthy-looking man hanging out in a suburban parking lot was sure to attract attention. Within minutes a tall, lanky stranger wearing a Redskins jacket got in the passenger seat. Speaking tersely, he told Mahmoud to keep quiet and follow instructions. He neither stated his name nor made significant eye contact.

"Where are we going?" Mahmoud asked.

"Listen to me, fella," said C.J. "Don't ask questions. Get back on the Beltway and drive west to U.S. 1. Get off there and go north to Alexandria."

"Do—" Mahmoud began, only to be silenced by the tall American's glower.

"I'll tell you everything you need to know. Now drive."

Mahmoud exited the parking lot and returned to the Beltway. Ten minutes later, after crossing the Potomac, they were in Virginia. U.S. 1 carried them into downtown Alexandria, where Mahmoud was told to get off at Russell Road and work his way up East Rosemont. Soon they parked in a downtrodden neighborhood near the railroad tracks. Trailing the stranger into a rundown apartment building, Mahmoud followed the man to a room on the third floor. The door was double-locked.

Once inside, Walker turned on the lights, revealing a shabbily furnished one-bedroom apartment. The main room smelled of stale tobacco and garlic, and its single grease-smeared window looked out onto a small park nearby. The man picked up a remote controller and switched the TV on to a local channel.

"You keep your ass here until I get back to you," he said.

"I don't know how long that'll take. Could be several days or several weeks. Everything you need is here. You have clothes, a lot of food in the kitchen, stuff to read, and the TV. Use it to practice your English."

"When will—?"

"What'd I say about questions?" the stranger said, raising his hand. "That phone there," he indicated, "only receives calls. You can't call out. It'd be better for everybody if you stayed inside, y'know? But if you've gotta stretch those skinny legs of yours, make sure it's dark first. You don't want to be attractin' any attention, now. If you do go out, make it short and snappy, and don't go far. This is a dangerous neighborhood, brother."

"I am not your brother."

Walker ignored him. "Two final things," he continued. "I was told you might ask what's goin' down. That, I don't know, but I'll let you know when the time comes. Just keep a cool head, all right? Finally, I'll deliver your tools once I get the go-ahead about the mission. That's everything. Got it?" He turned to leave. "And hey—good luck."

"Everything?" Mahmoud asked. "Am I to sit here watching television until I am contacted again?"

"No, not everything," the man said. He lifted a copy of the Koran from a nearby table. "You can also pray."

CHAPTER 15

The complex of buildings comprising the Smithsonian Institution was a short drive from the White House. At noon the following day, the first lady's limo pulled up outside the National Air and Space Museum. The short drive down Independence Avenue was a last-minute addition to her scheduled stop at the Smithsonian's African Art Museum, where she briefly attended an eleven-a.m. fundraiser.

Normally, once her Secret Service detail learned of a change in plans, two agents would be sent ahead for advance security. But inasmuch as the new destination was only several hundred yards away, there was no time for that. Security would be handled on the fly. All she said was that Dr. Townsend was in the area and she wanted to have a private word with him. She did not mention that her meeting was pursuant to a phone call she'd made last night.

En route, the museum's security chief was notified. The limo was instructed to pull around to a rear loading entrance. Simultaneously, space was made available in the museum's movie theater, which was between showings.

With a Secret Service agent guarding each aisle, Roxanne took a front row center seat. Minutes later, Dr. Townsend arrived and was escorted into the theater. He shook hands with the first lady.

"Don't get up, Roxanne," he said, sitting beside her. He looked around the empty theater. "Now this is service, the whole place to yourself. I'm impressed."

"Don't let the word get out. I wouldn't want the taxpayers to think I'm squandering their dollars."

"The taxpayers are crazy about you, and you know it." He paused. "What's up?"

"I apologize for calling so late, Jon. But I'm at my wit's end, and I don't know where to turn."

"That's a start. Go on."

"It's...it's Bob," she finally said with a sigh. "I don't really know how to put this diplomatically."

"Don't play politician, Roxanne. I'm his doctor. Just tell me what happened."

"What happened is that there's something wrong with him. He's...he's not himself. He hasn't been for months. I'm scared to death he's developing Alzheimer's."

"Hold on a minute. Diagnosis is my job, and I hardly think he qualifies for a diagnosis of Alzheimer's. Is he forgetting things?"

"Yes, but it's way beyond forgetfulness. Take last night. He was heating a sandwich, forgot about it, and cooked it to a crisp."

"So what?"

"He also forgot to take it out of its wrapper. He nearly set the room on fire. Then he accused *me* of cooking it and screamed so loud one of the agents came into the bedroom."

As precisely as possible, Roxanne related the events of the recent past, emphasizing the president's memory and personality changes. Jon listened with concern. From the tears that filled her eyes, it was apparent that the first lady was very upset about what was happening. Her husband's faulty recall, she went on, didn't upset her so much as his flashes of temper, irritability, and obstreperousness. At length, she stopped talking and looked him in the eye.

"Well?"

"I think I need to examine him," he said. "I don't want to venture a guess until then. The physical I just gave him was pretty basic—heart, lungs, EKG. I'm going to have to focus on neurological areas."

"But what do you think? *Could* it be Alzheimer's?"

"Anything's possible, but early Alzheimer's wouldn't be my first choice. His symptoms are too mild and varied."

"But they're getting worse!"

"Okay, but you're describing a hodgepodge. The jitters, memory loss, irritability, and personality changes are a neurological stew. There are dozens of possibilities, like organic brain syndromes, other dementias, infections, and psychiatric disorders, to name a few."

Deep worry lines etched her face. "Whatever it is, is it treatable?"

"I can't tell yet. I'm not trying to be evasive. It's just that everything depends on the proper diagnosis. He's going to need a thorough workup. Let me ask you this: does he know he has a problem? Is he aware of what's happening?"

She shrugged. "Yes and no. I think there are times he gets little glimpses of his behavior, like when he catches himself in the act of forgetting. I can tell it embarrasses him, because he changes the subject. Of course, if I point it out to him, which I try to avoid, forget it. It's denial with a capital D."

"That's not unusual. Most people who get trapped by memory loss find it painful and humiliating. But what about his moodiness? Does that embarrass him too?"

She sighed audibly. "I honestly don't know. When that happens, he's like an exposed nerve. Everything's so raw and angry, I can't tell what lies underneath."

"All right. By any chance does he know you're telling me about this?"

"No way," she said, shaking her head. "I'm doing this behind his back. I feel like I'm betraying him."

"That's not true, and you know it. You're a concerned wife who wants the best for her husband, president of the United States or not. What I don't understand is what took you so long to tell me about this."

"Actually, I've been wanting to tell you for a while. But Mitch Forbes begged me not to."

He was jolted. "Did he say why?"

"The re-election, mainly. He's convinced that if word gets out that Bob has a problem, it will kill his chances."

"Well, I can understand that. Mr. Forbes is one of the smartest guys around. I'll leave the politics to him if he leaves the medicine to me. But don't worry, this won't go beyond you, me, and the president."

"Thanks, Jon," she said with a wan smile. "I can always count on you."

"Yes, you can." Mind racing, he slowly stood up, not mentioning how alarmed he was that the president's symptoms resembled those of the late Mr. Phillips. "One more thing, Rocky. We've talked about your husband, but what do *you* hope will come out of all this?"

"It's very simple. I'm losing my husband, and I want him back. That's not too much to ask, is it?"

Jon left the museum and returned to work. The first lady went back to the White House. Outside the museum, their conversation was dutifully recorded by a sophisticated listening device within a nondescript government Ford Taurus.

The National Naval Medical Center was undergoing hard times. Although it was the flagship of Navy medicine, it had been criticized recently by members of Congress who reported numerous complaints of substandard medical care. Consequently, for over a year an outside panel had been conducting an independent review of operations. Nonetheless, the Bethesda hospital continued providing care for governmental VIPs.

The Presidential Suite in the outpatient building had been used for decades. The facilities were slightly altered to suit each chief executive, but the primary mission of providing an up-to-date treatment facility was unchanged. At the appointed time, the president and his Secret Service detail were waiting in the suite. Jon and a corpsman met the president in the examining room.

"Thanks for making the time, Mr. President. How're you feeling?"

"About the same as a few weeks ago. Too good to be here, that's for sure. This is an incredible waste of time, if you ask me."

"Why do you say that?"

"Because it's much ado about nothing. Sure, I might forget

something from time to time, but who doesn't? Jesus, that doesn't exactly make me senile, does it?"

It wasn't what the president said, but how he said it—little flashes of annoyance, like a flame's flickering blue spark. It was so out of Meredith's character that it was instantly noticeable. "Of course not, but I'm glad you're aware of it. What else?"

"Well, I've been getting pretty annoyed at Rocky lately. But she's really getting on my case, God knows why. If you want my opinion, she's the one who should be here, not me."

"Okay. What about your habits? Has there been any change in the amount you smoke or drink, or what you drink?"

"None at all. This has nothing to do with drinking, Jon."

"What about food? Are you eating anything differently—snacks, health food, whatever?"

"I'm not sure the chef's food qualifies as health food, but no. Nothing whatsoever."

"What about vitamins and over-the-counter products?"

Meredith shrugged. "Just the antioxidants you gave me."

There was an occasional twitch in Meredith's face, a fine muscular spasm near the eyes. For the first time, Jon noticed a subtle, intermittent tremor in the president's fingertips. Little things, to be sure; but combined with the memory and personality changes, they were enough to concern Jon. He began a lengthy review of systems, paying particular attention to questions that might relate to neurological findings.

Foremost among these questions were simple tests designed to evaluate memory, and it was here that the exam began. Realizing the topic's sensitivity, Jon asked the corpsman and the agents to temporarily leave the room. Jon started by asking the president to respond to commands. Meredith easily followed two-step commands, but some three- and four-step commands were hard for him. He could complete six digits forward and repeat a four-word list immediately, but his recall after one minute was substantially impaired. He had difficulty with serial sevens, in which seven was subtracted from one hundred and then consecutively subtracted from the answer.

The results were troubling enough for Jon to conclude that the president would require formal psychological testing.

Meredith had short-term memory deficits, but other aspects of memory, like semantic memory, were also questionable. Moreover, the president displayed very subtle paraphasia, or verbal comprehension, sufficient to warrant in-depth testing. Finally, Meredith's attention wasn't what it should be. When Jon finished this line of inquiry, he called in the others for the neurological exam.

The straightforward physical was similarly troublesome. Besides the fine tremors, the president had mild spasticity and muscular rigidity. His cranial nerves were intact, although there was questionable weakness in the lower extremities. On one occasion, Jon was able to elicit a coarse myoclonic jerk. Meredith's eyes had a beat of nystagmus, an oscillatory movement of the eyeballs. Finally, there were some soft visual-oculomotor and extrapyramidal signs.

The exam completed, Jon folded his arms in quiet thought. The medley of neurological findings was a medical stew of unrelated ingredients. The myriad of minor abnormalities was diagnostic of nothing in particular, but the variety of possible diagnoses ran across the medical landscape. At various points, Jon thought he was dealing with encephalopathy, then drug intoxication, then an Alzheimer's variant, only to conclude it was none of the above. The only thing that was clear was that additional testing was mandatory.

"Am I going to live?" the president asked.

"No question about that. But there are a couple of minor things that bother me."

"My memory's not the best, is it?"

"It could use some improvement," Jon said. "You won't ace the SATs, but you can still run the most powerful nation on earth."

"That's a joke, right?"

Jon smiled. "My humble attempt at humor. The point is, Bob, even though I think what you've got is pretty minor, I can't pin it down. In an ideal world, I'd send you to a hotshot neurologist. But there's nothing ideal about re-election politics, particularly where it comes to rumors. Mitch Forbes already asked me to keep a low profile on this, so this is what we're going to do.

First, the corpsman will draw some blood. Then we'll bring in an EEG, a brainwave test. It won't take long, and we can do it right here in the suite. Finally, I'll do a spinal tap. After you rest here a little while, you'll head back. How does that sound?"

"A spinal tap? That should be the most fun I've had in years. But if that's what I have to do to keep you and Rocky happy, so be it."

After the blood samples were taken, Jon checked off the tests he wanted and sent the slips to the lab. In addition to routine chemistries and blood count, he ordered hormonal, serologic, and metabolic studies, plus several exotic tests. It would take several weeks for all the results to come it.

Fifteen minutes later, the EEG arrived. For the president's comfort, they set it up by the bed in the sleeping area. The machine was a Neurofax 1110, a newer Nihon Kohden model with a sixty-four-channel display. It was a portable, high-end, easy-to-use PC-based system. Once the president was lying down, the electrodes were applied. The jumble of wires wreathed his head like an electronic Medusa.

"Can I move, or do I just lie here?" he asked.

"Just keep still so nothing gets tangled."

"You could get strangled in this thing."

"That's not going to happen," Jon said.

"Wanna bet?"

"Come on, Bob, take it easy. Close your eyes and relax. This'll just take a few minutes."

Steady old son, Jon told himself. *Bob's grown ornery, but you're the doctor, and he's the patient.* When everything was ready, he powered up the machine and began recording.

For this study, he only needed half of the machine's potential. Sixty-four channels were often needed for epilepsy evaluation, surgical monitoring, and subdural electrode placement. Routine studies like this one required only thirty-two channels. Inasmuch as EEG monitoring was a random assessment of cerebral electrical activity, it could take as little or as long as the examiner wanted. In some cases, a twenty-four-hour recording was advisable. But for routine screening, Jon knew he'd need only fifteen minutes.

Talking was kept to a minimum for the next quarter hour. Jon scrutinized the recording. The built-in computer software provided instant interpretation, but Jon knew he'd refer to it later. He preferred to perform an initial assessment on his own. As he examined the emerging waveforms, his eyes narrowed. What he saw was rather peculiar.

In general, the pattern showed what was called non-specific slowing of cortical activity. This in itself wasn't diagnostic. But every few minutes, there were peculiar spikes—biphasic, sharp-wave complexes reminiscent of EKG waves. These occurred three times in the fifteen-minute recording. When it was over, one thing was certain: whatever was ailing the president, it wasn't Alzheimer's.

Yet what it was remained unclear. There was a long list of interpretations that combined generalized EEG slowing with random sharp-wave spikes, a list that included infections, cerebral inflammations, toxic or metabolic disorders, and even tumors.

Clearly, Jon needed more information. When the electrodes were removed, the president sat up.

"So, what's the verdict?" he asked Jon.

"I don't know yet, Bob. It's like I said about your exam before. There are some minor changes, but nothing that tells me exactly what's going on. Why don't we do that spinal tap now?"

"We? The 'we' part isn't sticking a needle in my back, but what the hell. Do what you gotta do."

"It's no big deal. I'll talk you through it."

"Talk you through it…. Where did I hear that before?" the president asked. "Oh, right. You remember that hospital ship we were on?"

"The *Sanctuary*?"

"Yep. Just before the doctor probed my wound, without a damn drop of anesthesia, he said he'd talk me through it. God almighty."

Jon laughed. "At least your long-term memory's pretty good."

He had the president sit up, take off his shirt, and dangle his legs over the side of the bed. Jon pulled over a stool, sat behind

Meredith, and opened a disposable spinal tap tray. The self-contained unit had various needles and syringes, prep swabs, a sterile paper drape, local anesthetic, and collection vials. All it lacked was latex gloves.

The corpsman opened a pair of size eights for Jon. He daubed the skin over the president's vertebrae with iodine-soaked swabs and covered the lumbar area with the drape, which had a diamond-shaped fenestration. With his gloved thumbs, Jon carefully palpated the vertebrae, searching for the spaces between the bones. Locating what he wanted, he marked the area with his thumbnail, indenting the skin.

"Bob, you're going to feel a pinprick. Then the anesthesia might sting a little. But try to remain bent over."

"Fine, as long as you're not a proctologist."

With a tiny needle, Jon raised a wheal on the skin. After numbing it, he deadened the underlying inch of subcutaneous tissue, down to the ligament. Then he lifted a thin, twenty-five-gauge, three-and-a-half-inch spinal needle. The thinner the diameter, the less the likelihood of a port-spinal headache.

"What you'll feel now," he told the president, "is a little pressure."

Jon pierced the anesthetized skin and advanced the needle by pressing on its plastic hub with his thumbs. He'd selected a good spot. The needle moved forward without obstruction until it met the ligament. Jon gave a deft push, and the sharp tip penetrated the dura.

The president grunted. "Some little pressure."

Jon removed the inner stylet and was gratified when a glistening drop of spinal fluid welled up at the hub.

"We're in, Bob. Shouldn't be more than a minute."

After quickly checking the fluid's pressure, which was normal, he let the spinal fluid drip into sterile collection tubes. The crystal-clear fluid looked normal, but a battery of tests would have to verify that. Soon, when he'd collected several ccs into three tubes, he removed the needle. The procedure was over.

"That'll do it, Mr. President. Sit tight while the corpsman puts on a dressing."

"Then what?"

"Then, you lie flat for an hour. When you go home, take it easy for the rest of the day."

"What I mean is, when will you get the results?"

"First the fluid's cultured and checked for protein and sugar. They'll do a cell count, electrophoresis, and a few more chemistries. But I also ordered a few tests that aren't so common. They need to be sent out to reference labs, and that'll take time. All the results, including the EEG, bloods, and spinal fluid studies, should take three to four weeks."

"That's okay with me. I'm not going anywhere. But if there's anything seriously wrong, I want you to tell me first. Not Roxanne, not Mitch Forbes, but me, okay?"

"Yes, sir. That's the plan."

Alexandria, Virginia

When the call came, the phone's ringing was so jarringly unexpected that Mahmoud stared at the instrument like a frightened deer. He hadn't received any other calls. He finally gathered his wits and answered after five rings. When the caller asked for Mr. Abu-Zeid, Mahmoud said the agreed-upon phrase.

"There is no such person here. Who may I say is calling?"

"This is Saif Allah," the caller said in Southern-accented English. It was the code word for Allah's sword. "You listenin'?"

Mahmoud thought he recognized the voice as the man who'd met him in the Burger King parking lot. "Go on."

"Did your tools arrive?"

"Yes, the package arrived yesterday." He looked over at the rifle, which rested against a chair. The box of hand-loaded ammo was on a nearby table. "It was everything I expected."

"You ready to get on with it?"

"I am. All I have to do is check the rifle's zero somewhere, in case it shifted during transport. I'll need some targets."

"I'll take care of that. Meet me in front of your apartment at eight o'clock."

Precisely at eight, Mahmoud descended the apartment's front steps, carrying the rifle in a case. The nondescript plastic case was rectangular and could have contained anything. The driver, the man he'd expected, wore the same Redskins jacket as before.

Mahmoud put the case in the back seat and slipped into the front. As soon as the door was closed, the car drove away. They traveled in silence.

A mile later, they entered the Arlington National Cemetery. It was well after dark, and the site was deserted. Security at night was lax. The stranger drove to a hidden location and stopped.

"I already checked it out. Nobody's here. How long will you need?"

"Enough time for one shot. You brought the targets?"

"In the trunk," said C.J. "Let me see your weapon."

"That is not necessary."

"I said, let me see your weapon."

Meeting the American's unflinching stare, Mahmoud reluctantly unlatched the gun case. Snipers were jealous of their rifles and didn't like them touched by anyone else. He gingerly handed the weapon to the driver.

Even in the dark, C.J. could tell that the rifle was a finely made instrument. All potentially rough edges were highly polished, smooth and snag-free. It was light, weighing roughly half of his M40A1. He slowly worked the bolt. The rifle's lightly oiled action was like butter, the metal surfaces sliding perfectly over one another. Much as he hated to admit it, C.J. was impressed. He handed the weapon back.

"Now let's see what you can do with it."

With the driver remaining in the car, Mahmoud took the targets from the trunk.

He paced off one hundred fifty meters to an area lighted by a nearby lamp. In its dim light, the gray tombstones beneath it were ghostly markers. Mahmoud placed his targets atop adjoining headstones. First was a paper target, with a central orange bull's eye. Next was a gallon jug of water, and finally, a tangerine. Then he walked back to the car.

He spread a blanket on the vehicle's hood and took out his

rifle. He swiveled out a bipod attached to the stock and rested it on the blanket. Keeping the rifle's safety on, he loaded the magazine, chambered a round, leaned over the car's fender, and peered through the scope. Even in the faint light, the scope's excellent optics showed crisp, sharp images. Mahmoud cranked the magnification up to twelve-power and eyed the targets.

He could see everything clearly. Hitting the bottle of water would make the most dramatic display, but he was interested in accuracy, not showmanship. If the point of aim had shifted, he'd need several shots to re-zero it, and that called for paper. But if it hadn't, one shot was all he required. The tangerine had a two-inch diameter, and if he could hit it at this distance... He centered the crosshairs on the rind and flicked off the safety. Taking a deep breath, he gently squeezed the trigger.

The rifle bucked, and its roar shattered the graveyard silence. When Mahmoud looked back through the scope, the fruit was gone. He straightened up, folded the bipod, and returned the rifle to the back seat.

Inside the car, Walker had been watching through binoculars. He knew what the man was doing with the three targets, for it's what he might have done. When the tangerine exploded, he snorted in grudging admiration. This old boy could shoot, all right.

"It's perfect," Mahmoud said to the driver.

"Then get in, stow your gear, and let's go."

CHAPTER 16

The already-considerable pressure on Rocky increased daily. It was late November, with less than a month remaining before Christmas. As the re-election campaign began to unfold, Bob Meredith's eccentricities showed no sign of diminution.

It astonished her how her husband could seem so much in control at public appearances and yet privately be falling apart. It was painful to watch what was happening to him.

The effect on her was as much physical as emotional. Her whole body seemed swollen, a feeling of pressure. Her head felt ready to explode, as if it were being stretched. Her left arm had such persistent achy stiffness that she was worried it was her heart.

Their lovemaking was also a casualty. Over the years, their intimate life, while no longer lustful, had grown comfortably familiar. It was a refuge, a place of warmth, a safe haven to which two people could retire when the outside world was overwhelming. But now it was a casualty of the president's problem. For one thing, Meredith showed almost no interest. Rocky had the impression he could no longer be bothered. Because of his unpredictable reaction, she was afraid to ask him about it. She kept her thoughts and needs to herself.

Her official duties were a refuge. Although Rocky stayed out of politics as much as possible, she did represent the administration in a ceremonial way consistent with her status as a high-profile figurehead. She most often appeared at ribbon-cutting ceremonies, speaker introductions, cake cuttings, and silent support from the dais, roles some dismissed as fluff. Yet she enjoyed this and did it well. Today, in keeping with the administration's support of health care financing, she was scheduled to introduce a speaker at a major medical conference in nearby Baltimore.

Baltimore was home to two excellent medical schools in Johns Hopkins University and the University of Maryland. While Hopkins was more prestigious, Maryland was renowned as the leader in shock-trauma. Equally important, barring traffic, the University of Maryland campus was a direct forty-five-minute drive from 1600 Pennsylvania Avenue. The evening conference was scheduled to begin at seven p.m. in the modern Homer Gudelsky Building. Rocky could introduce her speaker, stay a while, and still be back at the White House by nine. She was to have been accompanied by Dr. Townsend, but at the last minute he begged off, citing an emergency.

Which was just as well. She knew they would talk about Bob the entire drive, and what she needed right now was distance from the subject. She had to get away from it. Her mind had been racing with preoccupation about her husband, and she longed for an opportunity to release her thoughts from the squirrel cage. A few hours' diversion would give her emotional breathing room.

It had been a quick, relaxing drive with little traffic. As the limo neared Oriole Park at Camden Yards, Rocky leaned back in her seat, grateful for the respite. She tried to think positively and soon convinced herself that, with luck, things could only get better.

Baltimore rush hour traffic was increasing when Mahmoud arrived at Redwood Street. It was five minutes of five when he walked into the newer of two buildings at the University of Maryland's School of Social Work, carrying a musical instrument case. His hands were sweaty, his throat dry. The case was shaped like a large string instrument, though if it were precisely measured, it would prove to be larger than a viola, but smaller than a cello. Most people were too caught up in their departures to notice the stranger or his parcel. Having studied the building's floor plan, Mahmoud avoided the elevator and entered the stairwell.

On the upper landing to the fifth and top floor, he waited until several minutes past five before stealing into the men's room. He sat in one of the stalls, trying to slow his racing heart. Mahmoud was no stranger to pressure. In fact, he usually found himself calmest under duress, when, as a member of the black-hooded Palestinian Tanzim, there were Israeli bullets whizzing overhead. Or when the authorities searched for him house by house. By mentally reciting phrases from the mighty Qur'un, Islamic scripture, he was able to calm his nerves and steady his hand. But in this country, things were different.

It was another world here. People were people the world over, but when in a strange land, one could not retreat to the refuge of usual places and familiar habits. Although Mahmoud spoke English, it lacked the fluid comfort of his native tongue, where words flowed from one's lips like water from a well. The frenetic pace here was completely different from his homeland's languid ways. And most important, if the situation deteriorated, he had nowhere to run. He and his contact had worked out possible escape routes, but they were theoretical, lacking the familiarity of a hidden wadi or a twisting alleyway back home.

And then there was his target. He had been kept in the dark all along, and now he understood why. When his contact had finally mentioned their target's name earlier that day, Mahmoud's heart wanted to explode. Surely this was a blow for freedom, the will of the Almighty! Yet Mahmoud dared not dwell on it, for thinking about something so awesome could tear him apart.

No one entered the men's room. At five forty-five, Mahmoud thought the building should be virtually vacated. He peered into the hall, found it empty, and returned to the stairwell with his case. The stairs, which went up to the roof, ended at an alarmed fire door. He bypassed the alarm and walked out onto the roof.

The steady westerly wind was blocked by University Hospital's main building directly across the street. At this time of year sunset arrived early, before five. On the roof, it was already cold and dark. Mahmoud was wearing a black ski jacket, and its collar was hiked up around his neck. Bent slightly forward, he quickly crept across the roof. The bright lights of University

Hospital reached out to structures nearby. Mahmoud hugged the roof's shadows.

From his vantage point, he could see several blocks down Greene Street. Two hundred yards away, the Gudelsky Building's brightly lit glass atrium was a shining beacon. Keeping to a crouch, Mahmoud hurried to the parapet and looked over. Three police cars were already parked near the building's entrance, and he had no doubt others would arrive soon. In addition, a handful of plainclothes security agents were already taking up strategic positions. So, he thought, *It has begun.*

Although keeping to the roof's edge offered the most direct shot, it also provided the greatest exposure. If he had any hope of getting away, he couldn't risk it. Mahmoud retreated to the shadows and opened the instrument case, removing a compact photographer's tripod. The tripod's top surface was fitted with a U-shaped cradle for supporting a rifle stock. Once its legs were locked in place, Mahmoud took out the rifle and placed it in the cradle.

He took off the scope's protective covers and put his cheek to the stock. Aiming the rifle toward the Gudelsky Building's entrance, he looked through the rear lens. Under magnification, the atrium gleamed like an incandescent gem. His target would be well illuminated. There might be changes in the bullet's point of impact due to the temperature, the downhill trajectory, and the wind, but at this distance, they would be minimal.

He'd thoroughly cleaned the rifle after the test firing. Now Mahmoud worked the bolt to chamber a round from the four-cartridge magazine. Everything was ready, and all he had to do was wait.

The results were in the hands of Allah.

The first lady's three-car motorcade drove west on Redwood and turned south onto Greene Street. The local police were temporarily diverting traffic, and Greene Street was deserted. The police had cordoned off the Gudelsky Building's entrance with funnels of rope reminiscent of those outside a movie theater. The three black cars slowed and pulled to the curb together.

The agents left the lead and chase cars and formed a protective phalanx outside the first lady's vehicle. As she slid across the seat, the head of her detail opened her door.

"Take your time, ma'am. We're a few minutes early."

"Do we have far to go, Chip?"

"No, the auditorium's on the first floor, just down the hall."

Roxanne tightened her collar and stepped into the cold night air. Much as she needed an evening diversion, she was tired. On the curb, she straightened up and smoothed her coat, suddenly feeling guilty for wanting time to herself. She was already looking forward to finishing this engagement and returning home to Bob.

The instant the limos rolled to a stop, Mahmoud thumbed off the rifle's safety. He was wearing woolen fingerless gloves that provided warmth while allowing good tactile sensation. When the motorcade rolled into view, a sudden calm settled over him like a blanket. His heartbeat slowed, and his hands were rock steady. Relaxed though he was, he also felt a steely resolve.

The scope's duplex reticle had heavy peripheral crosshairs that gave way to finer lines in the center. Mahmoud took a deep breath and held it. As soon as the woman stepped out of the vehicle, the crosshairs fixed on her hat. Mahmoud hadn't anticipated a hat, but it didn't matter. The edge of its brim made a good aiming point. When the target momentarily paused, he squeezed the trigger.

Secret Service agent Chip McNally was closing the car door when he heard the horrifying splat. It was a sickening noise, the sound of a hammer striking a side of beef. Out of the corner of his eye, he noticed the first lady's head jerk forward. As he reached her way, there came a sound like a backfire, and Roxanne Meredith collapsed in a heap.

His first thought was, *This can't be happening.* But then he acted reflexively, an instinctive reaction that stemmed from years of training. He leaped on the first lady and shielded her body with his.

"FLOTUS is down!" one of the agents screamed into his mike. "We're taking fire!"

Guns were quickly drawn. Apprehensive eyes peered up and out.

"Does anyone see the shooter?" another asked.

"Let's get her in, Chip!" said a third.

Normally, protocol called for returning the stricken person to the protective interior of the armor-plated limousine. But McNally's mind was racing. Even as he covered Mrs. Meredith, he could smell her blood. From the stillness with which she was lying, he knew the first lady was badly injured. If they put her in the vehicle, then what?

Mindful of a follow-up shot, he quickly rose to a crouch, keeping his torso between Mrs. Meredith and the street. He scooped her into his powerful arms and dashed toward the hospital and its shock-trauma unit. Chancing a wary look down, he spotted the dark entry wound at the top of Roxanne's neck, just behind the mastoid bone. *This is not good*, he thought.

As he raced through the atrium's opened glass doors, he was struck by how light Mrs. Meredith was. He knew he needed help, but the first order or business was to protect the first lady. Soon he knelt in a corner, still holding her in his arms, feeling the protective cordon surround him.

"Got to get her into Shock Trauma, Chip!" called one of his men.

"Which way?"

"Other corner, across the street. We alerted them. They'll bring a gurney." McNally chanced another glance at the first lady, who lay helplessly in his arms. The exit wound on the left side of her neck was a small dark hole that bled freely. "Fuck the gurney!" he cried. "Where the hell's the unit?"

"This way."

Forming a protective cordon, guns drawn and facing outward in a phalanx, members of the first lady's team guarded her as McNally carried their charge toward the R Adams Crowley Shock Trauma Unit. Once they'd crossed the street a gurney almost magically appeared, and a group of EMTs surrounded the stretcher as it neared the closest shock-trauma bay. As carefully as possible, McNally placed Roxanne back down on the still-moving stretcher. Her face was deathly pale.

A frighteningly ragged exit wound in her neck gushed blood profusely.

"Pressure!" someone shouted. "Put pressure on that wound!"

The unit was a warren of diagnostic and treatment rooms, some of them in use. Word of the shooting spread rapidly. A green-clad, scrub-suited man appeared beside the stretcher and pressed a heavy sterile white pad against the first lady's neck.

"Whoa, whoa," he shouted. "Where are you taking her?"

"Who are you?" McNally asked.

"Dr. Darmajian," he said. "One of the surgeons on staff here."

Darmajian, McNally thought. *Iranian*. But he couldn't afford to be choosy. Any port in a storm. "This is the President Meredith's wife, Doc." His tone implied caution.

"I realize that, but you can't just wheel her into the nearest open space. She's got to be examined. And that wound has to be explored before she bleeds to death." His fingers gently probed the back of her head. "Is this a pistol or rifle wound?"

"Rifle, we think."

"Jesus. All right, let's take her over to the spiral CT. And somebody get hold of Dr. Douglas."

"Who's that?" McNally asked.

"Cliff Douglas is chief of neurosurgery. I think he planned to attend the speech." Within literally seconds, other health care workers appeared and began cutting off the first lady's clothes. Fortunately for Roxanne, she was in the right place at the wrong time, for she could not possibly receive finer care anywhere in the world. Late in 1968, an elderly Western Maryland resident was transferred to the University of Maryland Hospital with abdominal pain and a presumptive diagnosis of severe pancreatitis. During his workup, he was discovered to have a ruptured cardiac muscle. The patient underwent cardiac surgery and a months-long rehabilitation, during which he was intensely monitored as the sole patient in a fledgling diagnostic and treatment unit. From such humble beginnings the Shock Trauma Unit at the University of Maryland Medical Center was born, later to become the preeminent such facility in the Northeast.

The agents were unceremoniously hustled toward the periphery of the care area. Shock Trauma's admitting area was essentially a massive intensive care unit where all effort centered on treating the patient quickly. Unlike other hospitals, where the patient went to an ER or trauma station and then had the necessary diagnostic tests performed elsewhere in the hospital, everything in Shock Trauma was located within forty feet. The Trauma Resuscitation Unit, or TRU, had ten identical resuscitation bays and six ORs, all connected by audio-video-data links to a telecontrol room. This included a spiral CT scanner that could take photographs of the brain from multiple angles with a single time-saving set-up.

In less than ninety seconds, the newly arrived, hospital-gowned patient had two large-bore IVs, including a central venous pressure catheter; a urinary catheter; an elaborate blood pressure and pulse monitor; and a pulse oximeter, a device measuring the blood's oxygen saturation. Her blood pressure had already fallen, and her pulse was beginning to rise. The next half-hour would be critical. Meanwhile, Darmajian continued his preliminary examination.

It was obvious that the patient had suffered a severe traumatic head injury. Using the well-established Glasgow Coma Scale, she was clearly in a coma, unresponsive to verbal commands or painful stimuli. The basic neurologic exam included an assessment of the GCS and evaluation of the pupils. Both pupils were mildly dilated, one slightly more than the other—not a good sign. In addition to this abbreviated physical examination, imaging the brain was important to patient evaluation. The spiral CT was best for this purpose. The first lady had just finished having the scan performed and her vital signs monitored when Cliff Douglas arrived.

Dr. Clifford Douglas, a 1968 graduate of the N.Y.U. School of Medicine, was the paradigm of an African-American success story. Growing up in Harlem, he was a gang member who seemed destined for a life of crime and imprisonment. At six-feet-four and two hundred fifty pounds, his imposing presence both inspired and terrified those around him. And he might well have gone down a path of self-destruction were it not for a retired cop who steered him toward the Police Athletic League. His success on the football field landed him on the high school varsity team, and Douglas soon earned college scholarships. It was in college that he managed to turn himself around and seek a career in medicine. More than thirty years later, just as tall and a few pounds heavier, he was every bit as impressive in the OR as he had been on the gridiron.

Even in triple-extra-large scrubs, his bulk seemed to burst at the seams. But his deep baritone voice left no question about who was in charge when he entered the room. "Just the details, Hamid," he barked to Darmajian. "I know the rough story."

"Then you know who our patient is," said the surgeon. "Her most recent 'crit's twenty-six. Vitals are low but stable. Her left pupil's become unresponsive. You'll want to see the CT."

"You pushed diuretics?"

"Yes, and steroids are on board. The cops don't know what she was shot with yet, but the entrance wound looks under thirty-caliber."

"Not that it matters." Douglas was addressing the fact that even small-caliber, high-velocity rifle bullets could produce devastating injuries; but if they were dealing with an elephant-killing caliber, chances of survival were negligible. Douglas performed a quick physical exam on the first lady, confirming the grave prognosis.

Surrounded by residents and staff, the two physicians evaluated the ultra-fast CT scan. Douglas' first impression of the films was that they were not dealing with an ultralightweight hollow-point bullet. Such a projectile rapidly expanded when it entered the cranial cavity, producing an explosion of brain tissue, fragments of skull, and shards of copper-jacketed bullet. Rather, from the neat, downward trajectory of the wound, it appeared that they were dealing with a solid projectile, often used to gain accuracy or penetration at the expense of expansion. For Roxanne Meredith, this was one small piece of good news. But the CT scan did reveal a significant, or growing, mass of blood called a hematoma, and the presence of considerable edema, or swelling. Bullets did more damage through edema and hematoma formation that from actual destruction of brain tissue.

"But no herniation, though," said Darmajian of the films.

"Not yet, anyway," Douglas agreed. "But we've got to get in there fast."

Unlike bone or cartilage, brain tissue was highly compressible. It responded to swelling and hemorrhage and clot by squeezing together more tightly. However, within the closed space of the skull, its ability to squeeze ever tighter was limited by space and pressure. If the swelling rose precipitously or became too great, it caused a phenomenon called increased intracranial pressure, or ICP. The effect of dramatically increased ICP on brain tissue was similar to squeezing a tube of toothpaste: the gray matter would shift, or herniate, following the path of least resistance. Unless relieved, severe brain herniations were fatal. Thus, Douglas' role as a neurosurgeon, in the case of traumatic brain injury, was to reduce that build-up of pressure by controlling hemorrhage and eliminating clot. That meant immediate surgery.

The technical term for such surgical gymnastics was exploratory craniotomy with debridement. In a sense, this kind of neurosurgery was akin to sophisticated plumbing. Although it was impossible to repair damaged brain tissue with cautery and sutures, the leaks could be controlled. Also, evaluation of the patient with a penetrating, traumatic head injury during the immediate post-operative period relied on frequent monitoring of the patient's neurological examination, the GCS score, the pupils, arterial blood gases, and in most cases, the ICP. This meant that Douglas had to insert an ICP catheter into the brain during surgery. And he had to do it soon.

The rifle bucked. When Mahmoud regained the image, he saw that the target was down. He wasn't certain his bullet struck the point of aim, because the woman moved the instant the rifle fired. Yet from the way she'd fallen, there was no question he'd done his job. He was filled with intense elation and gratitude. This was truly God's work.

He had to get out of there immediately. The plan was to make his way back through the building and leave through one of the first-floor office windows. From there he'd cross over to Paca Street, well behind the School of Social Work and far enough from the killing ground that the searchers would take a while to arrive. By then, he'd be long gone.

Mahmoud hurriedly repacked the rifle and tripod and closed the case. In spite of the cold wind, he was sweating. He felt more alive than he'd ever felt before. He was pumped, and the case no longer seemed heavy. As he crossed the roof to the fire door, there was spring in his step. But when he reached for the metal handle, the door unexpectedly swung open. Startled, Mahmoud stopped in his tracks. There was a man in the doorway, his features indistinct in the stairwell's dim light. Yet as Mahmoud's vision focused, fear set in.

"Who are you?" he said.

There was a sound like a muffled "pfft," and Mahmoud fell backward. The gunman stepped onto the roof and approached his victim. The thirty-two-caliber bullet had struck Mahmoud below the right eye and was probably fatal. Nonetheless, the man pointed the silenced semi-automatic at Mahmoud's forehead and fired twice more, finishing the job. Then he bent over, pocketed the three shell casings, and left.

Fifteen minutes later, Roxanne Meredith was in the OR, intubated, head shaved, and prepped for surgery. As Dr. Douglas backed away from the scrub sink, bent arms raised and dripping soapy water, he was aware of the awesome responsibility he carried. He had operated on thousands of patients with head trauma, some more critically injured than the first lady. But none had the added burden of being the wife of the most powerful man in the world. Accepting a towel from the scrub nurse, Clifford Douglas took a deep breath and concentrated on the task at hand.

In spite of driving wildly through rush hour traffic, Jon still reached the White House much too late. In the world of White House scheduling, punctuality was king. He was supposed to have been there at five-thirty; and now, at six-fifteen, he doubted the day's events had waited for him. As he pulled up at the gate, attired in his overcoat and dress uniform, he lowered the window.

"Have they left yet?" he asked the guard.

"Who's that, sir?"

"The first lady. I was supposed to go to Baltimore with her."

"Afraid they've gone, Doc. Left fifteen, twenty minutes ago."

Muttering under his breath, Jon parked and entered the White House. He was still shaking from what had made him late in the first place. He didn't think Mireille was still there, but it was worth a look. He needed a friendly face to talk to. Surprisingly, she was just putting on her coat when he caught her in the kitchen. He kissed her on the cheek and hugged her warmly.

"Am I glad you're still here," he said. "I was afraid you'd left."

"Weren't you supposed to attend a conference?"

"Yeah, I was. But just before I left the office at five, I got a call about Tommie."

"What kind of call?"

"It was someone from her school who said that Tommie was missing. I thought I was going to fall over. They said she'd stayed late to work on some kind of project, and the next thing they knew, she'd disappeared."

"Oh my God," Mireille whispered. "You wouldn't be here if they hadn't found her. Where was she?"

"That's just it, she wasn't anywhere. It was a prank call, but I only found that out after I drove over there. It turns out Tommie had been at Victoria's all along. By the time I discovered that, I was late getting here. I missed Roxanne's limo."

"That's terrible. Do you think someone did it on purpose?"

"You mean scare the hell out of me, or make me late getting here?"

"Both. Either."

"I doubt it," he said. "That's just too weird. It's probably someone with a grudge who wanted to piss me off. And he succeeded."

"Poor Jon," she said, taking his hand. "Is there anything I can do to un-piss you?"

"What a delightful thought. A drink would be nice. Followed by dinner."

"Okay. Where would you like to go?"

"Someplace casual, if it's okay with you."

"Sure. What about my place?"

When the Secret Service relayed word of Mrs. Meredith's shooting to the White House, security increased dramatically. Protecting the First Family was a well-rehearsed drill that was regularly practiced. The president, who was preparing for dinner, was immediately hustled to a secure room below ground. There, the chief agent in charge informed him of the events in Baltimore.

Meredith paled. He sat down and mumbled something incomprehensible under his breath.

"Can I get you something, sir?"

"We've got to get over there."

"Mr. President, the situation is very fluid right now. I think they're going to take Mrs. Meredith into surgery. We should wait until things calm down a bit."

The president slowly appraised him. "You're married, right?"

"Yes, sir."

"How long?"

"Sixteen years, sir."

"Well, I've been married twice that long. And I'll tell you something. Every time I've been ill, even if it's sniffles, the first lady's been by my side. And I've tried to do the same for her. So you see, son, staying here's not an option."

"Sir—"

"How soon can you get me there?" the president persisted.

"I'll look into it, Mr. President. I'm not sure about their landing facilities. We might have to use the limo."

"Then see to it. I want to leave in five minutes."

The helipad at Shock Trauma, normally used by the Maryland State Police helicopter system, was very sturdy, but it was not designed to support the weight of the presidential helicopter. Formally known as a Sikorsky VH-3D Sea King, the craft was simply called Marine One when the president was aboard. Instead, the Secret Service called in one of its many backup helicopters, a new Bell 412EP. On the south lawn ten minutes later, eleven agents and presidential staff climbed aboard for the short flight to Baltimore. At its maximum speed of one hundred forty miles per hour, the chopper was on site fifteen minutes later.

President Meredith wanted to see his wife before the doctor began operating. But despite their urgency, the operation was already underway when the helicopter landed. The Secret Service immediately cordoned off a secure area of Shock Trauma. While the first lady was a patient there, further admissions to the unit would be halted. The State Police were instructed to transport eligible patients to Johns Hopkins or the Greater Baltimore Medical Center.

With nothing to do but wait, the long vigil began.

CHAPTER 17

Twenty minutes after leaving the White House, Jon was in Mireille's apartment. She had a one-bedroom in a new luxury high-rise in Georgetown. Although she was on the ground floor, her living room overlooked the river, and at night, the lights on the banks of the Potomac were a glistening brocade. While he inspected the view, Mireille hung their coats in the hallway closet.

"Great view," he said. "How long have you lived here?"

"About a year. It's perfect for me. Can I get you some wine?"

He followed her into the kitchen, where she opened the wine. It had to breathe a while. She removed rounds of Brie and Camembert from the refrigerator, though these, too, needed to time to soften. While they waited, Mireille changed her clothes. She had worn a pants suit to work, but in a few minutes, she came out of the bedroom wearing a skirt and blouse. The skirt was short, and the long-sleeve blouse, made from a glossy, lightweight fabric, was partially unbuttoned. Jon smiled.

"That's a great-looking outfit."

"Thank you. I'll get the glasses."

A dining room table was by the living room window. Jon carried in the cheeses on a cheese board, and Mireille brought in the wine and two glasses. When she poured and swirled her glass, Jon did likewise. Then he tasted it.

"That's fantastic wine," he said, lifting the bottle and checking the label. "Clos de Vougeot. This is burgundy?"

"Yes, a Grand Cru, one of the great growths. It comes from a small vineyard run by monks. I fell in love with it when I was a teenager and my boyfriend introduced me to it. He moved on, but I always adored the wine."

"Looks expensive."

"About a hundred dollars a bottle. Too expensive for my budget, but most of my wines are gifts."

The cheese was mild, the wine full and mellow. As they drank, they spoke about life and love. Jon felt unusually comfortable in her presence. He considered Mireille remarkably feminine. She was pert and outgoing, yet undeniably sexy. After the first glass of wine, he felt more relaxed than he had in days. A grin crept over his face.

"I think I'm there."

"Where?" she asked.

"Un-pissed. It's a good place to hide for a while."

That made her laugh. "You are a wonderful man." She walked closer and kissed him softly on the lips. "And maybe a little high. Here, have some more wine," she said, filling his glass. "Let's see how much more relaxed I can get you."

Standing by the living room window, looking out over the river, they held hands and savored the vintage. Jon's earlier cares had vanished. He had no idea who had called him about Tommie, and right now, he didn't care. He was living in the moment, where all that mattered was that he was in the company of the most enchanting woman he'd known in years.

"Do you eat caviar?" she asked.

"Eat, yes. Like, that depends."

"I have one I want you to try. Beluga, from the Russian Embassy."

He followed her back into the kitchen, where she rummaged through one of the cabinets.

"That's funny," she said. "I was sure it was in here."

Wanting to help, he opened an opposite cabinet and searched among the foodstuffs. Mireille let out a discouraged sigh and turned around. Not realizing what Jon was doing, her head banged into the edge of his cabinet door.

"Oh!" she cried, hands flying to her face.

"Christ, I'm sorry, Mireille," he said, annoyed at his clumsiness. "Here, let me take a look." He gently pried her hands apart and looked at the injury.

"Am I bleeding?"

"No, it's just a little bump. Go sit down and I'll get some ice."

Back in the living room, Mireille sat on the table, near the cheese. The shoes slipped from her feet. Jon returned with several ice cubes wrapped in a dry dishtowel. He lifted her chin up and gently placed the towel on her wound. She grimaced at the chill but said nothing. As the ice went to work, she looked up at him for support.

"It doesn't look bad. A little bruise, maybe, but that's it."

She nodded, feeling warm and safe in his hands. His very closeness stimulated her. Despite their difference in age, Jon Townsend was undeniably masculine and attractive. He possessed a quiet strength that belied his stated insecurities, a decisiveness that was at odds with his lopsided emotional baggage. Mireille felt drawn to him. Her hands slid from his wrists to his elbows before coming to rest on his hips.

As he looked down at her tranquil face, Jon knew there was something lovely about this woman, an internal beauty that went past her obvious physical charms. She was a caring individual whose circle of compassion extended beyond basic politeness. She'd been there for Tommie on several occasions, and today she had reached out to him with such a supportive, reassuring hand that his own troubles faded. Feeling her palms on his hips, he bent forward and kissed her hairline.

Loosened wisps of her fine hair tickled his cheeks, and he tenderly kissed her bump, then her nose. Her flushed cheeks were red from alcohol and anticipation. Jon put the ice down and kissed her chin before his lips found the soft warmth of her neck. Mireille sighed, and her head rolled to one side.

"That feels so good," she said. "Do you do this with all your female patients?"

"Only the ones that I care for."

"Too bad. The rest don't know what they're missing."

The alcohol made her heart beat faster. She slowly lifted her head, raised her chin, and kissed him. His partially opened lips were warm and dry. She lightly pressed his upper lip between hers. It tasted salty, sweet with wine. Her hands came up and cupped his cheeks, keeping his face within reach. She wanted to take time with his mouth.

"Just stay as you are," she whispered. "Keep your eyes closed, and let me do everything. Don't kiss me back until I tell you."

She nibbled gently on his lip, moving her mouth from side to side. The tip of her tongue traced warm lines along the border where lip met skin. When she finished there, she began on his lower lip, tasting, delicately teasing. Then her tongue slipped between his lips and slid across his teeth.

Jon stood there mute and unmoving. He would stay like that as long as she wanted. He'd always thought it better to give than to receive, but this was heaven, and he knew he'd follow wherever she led. His own breath was coming more quickly, and he was growing aroused.

Mireille's lips worked up his face in slow, tender kisses. Her mouth touched his nose, his eyes, and his ears. She seemed intent on exploring every inch of his face with her lips, testing here, probing there, as if looking for something but not finding it. After several tantalizing minutes, her lips returned to his.

"You can kiss me now. Kiss me wet and deep."

He responded immediately, forcing her lips open and pressing his mouth into hers. A throaty moan escaped her, and Mireille's arms went around his back. In turn he held her tight, wanting to make his mouth a part of her very being. Soon they kissed one another hungrily, with the neediness of thirsty men suddenly given drink.

Their warmth and closeness increased desire. Mireille's hands found his uniform and began working on the buttons of his shirt. The dress blouse was made of a thick fabric that was difficult to unbutton. Bit by bit she got it open, revealing a white tee shirt. She slowly pulled out his shirttails and pulled the blouse from his shoulders. Yet when she began lifting his undershirt, he started on her own buttons. Mireille seized his wrists.

"No," she said. "Don't touch me yet. Just stand there."

She got off the table and, standing before him, pulled his tee shirt over his head. Then she caressed his chest, touching and stroking gently, finally kissing him with her soft mouth, wispy kisses that felt like silk on his skin. She kissed his breastbone and his nipples and the fine hairs that dove down his stomach in a V. Then she walked behind him.

Pressing herself into his back, Mireille circled his torso with her arms and once again ran her palms over his chest. This time she touched him harder, kneading and pressing with baker's hands. His abdomen was flat and firm and she squeezed as she rubbed, as if testing the resiliency of dough. Then her fingers fell to his belt.

Jon was incredibly turned on. He thought he was living a dream. The woman he cared for deeply was pressing her soft breasts into his bare back while her fingers undid his belt. She was doing everything for him, and much as her actions were unexpected, he found it oddly satisfying to be so completely doted upon. The role reversal was the stuff of other people's fantasies, and although new to him, he didn't object at all. And so, he stood there with schoolboy stillness, awaiting her intentions.

His belt undone, she unzipped his trousers. While she held him close, she kissed his neck and shoulders. He was now fully aroused. Perhaps sensing this, Mireille reached into his boxers and grasped him, squeezing once before removing her hand. She tugged at the clothing around his waist. Lowering his pants and shorts to his ankles, she made him step out of them. He was naked except for his socks.

"Turn around. Keep your eyes closed."

She spoke, he listened. He felt somewhat ludicrous blindly standing there in the altogether, but he realized this was her intention. There was vulnerability in his nakedness, and being deprived of sight forced him to rely on his other senses. The physiologic imperative was exquisite. Everything was unusually sharp and keen. His sensual acuity magnified, her scent became pronounced, intoxicating in its depth and overtones. His skin felt unusually sensitive, and every inch, every hair, responded to the delicate raking of her satiny nails. When she began stroking his inner thighs, each cell in his body wanted to reach out to her.

He sensed her kneeling and she finally took hold of him, using two fingers, no more. He felt the momentary softness of her lips, and she kissed away the moisture at his tip. Unexpectedly, she rose and walked away. Suddenly alone, Jon felt abandoned. Should he move or open his eyes? In his uncertainty, he did neither. But soon he sensed her presence once more, and she returned and again stood before him. Her hands grasped his shoulders and lightly pushed.

"Move back," she said. "Lie on the table."

The tabletop was cold against his bare skin, and he shivered. But then her warm hands were on his skin, caressing him with wispy movements that felt like warm feathers. She took hold of him once more and rolled a condom down his length. He heard the silky rustling of fabric and zipper as she removed her clothes. Then she surprised him by getting on the table with him, straddling his hips with her knees.

She lifted his hands over his head, pinning his wrists to the table. When she leaned over him, her breasts brushed his chest. He suddenly wanted to embrace her, but he resisted the temptation. Her bosom, meanwhile, rose to his face. Her nipples played about his nose, touched his mouth. Her breasts moved from side to side like a pendulum, tantalizing him, grazing his lips provocatively. Finally, he could resist no longer. His lips closed around one areola, and he took the stiffening nipple into his mouth.

Mireille sucked in her breath and groaned deeply. Without hesitation she took hold of him and placed him inside her. After all the sensory stimulation, Jon found their sudden joining so intense that he let out a long, satisfied sigh. She was all heat and softness, and her warmth drew him deeper.

But it was not nearly close enough. His arms finally went around her, and he seized her buttocks with such urgency that she was startled. It was as if he wanted to be part of her, to possess her. Mireille responded in kind, moving her hips against his with increasing frenzy.

The exotic ministrations were all too much for Jon. As he felt the warmth rising in his loins, he opened his lids just as her breasts fell away. He found himself looking into her eyes, hazel eyes so filled with tenderness that he wanted to curl up inside them. As they gazed at one another, Jon felt himself losing control. But he wouldn't look away. When the climax overtook him, his entire body stiffened. As it did, Mireille's hips began to shudder; yet she, too, wouldn't abandon the shared look that spoke more than could ever be put into words.

Several minutes later, they lay in her bed together, side by side, face to face. In the background, the TV she'd turned on while changing was a distant whisper. Jon continued holding her in his arms.

"Are you still un-pissed?" she asked.

"I am. Unstressed. And very relaxed. And," he said, kissing the tip of her nose, "happier than I've been in a long time."

"Is that the wine talking?"

"No, it's me. And I mean it."

"What about the cheese?"

"The cheese?"

She touched his head. "You have cheese in your hair. The Brie."

"Really? As your humble slave, I'm not responsible for that."

"There's some on your shoulder, too." She leaned over and nibbled it off. "Hmmm."

"Can I ask you something? Nobody ever did what you did to me tonight. It was so different. Fascinating, delightful. I loved it, and I hope we can do it again. But…do you do that a lot?"

She gave an amused sniff. "You mean, am I a dominatrix? Are you afraid of my whip, *mon petit chou?* Actually, I saw it in a movie for the first time last week. I've never done it before."

Just then, a news bulletin came on the TV. From force of habit, Jon turned toward the screen.

"CNN has just learned that first lady Roxanne Meredith has been critically wounded at around seven p.m. Eastern Time, the apparent victim of a sniper. We are told that she is undergoing emergency treatment at Shock Trauma at the University of Maryland School of Medicine in Baltimore, where she was to have delivered an address. President Meredith has been flown from the White House to be at his wife's side. There are no further details at this moment. We repeat…"

The covers fell away as Jon bolted upright in bed. Horrified, he simply stared at the screen, too stunned to utter a word.

CHAPTER 18

The first lady's surgery was a neurosurgical marathon that lasted until one in the morning. From the confines of Shock Trauma, President Meredith conducted what little he could of the country's business. The only calls he took were from the vice president and the chief of staff. In the streets outside the unit, it was a mob scene. By midnight, hundreds of journalists had assembled, essentially closing off traffic for blocks around. Interested passersby and ordinary citizens swelled their ranks. In addition to state and Baltimore City police, the FBI and Secret Service coordinated crowd control. Every hour or so the White House press secretary released a noncommittal statement to the effect that Mrs. Meredith was still in surgery.

On TV, talking heads, political touts, and Washington cognoscenti were in their speculative glory. Although no one knew precisely what happened, everyone had an opinion. Inside of Shock Trauma, the mood was somber. The medical staff went about its job without disturbing the president. Finally, at one-fifteen, Dr. Douglas came out of surgery and approached the president.

The two men shook hands. Meredith was immediately impressed, and comforted, by the physician. The man had unmistakable presence. Everything about Douglas was huge: huge hands, huge body, and a deep James Earl Jones baritone.

"Your wife is stable, Mr. President," Douglas began. "Critical, but stable. We're watching her closely."

"Thank God. The surgery's over?"

"For now," Douglas said with a nod. "The next forty-eight hours will be crucial. We've stopped the bleeding, and fortunately, there's not as much injury to the brain substance as I feared. But now, her biggest enemies are swelling and pressure. We'll do everything we can to keep those under control."

"I don't suppose she's awake, is she?"

Douglas shook his head. "No, she's in a coma. She's on a ventilator and probably will be for several days."

"Rocky was always a fighter, Doctor. Does she have a fighter's chance?"

"I'll level with you, Mr. President. If we're talking about living or dying, right now I'd say her odds are fifty-fifty."

"And if we're talking about...?"

"Going back to the way you've always known her? This is a very serious injury, sir. And if she survives, she'll face a long rehabilitation. As of now, every minute and hour that passes is in her favor."

Meredith's gaze fell to the floor. "I see," he said glumly, not really seeing at all.

"You might want to get some rest, Mr. President. There's not much you can do right now."

"But there is, Doctor. I can pray."

They gave him five minutes to spend with her. Clad in a disposable jumpsuit and a bouffant cap, Bob Meredith looked anything but presidential. Inside the recovery area, a similarly clad Secret Service agent stood against the wall. Two scrub-suited nurses hovered beside the ICU-style bed. When the president saw his wife, he wanted to weep.

She looked so helpless lying there. Her head was swathed in thick bandages that wrapped around her skull, both cheeks, and her neck. Her eyelids, though taped shut to prevent her eyes from drying, were swollen and puffy. A clear plastic breathing tube protruded from her mouth; and every few seconds, the bellows of a respirator contracted with a rhythmic hiss. Meredith struggled to fight back the tears.

"Can I hold her hand?" he managed.

"Yes, sir," said one of the nurses. Then they both backed away to give him privacy. Meredith took a seat by the bedside, taking his wife's hand through the raised side rails.

"Rocky," he softly began, his voice quaking with emotion,

"can you hear me, girl?" He gently squeezed her fingers, half expecting the familiar lightness of her return touch. Her still fingers were damp and cool. "Well, maybe not.

"I don't know what to say, Rock. A politician, figure that. For the first time in my life, I'm at a loss for words." He paused, eyes growing moist. "We've been through a lot together, haven't we, Rock? Thick and thin. Good times and bad. I just want you to know that I'm here for you now, for however long it takes.

"I'm not ready for you to leave yet, kid," he continued, voice choking. "I want more time with you. Call it selfish, but that's the way I feel. Don't go, Rocky, I'm begging you. Fight it—fight it with all you've got.

"When you're ready to wake up, I'll be here." As Meredith stood up, a tear rolled down his cheek. He leaned over the rails and kissed his wife on the cheek. "I'll always love you, Rocky."

Second only to international terrorist attacks, the assassination attempt on the first lady was the most moving event of the fledgling twenty-first century. The entire nation waited expectantly for any news about its beloved Roxanne Meredith. Regular TV programming was temporarily cancelled on all major networks, and news coverage of the shooting filled cable and the airwaves twenty-four hours a day.

Gifts, letters, and flowers sent to the White House numbered in the hundreds of thousands. The White House staff was overwhelmed. Federal funds were allocated to rent temporary storage and processing space for the gifts. The White House staff was edgy if subdued, and President Meredith was in seclusion.

The nation's sense of personal injury was balanced by its feelings of outrage. By seventy-two hours after the shooting, it was becoming clear what had happened. By correlating the wound channel in the first lady's neck with testimony of Secret Service agents on the scene, ballistic experts were able to trace the fatal bullet's trajectory. The shot unquestionably came from the roof of the University of Maryland's School of Social Work. Moreover, markings of the eighty-five-grain, six-millimeter projectile revealed that it came from the rifle found next to the unidentified dead man on the school's roof.

Although the manufacturer's name and serial number had

been filed off the rifle, it was obviously a custom weapon. FBI ballisticians were able to read the erasures and were soon in touch with the manufacturer, who confirmed that it was one of their products. The number of rifles made in that chambering was small. Within twenty-four hours, the FBI had tracked down all customers except one. The man who remained missing was the American-born man of Palestinian descent who sold firearms in California. A nationwide manhunt was immediately begun.

As each new piece of information became available, it was relayed to an incensed nation. The country demanded justice. Although the olive-skinned man on the roof was initially unidentified, on day three—with the assistance of Interpol and the Israeli Mossad—they got a fingerprint match. The dead man was identified as Mahmoud al-Abed, a Palestinian wanted by the Israelis for terrorism. That identity, coupled with the missing California man's purchase of the attempted murder weapon, clinched it for most Americans. The enemy had a face, and it was Palestinian. What was not nearly as apparent was who had killed the shooter, and why.

"This is not good, C.J. Certainly not what I expected."

"That boy was a shooter, Sean. A headshot, at that range? Damn," Walker protested, "I still can't see how he could have missed. Must've been that pipsqueak cartridge he was usin'. I told ya, if he'd a fired a decent .308...."

"That's ancient history now. The point is, we wanted to send a message. With her still alive, people are more sympathetic to administration policies than ever."

"You want me to take care of it? I might be able to figure out a way to get in there."

"No, it's too late for that," said O'Brien. "We had one chance, and that was it. No, I'm going to have to figure out a new angle. Maybe go after the man himself, who knows. But there's one thing we've got to be sure of."

"You name it."

"If anyone—and I mean *anyone*—gets close to what's really happening, that person's got to be taken care of immediately, understand?"

For twenty-four precarious hours post-op, Rocky clung to life. She was every bit as much of a fighter as her husband had predicted. On two occasions her blood pressure fell precipitously and her heart threatened to stop, but the team at Shock Trauma successfully juggled IV medications to bring her vital signs back to acceptable levels. Finally, early on the morning following her surgery, her condition was deemed to have stabilized.

The news was relayed by a pool reporter, the only journalist permitted in Shock Trauma. Over the airwaves, virtually all TV programming had been preempted by news of the assassination attempt and the first lady's condition. A grateful nation gave a guarded sigh of relief when her condition was updated. But she was in deep shock, still in critical condition.

Both the president and Dr. Douglas remained in the unit for thirty-six hours.

Shock Trauma had sleeping areas for staff, and the neurosurgeon managed to steal catnaps in one of the on-call rooms. Meredith, however, couldn't sleep. He alternately paced to and fro or informally attended to administration duties in the secure space reserved for him and presidential staff. By mid-morning, Douglas called the president aside.

"If I could be so bold, Mr. President, this is going to be a long, slow process. Your wife is gradually improving. I'm fairly confident that, barring some catastrophe, she's going to survive. But there's nothing to be gained by your hanging around every minute."

"It sounds like you're kicking me out."

"No, sir, but I wish I could. I'm not your doctor, but I can tell when someone needs rest. Also, you're making the staff here nervous as hell. They don't function like they should with the president looking over their shoulder."

"Come on, Doctor," Meredith protested, "I'm not looking over anyone's shoulder. I'm just a husband concerned about his wife."

"And I appreciate that. I'd do the same thing. But you're no good to her like this. You can't take care of someone else if you don't take care of yourself."

The president's head sagged, and he sighed deeply. "You're right. I just needed someone to tell me. I presume I can come back whenever I want, though? No silly visiting hours restrictions?" "You, sir, are welcome any time."

For the next several days, the president helicoptered back daily, staying three to four hours at a clip. Rocky's condition continued to improve, but in tiny increments. Importantly, she showed no signs of infection, and her critical bodily functions, such as cardiac output, kidney function, and respiration, were strong. Throughout, her ICP readings remained excellent. Unfortunately, however, she showed no signs of waking up. Douglas told the president that this could occur unpredictably. Rocky might open her eyes at any moment, or she could remain in a coma for many, many months.

President Meredith's intense worry was palpable. His shoulders sagged, and deep bags hung beneath his sunken eyes. To those around him, there was no question that his concern was profound. He delivered a brief, televised address about his wife's condition and promised the nation that with everyone's help, he would persevere. When he finished, his eyes were red and his legs weak.

Only Jon noticed that the president's tremor seemed more pronounced than ever. Jon also thought that some of Bob Meredith's difficulty standing was due to a balance problem rather than emotional weakness alone. He was still waiting for the results of the president's spinal tap, which should arrive any day. In the meantime, Bob had asked for something to help with his nerves. Jon wanted to avoid any drugs that might impair memory, like the benzodiazepines. He ultimately prescribed small doses of trazadone to help the president sleep, along with Zyprexa to control anxiety.

On the political front, there was a lot of posturing. The Palestinian authorities, while expressing condolences for the first lady's injury, vehemently denied any complicity in the assassination attempt. The Americans were friends and honest brokers, they claimed. What motive would they have for wanting Mrs. Meredith dead?

The reaction of the American people was equally vehement, although mixed, reflecting a split in approach. Half of the electorate demanded immediate retaliation, although how, and against precisely whom, wasn't clear. The other half favored a dump-the-Arabs approach in which the U.S. removed itself from any involvement with Arabic causes, Middle Eastern oil, and Islamic considerations. In the end, America renewed its centrist approach, favoring the president's former priorities—at least temporarily.

A week after Roxanne was shot, the president's final test results came in. The routine blood tests were of little diagnostic help. Blood chemistries, blood count, and the differential count were generally normal, except for slight elevations of BUN and creatinine. The neuroimaging studies, including the CT scan and MRI, revealed no tumor, but suggested increased T2 signals in the thalamus and the striatum. The "official" EEG report corroborated Jon's initial impression of background slowing, but the examiner's interpretation of the spikes was much more specific. According to the report, the sharp wave complexes were highly suggestive of CJD, or Creutzfeldt-Jakob disease.

When he first got the report, Jon was shaken. CJD was a degenerative neurologic disorder that might account for the president's dementing symptoms. Pathologically, it was characterized by deposition of amyloid material in the brain, eventually causing the brain to develop a spongy appearance. Taken as a whole, the spectrum of diseases like CJD were called transmissible spongiform encephalopathies, infectious cerebral amyloidoses, or prion diseases.

Such diseases were caused by the prion, a protein-containing infectious particle. The most notorious prion disorder was European mad cow disease, in which spongiform encephalopathy was transmitted to humans through contaminated beef. The tragedy of the disease was that it was progressive and invariably fatal. All that could be offered the patient was good nursing care, symptomatic relief, and palliative measures. Jon shook his head. He didn't relish the thought of conveying this sort of news to the president.

But however suggestive the EEG, it wasn't the final word.

Since the most definitive test—examination of actual brain material—was impossible, the spinal tap results would be crucial. The cerebrospinal fluid, or CSF, of patients with diseases like CJD often contained abnormal proteins, like neuron-specific enolase, S-100 glial protein, tau protein, and a significant player called 14-3-3 protein.

It took several weeks for the CSF results to come in. Waiting for them to arrive, Jon was very apprehensive. He didn't want to consider the fact that, on the heels of the first lady's shooting, the president might be diagnosed with a disease that could kill him within a year. Jon was in his office when the CSF reports were hand-delivered. When he looked at the values, he was crestfallen.

Levels of CSF 14-3-3 protein were definitely elevated. The test was not diagnostic of a prion disorder, and could be raised in cases of herpes, metabolic or toxic encephalopathy, metastatic cancer, and hypoxia. But his patient didn't have those other conditions. Given the 14-3-3 level, the EEG, and the president's symptoms, Jon was ninety-five percent certain that Bob Meredith had a prion disorder.

He shook his head as he let the report fall to his desk. This was precisely the sort of news an ailing country didn't need. Jon hadn't the faintest idea how to break the news to the president. Medical schools didn't teach precise ways of delivering bad tidings. Every physician developed his own method of conveying the worst. In Jon's case, when the need arose in terminal HIV or cancer patients, he delivered an upbeat version of the "there's always hope" approach. He thought it might improve the patient's attitude, or work by placebo effect. In any case, it certainly helped *him*.

Jon knew he also had to inform the chief of staff and the vice president. Both were pragmatic men who understood the political ramifications far better than he did. The news would undoubtedly derail the re-election process. A disease like CJD was far more significant than the Alzheimer's Mitch Forbes had postulated. With the president's permission, Jon would certainly talk with the chief of staff—but only once he was certain.

The problem with ninety-five percent certainty was that

there was always a loophole of doubt. Indeed, something about the diagnosis nagged the back of Jon's mind. He couldn't put his finger on it; and until he could, he'd keep his diagnosis to himself.

Equally important were the questions of how and why. Contrary to public belief, few cases of spongiform encephalopathy were contagious. Most were actually sporadic in nature or familial. But there were some notable exceptions, like mad cow disease and some disorders found in the South Pacific.

Could that be a factor? he wondered. The more Jon thought about it, the more he wondered if he already knew the answer.

One Year Earlier
Hanoi

"Air Force One, on heading one-six-zero degrees, descend and maintain flight level one zero zero," said Hanoi control.

"Roger. Air Force One descending to flight level one zero zero, heading one-six-zero," replied the captain.

"Air Force One, contact Hanoi approach control on one-two-one-point-zero."

"Roger. Approach on one-two-one-point-zero. Good day."

Air Force One was thirty miles from Hanoi and descending through the clouds for a landing on runway eleven at No Bai International Airport. President Meredith was a hands-on passenger who often flew up front with the cockpit crew. Nearing the end of their long flight, he and Dr. Townsend went forward as the 747 began its descent. They strapped themselves into jump seats behind the crew.

"What are you feeling, sir?" Jon asked.

"God, it's weird. When I left this godforsaken country, I never thought I'd return. But here we are survivors of a bygone age. And they're actually welcoming us back."

Through the cockpit windows, the coastline was rushing up toward them, and beyond it were the lush green hills of their former enemy. "This place still gives me the creeps. When I look out there," Jon confessed, "all I feel is terror."

"I hear you. But we're both Marines, and Marines get the job done. This time, on our own terms."

The long-delayed trip to Vietnam was an integral part of President Meredith's policy of economic globalization. The visit had two goals, both of which arose after the 1994 lifting of the trade embargo. One was to draw Vietnam out of its self-imposed economic isolation, and the other was to suggest that prosperity in the information age required a measure of political openness and the free flow of information. Ultimately, the president hoped to loosen state control that had choked the local economy and sent foreign investors fleeing.

The apprehensive body language of the men in the jump seats made it clear that the trip was more than a state visit. By facing the demons of their past, they were confronting their fears, putting closure on a chapter in their lives that should have ended a generation ago. As the airport became visible, they shared a feeling of déjà vu, for Air Force One was descending through the same skies that were once thick with B-52s.

"Air Force One, this is the final controller, turn left now to heading one-four-zero. Descend and maintain two-five-zero-zero feet, Intercept ILS/DMR runway eleven. Cleared approach."

"Left turn one-four-zero," said the captain. "Descending to twenty-five hundred feet. Cleared to intercept localizer, cleared for the ILS/DME runway eleven approach."

"Air Force One," said the final controller, "you are established on the localizer, runway eleven. Contact Hanoi tower at Charlie, frequency one-one-eight-point-two. Good day."

Slowly, the huge 747 lined up with the runway. It came in low over rice paddies once pitted with bomb craters but that now bore billboards advertising Korean-made electronics. Soon the jumbo jet landed and taxied to a stop near the hangar. There was a brief welcoming ceremony, and then a motorcade sped the president and his entourage over the Red River into Hanoi.

En route to the president's hotel, there were thousands of onlookers lining the streets. The curious bystanders waved constantly but didn't cheer. It was the largest motorcade the city had ever seen, and children were held aloft to glimpse the most powerful leader in the world. Curiously, the president's limo had Washington, D.C. license plates, with the Vietnamese flag on one front fender, and the Stars and Stripes on the other. It was to be a three-day trip. After the visit to Hanoi, the presidential party would go to Quang Tri Province on day two before heading to Ho Chi Minh City, the former Saigon, on the third and final day. Jon was in a limo several cars behind the president. He didn't notice he was clenching his fists until halfway through the drive.

The scene around him was surreal. Hanoi was a charming city that retained the flavor of France in its architecture and tree-lined boulevards. It was a city of orderly landscaping and a dozen lakes and the ever-present aroma of food prepared by street-corner vendors. People were everywhere, on foot, or on bicycles. Everyone looked young. If anyone besides Jon and the president remembered the war, it had to be a distant memory.

A gala state dinner was held the first night. The next day, while the first lady remained in Hanoi for a well-publicized shopping trip, Jon, elected officials, and the press helicoptered to the area of the abandoned fire support base Ross. The trip was intended to be symbolic of the American desire to keep the war in the past. But once on the ground in the hamlet that arose where the base had been abandoned, the sights and smells of the village carried Meredith back in time.

Flanked by Secret Service agents and Vietnamese security, Jon and the president strolled through the ratted dirt roads grown soft with winter mud. Insects buzzed around their heads, and pot-bellied pigs squealed when driven from their path. Occasional thatch-roof, stilted huts were beside the road, but most structures were the hauntingly familiar hooches. Women in colorful sarongs peered from doorways, and the silent, dark-eyed babies on their backs resembled dolls.

"Smell that?" asked the president, nose to the air. "This country never lacked for smells. Gotta be chicken."

"I'd bet on pork," Jon said. "Might be fish, but we're pretty far from the coast."

"What I remember most is the smells. The smells and the heat." His gaze slowly fixed on the villagers watching him, and as it did, a smile spread across the president's face. "Well, will you look at that. I don't believe it."

"Sir?"

"Last time I saw that guy, he was wearing a camo shirt, a loin cloth, and a bandoleer. At least, I think it's him."

Jon spotted the man Meredith was staring at. The short Vietnamese appeared to be Bob's age, although his withered face was deeply corrugated by the sun. "You recognize him?"

"We called him Joe. Then, we called everyone Joe. I never knew his real name. Dave," the president said to Agent Saunders, "see if that guy knows me. If he does, bring him over."

"Was he ARVN?" Jon asked.

"No, Hmong tribesman. Know anything about them?"

"Just the name."

"The Hmong were good guys. They're mountain people, over near Laos. They served in guerrilla units. A lot of them fought with the Special Forces. I met them on some ops way up into the mountains."

"This Joe, he was a guide?"

"A scout, mainly. He knew the territory, and we needed him on recon. The Hmong cooked for us, guarded us, and carried us when we were wounded. They wrapped up the bodies of guys who got killed. About twenty thousand of them were KIA."

The short, silver-haired man who accompanied Saunders had a smile that broadened with each approaching step. He wore a khaki shirt and trousers and carried a small lacquer box. He bowed when he reached the president.

"Is that you, Joe?" Meredith asked.

"Yes, Captain Bob. It is me."

"Well, I'll be damned. Come on over here!"

As the president stepped forward to bear-hug the smaller man, Saunders deftly pulled away the box, not knowing what it contained. Numerous cameras caught the embrace. Meredith towered over his old ally. At length, he pulled away.

"You haven't changed, Joe. I'd recognize you anywhere. Everybody," he said, addressing those around him, "this is my buddy Joe, an old friend of mine. He sure saved my ass a time or two. So, how're you doing, old friend?"

"Very good, Captain Bob. I know you are president now. I have family in Milwaukee. Someday, I will visit."

"I'm sure we can help you there. What's in the box?"

"You remember the night I cook for you, in the mountains? You tired, you not want to eat, but I cook for you, remember?"

"Oh Jesus. Is this what I think it is?"

"*Danh tor.*"

The president opened the lacquer box, which emitted a pungent aroma. "I remember all right. *Danh tor.*" He showed the contents to Dr. Townsend.

Jon squinted. "Looks like eggs in barbecue sauce."

"Actually, Doc, it's brains. Monkey brains in *nuoc mam* sauce. It probably saved my life in 1970, and I sure as hell am not going to refuse it now."

"Sir, I'm not so sure...."

"Don't worry, I'm just going to taste it. Let's go over to the hooch with the pork, and we'll have a little photo op for the press."

Thinking back, Jon wondered if the president's impulsiveness in Vietnam had been a deadly mistake. He didn't have to taste the gift; he only had to accept it. But Meredith was a very demonstrative man. Was it possible that he'd contracted a prion disorder from eating contaminated monkey brains?

Infected animal brains were a rare but recognized source of human prion infection. Members of certain tribes in New Guinea, for example, contracted a disease called kuru through cannibalism. In the U.S., isolated Appalachian hill-folk developed spongiform encephalopathy from eating infected squirrel brains. Although Jon wasn't aware of it, he thought it possible that the brain tissue of monkeys could also be a vector.

But even if it *were* possible, Jon doubted he could prove it. After the Vietnamese photo op, the Hmong known as Joe melted away, returning to his people. To now send research teams into the mountains searching for infected monkeys would take months, perhaps years. In the meantime, the president was deteriorating. Therefore, although this mode of transmission was theoretically possible, Jon couldn't be certain. He'd have to rely on his judgment. And his most educated guess said President Meredith had a prion disease.

Where it came to the president's life, no physician wanted to guess. But the art and science of medicine didn't always provide cut-and-dried answers. Sometimes, one had to go with one's best impression. For now, at least, an unusual prion disorder was Jon's diagnosis, and he was sticking to it. Yet the whole clinical picture nagged him, like threads hanging loose from a sleeve. He couldn't put his finger on it, but he had a sense of incompleteness, of something lurking, the way a distant memory hovers just out of recollection.

When he would ultimately convey his diagnosis to the president, Jon wanted to have maximum certainty about his professional opinion. Right now, he just didn't have it. He'd promised Bob an answer, but he hadn't been pinned down as to when. He needed a little more time—time to mull everything over, to let things sort themselves out, perhaps to gather more information. Considering Roxanne's illness, the president certainly had enough on his plate that delivering yet more bad news wasn't imperative. When the time was right, Jon thought he'd know it.

He was eager to see Mireille again. The time they'd spent together was a blissful memory that lingered in his subconscious. He wasn't sure where their relationship was headed, but he liked the general direction. Yet for everyone involved with the administration, there was such turmoil following the first lady's shooting that finding quiet time was a near impossibility. Everyone felt the strain, and they were all living on the collective edge. Jon did manage to speak with Mireille every day, however. They both hoped to get together as soon as possible.

As the CNN talk show was winding up, the moderator asked each participant to sum up his viewpoint. The subject that night was U.S. policy in the Middle East. Since the shooting of the first lady, the average American's opinion had changed considerably. The opinions of the guest congressman and senator differed considerably.

"The time has come to rethink our relations with all the

Arab states," said the congressman. "Time and time again, we've tried to be evenhanded in the region, and you can see where it's gotten us."

"So, you would have us withdraw from the region entirely?"

"Well, I certainly wouldn't put American troops in harm's way. We're not appreciated over there as much as we think. I'm not talking about geographic isolationism; I'm talking about retrenching. And maybe we should get tough with these guys instead of kissing their you-know-whats."

"I love it," said the senator sarcastically. "Excuse my French, but back in seventy-three they called it, 'nuke their ass and take their gas.' It didn't make sense then, and it makes less sense now. I agree with the president's strategy of constructive engagement. Now's the time to circle the wagons, not get out of Dodge."

"That's not what most Americans are saying," the congressman said.

"What about that, senator?" asked the moderator. "Since the assassination attempt on the first lady, most polls have shown that Americans want us out of the region by a three-to-one margin."

"That kind of knee-jerk reaction is understandable, but not helpful. The area is critical to us economically, politically, and militarily. Beyond that, hasn't the president suffered enough already? I think we owe it to him to give his policies more time."

"Congressman, you get the last word."

"What a bunch of baloney."

More quickly than anyone dared hope for, Roxanne Meredith's clinical condition stabilized. A week post-op, she showed no signs of infection. Her skin sutures were removed and her head wound was clean. Her ICP catheter was removed. Her vital signs were strong and normal. Yet she simply lay there in an ongoing coma, eyes peacefully closed, her shaved head just starting to grow stubble.

The president continued to visit no less often than every other day and was in nearly continuous phone contact with the unit. The first lady's remarkable physical recovery made unchanging mental status all the more discouraging. She continued to be the nation's most talked about female, but now all discussions about her regarded her coma. Everyone wanted Rocky to just wake up, make some lighthearted, self-effacing quip, and get on with mothering the nation. But it was not to be. President Meredith's impatience with her condition was growing obvious.

"What the hell is going on, Doctor?" the president asked Douglas. "You keep telling me she's getting better, but it doesn't look that way to me."

"With all due respect, sir, what I think I said was..."

"I know damn well what you said!"

"—what I said was," Douglas slowly continued, "that your wife continues to improve. But there are several aspects to improvement. The neurological aspect, the mental part, is the most unpredictable. There's simply no way I can tell when she's going to wake up."

"But there must be some kind of tests!"

Douglas struggled to remain patient. He'd already been down this road with the president. Usually, he was accustomed to throwing his weight around, both literally and figuratively, anywhere from the playing field to the OR. But this was the president he was dealing with. "As I've explained before, sir, we use several laboratory yardsticks. The imaging procedures, the MRIs and ultrasounds, have been helpful. We rely most on serial spiral CT results. These have shown definite improvement. There's no indication of further bleeding and the swelling is way down. There is some destruction of brain tissue in the wound channel, but it's not excessive. But unfortunately, there's no lab test that can predict the level of consciousness. We're just going to have to wait and see."

"Wait? How long is it going to be until I get my wife back?"

"I'm sorry, Mr. President. I just can't say."

Maggie Valley, North Carolina

The small hamlet of Maggie Valley lay ten miles east of the Cherokee village at Oconaluftee. This was bourbon country, and the acrid smells of sour mash and illicit fermentation hung thickly in the air above the meandering backwoods roads. The slow-moving Ford van weaved unpredictably, as its driver was intoxicated. On the van's front seat, between Smith and C.J. Walker, was a half-empty jug of white lightning.

"Ah cain't believe he holds you responsible," Smith growled. "Damn, warn't your finger on the trigger."

"If it had been," said C J., spitting out the rolled-down window, "that'd be one dead woman."

As he drove, smoke curled upward from the cigarette wedged between Smith's yellowed fingers. His gravelly voice was a harsh rasp. "Shit, so what the hell's he want us to do now? This was his bright idea to begin with!"

"He don't want us to do nothin', from what I can tell. 'Cept keep an eye out for anyone who comes too close."

"Just sit on our ass, huh? Fuck that," Smith grunted. "This is God's work, C.J. We've come too damn far to back off now."

"So, what're you sayin'?"

"I'm sayin' that if Sean O'Brien don't want to do God's will, we just might have to do it ourself."

It was now December. Sunset came early, and it was dark well before five. Jon spent long hours at work. The various parts of his professional life were equally demanding, yet he did his best to pursue them all. Perhaps most important, he went to the White House every morning to check on the president's physical and emotional health. Bob Meredith was a strong man of resilient character, and after several expectedly stormy days following his wife's admission to Shock Trauma, he managed to move on with his life. Still, he was grateful his doctor was keeping an eye on him.

Jon's patient load was as full as ever. As the winter neared and the temperature dropped, flu season was well underway. Many of his regular patients had become ill, including several VIPs, but not Senator Friedman. At her two-week follow-up, Jon was pleasantly surprised to see that she was doing well on the L-dopa. She was so impressed, in fact, that her committee was about to hold a round of hearings on fetal stem cell research.

Jon's own research was moving ahead rapidly. Two weeks

ago, when he had an abundant supply of fetal neural stem cells in purified culture, he began testing. Yet before he dared inject human beings—Ellen's son, and particularly Tommie—he needed some idea of efficacy. He was reasonably certain stem cells would be helpful because of foreign reports in the literature where they seemed to be successful. Equally important, it seemed to do no harm. First, however, he had to test his batch on lab animals.

He used albino Wistar-Hannover rats, a general-purpose species. Around Halloween, three weeks before he began testing the stem cells, he'd anesthetized the rats and transected their spinal cords to make them paraplegic. He disliked harming lab animals, but for the purpose he had in mind, it couldn't be helped. Dragging themselves around their cages on forepaws, the rats could feed normally. Once they'd recovered from their wounds, he could proceed.

Anesthetizing the rats once more, he used a hair-fine, thirty-gauge needle to inject their injured spinal cords with varying amounts of neural stem cells. Since this was an inter-species transplant from human to rodent, there would be considerable immune response. Therefore, he also administered anti-rejection drugs. He wasn't looking for a cure. That wasn't feasible between species, and even if it were, complete neural regeneration would take months. He knew he'd be satisfied just to see the nerves start growing again. This would only take several weeks. He should know by Christmas. If it were successful, he'd feel safe moving on with humans. When the injections were finished, all he could do was wait.

CHAPTER 19

For Jon, the weeks preceding Christmas passed with infinite slowness. President Meredith's odd behavior and foibles were partially masked by the medication he took after his wife was shot. Those times he did appear to act peculiarly, his behavior was attributed to ongoing stress and concern. Jon felt pressured to firm up his diagnosis with the lab results, but the reports were endlessly delayed due to their source. No one was willing to sign off on a presidential test without triple-checking the result and having it verified by a supervisor. For those exotic tests that had to be sent cross country, where specimens from the president had never been previously evaluated, the paperwork and duplication was even more pronounced. This was matched by the need for secrecy, which made the already-stressed lab workers nearly schizophrenic. There was little Jon could do to speed up the process.

The already-weeks-old investigation into the first lady's shooting was going nowhere. It was a journalistic field day, and speculation was as boundless as solid clues were absent. A thick blanket of tension covered the country like a smoky pall, and preholiday festivities were subdued.

Jon was under extraordinary pressure, particularly regarding the lab results. Still, he carried himself with great dignity in his frequent visits to the White House. His own workload was monumental. He looked forward to a time when he could lie unencumbered on some distant beach, basking in the sun. Until then, his twin rays of sunshine were his daughter and Mireille.

"Jon," the president said, calling him aside one morning,

"I've always trusted your advice. I want a second opinion."

"On what?"

"On Rocky. I know Dr. Douglas is supposed to be good—"

"He's the best there is, Mr. President. I checked his credentials myself."

"Then..." Meredith sighed and slowly shook his head. "Then why isn't she coming around already? And don't give me any of this 'it takes time' shit!"

Bob Meredith was anything but a stupid man. Jon knew that Douglas had emphasized the gradual nature of the first lady's neurological progress, and he knew that the president understood that, at least logically. But as Jon looked into the president's eyes, he detected just a hint of mania. He realized that the president's impatience was just another aspect of the medical problem that was affecting him.

"All right, Bob, I won't. But I can honestly tell you my opinion won't differ at all from Dr. Douglas'. And my advice would be the same."

"But there must be something else that can be done. For God's sake, it's been weeks already!"

"Mr. President," Jon calmly continued, "the standard medical treatments—"

"To hell with standard!" Meredith fumed. "We're talking about my wife here! Surely there must be something new, different. Experimental, even—isn't there?"

This caught Jon by surprise. "You'd be willing to try something experimental on the first lady?"

"If it meant the difference between her remaining in a coma and returning to the person I know and love, you're damn right I would!"

"Okay, Mr. President," Jon said, a new possibility suddenly occurring to him. "I'll look into it."

The week before Christmas, Jon was finally visited by good news. During his last visit to his lab at the NIH, Jon began his first test of the injected mice. He was using a miniature EMG, an electromyograph, a machine that recorded electrical currents in muscles. Atrophied muscles downstream from damaged nerves traced a characteristically flat, denervated pattern. If, after the stem cell injections, he could record restored electrical activity, he could conclude that the experiment was successful—and human treatments could begin.

In their cages, although the rats still weren't using their hindquarters, they looked particularly robust. Jon carefully immobilized one of the rodents in lab restraints and proceeded to hook up his equipment. When he made his recording, a gratified smile spread over his face. Small but measurable electrical impulses were returning to the legs, indicating neural regeneration. Three out of four rats tested showed the same results. Soon, if his nerves held out, he could start to work on Tommie.

When Jon finished work at six the next day, he left the building for the tiered parking lot. Moments later, he drove out of the lot and wound his way along the campus roads toward the Pike. Ordinarily, he was not the kind of driver who lived in his rearview mirror, but there was something about the car behind him that caught his eye. He'd seen it before, just a few days ago. The vehicle had unusually bright orange fog lamps.

In the darkness, he couldn't tell the make of the car, or indeed if it *was* a car, rather than a van or SUV. When he accelerated onto the main highway, the orange lights followed him. Sometimes they were several car lengths away, and they would fall back a hundred yards or so. But every time Jon turned, the fog lamps stayed with him. There was no question he was being followed.

Why would someone follow him? In the grand scheme of things, he wasn't all that important. The vehicle always stayed a prudent distance behind, seemingly uninterested in following him or cutting him off. Did it just want to see where he was going? That didn't seem very logical, for his life was an open book. He didn't go many places other than to and from work and the White House. Maybe the driver just wanted to scare him.

If that was the case, it was working. Jon wasn't as scared for himself as he was for Tommie. As a handicapped person, his daughter was already so vulnerable that she didn't need any more threats to her health or welfare. But the more he thought about it, the more he doubted Tommie was the focal point. It made little sense to follow him if his daughter was some sort of target.

Throughout the drive home, the vehicle remained behind him. Rather than pull into his driveway, Jon slowed and stopped at its entrance. His pursuer likewise pulled to the curb a hundred feet behind. Jon waited to see what would happen, but nothing did. No ski-masked stranger came up to his window or even got out of the vehicle. Jon waited several minutes. As he did, his pulse rate and his annoyance gradually increased. Finally, he got out of his car and stormed toward the other car in a fury.

When its driver saw him coming, the vehicle made a quick U-turn and drove in the other direction. Jon saw that it wasn't a car, but an SUV like a Chevy Tahoe, or maybe a Ford Expedition. The vehicle's squealing tires kicked grit in his face. Although he couldn't make out the license plates, Jon noted that there were two men inside. Their faces were indistinct, and he couldn't make out either of them.

He felt a growing rage. How dare these men try to intimidate him like that! Yet he *did* feel threatened, and more than a little worried. He had no idea what they wanted, and that ignorance scared the hell out of him. Even if he *had* caught up with them, what would he have done?

Although he acted decisively in his line of work, the idea of physical confrontation frightened Jon. Ever since Vietnam, the idea of going *mano a mano* with another man was profoundly intimidating. It was more a mental than a physical thing. Before going overseas, he'd gotten into his share of fights, and he'd emerged victorious more often than not. Yet his experience in Quang Nam Province crippled him emotionally. Where it came to fighting, he now wore a coward's mantle he didn't think he'd ever shake loose.

The phone rang as soon as Jon entered his house. It was Mitchell Forbes.

"Sorry to disturb you, Jon. You have a few minutes?"

His first thought was of Bob Meredith. "Did something happen to the president?"

"No, he's fine. But he is whom I'm calling about. I heard that all his test results are in. Can you share them with me?"

"I'd like to, Mitch, but I promised Bob I'd let him know first."

"And did you?"

"No," Jon said, "not yet. There's no hurry because—"

"No hurry? Excuse me, but this is a re-election campaign!"

"What I'm saying, Mitch, is that everything's pointing in a certain direction, but some of the data's a little confusing. I want to sit on it a while and mull it over."

"Sit on it? Did I hear you right? We're talking about the president of the United States here!"

"My hearing's fine, Mitch. You don't have to shout."

"But he does have a medical problem, did I hear that right?"

"Let's just say that all the data seems to indicate something in particular, but I'm not a hundred percent sure. Until I am, the president's got other things on his mind."

There was an uncomfortable pause. "For God's sake, man, while you're thinking it over, don't forget that the president's got a primary coming up next month, not to mention a country to run! It's very considerate not to bother him, but we're not talking about any ordinary patient, are we? So, I'd appreciate it, and I think the country would, too, if you got off your ass and told the man what he needs to know!"

"Is that all, Mitch?"

Forbes abruptly hung up. After staring at the receiver a moment, Jon replaced it in the cradle. Forbes was known for his single-minded intensity, and he was now nothing if not intense. But lately the man had a coarse veneer or roughness. The curtness with which Forbes addressed Jon was downright rude. Surely the man had a job to do, but Jon was beginning to wonder if there was more motive to the chief of staff's actions than was initially apparent.

Jon always worried that things that impacted him might somehow harm his daughter. After calling Victoria's house to verify that Tommie was okay, he wasn't sure what to do next. He supposed he could call the Bethesda police and tell them he thought he'd been followed, but he doubted they'd be interested, much less do anything. Instead, he decided to talk to

Dave Saunders. He knew the agent was quite busy in the wake of the first lady's shooting, but Jon was desperate. He entered his callback number on Dave's beeper and awaited a return call. Saunders called back twenty minutes later.

"What's up, Jon?"

"I hate calling you, Dave, but I really need some advice."

"Name it."

Jon related the earlier incident and his suspicion that the same car had tailed him once before. He didn't know what, if anything, to do. He just knew he was worried.

"How should I handle this?"

"First of all, definitely call the cops. There's not much they can do, but at least your complaint will go on record."

"Do you think I should be concerned?"

"Oh yeah," Dave said. "Two guys following you to your house? Doesn't sound like UPS to me. But it also doesn't sound like they're out to rob you. Most burglars make an effort not to be seen."

"What *does* it look like?"

"When people don't mind being spotted, it's like Western Union. They're trying to send you a message. I'd say they're out to frighten you."

"They've done a great job, because they frightened the hell out of me. What I don't understand is why. I haven't messed up with the president, I'm not sleeping with anyone's wife, and none of my patients has died recently."

"Mireille's not married, huh?"

"Don't go there, Dave. I'm serious."

"Sorry. The fact is, I don't know why someone wants to frighten you. There are all kinds of possibilities. When people are trying to scare someone, they usually want him to change his behavior. To do something, or to stop doing something. Does that ring any bells?"

"Not a thing."

"Then for the meantime, just be very careful. Do you have a gun?"

"No," Jon said. "Should I?"

"Can't hurt. How late are you going to be up tonight?"

A little after ten p.m., Dave showed up with a shotgun he'd brought from home. The twelve-gauge Mitchell Arms pump was a high-tech, all-business, defensive shotgun. The all-black firearm had a synthetic stock, an eighteen-and-a-half-inch barrel, and a six-round extended magazine. In a serious social encounter, it would be a manstopper. Dave reviewed shotgun functioning with Jon, who remembered the basics from his time in the Marines.

"You're all set," Dave said. "You've got six rounds of double-ought buckshot. Just rack the slide and shoot. You don't have a problem with that, do you?"

The icy fingers of the past clawed at whatever was left of Jon's courage. He silently shook his head.

"Good. Carry it with you. Put it in your car when you leave for work and bring it in at night. When this is all over, you can buy one for yourself."

"Okay. I appreciate it, Dave."

"Any time. Now, as far as repayment goes, are you up for a little fishing this weekend? Maybe you can drag Tommie and Mireille along."

Saturday was overcast but reasonably mild, with temperatures in the mid-forties. They planned to fly fish the Chesapeake. Temperatures were usually slightly colder on the bay, where a strong wind could defeat the most determined fisherman. But the marine forecast was favorable, with winds nearly calm.

Saltwater fly fishing differed from its freshwater counterpart in tackle more than technique. Rods, reels, and lines were stronger and heavier. The flies were more robust. As a lifelong fly fisherman, Saunders had the best equipment, and he'd brought enough for everyone. He'd easily invested ten thousand dollars in the sport. Today he'd brought along eight- and nine-weight G. Loomis and St. Croix rods with which to try their luck.

At that time of year, rental boats were plentiful in their starting point of Annapolis. Just south of town were numerous western-shore tributaries where submerged aquatic vegetation provided good cover for pickerel and yellow perch. But these were backup fish. Their main quarry was striped bass, which the locals called rockfish.

November and December were transition times for Chesapeake Bay anglers and the fish they sought. Baitfish and predators moved into the bay from river mouths, and many fish left the Chesapeake entirely for warmer waters to the south. As water temperatures dropped even lower, warm water shore discharges appealed to the fish that stayed home. A good deal of the stripers and bluefish followed the bunker as far south as the Outer Banks. But plenty remained.

Striped bass were a saltwater angler's prize because of their size and fight. Keepers ran twenty-eight inches and over, and trophy fish weighed over forty pounds.

But the younger fish, called snappers, were a pleasure to catch and release. There were often so many of the aggressive young fish that it could be hard to get a fly down to the trophies that lurked deeper. The fly fisherman had to know his craft.

Everyone dressed warmly, in layers. It was glove-and-parka weather, and Jon made sure Tommie had a ski hat, a heavy scarf, and a thick woolen blanket that could wrap around her wheelchair. When everyone was ready, Dave cast off from the dock. "All set?" he asked.

"Yes, sir, Cap'n Dave," Jon replied. "Open 'er up."

In the back of the boat, Mireille and Tommie were already too engrossed in chitchat to say anything. Jon took the wheel while Dave prepared the rigs. Traffic on the bay was light, which was better for fishing. The water was like glass. They headed for a spot fifteen minutes south of town, where Dave had previously had success.

"Roxanne's shooting must be a nightmare for you guys," Jon said. "They must be busting your butts. I'm surprised you got some time off."

"The first lady's detail is getting hammered. They're still going twenty-four seven. They gave my guys a little more breathing room, but this is still my first day off since Mrs. Meredith got shot. Believe me, there are a lot of agents with their tails between their legs."

"What's the latest? I'm sure you're following the local news, which says there aren't any good leads."

Dave looked at his friend askance. "Officially, as you know, I can't tell you a thing. Unofficially, we haven't got a clue. I mean, we know who did it, but we don't know why."

"Do you think it was an Oswald, that he was working alone?"

"That would make it easy, wouldn't it? But the truth is, what the assassin accomplished was too damn complicated for one person. Not to mention that whoever killed brother Mahmoud was in on it. For one thing, you'd have to know the first lady's schedule. Then there's the shooter's location, lines of fire, and the weapon. That's all big-time planning. Besides the shooter, there had to be at least one additional person, probably more."

"You're talking an organized plot."

"Looks that way. Now, were these two guys part of a larger plot to kill the wife of the president of the United States? According to the Mossad, they're just a couple of well-trained Palestinian crazies. Maybe there *is* no Islamic conspiracy. Maybe some rich old redneck hired these boys to pop her."

"But what about the California gun dealer?"

"Don't worry, nobody forgot about him. He's still missing, just like his cousin."

"What cousin?"

Dave looked at him. "Forgot to tell you that part, huh? His cousin is our old friend Marcel Al-Hakeem."

After a moment, Jon recalled the name. "The last-minute chef who disappeared after the White House state dinner?"

"None other. It turns out that the chef was raised in Algeria, but he was born near Hebron."

Jon whistled softly. "Do you think the chef was up to something then? Like, did the food have something to do with the president choking?"

"We thought of that, but the food had been discarded. We're looking at a thousand possibilities. The point is, we certainly don't have the answers. But we're working under the assumption that this *is* a well-organized plot, not some harebrained last-minute scheme. Finding out precisely what may take some time."

Soon, just north of Bay Ridge, Dave had Jon kill the engine. As they drifted along with the tide, the current carried the boat lazily offshore. Saunders was an avid fly tier, and he'd brought along an assortment of his own colorful epoxy-head flies. Their straight, three-inch hairs streamed backward and outward, a bristly funnel shape. Dave wanted them to try the white and chartreuse colors first.

After a few last-minute tips, they started fishing, casting at precise spots, trying to tease larger stripers up from the depths. Action was slow for the first half-hour. But when the boat came abreast of a rocky outcropping, the fish lurking in the boulders went for their bait. Fly color didn't matter, for the stripers were insatiable. Over the next hour, the foursome caught three dozen stripers. Most were shorts and had to be thrown back, but they landed two good-size keepers that could feed them for days.

They took a break at midmorning. Tommie was tired, and they decided not to stay out much longer. It had already been a good day's fishing and there was little reason to linger. Before they left, they made a picnic feast of another of Mireille's culinary creations.

"By the way," Dave said to Jon, "I suppose you would've told me if that SUV was still following you?"

"I haven't seen them, but it hasn't been that long. Maybe it was just a prank."

"I doubt it. Did you call the police?"

"Not yet, but I will."

"Hey, it's your life. I just don't want to say I told you so in front of your casket."

Canton, North Carolina

In the Ford van, the three of them drove east on U.S. Route 40, just outside of Canton, on the way to Asheville. They left the bingo halls and tepees and tomahawks of Cherokee town far behind. O'Brien had the other two men pick him up en route to a well-known eatery on Asheville's outskirts, some twenty miles away. They were in the valley now, with the striking ridges of the Great Smoky Mountains to the north and behind them.

"Turn right on the dirt road up ahead," said Sean.

Smith's eyebrows raised. "Ain't gonna get to Asheville this way."

"There's something I've got to show you."

"Your call, Sean," said C.J. "You're the man with the plan."

He was also the man with the money. Just two days before, O'Brien had wired them each five thousand dollars. It was an advance, he said, against further plans. They would discuss what he had in mind over ribs in Asheville.

The rutted, beat-up dirt road was bordered by a barbed-wire fence, beyond which an overgrown field of clover and fescue glistened with dew. The new road was rough. As they put distance between themselves and the highway, the only sounds were the groans and creaks of the vehicle's shocks and springs. The area had the look of abandoned farmland. Eventually they came to a large clearing in a grove of shady oaks. A new white rental car was at the far end of the clearing.

"What the hell?" said Smith, eyeing the other vehicle as he crawled to a stop.

"Drive on up to it," Sean said. "I had it dropped off."

C.J. looked around. "Ain't nobody else in sight."

"Good thing for that," said O'Brien. "What I've got in the trunk is for your eyes only."

The way he said it, with a slightly upward inflection, was too much for Walker's diminished mentality. He felt as if he'd been given permission to open his Christmas gifts early. Brimming with enthusiasm, he jumped from the van and ambled over to the parked sedan.

"Damn, Sean, whatcha got in there?" he asked excitedly.

O'Brien waited until Smith reached them and then flipped the trunk keys to Walker. "Open her up, C.J."

Growing curious, Smith edged closer to the rear bumper. C.J. inserted the key and had just popped the lock when Sean pulled the snub-nose revolver from under his windbreaker. Walker's last conscious recognition was that, except for a can of gas, the trunk was empty. But then his world went dark as a .38 special hollow point exploded inside his skull.

At the moment of the gunshot, Smith knew. As they'd

pulled off the main highway, a part of him was suspicious about the change in route. Although he'd followed orders, he never completely trusted O'Brien. But the money and the abundance of corn whiskey had dulled his edge. Now, as the barrel of the revolver swung his way, he conceded defeat.

"All, shit," he managed.

The two bullets slammed into his chest, toppling him over. Sean calmly walked over and fired a finishing shot into Smith's head. Then he slid the gun back into his waistband. He removed the keys from Smith's trouser pocket and returned to the van. Driving it over to the rental car, he opened the van's rear doors. With some difficulty, he managed to get both corpses onto the cargo bay's floor.

The rental car's trunk was still open. Careful to avoid spills, O'Brien removed the five-gallon gas can and carried it to the van. He liberally doused both men with gas, saving the remainder to saturate the front seat. Finally, he took a small cassette tape from his breast pocket and tossed it into the rear of the van. It was the same tape with which he'd secretly recorded Smith and Walker's conversation in the vehicle not many days before, a conversation that had sealed their fate. Then he struck the match.

The van went up with a violent whoosh. O'Brien felt its mounting heat on the back of his neck as he returned to the rental van. A few underlings remained, he thought, but that was essentially the end of the Southern Cross. Sean smiled to himself.

"God's fuckin' will be done."

It was midafternoon when Jon returned home after dropping off Tommie and Mireille. He planned to see Mireille again later that night. Despite the festive morning, he was chilled from the day on the water, and he felt grimy. Once he was indoors, the first order of business was to take a hot shower.

His bedroom had a bath-shower combination enclosed within a glass stall. Jon stripped, put his outdoor clothes in the hamper, slid the shower doors closed, and turned the shower to hot. Soon the water was scalding. He stepped inside and luxuriated in the spray, letting the soothing heat seep into his muscles.

In the steaming jets, Jon closed his eyes and let the heat work its magic. His internal chill slowly dissipated. The knots in his muscles softened and relaxed. He took full, deep breaths through his nostrils, filling his lungs with the warm, humid fog. And then he smelled it.

Jon's eyes jerked open in panic. He instinctively held his breath, for he knew that smell. He'd read about it hundreds of times, and he'd actually gotten a whiff of it decades before in Vietnam, when there was an accident fumigating surgical instruments. It was the odor of bitter almonds. It was the smell of cyanide.

As he twisted off the water, his mind was racing a thousand miles an hour. The odor was so distinctive that there was no question what it was. He understood that for some unfathomable reason, his bathroom was filling with hydrocyanic acid gas. Although he couldn't tell how much he'd inhaled, he *did* know that the gas was so lethal that unconsciousness would occur within thirty seconds and death within minutes.

In a fraction of a second, his racing thoughts fixed on the men who'd been following him. There was no possibility of an accident. Someone had booby-trapped his bathroom to release cyanide gas when he was in the shower. Following him was one thing; trying to kill him was something else entirely. But right now, he couldn't afford the luxury of thinking it through. Time was critical, and he couldn't hold his breath forever.

As he stood there wet and dripping and wide-eyed with fear, he was rocked by a wave of nausea. All of a sudden, his head started to pound, and his heart boomed in his chest. His logical mind realized that however little he'd inhaled, it was too much. He knew he had to do something—and he'd better do it fast, before he lost consciousness.

He threw open the sliding glass doors and leapt onto the tiled floor. The footing was treacherous, and he nearly lost his balance. Out of the corner of his eye, Jon noticed whitish fumes escaping from the medicine cabinet. His face was stroked by the first faint touch of vertigo. Steadying himself, he flicked on the bathroom exhaust fan and raced from the bathroom.

His face felt hot and flushed. As Jon sprinted nakedly toward the spare bedroom, his memory frantically regurgitated medical information. He recalled that the only approved antidote was the three-step Eli Lilly kit, not the sort of thing one ordinarily kept at home. But he did have a substitute that might work nearly as well. At least he hoped it would, if it were still there in the nightstand drawer. His life depended on it.

His increasingly unsteady feet left wet prints on the hardwood floor. Tiny dots twinkled across his retina like Christmas lights. He knew it was a symptom of oxygen deprivation, asphyxiation, or both. Now well away from his bathroom, he inhaled deeply, but the feeling wouldn't go away.

The guestroom seemed to grow darker. It was unconsciousness descending like a shroud. Jon stood by the bed and pulled open the nightstand drawer. His balance left him. The entire drawer fell to the floor with a clatter, its contents spilling across the rug.

Jon's legs grew wobbly, and he fell to his knees. Through increasingly tunneled vision, he spotted the amber vial and twisted off its cap. He knew only seconds remained.

The plastic cover finally came off in his leaden fingers, and he inverted the bottle. The tiny glass pearls spilled from the container like diamonds.

Despite the growing darkness, Jon somehow managed to pick one up between thumb and forefinger. Yet crushing the small glass popper seemed impossible. It suddenly occurred to him that he was about to die, and he thought of Tommie. With every last bit of strength, Jon squeezed the tiny sphere. It crushed with a snapping noise, and he held it to his nose.

He could no longer support his own weight. Collapsing onto his side, he took one last, deep breath. A veil of blackness swept over him, along with a sense of falling. But then, incredibly, the room began to brighten, and he inhaled again. All at once, his senses returned.

He was extremely fortunate that amyl nitrite worked very rapidly. Within seconds he could see clearly again, and he rolled to an upright position. He picked up another glass pearl.

His heart was still pounding, and he was shaking all over. He popped the sphere and inhaled its contents. He'd placed it in the nightstand two years ago, when his father had stayed with him shortly before the old man died.

Among its therapeutic uses—not including use during recreational sex as an inhalant rush—amyl nitrite was employed medically to reduce the pain of angina attacks. This was Jon's goal in treating his father, who found it more effective than nitroglycerine. The bottle had remained in the drawer after his father returned home. Mainly due to what it represented, Jon never removed it after his father's death.

As he sat there breathing deeply, nausea again overwhelmed him. Jon began to retch uncontrollably. Although his stomach was empty, green bilious contents spilled from him in waves, soiling the rug. Shivering, he stared numbly at the rancid stains, trying to think clearly.

He knew he'd been extremely lucky. This had been intentional, and someone wanted him dead. For the life of him, Jon couldn't figure out why. He thought it might somehow be related to his relationships with Victoria or Mireille, but he didn't see the connection. Then there were the incontrovertible facts of the first lady's assassination and Jon's service to the president. But what did they have to do with him? Could it be related to a disgruntled patient? He just didn't know.

Shaking with cold and anxiety, he got unsteadily to his feet. His knees were trembling. He shuffled to the hall linen closet and removed a beach towel, wrapping himself in it. Once he was dry, Jon went to the guestroom and wiped up the mess with the towel. He swept the unused pearls into the bottle and returned it to the drawer.

Going into the guest closet, he pondered the cyanide as he put on a pair of gray sweatpants and a sweatshirt. He reckoned the cyanide fumes were generated the same way they were in traditional gas chambers, when solid sodium or potassium cyanide was dissolved in hydrochloric acid. The rapid chemical reaction required a minute or less, depending on the quantity of solute. It was quick, easy, and lethal. By now, all the gas in his medicine cabinet should have long since been produced.

Before he went back there, an important question was whether or not the bathroom exhaust fan had completely vented all the toxic vapors. The fan directed room contents outdoors, where it would be safely dissipated. Jon got a new towel and pressed it to his face and nose. Ever so slowly, he tiptoed to his bedroom, cautiously peering into the master bathroom. The medicine cabinet came into view. The fumes and vapors were gone, but that didn't mean that lethal traces of cyanide had vanished. He'd have to give it a little more time.

When it came to attempted murder, Jon knew he was in way over his head. He needed assistance the way others needed medical help. He picked up the phone and called the Bethesda police. Then he called Dave Saunders.

The Secret Service agent didn't arrive until the local cops were nearly finished. Jon had also called Tommie and Mireille to make sure they were okay. Mireille insisted on coming over. They were both sipping scotch when Dave finished chatting with the police. When he walked into the living room, Jon handed him a drink.

"You're quite the popular guy," Dave said, shaking his head. "First, you've got them following you, and then they try to gas you. Can't take you anywhere."

"I don't think the cops believed me."

"Maybe not at first, but that contraption in the medicine cabinet was pretty convincing. Did the detective tell you?"

"He mentioned seeing one before."

"And I believe him," Dave said. "He was a district homicide detective before coming out here. That thing like a teapot is actually an old Soviet-style steam generator. The one he saw was used to kill a defecting diplomat."

"Great. Now the Russians want me dead. I wonder what I did to piss them off."

"Probably nothing. First of all, as notorious as you think you might be, you're just not that important. Second, our Russian friends don't do that anymore. Any well-connected hoodlum can get his hands on one of those things."

"I am wondering," Mireille said. "The other recent attempted murder we all know about was Mrs. Meredith. Could this be related to her shooting?"

"Funny you should ask, because everyone at work is wondering the same thing. Obviously, I haven't told them about this yet, but I did mention the guys in the SUV. They want to check out any possible connections to the first lady. After this, I don't think there's any holding them back."

"Isn't it a little far out," Jon said, "to think this is related to Roxanne?"

"Hey, anything's possible. But you have to remember the way guys like me think. To us, everything's a conspiracy. That's the way we're trained. And you know what, sometimes it is, okay?"

"All you're saying is you're making no progress on her murder attempt, which is what you told me before."

"That's the God-awful truth. FBI's in the same boat we are."

"So, what's all this crap on TV about progress in the investigation?"

"Crap is the operative word. But you, well...you're a connection nobody seriously considered before."

Mireille put her hand on Jon's arm. "While they are considering it, what about Jon? After today, I don't think he's safe."

"He's not. But short of taking him into protective custody, there's only so much that can be done. You've still got that item I gave you?" he asked Jon.

"I've got it."

"Beginning tonight, the police are starting extra patrols," Dave continued. "I'm going to phone this in, and I'm pretty certain the Agency will contact the FBI about surveillance. The fibbies are going to want to talk to you. How do you feel about that?"

Jon thought about it. "Like a kick-me dog."

"A what?" asked Mireille.

"I used to go to the Caribbean a lot," Jon explained. "On almost every island I visited, there were packs of these little dogs. They were strays, pretty pathetic. A lot of them had sores, and you could almost always see their ribs. They were all different colors, but I remember tan the most. They were a nuisance to the locals. Their only function in life was to get kicked. But to me, well, my heart went out to those poor dogs. They used to walk up to me with these soulful eyes, and all they seemed to want was a little help. That's how I feel now—like a kick-me dog who could use a hand."

Dave smiled. "That's what I'm here for, my friend. All you've gotta do is ask."

"Me too," said Mireille. "In fact, I'm not leaving."

"That's my goodnight signal. Call me tomorrow morning," said Dave, heading for the door.

After the agent left, Jon looked at Mireille. He saw the look of worry in her eyes, an expression that matched his own fear. He'd become involved in something beyond his control, and he felt utterly helpless.

Andover, New Hampshire

In an unlit bedroom of the chic bed and breakfast, an old black-and-white movie played on TV. It was one a.m. The volume was turned down low, and the flickering images sparred with the darkness. A disjointed choreography of ever-changing shadows danced across the papered walls. The couple in bed wasn't watching the movie. They were too absorbed in one another.

America's Christmas holiday had been subdued due to the emotional pall cast by the first lady's illness. Roxanne's condition remained the same—physically strong, but neurologically going nowhere. Nevertheless, the president proved a stalwart. While he was constantly concerned about his wife, he nonetheless went on with the country's business. By the time of the week between Christmas and New Year's, less than a month remained until the Iowa caucuses. Although the president was unopposed for his party's nomination, he still made a brief Iowa appearance during the vacation week, staying overnight at the Des Moines Marriott.

Others of various political persuasions, however remotely involved in the political process, were already in New Hampshire, preparing for the nation's initial primary election the first week in February. Most stayed in the Concord area, but some chose the historic inns in towns like Andover. The state's hostelries thrived on the quadrennial increase in business. The politics went hand in glove with revelry that lasted well into the night. In the bed and breakfast, however, the couple chose to celebrate with one another.

The woman was not particularly old, but nor was she young. Yet owing to regular workouts, she still had a young woman's figure, grown softer and less angular over the years. She lay naked beside the man who had just made love to her. Her skin was damp with perspiration, and in the chiaroscuro lighting, the sweat twinkled like rosettes of pearl.

Time had not quite been so kind to the man's body. His true fitness was the internal variety, wrapped around a core of steely resolve. But that didn't stop him from admiring his lover's shapeliness. Lying beside her, he explored her skin with his finger, gently sliding it across her flesh as if tracing a map. His finger trailed up her abdomen toward her sternum.

He adored her breasts. Her full bosom had known childbirth but had not succumbed to childbearing. His finger slowly circled her areola. The recently softened nipple, stimulated once more, responded to his touch. He gave it the gentlest kiss.

"We're animals," the woman sighed.

"I hope that's not regret."

"Not at all. I've never been more satisfied in my life. I just don't know how long we can keep this up."

"Don't. We've already been through that. Let's just enjoy one another as long as we can."

"You're right," she said. "You're absolutely right. You know what's so funny? I've never been much of a risk-taker. But this— us, the other things we're doing, my God. A year ago, I never would've…"

"I know," he interrupted, shushing her with a finger to her lips. "That's the way I feel. But everything's going so smoothly, why rock the boat?"

Directly above the bed, a miniature wireless video camera was hidden inside a ceiling-mounted smoke detector. The couple's renewed embrace was dutifully recorded electronically, along with their entire assignation.

CHAPTER 20

The most perplexing thing about fetal neural stem cells was that the concepts behind them were about as easy to understand as the Big Bang. For centuries, prevailing medical opinion held that mature neural tissue was a terminal end organ, incapable of regrowth. Once destroyed, it was incapable of functional viability. Boxers became punch drunk because of a progressive reduction in cerebral tissue. A severed nerve disabled the muscle dependent on it because the nerve could not regrow. Or so the thinking went. Only recently had it been discovered that under some circumstances, certain neural tissues might be capable of limited regeneration.

If that discovery were not startling enough, there came the wonder of fetal stem cells. Their capabilities seemed nothing short of miraculous. The idea that they might be able to restore function to parts of the body deprived of innervation was almost inconceivable. To take someone destined to a handicapped existence and return them to a semblance of normality was the very essence of healing.

For Tommie, that time had now arrived. For her father, performing a stem cell transplant was at the foundation of everything for which he'd become a doctor. Helping the sick and suffering was medicine at its noblest. Yes, what he planned was experimental; and the knowledge that all experimentation carried some risk was a concern to him. It helped that he was nowhere near the first to attempt such a thing.

Researchers much more courageous than he had made the first efforts years ago. The most famous work, and also the most notorious, had been performed in Mexico, where physicians injected dopamine-rich fetal adrenal tissue into the brains of patients with Parkinson's disease. Unfortunately, after much initial hoopla, the results were not quite as wondrous as had been expected.

Nonetheless, the methodology and performance details had been worked out. Although there were expected variations in technique, the procedure most commonly employed called for direct injection of the fetal cells into the target area. Experimenters differed on the cellular amounts transplanted and the mechanics of injection. But having devoured every written report he could find, Jon became comfortable with how to proceed.

There was also the very real issue of being doctor to one's relative, particularly when it was a child. Those who disapproved pointed out that managing a sick child was an emotionally charged situation that could overwhelm a caring parent and thwart the objectivity of the most skillful physician. Because of this, medical ethicists frowned on situations where parent and doctor were one and the same. And yet, its proponents argued it was only the parent/physician who truly had the child's best interests at heart. What ended the philosophical discussion for Jon was his knowledge that what he was doing was illegal. In Tommie's case, not only could father and doctor be the same, they *had* to be the same.

Of course, nothing could happen without Tommie's knowledge and consent. The seed for Jon's efforts was actually planted a year and a half ago, when the usually upbeat Tommie was lamenting things she'd never be able to do. As the months went by, Jon drew her out on this. Realistic though she was about her disability, Tommie regretted the unfairness of never being able to ski, or the finality of not being able to dance. It was then that her father gently broached the subject of what she was willing to do about it.

Over the ensuing months, Jon explored the therapeutic options with his daughter. When he discussed a fetal stem cell transplant, he was careful not to sugarcoat the fact that it was an as-yet-unapproved, experimental procedure. But Tommie was a child, and he was aware that she was relying on him. However bright she might be, and however much he might want her to be a full participant in the decision, she was still a ten year-old girl who depended on her father.

Primum non nocere, went the medical dictum: above all, do no harm. This was always Jon's primary consideration. He couldn't deal with the idea of taking a bad situation and making it worse. But the beauty of the stem cell transplant was that it carried little risk. The injection might provoke a mild host immune response, but little more. It might not work, he reasoned, but it shouldn't cause any harm. In the end, that knowledge carried the day.

Yet although the cells themselves were harmless, the injection needle could cause trauma. Where it came to the spinal cord, a slip of even a few millimeters could lacerate delicate nerve tissue. Therefore, careful technique would be critical.

It went without saying that this had to be a father-daughter secret not intended for sharing with anyone, particularly Victoria. Jon wound up saying it anyway. If his ex-wife ever got wind of what was about to occur, the results would be catastrophic. She'd go right to her lawyer. Once attorneys became involved, Jon would never see Tommie again.

The time to proceed was now. It was a holiday week, and hospital staffing would be light. Victoria was out of town for several days visiting her parents, so no suspicions would be raised when Tommie stayed with her father. Most important, the purified cell culture was ready to go. Jon extracted an ample amount of fetal neural stem cells and placed them in an isotonic buffer for injection.

In the various published reports, there was disagreement on how many cells to inject. Jon therefore relied on his own calculations and decided on a concentration of a billion cells per cc. This time—and he hoped it would be the only time required—he'd inject no more than one cc.

They were going to perform the transplant that morning. It seemed rather silly calling a simple injection a transplant, but that was its technical term. Jon needed a trustworthy assistant. Earlier, when he'd tactfully sounded out Mireille, she was eager to help. She'd taken the morning off to assist.

"Is it going to hurt, Daddy?" Tommie asked after getting dressed in the guest bedroom.

"Maybe the tiniest bit, princess. All you're going to feel is a little pinprick from a baby needle. After that, all you'll feel are my big thumbs."

"I'm really starving."

"Honey, as soon as we get back, Mireille's going to make something special. Right now, just hang in there."

When they were ready, Jon peered out the front window's drawn blinds. He was still shaken by the attempt on his life. The police lab had confirmed traces of undissolved sodium cyanide in the bizarre generator, and ever since, police patrols were very much in evidence. The FBI notified him they wanted to interview him soon. Outdoors, there was no one in sight. Jon nodded to Mireille and opened the front door.

Jon followed closely behind Mireille, who pushed Tommie in the wheelchair. Jon was wearing a long, lined raincoat. Neither Tommie nor Mireille was aware of the shotgun that hung under his armpit, attached to a strap. Outside, Jon quickly looked right and left and saw nothing suspicious. After the women were in the car, he got in the driver's seat and set off. During the drive, his eyes had a cat burglar's nervousness, flitting between the side and rearview mirrors. He didn't think he was being followed.

He'd decided to perform the transplant in his office at the medical center. In truth, the intra-spinal injection could have been done almost anywhere. Still, he was treading in poorly charted territory. In the event of an unforeseen emergency, the proximity of a hospital was reassuring. No matter how careful the operator might be, complications like a traumatic injection and allergic reactions were an inescapable part of medical life.

He'd already taken the purified neural stem cell suspension from the NIH and placed it in his office. Living tissue didn't keep well and had to be used within one to two days of harvest. Jon stored it overnight in an incubator, because lower-than-body temperatures would kill the cells. Once they reached the medical center, he dropped the women off in front and parked in the garage.

Few patients had elective appointments that week, and there were relatively few staff. Jon gave warm but abbreviated greetings to those he met and wheeled Tommie to the office. To ensure privacy, he'd decided to do the procedure in his consultation room. After they took off their coats, Jon spoke to the women.

"Let me go over what I'll do once again," he began. "It's very simple."

"You sound like you're in a hurry, Daddy."

"Do I? I certainly don't mean to be. Everything's going to happen slow and easy. Tommie, honey, you're going to sit right in this chair." He wheeled over a cushioned stool. After adjusting its height, he and Mireille helped Tommie onto it.

"How can I help?" Mireille asked.

"When I'm ready to go, you stand in front of her and hold her shoulders. All she needs is a little support. Then I'll do the injection, and after that, we're outa here, okay?" Tommie and Mireille nodded. Tommie's chin was quivering. For all her good-natured strength, she was still a frightened little girl. Jon bent over and hugged her.

"I know you're scared, baby. But it's going to be all right, you'll see."

"It's going to hurt, isn't it?"

"First, I'm going to numb up the skin. The needle won't hurt, except for a little pinch. The injection might sting a little, but it'll be over so fast, you won't even notice it. I'll be finished before you can say Rumpelstiltskin."

These were the words he'd used when he'd given her injections as a younger child. It was a deliberate ploy, but it usually worked.

"You don't have to say that, Daddy. I'm not a baby anymore."

"Don't I know it. You're a tough, butt-kickin' *señorita*. Which is why I know you'll be okay with this." He kissed her cheek. "So, you ready?"

She nodded bravely and managed a smile. Jon wished he were as courageous as she. Tommie had the kind of inner strength he'd never known. The fact was, he was a desperate father about to perform a desperate act. His confident words were all bluster; and if Tommie realized how uncertain he really was, she would never have agreed to the procedure.

"Mireille, if you would, just help her get her shirt up in the back. After that, Tommie, I want you to lean forward a little against Mireille's hands. Remember, I'll keep explaining as we go along. Okay, let's do it."

Tommie took off her NSYNC tee shirt. She wore a tank top underneath, which Mireille helped pull up to the shoulders. Meanwhile, Jon opened a disposable lumbar puncture tray, which had all the required equipment. When he was ready to proceed, he removed the tissue culture vial and aspirated its contents into a sterile plastic syringe.

"First, you're going to feel something cold, princess. Here goes." He swabbed her upper back with antiseptic.

"That's freezing!"

"Told you. Now, I'm going to put something called a sterile drape on your back. It's really just a big piece of paper. How're you doing, honey?"

"I can't wait 'til this is over."

"Won't be long. How about you, Mireille?"

"I have her, Jon."

"All right." With his leg, Jon moved another stool into position behind Tommie. He sat down and readied a syringe with local anesthetic, placing it beside the syringe containing the fetal cells. "Okay, Tommie, here comes that little pinprick." He was using the tiniest needle available, a thirty-gauge. After raising a wheal on the skin, he switched to a twenty-five-gauge needle and numbed the deeper subcutaneous layers. "Does that sting some?"

"A little."

"Now I'm up to the important part. All you should feel is a little pressure. Stay just like that."

Previous studies had shown that Tommie's spinal cord injury was at the level of the second thoracic vertebra, T-2. The damage was as complete as if the cord had been severed with a knife. The purpose of the transplant was to place the new cells in a location where they could literally regrow neural connections across the gap. Therefore, the injection would be made at T-1.

Jon lifted a long, slender spinal needle and checked the location on his daughter's back.

A tiny dot of blood marked where he'd made the wheal. He was satisfied with its anatomic location. The problem, and the challenge, lay in the precision of needle placement. Ideally, an intra-spinal injection should be performed with imaging guidance, like ultrasound. The illegality of what he was doing prohibited that. Not only would it get the technician in trouble, if one were foolhardy enough to agree to help, but the paper trail generated could be incriminating. Therefore, Jon would be working through his daughter's back by sight, touch, and spatial orientation.

"Keep very still, Tommie." With the needle tip, he punctured the anesthetized skin and slowly advanced the needle. For a person his daughter's size, he had to transverse three-quarters of an inch of subcutaneous tissue before reaching the cord's protective covering. Once he went through it, he would come to a space containing cerebrospinal fluid before reaching the spinal cord proper. He intended to inject in the middle of the cord.

To do that with precision, he couldn't simply estimate the distance from the skin and then inject. He was working on his daughter here, and that would involve too much guesswork. Not only couldn't he risk imprecision, but he might only get one chance at this. Therefore, he'd rely on a neurologist's old tricks to reach the target area.

He felt a little pop as the needle pierced the protective ligament. As with the president's tap, a small drop of glistening spinal fluid appeared at the needle's hub. That told Jon he was on the right path. He advanced the needle slowly, cautiously. Seconds later, Tommie gave a little yelp.

"Daddy, I feel something hot on my leg."

"That's okay, honey. It means the needle's in the right place. Hold on."

Her voice had a nervous warble. "This is a lot worse than stinging!"

"Don't move. I'm almost finished."

"Daddy, hurry!"

Jon carefully advanced the needle the final half-inch, directly into the center of his daughter's spinal cord. His trembling hands reached for the syringe containing the fetal cells. Although he wanted to get this over with as quickly as possible, he realized he was on the edge of the medical envelope. What he was doing for such disastrous finality that he proceeded with utmost caution. Attaching the needle to the syringe, he took a deep breath and injected. "That's it."

Tommie let out a high-pitched wail. "Daddy, stop, stop!"

He quickly withdrew the needle. "It's all over, honey. Everything's out."

"No, it isn't!" Tommie cried, a piercing shriek of pain. "I still feel it! Daddy, *please*, take it out!"

Mireille pulled Tommie's head to her chest, stroking the child's hair. "It's all right, Tommie, it's over."

"Oh my God!" Tommie screamed. She reached up and started frantically pulling her own hair. Her body writhed in agony, and her screams became tortured cries that seemed to go on forever.

Jon was beside himself. He jumped up, kicked his stool away, and grabbed his daughter's shoulders. "What is it, Tommie? *Tell me!*"

As tears streamed down her cheeks, Tommie babbled incoherently. She said something about her legs and burning and fire, but Jon couldn't concentrate on the words. Seized with overwhelming panic, he couldn't think straight. Menacing thoughts of intravascular injection and allergic reaction lurked in the back of his mind, but his overriding fear was that he was killing his own daughter. Not knowing what to do, he simply hugged her small body, holding her tight.

For a short while, Tommie was inconsolable. Her heartrending shrieks continued for several more seconds before finally slowing. Thinking she might be losing consciousness, Jon abruptly shifted gears from parent to doctor, mentally racing through a checklist of emergency procedures. But before he could act, Tommie stopped crying altogether. Jon just kept holding her. Soon she was sniffling, and her head jerked with little spasms.

Jon looked at her eyes, which were clear, the pupils focused. "Is it gone, honey?"

"Yes," she said softly, giving one last sniffle. "I'm sorry, Daddy."

He suddenly felt like crying himself. He leaned against Mireille, holding Tommie protectively between them. He wasn't sure precisely what happened, but he *did* know that he was more relieved than he'd ever felt in his life. He slowly bent to Tommie's level, wiping her tears with his finger.

"*You're* sorry?" he said, his tone somewhere between laughter and astonishment. "Believe me, the sorry one is me! I can't believe I hurt you like that. Is the pain completely gone?"

"It's over," Tommie said. "But it really, really hurt. I'm glad you didn't tell me, because I never would've gone through it."

"Why was it so painful, Jon?" Mireille asked.

He straightened up, taking a deep breath. "I didn't expect it to be. It must have been a severe reflex irritation. When you're in the middle of the cord, there are millions of sensitive synapses. I guess it takes less than I thought to trigger them."

"She'll be all right, won't she?"

"She will now. It's like sticking your finger in an electric socket. But if I'd known, I never would've put her through that."

Tommie looked up at him, tears drying, a trusting look on her face. "But Daddy, if the needle was in exactly the right place, that gives it a better chance of working, doesn't it?"

When Jon gazed into his daughter's eyes, he could tell that all the pain was gone. Hope and love replaced it. He suddenly knew why they were all going through this, and he swelled with pride. Looking at Mireille, he affectionately stroked Tommie's neck. "What did I do to deserve a kid like this?"

Afterward, he insisted they remain in the medical center thirty minutes to guard against the unforeseen. While Mireille took Tommie to the bathroom and the food court, Jon retreated to the familiar comfort of his desk. Still teetering on the edge of emotional calamity, he sought refuge in the paperwork in his file tray. *Never again*, he thought. The mixture of parenting and medicine could be a toxic brew.

Unlocking his central desk drawer, Jon removed the

president's folder. With all the written tests and lab reports now in final form, he had to prepare a written report. Forbes continued pressuring him to do so. He idly leafed through the pages, still not completely satisfied. At best, his report would be medical speculation, an educated guess. His conclusion would draw as much from art as from science.

Once his report was submitted, Jon would be on record contending that President Meredith was suffering from a prion disorder. He wished he were more certain of that. In reality, all he had was bits and pieces—hints, suggestions, likely possibilities in a long list of differential diagnoses. What he really needed to firm the diagnosis up was a medical smoking gun. He wanted something pathognomonic, incontrovertible evidence of a specific disease.

He put down the printed reports and thought back to the president's exam. The finding he most vividly recalled was Meredith's irascibility. Jon forced himself to rethink the entire examination, especially the neurological details. He couldn't think of anything he'd missed except, perhaps, for a rectal exam, which he didn't think would add much. Organ system by organ system, he reviewed his findings. Meredith's skin and hair, he recalled, were unremarkable. The oral exam was normal. The president's breath was somewhat rancid, but...

Knitting his brow, Jon dwelled on that a moment. He remembered that when he'd gotten close to examine Bob's eyes, he'd been turned off by Meredith's breath. And it wasn't just from tobacco and alcohol. Jon couldn't recall what about it bothered him, other than that it was foul. Breath odor was the province of the dentist, the pulmonologist, and the gastroenterologist. A Navy internist had little expertise in the area.

Removing several texts from the shelves, he leafed through their indices. There were occasional references to breath tests, such as for the *helicobacter pylori* related to gastric ulcers, but there was no general table of breath smells in various disease states.

Not finding what he wanted, Jon went online.

Mireille wheeled Tommie back into the room. Both were smiling, and Jon was glad to see that Tommie looked none the worse for wear.

"How're you feeling, kiddo?"

"Good. Can we go now, Daddy?"

"Give me a few minutes. I have to check on something."

"I think the injection's working already."

"What makes you say that?" he asked.

"I don't know, I just do."

As the women resumed chatting, Jon logged on to a physician's medical information system. Through it, he was able to access most major medical journals online. Using the keywords "breath," "halitosis," and "disease states," he began a literature search. Soon he had several dozen computer hits. He briefly looked at the abstracts.

There were a number of references to breath in specific diseases. Foul breath was common in children with tonsillitis and sinus conditions. In substance abuse, various inhalants had specific odors. Diabetic ketoacidosis was associated with a characteristic fruity odor. Certain poisonings, like the cyanide with which he was all too familiar, had distinctive smells. Under the general heading of poisonings, certain heavy metals could produce distinctive breath smells. Jon pondered that, frowning.

"I'm ready to make that snack, Jon," Mireille said.

"How much longer, Daddy?"

"Almost finished, guys. Give me a minute."

He suddenly recalled something about the president's halitosis. Unless he was mistaken, Meredith's breath had a vaguely metallic odor. Could that be significant? Certainly, there were types of inadvertent metal intoxications that might be related to the president's symptoms, but…he'd have to read up on that. For the sake of completeness, he'd have to check it out.

Jon picked up his phone and called the lab, asking for the manager. The lab's head, Chris Leadbetter, was a longtime patient and loyal friend. All of the president's lab specimens were closely guarded and stored for months, perhaps years.

"Chris, this is Jon Townsend," he said. "I want you to do me a favor. This is probably a wild goose chase, but I'd like you to get hold of what's left of the president's serum from the bloods I ordered. You still have it, right? I want you to test it for heavy metals. That's right, lead, manganese, mercury, the works."

That night, Jon slept alone. Victoria had returned, and Jon took his daughter back to her mother. After the injection, Tommie had no lingering side effects. Mireille, also, spent the night in her own apartment. As the night hours slowly passed, Jon tossed fitfully in bed, listening to the house's every creak and moan. The shotgun was propped up at his nightstand. In his fantasies, a crazed gunman might break into the house at any minute.

Just before he was about to get up at six, the doorbell rang. Jon wasn't expecting any visitors. He grabbed the shotgun, put on a robe, and cautiously approached the front door.

Three men were visible through the peephole. With their inexpensive suits and short haircuts, they had the look of government employees. Shotgun under his arm, Jon unlocked the deadbolt and cracked open the door. The man in the lead thrust his ID into the opening almost immediately.

"FBI, Dr. Townsend. Special Agent Johnson. May we come in?"

Jon glanced first at the ID, then at the man. He'd seen enough FBI credentials to think this one legitimate. "Who's with you?"

Both men produced IDs. "This is Agent Fitzpatrick," Johnson said of the man behind him. "And this is Special Agent Lewis of the Secret Service."

Lewis was black, and he looked familiar. As he scrutinized the man, he recognized him as one of the agents who'd attended the president the night Jon performed the Heimlich maneuver. Lewis met Jon's gaze, then looked away.

"We know what happened the other day," Johnson continued. "We'd like to go over that with you. And I'd appreciate it if you'd put that weapon aside."

Jon leaned the shotgun against the wall and opened the door. The men followed him inside, and he led them to the living room. He and Agent Johnson took seats, but the others preferred to stand.

"Are you working today, Doctor?" Johnson began, removing a small notepad.

"I hope to."

"This shouldn't take very long. There are a few things we want to clear up, okay?"

"Go ahead."

"First, about the cyanide. We've gone over the detectives' reports, and one thing that puzzles us is how the stuff came to be in your house."

"It didn't walk in, I'll tell you that."

"Then how did it get in here?"

The question puzzled Jon. "Obviously, whoever put that metal thing in my bathroom brought it in with him."

"But you see," Johnson continued, "there were no signs of forced entry, and there weren't any footprints outside. You told the detectives you were sure everything was locked when you left, right?"

"That's right."

"Is it possible that your daughter or Miss Courtois left something open?"

Jon didn't like bringing either of them into this. "No, it's not."

"Help us out here, Doctor. We're trying to make some sense out of this."

"So am I. The way I see it, whoever did this is a professional who knew how to break in without leaving any traces. I'm sure that sort of thing happens all the time."

"Not as much as you think. Most break-ins leave some evidence, and the cops who investigated were pretty damn good. They didn't find a thing."

Agent Lewis, who'd been looking around the room, slowly strolled into the hall. "Excuse me," Jon called, "can I help you with something?"

"Just trying to get a feel for the place, sir. Okay if I look around?"

It wasn't, but Jon didn't want to appear uncooperative. "You're not going to turn my closets inside out or anything like that?"

Lewis laughed. "No, sir. Nothing like that."

"All right, go ahead."

"You're right about it being professional," Johnson went on. "What was your major in college, Doctor?"

"Biology."

"Know much about electrical circuits?"

"No, but I can change a light bulb."

"Whoever was in your medicine cabinet rigged a sophisticated timer hooked to a temperature sensor. The sensor was in your showerhead. When the water temperature hit a hundred twenty degrees, a three-minute timer was tripped. There was a lever in the gas generator that supported the cyanide. A hundred and eighty seconds after the water got hot, the lever dropped the cyanide into the acid. Simple and effective."

"Not completely effective, thank God."

"And you say the reason the gas didn't kill you," Johnson said, "was because you knew what it was?"

"It has a very distinctive smell. If you ever smelled it, you'd recognize it. But I was lucky. I'm sure you know about the antidote."

"Just happened to have it lying around, huh?"

Jon didn't like the suspicious tone of the question. "It was my father's. Check the prescription label. It's real."

"Where is your father now, Doctor?"

"He's dead."

"I'm sorry." Johnson paused. "I've heard people also use amyl nitrite poppers in recreational sex."

"So I've heard."

"What about you, Doctor Townsend? Ever use it that way?"

"I don't have recreational sex, Agent Johnson. Mine is the serious variety."

"Do you mind if I ask with whom?"

"Yes, I do mind."

"Other than Miss Courtois, I mean."

"If you're trying to be objectionable, you're doing a great job."

Johnson flipped the pages of his notepad. "Doctor, do you have access to cyanide, in your work or otherwise?"

"Now wait a minute! I really resent the direction this is

headed. Do you honestly think I'd try to commit suicide and make it look like murder?"

"I don't think anything, Doctor. It's my job to ask questions."

For the first time, Fitzpatrick spoke up. "Some people think it's peculiar that you just happen to recognize the smell of cyanide, Doc, and you just happen to have the cure in the next room."

"I see. So now I did it on purpose, huh? I'd just come home from a great day with my friends and my kid, and out of the blue, I try to set up my own murder, is that it?"

The agents stared at him, saying nothing.

"Why on earth would I want to do that?" Jon said.

"I don't know, Doctor," Johnson replied. "Why would you?"

Jon watched Agent Lewis return to the room. "This is ridiculous!" Jon continued. "I don't know what you guys are after, but I sure as hell didn't do what you're implying. And I suppose I imagined the people who were following me?"

"You tell me, Doctor. You're the only one who saw them."

"That's just great," Jon said, shaking his head. "Next thing I know, you're going to accuse me of being involved in the first lady's attempted assassination."

The three agents shared a look. "Now that you brought it up, Doctor," Johnson said, "maybe you *should* tell us where you were the night of her shooting."

Jon leapt to his feet. "You're out of your mind!"

"Sit down, Doctor Townsend. This shouldn't take very long. I'm sure you're more comfortable talking about it here than at the agency."

Jon sat down, fuming. Indeed, the remainder of their questions took all of five minutes. Jon told them his alibi, which he believed unshakable. His increasingly hostile attitude made it hard for him to be the least bit cooperative. After the agents left, the first thing he did was to phone Dave Saunders. Saunders wasn't available, and Jon left voice mail to call as soon as possible. Ten minutes later, while Jon was getting dressed, Dave called back. Jon quickly explained what happened.

"I know Fitzpatrick and Johnson, but I never met Lewis," Dave said. "The first two are behind-the-scenes types. They don't pull regular details. I can try to find out what they're after."

"I *told* you what they want. They think I set up my own murder, and they think I'm involved in Roxanne's assassination attempt!"

"Take it easy, Jon. They probably have an ulterior motive."

"Such as?"

"I don't know. But it's standard interviewing technique to try to provoke someone, to see what kind of response you get. Sounds like they succeeded."

"That's just wonderful. So, what am I supposed to do now?"

"Go to work, as usual. You have three reasons not to worry about a thing."

"What reasons?"

"First, they've got no evidence. Second, you've got a powerful alibi. Finally, you didn't do it. So, stop worrying."

That was easier said than done, for worrying was second nature to a physician. Nonetheless, Jon managed to finish dressing and get to work on time. His first appointment that morning was Senator Friedman. Stylishly dressed, not a hair out of place, the senator greeted him warmly.

Hands folded in her lap, she looked at Jon across the desk. "It may not be my place to ask, Doctor, but you seem distracted. Is everything all right?"

He didn't know it showed. "Just year-end loose ends, Senator. Budget, supplies. I appreciate your asking. So, how long have you been on the medication now?" He opened her chart. "A month?"

"Five weeks. I have to tell you, I can definitely notice the change."

"In what way?"

"My movements feel smoother. More relaxed. For some reason, I feel calmer. Is that unusual?"

"To be honest, the most common side effects go in the other direction—depression, even psychosis," he explained. "But I've seen a whole spectrum of reactions. Some patients get euphoric. I'm glad what you feel is positive. You don't have any twitching, or unusual movements?"

"None at all."

"Great. Come on, let's check things out, do some blood work, and get you out of here."

The senator's brief exam was encouraging. Her fine tremor had become undetectable. Her prior muscular rigidity was significantly reduced, and her hint of spasticity was no longer there. Soon, they returned to the consultation room.

"Your exam is as good as can be expected, Senator. Assuming your liver function tests are okay, we may as well keep your medication right where it is. At some point, things may change. But we'll deal with it at that time, all right?"

"I'm very satisfied with the way things are turning out, Doctor. But I'm not a Pollyanna. We'll see what the future holds, and I'll take your suggestions. Speaking of which, the vote on fetal stem cell research should be coming up soon in my committee. I've already spoken with other members, and I think you can count on majority support. When the legislation comes up, it should easily clear the Senate."

"I appreciate your help, Senator. And your friendship."

Shortly after she left, his phone rang.

"Jon, go out to the bank of pay phones," said Dave Saunders. His voice had an urgent tone. "I know the numbers. I'll call you in thirty seconds."

"Dave, what's—?"

"Just do it."

In the nearby lobby, one of the wall phones near Jon's office rang. He immediately picked up. "What's going on, Dave?"

"Listen closely, because I can't talk long. There's something weird going on around here. I've talked to a few people about Johnson and Fitzpatrick, and I'm hitting a brick wall. Nobody I really trust knows a thing, but everyone else is stalling. I'm worried. I don't really know how to explain it, except that you get a feel for these things."

"Does it involve me?"

"Maybe, but I can't say for sure. All I know is, I'm running into major stonewalling over pretty insignificant questions. That shouldn't happen. We're all supposed to be working together around here."

"That doesn't sound good."

"No, it doesn't," said Dave. "And I've got to go slow. If I push it, I'll be going out on a limb more than I already have. Jon, listen to me. I may be wrong, but consider all your phones tapped—"

"Are you serious?"

"Serious as a stroke, my friend. Work, home, or car phones. My guess is your ex-wife is bugged too, and probably Mireille. This is what I want you to do. First, if you have to call me, I have a new, untraceable beeper number. Got a pen?"

"Go ahead." He quickly scribbled down the number.

"Get yourself a new cell phone today," Dave quickly continued. "May as well get one for Mireille, too. Try not to talk on it for more than thirty seconds. Use cash to buy them, not credit cards, okay?"

"Jesus, who can live like that?"

"The point is, Jon, you may not live without it. Whoever they are, they already tried once, and you can't afford a second time. They might not miss. So, just do what I say."

As soon as the agent rang off, Jon called his daughter. He'd been in twice-daily contact since her injection, so his calling wasn't unusual. But given what Dave had said, he just wanted to hear the sound of her unfettered voice. Judging from her words and tone, nothing was amiss. He found this very encouraging. In the back of his mind, Jon was toying with an idea involving the president's wife. Every bit of good news about Tommie was a step in the right direction.

The morning dragged on until Jon finished with his last patient at noon. Instead of going out to lunch, he drove to the area's largest mall. The holiday week was shopper's heaven, and the mall would be packed. Being able to lose himself in the crowd was precisely why Jon had chosen to shop there. In general, he couldn't tell if he was being followed, and he could ill afford being trailed to some isolated electronics store, where his purchases and new phone numbers could be easily learned by someone with the right credentials.

The mall was wall-to-wall shoppers. Joining the throng, Jon was reasonably sure he was inconspicuous. Ducking into a telephone retail store, he purchased two quality cell phones and had them activated. He put them in his pockets. He didn't want to be seen carrying around an incriminating shopping bag.

When the day's office hours were finished late that afternoon, Jon drove to the White House, ostensibly to see the president. He knew full well that the chief executive was out of town on a campaign swing. Mindful of Dave's words, Jon hadn't wanted to phone Mireille, hoping to speak with her in person. But as he walked through the halls heading for the kitchen, he bumped into the chief of staff.

"What are you doing here?" asked Forbes, looking surprised.

"Happy Holidays to you too, Mitch."

"Sorry," said Forbes, stung. "Merry Christmas. I didn't expect you to be here when the president's away."

"So I just found out. I should've called ahead, but I thought I'd just stop by to see how he's doing. How does he seem to you?"

"About the same."

"Which means, not so good. Every time I see him, the president seems a little more forgetful, a little more irritable. He sticks to quick stump speeches he doesn't even write. I think the reason nobody's caught on is because they're still treating him with kid gloves after Rocky's shooting."

Forbes shrugged. "You're the doctor. But what about his test results? Didn't you say they'd be in by now?"

"In fact, they are—at least, all the original tests. I asked the lab to run one more."

"There's always one more with you, isn't there?"

"Mitch," Jon said with an innocent sigh, "these things take a while."

"How do the original test results look so far?"

"Come on, Mr. Forbes. You know the rules. As soon as I find everything out, I'll tell the president, then you."

Forbes eyed him icily. "I know the rules, all right. The question is, do you?"

He stormed away, leaving Jon to wonder what he'd done to incur the man's enmity.

He didn't have time to dwell on it. He worked his way to the kitchen, where Mireille was just finishing up for the day. Jon kissed her on the cheek and pulled her aside.

"We have to talk," he said. "But not here. Can we go to your place?"

She saw the urgent look in his eyes. "What's wrong, Jon?"

"Something's going on around here, and I don't know what. It's serious. What do you say—half an hour, in your apartment?"

They traveled by separate routes. Once they were at her place, Mireille sat him down and looked him in the eye. "You're scaring me, Jon. Talk to me."

He turned on her sound system, and soon an old Coltrane hit masked the background. When he began speaking, it was in a low whisper. "The Secret Service and FBI questioned me this morning. I think I'm being bugged. Maybe I'm paranoid, but the people close to me might be bugged, too."

She gave him an incredulous look. "Jon, I...do things like that really happen?"

"They can, and they do. This is the United States government I'm talking about. They're not beyond doing something underhanded."

"But why would they do that to you?"

"They weren't about to tell me, in so many words. But the gist of their questions was that they think I'm lying about the cyanide thing and probably set it up myself—"

"That's ridiculous!"

"They also hinted that I had something to do with Rocky's shooting."

Stunned, Mireille looked at him wide-eyed, at a loss for words. She slowly shook her head as she struggled to comprehend. "Do you have any idea at all what's behind this?"

"Not in the slightest. But I did speak to Dave, and he's worried, too. He says he thinks there's something going on that involves me, but he doesn't know what. This is what he wants me to do."

Jon gave her the new cell phone, and they exchanged numbers. He also let her have the number of Dave's beeper. He cautioned that the numbers were for emergency use, but she shouldn't hesitate to call whenever she thought necessary.

"Did you speak with a lawyer, Jon?" she asked.

"Do you think I should?"

"For something like this, absolutely. You have one, don't you?"

"Not anyone I call regularly. The last time I used an attorney was for my divorce."

"If I were you, I would get in touch with one soon. If you're in trouble, you need legal protection."

Jon put his arm around her, drew her close, and kissed the tip of her nose. "Sometimes I think you're all the protection I need."

Throughout the evening, an ominous sense of foreboding stalked the apartment like an unwelcome visitor. Jon felt it more than Mireille, but his tenseness was contagious. Nonetheless, they continued about their business, trying to pretend the anxiety was imaginary. When that didn't work, they distracted themselves with board games, DVDs, and cooking. But everything had an edge to it, leaving them unable to concentrate. The inescapable stress was palpable, an emotional tension that didn't wash off.

What made Jon's predicament all the more frustrating was that he didn't know what it was all about. He was left with a formless sense of impending dread, much like the feeling one might have before entering a ghost-inhabited forest, or receiving an unexpected certified letter. All Jon really understood was that he was caught up in something beyond his control. That futile sense of helplessness vanquished the serenity he might otherwise have in Mireille's company.

Curiously, in some ways the apprehension drew them closer. They were soldiers in a foxhole, convicts sharing a cell. Although it was hard to concentrate, the jitters heightened other senses, and they developed the eroticism of caged animals. They shared a night of repeated passion which was at once needy yet unfulfilling, an itch incompletely scratched.

Jon slept poorly. He pondered and ruminated, tossing uncomfortably in bed like a sunburned child. With Mireille snoring softly beside him, he stared up at the ceiling, listening to the ever-changing nighttime sounds, not knowing who or what was coming for him—or when.

The next morning was cold and overcast. As Mireille got ready for work, Jon returned home. The leaden skies opened, and it began to snow, large, thick flakes swirled by the rising wind. When he reached his office later, he was going to take Mireille's legal admonition to heart. He'd needed a good lawyer for a while, for mundane things like estate planning and a will that guaranteed Tommie's future.

In his bedroom, he put the new cell phone on his dresser while he changed clothes. The phone's slender owner's manual fell onto the floor behind the dresser. Once he was dressed, Jon got down on all fours to retrieve it. A small red package lay beside the booklet. Jon recognized it as the crumpled Marlboros pack that had belonged to Mr. Phillips. He took both items and stuffed them, along with the phone, into his overcoat pockets. When he was ready, he went to the front door and stepped outside into the steadily increasing snow.

In retrospect, he thought that maybe he hadn't first checked the outdoors because he was preoccupied, or that he'd forgotten about his shotgun because he was tired. But no sooner did he close the door than strong hands grabbed him and swung him around. He had a momentary glimpse of Fitzpatrick and Lewis before his face smashed into the front door. His arms were pulled roughly behind him, and his wrists were squeezed when the plastic restraints were tied around them.

"All right already," Jon managed, his eyes half-closed in pain. "Take it easy."

"This is easy, Doc. If it was the hard way, you wouldn't be standin' here."

"I already answered your questions. What do you want?"

"We want your ass in our car. Dr. Townsend, you're under arrest for the murder of Mahmoud al-Abed, and for conspiracy in the attempted murder of Roxanne Meredith, first lady of the United States."

Although he'd been expecting something important, Jon was stunned. When it was actually put into words, the outrageousness of the allegation was mind-boggling. His mind was racing. In the flat light of a dreary, sunless morning, as the agents dragged him to their waiting vehicle, Jon felt confused, beaten, and utterly alone.

CHAPTER 21

In the mounting storm, the rising wind froze the snow into crystals of ice. Hands tied behind him, Jon lowered his face protectively as the agents pushed him toward their vehicle. The driven flakes stung his face like pieces of glass. One of the men unlocked the rear door, and the other forced Jon's head down and shoved him into the back seat. The agents got in the front.

They were in a nondescript navy-blue Taurus. Agent Johnson drove. As the car pulled away from the curb, Jon sat glumly, struggling to become comfortable with his hands locked in place. He was still too stunned to say anything. Outside, the fallen snow quickly coated the road with a glassy rime. The car's wheels swerved as the vehicle accelerated.

"Careful, cowboy," said Fitzpatrick.

Johnson gave him a look. "Who's doing the driving?"

"Where are we going?" Jon finally asked.

Both men turned to him. "Shut the fuck up."

Their intensely dark looks persuaded Jon to keep silent. Unable to lean straight back, he listed to his left, keeping the weight off his hands. He was suddenly eager to reach headquarters and get on with it already. But looking through the car window, he was confused by their direction. The increasingly circuitous route took them down back roads nowhere near the main highways.

"You'll never reach the Beltway this way."

In the rearview mirror, Johnson glared at him. "What'd we tell you?"

"I just don't want to be in this car longer than I have to, and I'm telling you, this is the wrong—"

Without warning, Fitzpatrick turned around and punched him flush in the mouth. Jon momentarily blacked out but quickly awoke to a harsh ringing inside his head. The inside of his lip was deeply cut. Blood immediately filled his lips. Rolling onto his chin, it soon dripped onto his coat. He pressed his lips tightly together to stanch the flow.

For the first time since they'd questioned him, Jon realized something peculiar was going on. Like most knowledgeable adults, he knew that some law enforcement officers abused their prisoners. It was a fact of life. But in his wildest imagination, he couldn't believe an FBI agent would strike a Navy admiral—the president's doctor, to boot.

Not only would charges of police brutality jeopardize the government's case, but it would also turn the suspect into an adversary. No, federal agents—especially the ones he knew—didn't behave that way. All of which suggested that something else was afoot here. The fact that they were taking back roads made their intentions all the more ominous.

From Bradley Boulevard, they turned left onto Persimmon Tree Road. Jon wondered if they might be trying to avoid the heavier rush hour traffic by taking less-traveled streets. The road hugged the Congressional Country Club and they went south, as if toward Macarthur Boulevard. Indeed, traffic was sparse, perhaps due to the storm.

A strong wind buffeted the car. The storm was becoming a true nor'easter, and the winds were increasing to gale force. The snow now blew horizontally, and icy flakes peppered the vehicle like grains of sand. The driver's vision had to be impaired. Jon thought that continuing at their current pace was reckless. He didn't see what Agent Johnson had to prove, but he wasn't foolish enough to voice his objections any more.

On its way to Macarthur, the Taurus rounded a bend and headed downhill. There were no other cars in sight. All of a sudden, what Jon had feared came true. Taking the curve too fast for the conditions, the vehicle hit an icy patch and fishtailed. The rear wheels spun out. Before Jon knew it, they were skidding sideways down the hill.

"Shit!" Johnson cried, frantically working the wheel.

To Jon's surprise, Fitzpatrick let out a scream—a high-pitched, fear-filled warble Jon rarely associated with tough guys. He sat there in silent disbelief, an observer who watched events unfold in slow motion. As the car continued its sickening spin, Johnson struggled, Fitzpatrick wailed, and Jon was a spectator. Ahead, the road continued to bend, but the car went straight. Inevitably, the sliding wheels hit the side of the road.

In his peculiar detachment, Jon was thinking with unusual clarity. He knew what was going to happen next. He threw himself onto the floor just as the rear wheels hit the shoulder. Torque and momentum did the rest. The car flipped over. It spun through the air as its wheels left the ground, completing three-quarters of a revolution before crashing heavily onto the driver's side.

The initial impact boomed explosively. Wedged on the floor between the front and back seats, Jon was shielded from the worst of the impact. The car continued its catastrophic roll, flipping over and over, the harsh tearing of metal merging with Fitzpatrick's terrified screams. Jon's body was pummeled mercilessly. But within another second, the front of the Taurus smashed sickeningly into something and abruptly stopped, but not before a blizzard of fractured glass rained through the vehicle.

In the near silence that followed, the only thing Jon heard was the whirring noise of a front wheel that continued to spin. Agent Fitzpatrick was no longer screaming. Jon shifted painfully in place, trying to regain his senses. As his blurring vision cleared, he opened his eyes and took stock of his predicament.

Snow filtered through the car via a missing front window. Jon felt the blood rising to his head. As he oriented himself, he realized that the car had come to rest on the driver's side, upside down. He felt something wet and slick against his scalp and feared that it was blood. But then he felt the cold. Craning his neck to one side, he saw that it was snow. The window on his side had been likewise blasted out by impact.

"Hello up there?" he called.

There was no answer, no moan, no sound. It suddenly dawned on Jon, as he lay there with his arms behind him and his feet up in the air, that this might be a freakish opportunity. Never having been a prisoner before, he never had to think like one. Yet as he mulled over the agents' peculiar actions and equally bizarre back-street driving, Jon knew he might have been offered a gift.

Shifting uncomfortably in place, he found nothing broken. Jon again looked over his shoulder and noted that the Taurus was at a fifteen-degree angle to the ground, leaving an eighteen-inch opening he might be able to wriggle through. He inched toward it, listening all the while. Outside, the wind picked up. In its roar, he heard no passing cars. Despite the morning rush, traffic on Persimmon Tree had been sparse. He didn't know how far they were from the road, but given the weather and the traffic, he doubted they could be seen.

His head swelled from being inverted. The front seat was pushing backward into his hips and chest. Nonetheless, Jon managed to wriggle his upper torso into the window opening. By shifting his weight between his head, neck, and shoulders, he was able to slowly inch his way through the aperture onto the snowy ground. It was painful but steady-going. At length, he was completely free of the car.

Lying on his back was hurting his hands. Rolling onto his side, facing the front of the car, Jon immediately saw what had happened. The Taurus' forward momentum was arrested by a huge tree. As the vehicle had skidded on its side at forty miles per hour, its windshield collided with a massive oak. The car was effectively stopped, but not before its front-seat passengers had been crushed.

Both front air bags had deployed, but it wasn't enough. The oak's yard-wide girth had virtually eliminated the front-passenger compartment. Both of the agents were crushed beyond recognition. A gristly crimson ooze covering seat back and car frame dripped slowly downward, forming a widening scarlet stain in the snow. Jon felt sick. He realized how incredibly lucky he was for the car to have stopped when it did.

He looked back toward the roadway. The snow was blowing so hard that he couldn't tell where they'd gone off the road. In the gale, he couldn't see any cars, and he knew passing motorists couldn't see him. Unless someone had been right behind them, no one would come looking until the weather cleared. His chances for escape would never be better than they were now. The driver's-side door had been buckled by the impact. A portion of its mangled frame had been torn, leaving a jagged edge of metal just off the ground. To Jon, it looked as good as a serrated knife for severing his restraints. Staying on his side, he slithered backward toward it until his hands touched the cold, bare metal.

He had to do this blindly, working by touch. The durable plastic band was meant to be released by cutters, not twisted metal. It was also dangerous work: one slip could sever his radial artery, and he would bleed to death in the snow. But he didn't have much choice. Quickly but carefully, Jon sawed his restraints against the sharp steel edge. It was difficult, tedious work, and he soon began to sweat. Finally, the plastic gave way.

Wrists freed, Jon momentarily sagged against the snow, breathing heavily. Bringing his arms forward, he pushed himself to his hands and knees and then stood up. His legs were trembling. His whole body felt bruised, and he knew that tomorrow, he'd be painfully sore. That is, if there *was* a tomorrow. Right now, the most important thing was to get away from the accident scene as quickly as possible.

Jon's hands were freezing. The stinging, wind-driven flakes pelted his exposed skin. He didn't think the temperature was all that low, but the wind-chill effect was excruciating. Fortunately, his heavy coat shielded him from the worst. He patted his pockets for the cell phone, which he found intact. Once he got away from there, he'd make some important calls. Before he left, he bent over again and reached inside the driver's compartment.

Owing to the spilled, warm blood, a macabre vapor rose from Johnson's body. Jon's hand passed through the mist and onto the agent's sodden, sticky clothing. He found a gun in a shoulder holster and wrested it free, wiping off the bloodstains in the snow before tucking the gun in his waistband. Jon didn't know if he was going to need it, but he felt more secure having it available.

The sudden noise of a diesel engine startled him and

made Jon twist toward the roadway. It was the signature of an eighteen-wheeler, and it was soon gone. Jon realized that the storm could abate at any moment, and he couldn't continue standing there. Hiking up his coat collar, he lowered his chin and trudged off.

The footing was treacherous. Jon's regulation black leather shoes had slick new soles that made the going even more precarious. But the cold and his mounting rage spurred him on. He was soon walking as briskly as the conditions would allow. He hadn't realized it when he'd first left the car, but it was soon apparent that he was heading home.

He had nowhere else to go. Here he was, just having escaped after being arrested. He was physically battered, emotionally strained, and freezing. He couldn't aimlessly wander around in that condition. At the very least, he needed shelter and dry clothes. Once he had them, he wouldn't go to work. Nor could he go to a friend or Mireille and put them in jeopardy. Until he had a better idea of what was going on, he had to keep to himself. Beyond that, he desperately needed time to think.

He was two miles from home. Given his current pace, the walk would take about twenty minutes. He didn't plan to stop, and he doubted anyone could see him in the near whiteout. His brain churned with each stride. If he could get a handle on what was going on, he might be able to figure out what to do next. So far, all he knew was what they'd told him. The more he dwelled on it, the more outlandish their allegations seemed.

He began with what little he knew. There was no disputing the fact that legitimate agents of the FBI had arrested him. Prior to that, someone had tried to kill him in his own home. In Jon's mind, the connection between the two was now as obvious as it was absurd: someone wanted him out of the way. Yet that implied he was in the way, involved in something that threatened others.

He'd already wracked his brains trying to figure out what that was. He'd toyed with explanations involving Mireille, a malpractice scenario, and a disgruntled patient. If he let his imagination run wild, Jon supposed he could come up with a scenario involving infuriated patients or jealous ex-lovers, even up to the point of attempted murder. It went without saying that such an individual would be seriously deranged. Yet there was nothing deranged or haphazard about what was happening to him. The events of his recent life were methodical to the point of exact planning.

Moreover, such fanciful explanations were intensely personal. The more Jon mulled it over, the more he concluded there was nothing personal about what was going on. Everything had been professional and businesslike: sorry, sir, just doin' my job. No, he was in the way of something—something that threatened others—and people trained in mayhem intended to get him *out* of the way. And if he wasn't interfering with something personal, Jon's only reasonable conclusion was that he was interfering with something involving his line of work.

Okay, he said to himself, *let's run with that.*

Agents of the United States government are out to stop me from interfering with something. I don't know what it is, but they're dead serious. What could I be dabbling in that's so important that people want me eliminated? I'm just a simple internist. Is there another aspect of my work, maybe something that involves the Navy, or a project that—

He thought of Tommie and abruptly stopped walking. The fierce wind straightened him up, and the swirling snow danced around him in ghostly eddies. The stem cell research, he suddenly remembered. It was a controversial area that aroused strong passions because of its relationship to abortion. In that charged arena, some people had been killed because of their views. Perhaps Jon hadn't covered his tracks as well as he thought.

Lowering his head, Jon proceeded into the wind. While his involvement with stem cell research was irrefutable, he thought it unlikely to involve the FBI. That was not within the Bureau's purview. No matter how Jon looked at his research, he couldn't see why the Bureau would be concerned. By the time he reached his street, Jon was left with only one conclusion: that an aspect of his day-to-day work threatened someone or some people unknown.

And it was something worth killing for.

Once he'd reach home, Jon knew he couldn't afford to stay there. The main reason he was going was to get dry clothes. En route, the heavy snow provided good cover. As he trudged through the steadily increasing accumulation, he saw that traffic had slowed. No doubt many people had decided to take the day off or to go to work late. The few remaining motorists were too intent on their driving to notice a lone pedestrian in the storm.

Jon half expected more agents to be at the house. The ones who arrested him should have arrived at their destination by now, and when they didn't show up, it wouldn't be long before a search was begun. Once the agents couldn't be located or contacted, others would come looking, and one of the first places they'd search would be the Townsend home. Yet so far, his home looked unvisited. As he approached the house, Jon saw no strange cars on the street or in the driveway.

It would be foolish to leave footprints in the snow leading to the front door. Sticking to the property's edge, Jon made his way through the perimeter shrubs and trees to the back entrance, where he let himself in. Between the wind and the snow, he felt frozen. The snowflakes, melted by his body heat, had soaked through his clothes, and he was shivering violently. In the rear laundry room, he removed his wet garments and left them in a pile on the floor. He placed his cell phone, the gun, and his other belongings on the washing machine.

There was no time to waste. Turning on the shower, Jon needed several minutes of steaming spray before the chill left his body. As he bathed, he tried to figure out what to do next. Clearly, he couldn't live life as usual. Until he found a solution to what was happening, he couldn't go to work, he couldn't remain at home, and he couldn't go anywhere he might be seen. He needed to lay low somewhere. The question was where.

Once Jon dried off, he quickly changed into warm outdoor clothes: wool socks and long johns, wool pants, a heavy sweater, work boots, a parka, and a ski hat. He knew the wrecked Taurus might be discovered any minute. Once dressed, he tucked the cell phone into his jacket but debated taking the handgun. As he thought about it, he jogged to the front of the house and found the shotgun where he'd left it. He cautiously peered through the front window.

Outside, the wind still shrieked, but the snowfall was lessening. To Jon's horror, a sedan with a flashing red dome light skidded to a halt at the curb. *My God*, he thought, *they're here already!* Before anyone got out of the car, he grabbed the shotgun and ran back through the house. He was out the back door in a flash, sprinting wildly through the snow, clutching the shotgun in one hand.

He expected shots at any second, but the only sound was the slap of his footfalls in the snow. He was quickly into the copse of fir trees at the back of his yard, where the heavy snow was already bending the evergreen boughs. Once completely concealed he stopped, gasping for breath. The men were probably still at the front of the house, about to break in.

Jon's car was in his garage. When he'd come home to change clothes, he'd only planned on using it to leave the neighborhood. Now that was out of the question. But so was wearing a ski cap while carrying a shotgun in a residential district. At his feet lay a folded blue tarp that he'd used during the summer. Jon bent over, wrapped the shotgun inside it, and left the bundle beside the tree trunk. Then he was off again, winding his way through the trees that bordered the neighbor's property.

Jon wasn't sure if the cell phone would work in the storm. Taking refuge under a maple, he dialed a cab company he knew to be reliable. The call went through. Jon ordered a cab, requesting a pickup in ten minutes at a corner five blocks distant. Then he set off, chin against his chest, not really sure where he was going, or what he would do once he got there.

CHAPTER 22

"I don't have to remind you that the Southern Cross thing was your idea, do I?" the man asked.

"No, sir," said Sean. "I just thought it would be a lot more effective than it was."

"And it would've been, if the shooter was a little more accurate. Without his wife needling him, the president would've backed off domestically. The damn Arabs would be right where we want them. But now, forget it. The first lady's sympathy factor is off the charts. She's more effective in a coma than she ever was alive and well. Jesus, what a mess."

"You know, I've been thinking—"

"That's the problem, Sean," the man interrupted. "There are thinkers and then there are doers. Right now, you think too much. This is Boston all over."

Though stung by the comment, O'Brien had to admit that the man was right. A decade ago, he had been a rising star in Irish organized crime, already on the radar screens of federal prosecutors. For reasons that weren't clear even to him, he had tried to reach out to other criminal factions, working with them to avoid competition. But in doing so he had trashed the idea of established criminal neighborhoods. The ensuing turf battles cost lives and reputations. Sean was on the road to being killed himself when the politician with whom he was speaking managed to whisk him out of Boston at the last moment. Now, once more, it was time to stop thinking and start taking orders. "I hear you. What've you got in mind?"

"Right now, we've got to limit the threats to us. And there's one annoying snooper who's become a real pain in the ass. I have other assets working on him—but just to be sure, this is what I want you to do."

The cabbie tried to engage him in conversation, but Jon wouldn't bite. He peered out the window at the storm, huddling in the back of the cab, hiding his face. Face averted, speaking softly, he called Dave but only got voice mail. He left a message to contact him as soon as possible.

When Saunders wasn't in the White House, he worked nearby in Secret Service offices in the Treasury Building on Fifteenth Street and Pennsylvania Avenue. Jon couldn't risk going to either place. Although his arrest that morning was probably a ludicrous mistake, it also reeked of trumped-up paranoia, perhaps even conspiracy. If Johnson and Fitzpatrick were involved, other agents might be, too. Until Jon learned the answer to that, it was better to keep a low profile than to go charging into the lion's den.

There was a coffee shop on the corner of I Street and Fifteenth. Jon tipped the driver well and had the cab drop him off there. He took a rear table that had a view of the front door. Nursing a mug of black coffee, he halfheartedly sipped and watched, growing edgy. Feeling like a fugitive came with an uneasiness that made reflection difficult. It was a nervous, minute-to-minute state of finger-tapping and darting gazes. For a long-range planner like Jon, it was a frustrating existence.

Jon knew that, while Secret Service special agents frequently used cell phones in their work, personal calls—especially when on presidential detail—were discouraged. It might be a while before he heard from Dave. Still, Saunders must check his messages. Besides, since what was happening to Jon might somehow be connected with the presidency, Dave's call wouldn't be strictly personal in nature. Finally, after an exasperating forty minutes, the agent called.

"Thank God, Dave! I was going nuts waiting for you to call."

"What's up, Jon? You sound pretty stressed."

"That's because I am in a shitload of trouble. I'm not going to work today, and I can't go home. I need to talk to you, man. I'm not far. Any chance you could get away for a while?"

"Give me half an hour. Where are you?"

Jon told him. After ringing off, Jon refilled his mug for the third time, not really needing more caffeine but unable to sit still. Fidgeting, he squirmed in his seat. He took off his coat, felt cold, and put it on again. In his edgy impatience, nothing felt comfortable. He wanted to *do* something about his predicament, not simply to wait for the troops to arrive.

He had to force himself to concentrate. It required the kind of considerable effort a man under stress should avoid, but Jon finally distracted himself enough to think about other matters. The first thing that came to mind was the president. Jon had been so preoccupied with his own problems that he'd temporarily forgotten his professional obligations. Not wanting to overuse his new cell phone, he found a pay phone near the men's room. He dialed the hospital lab and asked to be connected with the manager.

"Chris, it's Jon Townsend."

"Thanks for calling back, Doc. Guess you got my message."

Jon gripped the phone tightly. "Actually, I didn't. I'm not in the office yet. Is it about those additional tests on the president?"

"Sure is. We finished this morning, and you were right. It's hard to believe."

"Go on, I'm listening."

"The president's serum contains mercury, Dr. Townsend. Inorganic mercury. We got a level of thirty-seven micrograms per liter, which is over twice the toxic limit."

Jon's mouth went wide. He couldn't believe it. "Is there any chance of a mistake?"

"Sure, but we ran it three times. Same results. We also cross-checked it against his urine, and it's in there, too." He paused. "You still there, Dr. Townsend?"

"Of course. I…I'm just a little stunned. I knew it was always a possibility, but I never really thought a heavy metal would turn up. It would be nice to know how long it's actually been in his body."

"Yeah, I thought about that, too. But we have all his serum frozen, going back three years. If you want, I could go back and check it. Just give me the order."

"Do it, Chris. As soon as possible."

"After I first called, Doc, I did a little reading on this. At this blood level, mercury should definitely cause symptoms, right? All I can tell of President Meredith is what I see in the news. Do you mind if I ask—?"

"I'm sorry, Chris, I can't talk about that. I'm sure you can glean a lot from the texts. And not only can't I talk about it, but you can't, either. Who else knows about these results?"

"Just the tech who actually did the tests," Chris said. "She has a top clearance and knows she can't discuss anything involving the president."

"Remind her anyway. And get back to me as soon as you test those old sera." Feeling overwhelmed, Jon returned to his seat. Like most good doctors, he realized that one of the keys to being a good diagnostician lay in having a high index of suspicion. This he had. Something about the president's prior diagnoses, be they Alzheimer's Disease or a prion disorder, had never entirely fit for him. Out of neurotic compulsion as much as a sense of completeness, he always felt he needed a little more clinical information, one more test. Yet as much as he felt compelled to order the heavy metal analysis, he never suspected it would be positive.

Although he was no expert on metal intoxications, as a competent internist Jon understood that mercury could explain many of the president's symptoms. High mercury levels could cause neurologic and psychiatric changes virtually identical to those exhibited by Bob Meredith. If the discovery was true, Jon's line of reasoning about the prion disorder was way off base. His prior deductions were understandable but inaccurate. But he didn't yet know that much about mercury to make such an abrupt about-face. First, he needed more facts.

Information on the effects of heavy metals could be found in any up-to-date medical library. Unfortunately, Jon couldn't risk walking around in public. Besides, before he did anything further, he needed Dave's advice. After libraries, the Internet should be able to get him what he wanted. Fortunately, his pricey new cell phone came with Web access. It was the last thing he thought he'd need when he bought it. Now, it seemed remarkable foresight.

While he waited to hear from Saunders, Jon went online and accessed a physician's medical information source. The website had a wealth of facts and data of particular interest to doctors, including recent journal articles and texts. The textbooks were listed by medical specialty. Under the emergency medicine category, he selected a recent text on medical toxicology. Soon, he was engrossed in reading the details of the effects of inorganic mercury on the human body.

The details were sobering. Mercury poisoning could cause acute and chronic effects ranging from mild skin changes to death. Like syphilis, mercury intoxication was a great mimic, and unless there was a history of exposure, diagnosis could prove very difficult. The major affected organs were the kidneys and the brain, and the possible symptoms were legion. As Jon digested the text, he felt he could just as easily have been reading any standard reference in psychiatry, nephrology, or neurology. He was so engrossed in the information that he didn't see Dave walk in.

"Am I interrupting your love affair with technology?"

Jon was startled by his sudden appearance. "Christ, am I glad you're here! There's so much going on, I don't know where to start!"

Saunders took a seat and signaled the waitress. "Start with the trouble you're in." Jon kept silent until the waitress took Dave's order and walked away. "Your friends Johnson and Fitzpatrick came by this morning while I was getting ready for work. They arrested me."

Dave eyed Jon obliquely but quickly saw that his friend wasn't joking. "They charged you with faking your own attempted murder?"

Jon fixed him with a stare. "The charge is conspiracy to murder Roxanne Meredith."

Saunders gaped, his expression the stunned look of someone who'd been slapped. "You'd better start from the beginning."

Concisely yet completely, Jon related the morning's events, from his sudden arrest to the snowy collision. Dave listened without comment. The expression on his face changed from minute to minute, alternately reflecting consternation, anger, and confusion. By the time Jon finished, the agent was shaking his head.

"No one saw the crash?"

"I don't think so. It's not a main road, and it was snowing pretty hard."

"So as far as you know, the Ford might still be lying there on its side?"

"I suppose," Jon shrugged. "But when the storm lightened up, I think someone would've spotted it and called the police. Maybe that's why the other guys showed up at my house."

"You didn't get a look at the second team?"

"Christ, at that point I was running for my life."

Dave got up. "I'm going to use the pay phone."

Jon's coffee was cold, and he pushed it away. He was too nervous to drink it anyway. Through the coffee shop's window, all the passersby looked suspicious to him. He sat hunched over, hat pulled down to his ears, chin folded into his parka. In a short while, Saunders returned.

"This is not looking good," Dave said. "I think there's some freelancing going on."

"What do you mean?"

"This sort of thing isn't supposed to happen in government service. Most federal security officers are pretty dedicated. But every once in a while, some hungry agent falls for the money. Usually, a lot of it."

"I don't get it. Are you saying those guys were paid to arrest me?"

"I'm saying that no one at FBI headquarters is aware of an order for your arrest. That means that Johnson and Fitzpatrick were working on their own, outside of their normal duties. On the rare occasions that happens, it's usually because someone's paying them big bucks."

"What's to say it's not a behind-the-scenes operation that no one knows about?"

"A lot of things. Mainly, it's hard to keep things like that really quiet. I'm high enough in the hierarchy that I would have heard, and I didn't, okay?"

"Okay so far."

"Second," Dave continued, "normal arrests follow rules and procedures. No federal agent is going to pop a prisoner in the mouth. Well, maybe for a cop killer, but not for an admiral."

"What about for someone they claim tried to kill the first lady?"

"*Especially* for him. In a high-profile case, no one wants to hand the defense attorney any ammunition. Finally, nobody I spoke with is aware of a backup team sent to your house or anyplace else."

"But they were."

"Not officially, they weren't," Dave said. "Which is precisely my point. The way I see it, Fitzpatrick, Johnson, and maybe someone like Lewis are acting on their own. I never use the term 'rogue agent,' but that's exactly what they are. Someone got to them for freelance work, meaning you."

"What for? Why pretend to arrest me?"

"That's simple enough. The arrest was just a ruse. They were going to kill you."

The way his friend said it, so casually matter-of-fact, was chilling. He looked at Dave oddly, searching for a hint of jesting or insincerity. But there was no levity in the serious mask of his friend's face. After several seconds, the enormity of Dave's words began to sink in. Throughout Jon's life, not everyone had wished him well. Some people had tried to harm him, both physically and emotionally. But outside the jungles of Vietnam, no one had tried to kill him—until now.

"Any way they could have been acting on their own?"

"Get with the program, Jon. Look at the big picture. This is a well-organized plot that probably involves dozens of people. I'm more certain than ever that you're one of them—I don't mean a player, I mean caught up in it. This also involved the first lady, and maybe even the president."

"How does he fit into it?"

"Just listen. Start with what we know, okay? We have a known Palestinian terrorist as Roxanne's shooter. Then we have the missing California gun dealer, and his cousin the guest White House chef, also gone missing. Both Palestinians. And the chef, you remember, disappeared the day after Bob

Meredith choked on some unusually spicy food. See what I'm getting at?"

"That everything's connected."

Dave pointed a finger at him. "You got it. The 'whys,' we don't know yet. But as of today, the other thing that we know is that this isn't limited to militant Muslims. Someone else, probably here in Washington, is part of this. Maybe behind it. Someone connected well enough to know the first lady's schedule. Someone wealthy enough to buy off supposedly incorruptible FBI and Secret Service agents. So, the long answer to your question is, no, the agents weren't acting alone. This is a coordinated, well-orchestrated effort. You got in the way of something, my friend. And they want you dead."

"But you don't know why."

Dave shrugged. "Not yet."

"On the way home after the crash, I kept wondering about that. All I could think of was that I must have been a threat to someone, enough of a threat for them to want me out of the way."

"That goes without saying."

"But how, and why? It can't be me personally, as Jon Townsend. It's got to be something I'm *doing*, wouldn't you think?"

Dave slowly nodded. "Makes sense. You tell me. What are you doing that's threatening?"

"The only possible thing has to be my work. But no matter how I look it, I don't see what."

"Then look harder."

"Believe me, I am. But enough of my problems. Listen to what I just found out about the president."

Special Agent Saunders' ears perked up at the mention of the president. "Go on."

"You know what I told you about his neurological symptoms, and how I thought it might be this prion thing?" Off Dave's nod, "It turns out I'm wrong. I thought he'd contracted an Oriental form of something like mad cow disease from something he ate in Vietnam. But it's not that at all."

"Then what is it?"

"It's mercury, Dave. Bob Meredith is suffering from mercury poisoning."

Saunders squinted. "What?"

"That's the same reaction I had. But it's true."

"You sound pretty sure of that."

"I am. It's in his blood, in toxic amounts. I ran so many damn tests on him—urine, spinal fluid, blood, and saliva—and they were all fairly normal. But the very last test was an assay for heavy metals. The results just came in, and guess what? They're positive for mercury."

"Christ," said Saunders, "you can get that ill from mercury? I thought you could just get a little sick from contaminated swordfish."

"Too much mercury can kill you, Dave. It's a major environmental pollutant, and it's used in a lot of manufacturing processes. In acute, high-level intoxications, victims bleed into their guts and get kidney failure. But chronic mercury poisoning can also really mess you up. And it causes neurological problems just like Bob's."

"You're sure about this?"

"As sure as I can be. I probably should've been more suspicious when I did his exam. His breath had a funny smell, but I couldn't place it. Now I realize it was the odor of metallic mercury."

Dave shook his head, perplexed. "How could this happen? Is it some industrial source he came in contact with?"

"I don't think so. He has absolutely no history of industrial exposure. And I know he's not eating huge amounts of contaminated seafood."

"So, what does that leave?"

"Well, Roxanne didn't have it, and no one else in the White House got sick..." He looked away with a frown. "Except maybe Mr. Phillips."

"Come on, Phillips died of a heart attack. You were there yourself."

"Yes, I was, and I'm sure that was the immediate cause of death. But Mireille mentioned that, for a few months, he had neurological and personality changes that were just like the president's."

"I still don't see how an accident like that could happen."

"Who's talking about an accident?"

A twitch developed in Saunders' cheek when he saw what Jon was driving at. "Now wait just a minute, Jon," he said. "Think carefully about what you're saying."

"I am. I don't like the conclusion any more than you do."

"You're suggesting the attempted murder of the president of the United States!"

"Are you forgetting that for the past fifteen minutes we've been discussing a conspiracy involving me, the first lady, and a couple of Palestinians? That two dirty FBI agents just got killed, and that a now-missing chef may have already tried to poison the president? Of course I know what I'm suggesting!"

"Keep your voice down," Dave said, looking around. "I see your point. Now, enlighten me further. Just how is the president getting poisoned?"

"Food and drink are the usual routes. Mercury vapors can also be inhaled, but that's getting complicated."

"So, someone's poisoning his food? I have to tell you, Jon, that's pretty damn unlikely. Everything the president eats is closely scrutinized. Without going into tradecraft, suffice it so say that the Service has plans to protect against poisoning. All supplies and vendors are vetted, no strangers get in, and the kitchen is thoroughly watched and monitored."

"The ways and means are your business. I'm just opening the door."

Deep in thought, Saunders scratched his cheek. "Can mercury poisoning be treated?"

"Yes, it can. Most of its manifestations are reversible. That's the whole point. The sooner the president gets treated, the sooner he gets well."

"Great, Jon. Just what I need, some more job-related stress. You don't do things the easy way, do you? This is a fucking bombshell. I've got to talk to my boss about this, and I know he's going to want to get the best people on it, as of yesterday."

"That better include you."

"I'd like to think it would."

"I hope your boss realizes the best people also have to be the *right* people."

"I hear you," said Dave, preparing to go. "All right, what are we going to do about you? We should get your ass someplace safe."

"My first priority is to let the president know. Timing is critical now. Every passing hour jeopardizes his kidneys."

"I hear you, but I don't recommend going to the White House. People want you dead, and nothing has less value than a silent messenger. Give me a day or two, let me get the lay of the land. Then we'll have a better idea what to do."

"If not at the White House, you think you could arrange a private meeting between me and Bob?"

"I'll work on it. Meanwhile, keep out of sight. You know the drill. Cash only, no credit cards, and stay off the phone unless absolutely necessary. Call me later, okay?"

To Agent Lewis, time was short. Dr. Townsend had to be found and eliminated immediately. Every minute Townsend remained alive was yet another opportunity for him to interfere with their plans. At this point, it was doubtful the doctor knew very much. But the longer he stayed around, the more he was capable of piecing things together. Townsend was an intelligent man, far more resourceful than they'd expected.

Precisely how he'd eluded Johnson and Fitzpatrick was a mystery. The two agents sent a coded message that they'd picked the doctor up, but they never arrived at their destination. Then, half an hour later, their car had been discovered by the Bethesda cops—off the road, smashed into a tree, and with two dead occupants. There was no sign of Townsend. Lewis had immediately sent a backup team to the doctor's house, but he wasn't there. The local police were playing the accident as a weather-related mishap.

With the proper spin, the incident could be portrayed as a deadly assault by a homicidal fugitive.

Where had Townsend gone? There was no sign that he'd been injured in the crash, so they had to assume he'd escaped unharmed. He wasn't at home, and he wouldn't be foolish enough to go to work. Lewis considered it carefully. The doctor knew he was running for his life, but he was also an idealist who insisted on doing the right thing. That suggested he'd remain in the area. Thus, they'd continue the search, as discretely as possible. Very few people really knew what was going on, and it had to stay that way.

If he were Townsend, Lewis thought, where would he go? Near his daughter, to his ex-wife? Most fugitives relied on a support network of friends and family. That was worth checking out. Failing that, they'd have to convince him to come to them.

Jon finally risked calling Mireille. When they spoke, he stressed that she act as nonchalant as possible. Many people knew they were seeing one another, and she couldn't afford to arouse suspicion. Fortunately, Mireille often took off at midday to check out fresh produce at local markets. For her to leave today would seem part of her normal routine. Jon told her where to meet him.

A weather front had come through from west to east, forcing the storm clouds out into the Atlantic. The strong westerly wind that remained whipped the fallen snow into swirling gusts that danced across the street like tumbleweed. For Jon, the weather was an ally. Hunched over, he wanted to seem like any other pedestrian braving the elements to get from one place to another. He left the coffee shop and headed north. Head lowered, he made eye contact with no one.

The Georgetown Park mall was a short distance from the John F. Kennedy Recreation Center. Jon went in and quickly mingled with the shoppers. The mall had over three hundred stores in which to lose himself. He pretended to browse, never lingering long enough in one place for anyone to notice. Nervous and impatient, the morning hours passed far too slowly. Finally, at noon, he headed toward the food court.

As he'd instructed, Mireille was already sitting alone at a table. Jon bought pizza and Cokes from one of the vendors and sat across from her. Her face had an intensely troubled expression. He gently took her hand and began his explanation. As he filled her in on everything that happened, her eyes never left his.

"You should leave, Jon. Go somewhere. Take a vacation. It's not safe for you around here."

"Believe me, I've thought about that. But I'm a doctor, Mireille, and President Meredith is my patient. How would it look if I just up and left?'

"Look? Who cares how it would look? Those men want to kill you!"

"And I won't let that happen. I have no intention of letting them get anywhere near me. If I'm careful, they'll never find me."

"Then how are you going to help the president? To help him, you have to get near him. If these men are as ruthless as you say, they will shoot you on sight!"

"Dave's working on that for me. Look, Mireille, the president is a sick man. He needs help, and I'm the only one who knows what's wrong."

Exasperated by his stubbornness, she shook her head. "I can see your mind is made up. But how did this happen, Jon? How did he get poisoned?"

"That's what I need you to tell me. The most likely way of poisoning someone is in their food. But Dave thinks that'd be hard." He went on to explain what Saunders had said about the kitchen's security checks and balances.

"Everything he claims is true," Mireille said. "They watch food preparation very closely. Nothing sneaks in. Besides, if someone poisoned, say, the veal, how would he know that only the president would eat it? It would never work."

"What about what he drinks? Beer, soft drinks, coffee, even water?"

"The same as the food. Everything is checked. That includes snacks in the private residence and Oval Office. All the water is bottled. Even if he drank from the tap, I'm told the White House supply is specially filtered and monitored."

Finishing his pizza, Jon scanned the crowd with a pensive expression. In the sea of passing faces, no one looked suspicious. "Well, it has to be getting into his body somehow. He's not on any prescription medications, but maybe he's taking something over-the-counter." He paused. "I told you about his symptoms. What if he's not the only one?"

"Are you thinking of someone else?"

"From what you told me, Mr. Phillips had some of the same problems as President Meredith. Could they have eaten the same food?"

Mireille made a roach-rolling gesture with thumb and forefinger. "Maybe they had the same taste in cigarettes."

"Hmmm..." Jon squinted, looking into the distance. "The president smokes a pipe, you know."

"Really? I never saw him smoke."

"He doesn't, in public. Same as Jackie Kennedy. Bad for his image," he said slowly. His expression turned contemplative. "I wonder if that's possible."   .

"What?"

"I've been concentrating so much on oral intake that I forgot the inhalation route. But if someone inhales metallic mercury, it can be as toxic as if he eats it." Jon reached into his pocket and removed the crumpled Marlboro packet containing the Phillips roll-your-owns. He unrolled one, picking at the brown shreds of tobacco. "Mr. Phillips had access to the private residence, right?"

Mireille nodded. "He was one of the main ushers."

"It wouldn't surprise me if this is pipe tobacco. It's easy for smokers who roll their own to try different tobaccos. I realize he died of a heart attack, but if he helped himself to some of the president's stash.... You follow what I'm saying? That could account for some of his symptoms."

"Can you get it tested?" she asked.

"That's what I have in mind. But alone," he said, lifting the pack, "this doesn't prove a thing. We'd need a comparison sample from the president's humidors. There are at least two I'm aware of, one in the Oval Office, and one in the study off the bedroom." He looked her in the eye. "This could be risky, Mireille. But is there some way you could get me a sample?"

She gave a Gallic shrug. "Maybe. In fact, I'm serving dinner in the residence tonight."

It was midafternoon before Agent Lewis heard from his contact at the NSA. The National Security Agency—the nation's cryptographic organization headquartered at Fort Meade,

Maryland—was charged with protecting U.S. information systems. Through its network of overhead satellites and land systems, it had a formidable ability to perform electronic eavesdropping. The White House, along with executive agencies like the CIA and the State Department, were its primary clients. Thus, when the request for surveillance came through routine channels, the NSA immediately complied.

Since it specialized in SIGINT, or signals intelligence, the NSA's technicians had an unparalleled ability to intercept and evaluate telephone transmissions anywhere in the world. This included cell phones. Knowing Dr. Townsend's cell phone number would have simplified Lewis' job, but apparently the doctor was using a new number. Lewis had traced Townsend's recent credit card purchases, and none of the charges matched a phone vendor. Moreover, the regional phone companies didn't have a new listing for Townsend, suggesting he'd used a different name. Still, Lewis knew that if he was patient and the NSA computers did their job, they could decipher and locate the new number within twenty-four hours.

But twenty-four hours was more than Agent Lewis wanted to spend. There was, however, another method of locating cell phone users, one that relied on keywords. Spy satellites had the ability to listen in on cellular conversations anywhere in a given locale. These conversations were relayed to the NSA's computers, where sophisticated voice-recognition software programs sifted through millions of spoken words searching for matches, or hits. Of the several keywords Lewis had submitted, the one that proved successful was "Mireille."

By three p.m., Lewis was inspecting a ten-page transcript of that morning's conversations in which the word Mireille appeared. Lewis quickly found the exchange he wanted. Although the call had taken place four hours earlier, there was a remote chance that Dr. Townsend was still at the agree-upon location. Lewis quickly organized a team and headed for the mall.

His men scoured the shops, walkways, and open areas. By now the chef was known to have returned to the White House, but Lewis hoped the doctor had remained behind. But after a thorough search, nothing turned up. Still, by making the proper inquiries, Lewis learned that Townsend had been there. He also got a description of what the doctor was wearing.

It was now just a matter of time. Once they had the doctor's new cell phone number, they could directly monitor the conversations in real time. Sooner or later, the phone would lead them to him. When it did, they would converge on his location, arrest him, and take him away.

And then they would kill him.

CHAPTER 23

"This is superb, Chef Courtois," Forbes said, cutting another piece of the entrée. "What did you call it again?"

"Galantine de canard, monsieur."

"That's duck to you," said Vice President Doria.

"Thank you, Tony. That nearly escaped me. What do you think, Mr. President? Is this great, or what?"

"Hmmm."

The president's noncommittal grunt did not go unnoticed by Mireille, who was there for main-course presentation. The president, vice president, and chief of staff were having an early working dinner in the study off the bedroom. For informal meals, especially when Roxanne had been around, small presidential groups often dined there rather than in the dining room. On most of those occasions, the president had been in good spirits.

Mireille thought he had changed considerably in a relatively short time. Gone was his spark, and his personality seemed flat, lusterless. Mireille could tell he was distracted, preoccupied with his wife's prolonged coma. But for the first time she also noticed that he had some of the same physical quirks that afflicted the late Mr. Phillips. The tremor in his hand was pronounced. He was drinking bourbon steadily, and whenever he lifted his glass, some of the liquor spilled. His muscular movements lacked fluidity. The slightest gestures looked spastic and uncoordinated. Mireille thought the jerky mannerisms inescapable. But if the other guests noticed, they were either unusually polite or else so accustomed to the change that they overlooked it.

She also detected emotional changes. Fidgety and impatient, President Meredith looked distracted. He didn't appear to pay that much attention to what the others were saying. He gave the impression of not caring as much as he used to. Also, there was an undertone of annoyance to his squirming, as if he was going to snap at someone at any minute.

So, this is mercury, she thought.

"Is there a problem with the duck, Monsieur le President?"

"Duck?" He looked at her oddly, as if not understanding. "No, no problem. Not hungry, that's all." He pushed his plate away.

"Can I refresh your drink?"

He drained the glass and handed it to her. "Thank you."

This was exactly what Mireille had been hoping for. Ever since she'd wheeled the food cart into the study, Mireille had been looking for an opportunity to get a sample of presidential tobacco. The president didn't use a pouch. Rather, he filled his pipe directly from the humidor. The masculine, custom-made box, crafted of mahogany and leather, lay atop the liquor cabinet next to several bottles of whiskey and an ice bucket.

She'd needed a pretense to approach the cabinet. Since there were five other people in the room—the three politicians, a kitchen helper, and a Secret Service agent—she couldn't simply waltz over and help herself. Refilling the president's glass was the perfect excuse. But she was startled when the kitchen helper moved to take the glass.

"I can get that, ma'am."

"Refill the water glasses, please," she quickly whispered. "I'll take care of this."

She approached the liquor cabinet before anyone else could interfere. She remembered what Jon had told her about Lewis, and she didn't know if the Secret Service agent was one of his men. Hazarding a glance over her shoulder, Mireille was relieved to see that the agent was watching the dinner table. At the liquor cabinet, she put down the glass, which she'd been carrying in a linen napkin. The ice bucket was next to the humidor. Mireille removed the bucket's lid and used tongs to place three large ice cubes in the president's glass. Then, as she reached for the bottle of bourbon, she knocked over the glass. She made no fuss about it. To the casual observer, she wanted it to appear like one of those little mishaps that merits no attention. Mireille's back was to the room, shielding her from view. Working quickly, she wiped away the ice with the napkin. As she did, she casually mopped away imaginary spill stains that soiled the humidor. When she dabbed its sides, she nonchalantly lifted its top and squeezed a pinch of tobacco with her fingers. She casually deposited her catch in the napkin. Then, after successfully refreshing the president's drink, she slid the napkin into her pocket.

Before she brought the meal to the study, she had only Jon's word that her sleight of hand was required. For her, that was all that was necessary. But half an hour later, as she left the room with the serving tray, Mireille was convinced Jon was right. President Meredith was a sick man. Physically and emotionally wounded, he desperately needed help.

"Disturbing news, Mr. President," said Forbes.

It was nine p.m., well after the last vestiges of the meal had been cleared away and the guests departed. The president had remained in the study to review campaign paperwork. There were dozens of advance reports, projections, and pages that needed his signature. He had changed into his pajamas and was sitting in a recliner, puffing away on his pipe, when Forbes knocked and entered.

"What's disturbing?"

"It's about Dr. Townsend."

"Jon? Did something happen to him?"

Forbes paused, making a steeple of his fingers. "This is a difficult subject. Let me start by saying that the Secret Service has been keeping an eye on him for a while—"

"Watching Jon Townsend? What the hell are you talking about?"

"Please, Mr. President, let me finish. This is complicated. Not long ago, Dr. Townsend reported that someone tried to murder him in his own home using cyanide gas. There was some evidence of that, but a few of the investigators thought the report a little farfetched. Basically, our in-house intelligence concluded that Townsend may have rigged the whole thing himself to look like an attempted murder."

Meredith exhaled a plume of smoke. "That's the most ridiculous thing I've ever heard. Don't tell me you actually believe it."

"I hear you, sir, but there's more to it than that. I'm sure I don't have to remind you that Townsend's actions have always been hard to predict, going back to when he was under your command in Vietnam."

"That was thirty years ago, for God's sake. He was a young kid."

"I realize that, Mr. President," Forbes patiently continued. "All I'm suggesting is that not everyone changes with time. Just assume for a minute that what I'm saying is true. It has to do with Roxanne."

A flash of anger tempered Meredith's curiosity, but he kept silent.

"You may not be aware of it," Forbes went on, "but on the night of the first lady's shooting, Dr. Townsend was supposed to have accompanied her to Baltimore. He was a last-minute no-show—"

"I'm sure he had a good excuse," Meredith said, although his tone didn't have quite the conviction as before.

"He had an excuse," Forbes agreed with a nod, "though the Agency thought it might be a little *too* convenient."

"I presume you're getting to the point."

"Just this, Mr. President. Since your wife's shooting, the intelligence services are leaving no stone unturned. *Everyone* who knew the first lady has been under suspicion, and that includes Dr. Townsend. Recently, his activities have been more and more bizarre. This morning, two FBI agents went to his home to question him." He paused. "I'm sorry to have to tell you this, but they were found dead in their car a short distance away."

Meredith's whiskey-reddened eyes widened with incredulity. For a long moment he stared intently at his chief of staff. "You're a good man, Mitch. I don't doubt your intentions.

But you don't know Jon Townsend like I do. Sure, I remember what happened in Vietnam. And I'm telling you, the man is incapable of murder."

"Mr. President, no one questions your allegiance. It's one of the reasons your staff is so loyal. And again, I'm sorry to tell you the bad news, but it gets worse. Dr. Townsend has disappeared, sir. The Justice Department issued a search warrant for his home. I'm afraid they found evidence directly linking him to the death of Mahmoud Al-Abed."

"You're joking," Meredith said. "They found the gun in his house?"

"Not the gun, sir. They found the ammunition."

Slightly pale, Meredith got up and started to pace. "I'd like to see this so-called evidence myself."

"You will, Mr. President, just as soon as they—"

"Shut up, Goddammit, and let *me* finish. I couldn't ask for a better chief of staff than you, Mitch. But I know Jon Townsend, and what you're suggesting is totally out of character. He's always been there for me, and God knows Rocky trusted him like a brother. Still, I suppose stranger things have happened. So, if the spooks have done their jobs properly, let the chips fall where they may. If a court finds he's guilty of something, so be it. But until then, I want him given the benefit of the doubt. Extend him every courtesy and trust him like an officer and a gentleman. Do I make myself clear?"

"Yes, Mr. President."

"God knows he's earned it."

In luxury high-rises, less-expensive ground-floor apartments were usually scorned because of their inferior views. Mireille agreed with that premise, but when she came to town, it was all she could afford in her price range. Nonetheless, the building's rear grounds gently sloped down toward the Potomac, and low as her apartment was, it still had a delightful river view. When she moved in, it never occurred to her that the ground floor might have unexpected benefits.

Earlier, when Mireille met Jon at the mall, one of the things they discussed was how to safely meet again. Jon knew his luck couldn't hold out forever. He was a hunted man just one step ahead of his pursuers. Although he thought the conspiracy was limited, it stood to reason that the plotters' manpower assets were considerable. There were doubtless people scouring the city for him, talking with informants, watching the areas he frequented. In addition to his home and office, another place was undoubtedly Mireille's apartment. Therefore, Jon and Mireille agreed that he would avoid the front entrance.

He called her at home from a pay phone. They spoke simply and avoided using each other's names. Mireille indicated she couldn't spot any surveillance. Thus reassured, Jon took a cab down Wisconsin Avenue, getting off at the intersection with K Street. Mireille's building was several blocks to the west. Walking with an easy if furtive stride, Jon headed away from the streetlights and toward the river, a few hundred yards away. Combined with the recent snowfall, the chill wind off the Potomac kept passersby away. Soon he was directly behind her building.

The high-rise's designers had tastefully landscaped the grounds approaching the river. Tall plantings and trees provide good concealment, and Jon used the natural cover as he approached the building. Nearly there, he had to cross a fifty-foot open area bathed in security lights. Undaunted, he sprinted through the untouched snow and soon vaulted the railing to Mireille's narrow patio porch.

The interior blinds were closed. Looking behind him, Jon detected no threats. He rapped softly on the sliding glass door. Almost immediately, Mireille separated the blinds, spotted him, and unlocked the door. She was wearing a long robe. Jon slipped into the apartment and was in her arms at once.

"I was so worried!" she said, hugging him tight. "Did anyone see you?"

"I don't think so. I was pretty careful, but the tracks in the snow are fairly obvious. They lead right to your door. I doubt anyone will notice tonight, but it'll be a different story tomorrow. I'd better not stay too long. So? How'd you make out with the tobacco?"

"Perfect. It was just sitting there, begging me to take it. So,

I did." She pulled away. "You feel so cold. Are these clothes warm enough?"

"Barely. But it's not their thinness that bothers me, it's their appearance. If someone spotted me, they might have given out my description."

"Then you should change into something else."

"And where, pray, am I supposed to find the apparel?"

Smiling, Mireille raised her eyebrows. "Remember Jean Claude?"

"Your brother, the Air France co-pilot?"

"Yes," she nodded. "He has some clothes here, even a winter coat. I'm sure they'll fit." She took his hand and led him toward the bedroom. While he sat on the bed, she rummaged through her closet and removed a pair of jeans, undergarments, and a designer shirt. She handed them to Jon to try on.

He looked them over. The fabric was expensive, the labels European. But the sizes looked right. "Perfect. And even if there is no Jean Claude, I'm grateful."

"I guess you'll have to stick around long enough to find out," she said lightly. "Go ahead, put them on."

"Now?"

"Now. Need help?"

Jon stood up and removed his shirt. "I think I can manage."

He expected her to walk away. Instead, Mireille stood there watching him, arms akimbo, a devilish smile on her face. She was staring into his eyes, amused by his uneasiness. As he removed his belt and pants, he periodically hesitated.

"Does this make you uncomfortable, Jon?"

"This? No. Been undressing all my life."

"You don't mind if I watch, do you?"

"Hell no. Watch away." But as his thumbs hooked the elastic of his boxers, he paused and sighed. "You're just going to stand there, is that it?"

"Yes, I am. Do you know why?"

"I have a feeling you're going to tell me."

"Because I love your body. I always have. Maybe if I look closely, I can see why it turns me on so much."

"Okay." He pulled down his shorts, stepped out of them,

and stood there. "All right, look closely."

She did, slowly eyeing him up and down. Mireille untied the sash of her robe, slid the cloth off her shoulders, and let it fall to the floor. Underneath, she was naked. "You don't have to leave right away, do you?"

"It's not safe to stay too long."

Mireille took slow, provocative steps his way, stopping inches from him. She could see the gooseflesh on his skin. As she reached up to touch his face, her nipples grazed his upper abdomen. "Five minutes isn't very long, is it?"

Half an hour later, as they lay in one another's arms, they both knew the time had come for him to go. Mireille snuggled up closely.

"You feel much warmer now."

"I am, thank you."

"What are we going to do with the tobacco?"

Jon propped himself up on an elbow. "We've got to get it to the lab. The head technician, Chris Leadbetter, is an old friend of mine. Despite what he may have heard by now, I think I can trust him. He's the one who clued me in on the president's mercury level."

"Are you going to take the samples over there?"

"I'd like to, but one of the first places they'll be looking for me is where I work. Think you could do it for me?"

"I thought you said they'll be watching me, too."

"I'm sure they are, but all they'll do is watch and report. They wouldn't dare arrest you, especially when they're not sure what you're up to."

"Exactly what do you want me to do?" she asked.

After he told her, Jon left the same way he'd arrived. Retracing his tracks through the snow, he made his way along the riverbank and then, eventually, through Georgetown proper. There was still no one following him. In Georgetown's narrow streets, there were several all-night cafes to choose from. Jon selected the least conspicuous and walked in.

Back in her apartment, still savoring the warm afterglow of their lovemaking, Mireille thought about Jon. She knew she loved him deeply and would do anything to help him. What he asked of her should be simple enough. In the atrium near his office in the outpatient building, she was to leave both tobacco samples. She would tape them to the underside of a table and leave. After she was gone, Jon's friend Chris would do the rest. Mireille didn't think it would prove too difficult.

Unable to sleep, she rolled over and used the remote to switch on the TV. As the indistinct image sharpened, Mireille's heart started to pound, and she sat up. The sheet fell away as she turned up the volume.

"To repeat our breaking story," said the newscaster, "Washington police and the FBI are searching for Admiral Jon Townsend, noted Bethesda doctor and personal physician to President Meredith. Dr. Townsend is wanted for questioning in the murder of Mahmoud Al-Abed, who is alleged to be the attempted assassin of First Lady Roxanne Meredith. He is also accused of complicity in the first lady's shooting. In addition, police hint at his involvement in the deaths of two FBI agents whose bodies were found this morning after they had gone to arrest Dr. Townsend at his home. Late this afternoon, a joint strike force executed a search warrant on Townsend's Bethesda home and discovered thirty-two-caliber shell casings that are ballistically linked to the Al-Abed murder weapon. Dr. Townsend should be considered armed and dangerous. Authorities are asking anyone with information on the suspect's whereabouts to contact—"

Dumbstruck, Mireille switched off the TV. She felt cold and utterly alone. Things like this weren't supposed to happen. The allegations were so outrageous that she felt incapable of responding. She got out of bed, put on her robe, and began to pace. She doubted Jon heard about the story, although he would, soon enough. She wished she could protect him, or at least warn him, but that wasn't possible. He told her not to dare risk contacting him. And so, she just paced, a victim of her own fears, helpless and terrified.

In the cafe, despite the late hour, Jon wore sunglasses and kept his ski hat pulled low over his forehead. The few other patrons were too absorbed in their own activities to pay him any attention. Jon quietly went online and composed his email.

"Dear Chris," he typed. "I'm sorry to have to reach out to you electronically rather than in person, but the fact is, I'm in trouble. By the time you read this, you may have heard some disturbing rumors about me. Let me reassure you that they are absolutely untrue. I've become dragged into something I don't really understand, but it's dead serious. All I can say is that it involves the president's health. I'll explain everything when I can, hopefully in person, once I fully understand it. But for now, I need your help. I'm going to rely on your trust and friendship for a big favor."

In detail, Jon related where Chris should look for the tobacco samples and what he wanted done with them. Jon knew it was a rush job, both for himself and the lab workers. But he didn't know any other way to go about it. If he wanted the result, he needed Chris' skill and savvy. Without them, there was no way he could save himself—or the president.

The Bell 2063B helicopter hovered in the cold gray skies above Georgetown, searching the ground below. The observer in the co-pilot's seat trained his Steiner binoculars on the area behind Mireille's apartment.

"We have fresh footprints leading to the chef's apartment, lead," the man said, using Mireille's code name. "Looks like one set going in and out, copy?"

"Copy that," said Lewis, listening from his ground car. "Any sign of Dr. Townsend?"

"The tracks look at least a couple hours old. I'd say he was here and gone."

"Copy. Hang for another ten minutes and then move off site."

Lewis radioed one of the ground surveillance teams and informed them of the discovery. If Townsend had visited Courtois, there had to be a reason for the rendezvous. The two were known to be romantically involved, but since the doctor was doubtless aware he was being sought, he'd have been a fool to visit simply for sexual favors. And Townsend was certainly no fool. No, the doctor was up to something. And if they couldn't locate him, perhaps the girl could lead them to him.

Of the surveillance units in the area, one was assigned to Chef Courtois. Shortly after eight a.m., the chef left home and headed for the White House. This was her normal going-to-work time. The in-house team picked her up and reported business as usual. But at ten, she abruptly exited the kitchen and left the White House. The mobile unit picked her up and followed her to the National Naval Medical Center, where she parked.

Worried that Townsend had evaded them and was back at the outpatient building, two teams converged on it, hoping to catch him unawares. Taking no chances, they kept out of sight as they carefully tailed Courtois to the indoor eating area. But she was alone, and no one joined her. Mireille bought a cup of coffee and took a table by herself. After nursing her beverage for ten minutes, she slowly got up and left. Once outside the facility, the team trailed her back to the White House, where she resumed work. There was no sign of Townsend.

The events left Lewis confused and annoyed. It rankled him that he didn't know what Courtois was up to. He felt pressured. Time was not on their side, and those running the show wanted results.

And they wanted them now.

Like Agent Lewis, Chris Leadbetter was confused. He'd heard the same news as everyone else about Dr. Townsend, news that was the talk of the hospital. The story seemed preposterous. He'd known Dr. Townsend for years and found him to be a compassionate physician and loyal friend. Townsend was not only Chris' own doctor but also the Leadbetter family physician. He'd been there throughout Chris' mom's long and arduous battle with colon cancer, often coming in on his nights and weekends during his off-time. Chris was deeply in his debt.

Yet, once aware of the monumental crime of which Townsend had been accused, Chris also understood his role as a key government employee. Being paid by the government left him with certain obligations. Underlying his confusion was the struggle between allegiance and gratitude. And then there was the matter of the email. At least Dr. Townsend hadn't tried to deny that a problem existed. In matters like this, Chris thought, where there were two conflicting viewpoints, it often boiled down to a matter of conscience. For him, there was no question where his conscience led him.

At precisely, eleven a.m., following Dr. Townsend's instructions, Chris left the lab and went to the lunch area. The midday crown hadn't yet arrived. Chris bought a Diet Coke and sat down at the table nearest the cashier. For the next five minutes, he was a study in casual break-taking. Then, as nonchalantly as possible, he slid his hand under the table. He located the letter-size envelope, stuck in place with a wad of chewing gum.

Chris pried it free and carried it, along with what remained of his drink, back to the lab.

It didn't feel like New Year's Eve.

The fact that the holiday fell on a weekday put a crimp in plans for festivities. Then there was the emotional fallout from the first lady's illness. The countrywide letdown persisted through Christmas and lessened customarily high spirits. The weather was also a factor. Although the snow had long since stopped, a stalled low-pressure front kept the clouds low and the skies uniformly gray. By three p.m., those still at work left their jobs for subdued holiday celebrations.

After Jon left Mireille, he called Dave, hoping that the Secret Service agent could come up with an idea of how Jon could inform the president. Dave was still working on it but thought he might have something by later that afternoon. In the meantime, Jon had to kill time and keep out of sight. Wearing Mireille's brother's clothes, he took a cab to nearby Chevy Chase, Maryland. The area had a cineplex that began showing movies at midmorning. With his thoughts light years away, Jon spent the next few hours staring at the big screen.

He knew it would take a while for Chris to perform the tests. Still, he'd lucked out in this regard because the National Naval Medical Center's lab had recently procured the atomic absorption equipment required for the testing. Previously, heavy-metal requests had to be shipped to reference labs in Los Angeles or Philadelphia, a process that would require several days. Jon didn't have several days. He thought he'd be lucky to elude detection for another twenty-four hours.

At four p.m., he left the theater and called the lab, where he was immediately put through to Chris.

"How're the tests coming?" he asked.

"Just finished, Dr. Townsend. Now, these are supposedly two separate samples, right?"

"Why do you ask?"

"Because even though one's rolled in cigarette paper and the other's loose, the tobaccos are identical."

Bells started ringing in Jon's head. "Identical, how?"

"Microscopically, the tobacco cut and textures are the same. These are pipe tobaccos, and it looks to me like they're from the same source. And then there are the test results."

"What'd they show?"

"Unless I made an error, both samples are impregnated with toxically high levels of mercury," said Chris. "And the levels are exactly the same."

Bingo, Jon thought. "That's great, Chris. Do me one last favor. Write all this down and lock it up somewhere safe. Don't show it to anybody, okay?"

"All right," Chris slowly agreed. "Dr. Townsend, could I ask—?"

"Not now. But I'll let you know everything soon. Just rest assured you haven't done anything wrong. I owe you big time, my friend."

With that, Jon rang off. He silently thanked God there were still people he could trust. Without Chris' information, he'd just be spinning his wheels; with it, he knew precisely what had happened. It was now clear that someone had placed poisonously high amounts of mercury in the president's tobacco. Every time Bob Meredith lit his pipe, he was inhaling toxic mercury fumes. And as the months went by, those fumes were causing an organic brain syndrome whose features were indistinguishable from better-known neurological disorders.

It was a remarkably clever way of incapacitating someone.

For the victim, it would be business as usual. Although everyone knew smoking tobacco was unhealthy, never in his wildest dreams would President Meredith suspect that he was committing suicide by lighting his pipe. And then there was poor Mr. Phillips, who must have loved the tobacco's aroma. Or perhaps the president had given him permission to borrow from the humidor. But by smoking the president's tobacco, Mr. Phillips was killing himself just as surely as if he'd swallowed cyanide.

Cyanide...the reason behind Jon's own murder attempt was now clear. He must have been getting close, too close. Once Roxanne's concerns had triggered her husband's in-depth evaluation, Jon was doomed. The more he thought about it, the more everything was falling into place. Roxanne *had* been right, after all. She knew her husband, and she realized something dreadfully wrong was happening to him. Her major blunder was to get hysterical about it. Whoever was poisoning the president wanted it to look like a slow, inexorable, and rather benign neurological condition, one that wouldn't interfere with the re-election. Once the first lady started making verbal waves, her fate was sealed.

As for himself, Jon thought, he'd become expendable once he started digging.

The president's enemies must have reached that decision when Jon ordered test after additional test. They probably realized that he'd stumble across the answer at some point. Before he did, he'd be eliminated with a few whiffs of cyanide.

How lucky he'd been! Sure, he'd been determined, but his father always told him it was better to be lucky than smart, and he'd been fortunate indeed. But he wouldn't stay lucky forever. The same people who'd sent men to kill him were undoubtedly behind what happened to the first lady and the president. If they had the ability to control supposedly dedicated agents of the nation's intelligence services, they had to be powerful men indeed. And the fact that they were trying to engineer events around the presidential election process suggested they were politically connected—and probably very high up.

As for precisely who, that was not for him to say. His job as a physician was to be a medical diagnostician, something that now, through persistence and luck, he'd been successful at. Still, Jon had his suspicions. The one person who most clearly tried interfering with the medical workup was Mitch Forbes. The chief of staff was certainly powerful and politically connected, but he was also the president's man. Bob Meredith liked and trusted Forbes, and if the president were out of the way, Forbes would be out of a job. No, Jon thought, he doubted it was Forbes. And there must be something else going on, something that eluded him.

He dearly wanted to go over all this with people he trusted, like Dave and Mireille. But first he had more pressing matters. He had to let Dave know what the tests revealed, and he hoped Dave would come up with a way for him to get to the president. Soon after he finished speaking with Chris Leadbetter, Jon called Saunders outside of the movie complex.

"Dave, my man," he said when the agent picked up. "I hope you're ready for this, because I just heard something that's going to knock your socks off."

Over the next few minutes, Jon related what he'd learned about the plot to poison the president. Dave listened in stunned silence.

"Are you sure about this?" he asked.

"It's a very accurate test, so I guess I am."

"Jesus. This is scary stuff, Jon. Are you certain you can trust Leadbetter not to say anything?"

"I think so. What I'm wondering is, who put the mercury in? It'd have to be someone with access to the humidors, right?"

"Not necessarily. The tobacco could have arrived already spiked. A lot depends on where it comes from."

"You don't happen to know, do you?"

"I'm afraid not," said Dave.

"Then I guess I'll have to ask Bob myself. How're you doing on that front?"

"I think I've got an idea."

The president's original plans for the holiday, Dave explained, had been cancelled after Roxanne's shooting. No one on the White House staff pestered the president about subsequent arrangements, and he didn't volunteer any—until today. Several hours ago, the president said that, after a visit to Shock Trauma, he wanted to spend the rest of the holiday at Camp David. Saunders would be accompanying the presidential detail. Since it was a last-minute trip, Dave said, the normally light holiday security contingent would be further reduced. Dave thought he could safely get Jon in to see the president.

Dave's plan was simple. Camp David wasn't far from Washington. Jon would rent a car under an alias and drive up to the state park to arrive at nine p.m. Rather than try to sneak into the facility, which would be virtually impossible, Jon would simply show up at the main gate. Dave would clear Jon's entry with the Marine sentry on duty.

Jon had no doubt he could rent a car and arrive on time, but the plan seemed almost too simple. Yet he was in no position to argue. He trusted Dave implicitly. Time was short, and his pursuers were doubtless closing in. This was his last, best shot, and he was determined to take it.

Still, he didn't want to go completely unprepared. It might be a good idea, he thought, if he wasn't wearing civilian clothes. He'd been a guest at Camp David before, and he felt the security personnel would be more receptive to someone in uniform than in civilian clothes. He stored uniforms both at work and at home. Although he was certain they'd be looking for him at the medical center, he sincerely doubted that, after his arrest, anyone would think he'd dare return home. Yet this was precisely where he would go.

Then there was the question of weapons. He still had Agent Johnson's automatic, but if he was heading home, it might behoove him to pick up the shotgun, for more stopping power. He certainly couldn't lug it through Camp David, but only a fool would overlook personal safety. And Jon had been a fool long enough not to have learned his lesson.

"Agent Lewis, this is Specialist Nugent at the NSA, come in please."

"Go ahead, Nugent."

"Sir, Lorsat recorded a cellular transmission from the suspect cell phone. Location is Chevy Chase, Maryland. I can give you coordinates, and I can send you the transmission. What's your preference?"

As he sat in his car, a smile slowly spread across Lewis' face. *Finally,* he thought to himself. For a man labeled a gutless coward, Dr. Townsend was proving to be a far more resourceful adversary than they'd anticipated. But while their operation wasn't large, their resources were abundant. Once they'd leaked the phony news story, their numbers were augmented by thousands of police and public-spirited citizens. It was only a question of time before they were on to him. "Are you ready to transmit?"

"Yes, sir."

"Switching to secure frequency, channel eight."

Over the next several minutes, Lewis and the man beside him listened to a recording of the recent Townsend phone conversation. So, he finally figured out what was happening to the president, Lewis thought. He'd only been recently told all the details himself. His bosses knew that the doctor was an excellent diagnostician who'd eventually piece things together. Clearly now that Townsend had pieced things together, he had to be stopped before he revealed what was going on.

Lewis thought that the other voice's Camp David idea was ingenious. And as much as it presented an opportunity for the doctor, it also presented an idea for them. When the transmission ended, Lewis thanked Nugent and signed off.

"There's light at the end of the tunnel," Lewis said.

"So it would appear," said the powerfully built man beside him. "It all comes down to this."

Lewis put the car into gear and cruised away from the curb. "Let's get started. I'll drop you at your hotel."

"That'd be fine," said O'Brien.

"Can I help you out with anything else?"

"You've been more than enough help as it is, pal. I think I can handle things from here on out. Why don't I call you when it's over?"

"When you are *sure* it's over," said Lewis. "I'm under orders not to report back until I'm convinced."

Lewis dropped Sean off at the Hotel Harrington, a modestly priced tourist hotel on Eleventh Street. One hundred dollars per night was all the leader of the now-defunct Southern Cross was willing to spend. But in truth, Sean rarely needed luxurious lodgings. At heart, he had a beer drinker's inexpensive tastes cultivated during his Beantown boyhood.

The sum he was being paid for this job, although not insubstantial, was not the reason he was in town for this job. He wasn't here for the money or to fulfill lofty personal goals. Rather, what impelled him was a profound sense of loyalty to the man who had saved his life. It was a loyalty that went beyond issues, causes, and fundamentalist beliefs. To Sean's way of thinking, such beliefs didn't empower a man, but crippled him. When one became wedded to a cause, he lost his own identity. Not that there weren't plenty of young men willing to martyr themselves in the name of one extremist belief or another. Indeed, there were more than enough Palestinians like Mahmoud Al-Abed, and right-wing religious fanatics like C.J. Walker, to fill several lifetimes. Sean saw little difference between them. In his scheme of things, such men had a place and served a purpose. They were the cannon fodder necessary to get the big jobs done. Sean wondered if Mahmoud had a better insight into that purpose the instant before his death, when their eyes met on that rooftop in Baltimore.

When he left Boston, the man he now worked for had given Sean a calling: listen to what I say and follow my orders. We will ultimately become wealthy, comfortable, and fulfilled. And Sean had done just that. The transition from idealist to pragmatist proved rather easy. He became task- and goal-oriented, doing what was asked of him. And now, achieving his goals meant leaving no loose ends. Dr. Townsend was one such loose end who threatened everything his boss had accomplished. And while it was fine to let disenchanted agents of the FBI and Secret Service discover the good doctor's whereabouts, Sean could not be certain they would take him out. O'Brien knew from long experience that when in doubt, it was best to enter the hunt oneself. So, as soon as Agent Lewis drove away from the hotel, Sean caught a cab and had it take him to the government car he'd left in Bethesda, Maryland.

He had a hunch about the doctor, and his hunches were rarely wrong.

CHAPTER 24

Sunset officially arrived at four forty-six p.m., and by five, it was completely dark. Jon waited until nightfall before returning home. Still dressed in Jean Claude's jeans and topcoat, he might have been any resident strolling through the neighborhood. Except that he wasn't strolling. When the cab dropped him off, he moved stealthily from one area of concealment to the next, slowly working his way to the back of his house.

The temperature dipped below freezing. Underfoot, the snow crunched wherever he stepped.

In the dark, Jon could barely make out the footprints from the day before, when he'd fled the house in the snow. There were no other tracks around his. In front of him, the unlighted house looked like he'd left it. Staying in a crouch, Jon slowly made his way to the back door. He tested the knob and found it unlocked—again, as he'd left it.

Turning the knob slowly, he eased the door open and listened for a minute. There was nothing but the stale silence of an abandoned dwelling. Satisfied, he pushed the door open and let himself in.

He was already looking ahead toward that evening. The way Jon figured it, whoever was looking for him was searching for Admiral Jon Townsend. While this was probably not the most important consideration for getting into Camp David, it couldn't hurt to dress down. In fact, he still had his enlisted man's uniform from his days in Vietnam. In all those years he'd only gained ten pounds. He was sure he could still fit into the uniform.

It felt odd sneaking into his own home. Yet sneak he did,

creeping cautiously, slowly stealing through the halls and rooms. He sifted the silence for the slightest sound, straining to hear the unacceptable. The only noise was his own cautious footfalls and the occasional creak of a floorboard. Reaching the basement door, Jon opened it, turned on the light, and proceeded downstairs.

He kept the old uniform in the basement cedar storage closet. The dry wooden staircase seemed to make a frightful groan with each passing step. When he reached the ground floor, he approached the closet and swung it open. The musty interior smelled of mothballs. Jon found the drawstring of the bare light fixture and yanked. The forty-watt bulb outlined the garments in its pale-yellow glow.

It had been more than a year since he'd last been down here. Most of the items should probably have been discarded, but he never had the desire to go through them. Most things not encased in clothing bags were covered with a visible layer of dust. Several of Victoria's old coats hung limp and untouched, and their sight gave him pause. But soon Jon pushed them aside, locating his decades-old uniform in the back of the closet.

The appearance of the green serge flooded him with memories. In a split second Jon pictured himself back on a parade ground thirty years earlier, standing with his platoon buddies under a hot sun. The memories were unwanted cobwebs he brushed aside. He had things to do and little time in which to do them. Lifting the clothes hanger, he coughed at the swirl of dust that filled his nostrils. Then he turned off the lights and went upstairs.

Once there, he left the lights off. There was no point in alerting anyone who might be out front, and besides, he knew his way around blindfolded. He went to his bedroom and slipped out of Jean Claude's clothes. When he stepped into the uniform, the wool's familiar feel and smell returned. It surprised and flattered him that the uniform still fit, albeit snugly. He unconsciously brushed at unseen wrinkles and walked out of the bedroom.

In the hall, when he was abreast of the laundry room, the lights suddenly switched on. Jon froze. His heart pounded wildly, and he broke out in a cold sweat.

"You look very convincing in that uniform, Dr. Townsend," came a man's voice from behind him. "No doubt they would have been impressed at Camp David. Turn around. Slowly, please."

Jon's mind whirled, and his brain was on fire. He was completely unfamiliar with the voice behind him. The slight New England accent was deep and thoroughly threatening. Worse still, the stranger knew about Camp David! How was that possible? Jon was sure Saunders hadn't told anyone. His only conclusion was that they must have listened to his cell phone transmissions—something he knew the techno-geeks were capable of doing, but only, he'd believed, with other people. Ever so slowly, he began turning around. As his gaze swept over the laundry room, he caught sight of the washing machine. And there, atop its lid, was Agent Johnson's automatic.

When he'd fled the house a day and a half ago, shotgun in hand, Jon had forgotten about the handgun. All he'd been concerned with was getting away. Now the pistol was within easy reach, but he resisted the impulse. Finishing his about-face, Jon found himself looking at a powerfully built man, whose own gun was pointed at Jon's midsection.

"Who—?" Jon began.

Sean's gaze was icy. "To a dead man, that doesn't matter." With that, he fired.

In the narrow hallway, the gun's explosive roar coincided with a hammering blow to Jon's abdomen. The force of the bullet knocked him backward and spun him around, toward the laundry room. Off balance, Jon twisted into it, spinning as he fell. He spotted Agent Johnson's automatic and reached for it as he went down.

He hit the floor hard. The air was knocked out of him, and he gasped for breath. But curiously, there was none of the spreading paralysis or growing weakness he associated with a mortal wound. Before he could dwell on it, he saw the stranger close in for the coup de grâce. Jon's fingers tightened around the pistol's butt. Without aiming, Jon pointed up and fired as the stranger loomed over him.

The man had been pointing his gun at Jon's head when Jon's gun roared. The bullet tore into O'Brien's shoulder, striking bone just as he himself fired. The impact made the big man's body torque. This deflected Sean's aim, and his return volley struck Jon's automatic on the hard metal frame above the trigger guard. Jon's gun spun away.

He didn't hesitate. Before the stranger could react, Jon lashed out hard with his foot, striking the man's knee. The leg buckled, and O'Brien went down. Realizing the reprieve was temporary, Jon wasted no time. He rolled onto his knees and quickly leapt to his feet, running down the hall to the back door. Behind him, the big man grumbled and cursed as he righted himself. Jon had just grasped the doorknob when another bullet punched a hole in the glass beside his head.

Desperate to escape, Jon yanked the door open and dashed toward freedom, out into the snow. But the soles of his dress black boots were still warm from the storage closet, and he immediately went down on all fours. From inside the house, he heard footsteps running toward him. There was another loud crack. A whining buzz whizzed past his ear, and a geyser of snow erupted upward. Driven by terror, Jon forced himself up as yet another shot tore through his sleeve. He frantically sprinted toward the trees.

Behind him, Sean raced after his prey, through the back door. He couldn't understand how Townsend had survived the first shot, which had clearly hit him mid-torso. And where had the doctor gotten the gun? Making matters worse, the initial numbness in his own shoulder was starting to wear off, replaced by a searing pain. Up ahead, his quarry's olive uniform was growing indistinct in the darkness. Sean had already fired wildly, something prohibited by the discipline of his craft. No, he had to catch up with Townsend first. And then he would kill him.

Sean watched the doctor reach the thicket at the rear of the property. The big man's legs pumped furiously, lessening the distance. All at once, Townsend slipped and fell flat. As the doctor struggled to right himself, O'Brien grinned, quickly closing the gap. His gun hand went up.

Jon had tripped on something even more slippery than the snow itself. His falling body brushed away the ground snow—and there, to his astonishment, was the tarp he'd found yesterday morning, the same tarp on which he now lost his footing. In the darkness, he frantically clawed at what lay within it, expecting another bullet to find him at any second. Behind him, the stranger's footfalls slowed.

Although it was hard to see in the darkness, Sean kept his gun pointed at the doctor's central mass. He would shoot the instant he got close enough. Curiously, the doctor seemed to stop struggling. They did that sometimes, toward the end. He could tell that Townsend was now sitting, turning his way.

"I hope you were a better doctor than a runner," Sean said.

For some unreason, Jon suddenly felt as if he'd been raised with shotguns all his life. It was now a part of him, an extension of his arm. A strange calm came over him. As he raised the weapon to waist level, he casually thumbed off the pushbutton safety. Without giving it another second's thought, he pointed the shotgun at the stranger and fired.

Even unconfined, the shotgun's concussive roar was considerably louder than either handgun. A sheet of bright-yellow flame reached out from the muzzle and momentarily lit up the darkness. Before the recoil knocked Jon backward, he could see the stranger topple. The darkness returned; and with it, a heavy silence.

Jon lay on his back, winded. His ears were ringing, and bright spots danced before his eyes. The shotgun slipped from his hands. His hand slid across his midsection, toward where he'd been shot. His abdomen ached. He expected to find the wetness, feel the wound. Yet, as his hand crossed his belt line, his fingers touched the heavy brass buckle of his uniform's belt. To his surprise, the thick metal was deeply indented, turned almost inside out by the impacting bullet. But it had not been penetrated. Jon laughed aloud, letting his head fall back into the snow.

He lay there for a minute or so, collecting his thoughts, feeling incredibly lucky. All he'd get from being shot at close range would be a bad bruise. But he couldn't afford to push his luck. Someone may have heard the shots, and besides, he had an appointment to keep. He pushed himself up and approached his pursuer, shotgun ready.

He needn't have worried. Beneath the big man's neck and shoulders, a widening liquid stain crept darkly outward in an expanding circle. The shotgun pellets had struck the man in the chin, nearly decapitating him. The metallic smell of draining blood rose upward with a warm, heavy stench. *Who was this man,* Jon thought, *and why did he want to take my life?* He bent over and rummaged through the man's jacket and pockets.

Half a minute later, he re-entered his house carrying the man's gun, keys, and thick billfold. The first thing he did was check out front. Peering past the drawn curtains, he found the street empty. His own snow-covered car was still there, seemingly untouched. In addition, there was a gray sedan of the type used by the Interagency Motor Pool. It had U.S. Government plates. The stranger obviously had both political clout and connections.

Keeping the shades drawn, he switched on one of the dimmer lamps. The stranger's gun, he noted, was a thirty-two-caliber automatic, a pocket pistol. But the instant he saw the caliber stamped into the frame, Jon knew it was the same pistol used to kill Mahmoud Al-Abed. It was probably also the same gun whose spent shell casings were "found" in the house, no doubt planted by Agent Lewis when the man conveniently disappeared during his first visit. Jon stuffed the gun in his pocket and opened the billfold.

According to his passport and North Carolina driver's license, the stranger was a man named Sean O'Brien. The name meant nothing to Jon. Turning the passport pages, he checked the visa stamps and found that O'Brien's most recent journeys abroad had been to Israel, Tunisia, and Jordan. He looked up, wondering. A man with an Irish name who lived in a Southern state and who spent time in Arabic-speaking countries. A man who probably also used the thirty-two-caliber automatic to kill a would-be Palestinian assassin. Jon began to see crosscurrents, political linkages. Bit by bit, the hazy Palestinian connection was slowly becoming clearer. A Palestinian had tried to assassinate

the first lady, only to be murdered by someone else shooting a
.32, someone Jon now thought was Sean O'Brien. And O'Brien—
aided by Agents Lewis, Johnson, and Fitzpatrick—wanted Jon
dead, presumably because he knew about the conspiracy to
poison the president.

Who, Jon wondered, stood to gain from such actions? For
now, the answer wasn't the least bit clear to him.

Perhaps the one person who could best make sense of things
was now at Camp David. Bob Meredith had the savvy, nose,
and the smarts for political riddles. Presented with all pieces
of the puzzle—if he were still mentally capable—the president,
Jon thought, should be able to come up with the whys and
wherefores. All of which made it even more essential that Jon
tell the president what was going on as soon as possible.

He glanced at O'Brien's key chain. There were two obvious
vehicle keys on a separate slender ring. *Why not?* Jon asked
himself. They'd still be looking for his car, which he wouldn't
be taking. And the stranger's body wouldn't be discovered
until daybreak. By then, one way or the other, Jon's Camp
David adventure would be over. It was highly doubtful that
his watchers would be looking for a nondescript government
vehicle.

Shotgun in hand, he crept out the front door. O'Brien's
footprints were prominent on the snowy walk. Jon nervously
followed the tracks to the curb. He half expected a caravan of
vehicles to come screeching toward him with sirens blaring,
but the only sound was the cold breeze that gently stirred the
nearby boughs. He quickly got in the car and started the engine.

Under ideal conditions, the sixty-mile trip to Camp David
could be driven in slightly more than an hour. But owing to
the storm, conditions were hardly ideal. Jon decided to drive
cautiously and allow two hours for the trip. He proceeded
slowly through local streets until he reached the interstate,
following the on-ramp to I-270 North.

The longest leg of the trip would be the straight northwest
shot to Frederick, Maryland. Traffic was sparse. The highway
was well ploughed, but Jon kept to the right-hand lane at a
sedate fifty miles per hour. He constantly checked the rearview

mirror, but no one seemed to be following. There was a briefcase on the passenger seat. As Jon settled in for the drive, he opened the briefcase. Keeping one eye on the road, he leafed through its contents.

The dashboard lamp made for dim but ample illumination. Jon pulled out a handful of paper pads, individual single-page documents, and manila folders, spreading them out on the seat. One of the folders, labeled with "The Doc" in handwritten script, contained a number of seemingly unrelated documents. There was a Baltimore/Washington International Airport concourse map, a Baltimore street atlas, brochures from the Johns Hopkins Medical institutions, a *Washington Post* article, and a grainy photo. When Jon peered closer, he saw that it was a picture of the murdered researcher, Dr. Jeremy Raskin. All of a sudden, the documents didn't seem unrelated at all. *Good God,* Jon thought, stunned.

Another folder contained photos. They were glossy, black-and-white eight-by-tens, professionally done. Some were telephoto shots. In the car's dim ivory light, Jon could see himself in the pictures—entering the house, or at the Naval Medical Center.

But what made him frown were the two-week-old pictures of him and Mireille leaving her apartment building. Obviously, the watchers had been interested in him for quite some time. He quickly pulled out the remaining photos, curious to see where the photographic trail led. What met his eyes nearly made him drive off the road.

Stunned, he had to tightly grip the wheel. His pulse was racing, and he momentarily had to focus on the road ahead to soothe his shrieking brain. *This can't be happening,* he thought. Regaining his composure, he glanced back at the telltale photos. He knew the pictures didn't lie. They were evidence, key pieces of the puzzle that was starting to come together in his mind, but that was as yet incomplete. He lifted the nearest picture and held it closer to the light for inspection.

She looked remarkably good for someone her age, he conceded. Then again, she was the same age as he. She had the full breasts and lithe figure of a woman two decades younger.

Then again, she had always looked good in her designer jeans and form-fitting tops, but until he saw her naked, Jon hadn't appreciated precisely how great. And it was abundantly clear, from the way her lover seemed fixated with her breasts, that Mitchell Forbes was also bedazzled with Amanda Doria.

Jon looked at another picture, similarly taken from above. A hidden surveillance camera had obviously taken the photos, which bore a digital date of approximately three weeks ago. From their grainy texture, Jon deduced that they were stills made from video camera footage. In the second photo, a deliriously aroused chief of staff lay on his back with his eyes closed, Amanda straddling him from above, back arched and head thrown back toward the camera. They both looked ecstatic.

He was sure the Secret Service logs could tell him when the pair had access to one another. *What am I supposed to make of this?* Jon asked himself. The chief of staff, the president's most trusted adviser, is secretly photographed having carnal knowledge of the vice president's buxom wife. All of which occurred at a time the entire nation was concerned about its beloved first lady. Yet Jon Townsend was a realist who understood that deep grieving never stood in the way of serious fucking.

From the expressions on their faces, the two lovers seemed deeply committed to one another, at least physically. Jon briefly wondered how long the affair had been going on, and who knew. Such *affaires du coeur* could not be concealed indefinitely. For a moment, Jon felt sorry for Vice President Doria. He didn't know Tony Doria that well, but the man always struck him as a decent guy. More to the point, what were the pictures doing in a trained killer's briefcase? On this point, he hadn't a clue.

The one thing of which he was certain was that it was all part of a larger conspiracy. It was a plot that, until just now, seemed to involve rogue government agents, Roxanne's shooting, a Palestinian hitman, a bizarre and ongoing attempt to kill the president, and efforts on Jon's own life. Add to that the murder of a noted researcher and an explosive love affair, and one had the kind of mind-boggling political intrigue that hadn't been seen since the days of the Kennedy Administration.

Reaching Frederick, he took U.S. 15 North to Thurmont, then

turned onto Maryland Route 77, toward Hagerstown. Following
the banks of Hunting Creek, Jon eventually reached Catoctin
Mountain Park and turned right at the visitor's center. The park
contained the presidential retreat. Continuing, he turned onto
a road that was the start of the security fence that encompassed
the camp's one hundred twenty-five acres of rocky, wooded
terrain.

His palms were sweating. Jon knew he was taking an
extraordinary, anxiety-provoking risk, but he didn't see that he
had much choice. Remaining on the run wasn't an acceptable
option, and besides, he had a duty to his patient. In the back of
his mind, he also thought he might be able to help the first lady.
Slowing the car, he looked at his watch. It was eight-fifty. In
the glare of his vehicle's headlights, the desolate approach road
was starkly beautiful. The bare tree limbs glistened with frost,
and the fir boughs drooped under the weight of their snowy
burdens.

Jon pulled over to the side of the road to wait. He didn't
want to arrive early.

Once he'd reach the camp's entrance, there was no turning
back. If for some reason Saunders wasn't at the main gate, Jon
was in serious trouble. Despite his old enlisted man's uniform
and the government car, it wouldn't take long for an alert guard
to associate him with the murder suspect sought by the police.
He couldn't let that happen. If Dave weren't in sight, he'd hang
a U and pray for horsepower. He squeezed the shotgun's grip,
hoping he wouldn't have to use it. Finally, at nine, he drove on.

The high, well-lit metal gates at the main entrance made it
clear that this was a maximum-security installation. The STOP
sign on the right-hand side of the road was superfluous. As
he approached, Jon saw the Marine sentry straighten up. Jon
tensed, tightening his grip on the weapon. But then he spotted
Dave behind the sentry. Jon braked to a halt before the gate,
clearly visible in the security lights. The gate opened.

The sentry waved him on.

Saunders came out of the guard post and pointed to
where Jon should park. Inside the compound, the roads were
well ploughed and relatively snow-free. Jon pulled up behind

an electric golf cart and waited for Dave to get in the car. He gathered the front-seat documents and replaced them in the briefcase. Dave opened the door and settled into the passenger seat, raising his eyebrows.

"I give up," he said. "What's with the uniform and the car?"

"Some people are still looking for me, right?"

"Yeah, but we told the TV people to back off the story."

"Fine. But until they do, I figure it might be safer not to wear the admiral's uniform. Is the president here?"

"Yes, up at Aspen."

At Camp David, all the rustic buildings were named after native American trees. Aspen was the presidential lodge.

"Does he know?"

"Not yet. I figured you'd want to tell him yourself. Where'd you get this car?"

"It's a loaner from someone who tried to kill me at my house." He handed Dave the passport. "His name was Sean O'Brien."

At the mention of the name, Dave's hooded lids narrowed. He slowly opened the passport and studied the photo.

"You know him?" Jon asked.

"Heard the name," Dave said slowly. "An unsavory prick, an Irish tough guy who was run out of Boston. Did some sort of low-level bullshit." He looked up. "Okay, what do you have to tell me?"

Jon quickly related what had happened earlier. Dave shook his head, astonished. "They want you bad, man. Did he say anything before you took his head off?"

"He knew that I was coming up here."

"You're kidding." Dave paused. "This is not good, Jon. If this O'Brien's part of a team, then some of the camp guests must be in on it. Which means they're expecting you, too. No, this puts a serious crimp in my plans."

"Who'd you tell I was coming?"

"The president, of course. He's the only one. But he's been very sociable tonight, his old charming self. Now that I know he's a little off," Saunders said, tapping his head, "there's no telling who else he let in on it."

"Who else is here?"

"There's about a half-dozen White House staff. A skeleton camp crew of maybe fifteen Navy personnel, and the same number of White House Communications Agency. The Secret Service—"

"Not Agent Lewis, I hope?"

"Don't be an idiot. And Vice President Doria, his wife, and Mr. Forbes tagged along."

"Oh, wonderful." Jon reached down and opened the briefcase, removing the folder with the photos. "You might want to take a look at these."

As Saunders slowly leafed through the glossies, Jon switched on the overhead light. The agent's expression went from perplexed to wide-eyed as he took in the pictures of the chief of staff and Amanda Doria. Dave slowly whistled and shook his head.

"What do you think?" Jon asked.

Dave whistled softly. "Some rack on this woman. I knew she had tits, but Jesus."

"I'm talking about motive."

"That, I'm not going to touch." Saunders let the pictures fall away. "But it *does* explain why Mitchie and Mandy have been spending so much time together."

"Does Bob know?"

"If he does, he hasn't let on."

"So, what's the plan?"

"I *was* going to bring you up to Aspen and let you talk to the president when he was by himself. That's the key, his being alone. There's hardly anybody in the camp, but there's still too damn many people around." He looked away, pensive. "Okay, here's what we're going to do."

Briefly, Dave explained what he had in mind. Then, leaving the shotgun in the car, Jon took the briefcase and followed Saunders into the golf cart. Jon's thin Navy pea jacket was scant protection against the steady wind. Fortunately, they weren't going far. The whirring cart carried them north through several crossroads and wooden one-story cabins called Cedar and Rosebud, Poplar and Hickory. Except for the building that housed the White House Communications Agency, few lights were on, and the camp had a subdued appearance. The road wound past Poplar toward the presidential area of the camp.

Jon wondered what President Meredith was doing on this cold and lonely New Year's Eve. The Aspen cabin, the first lodge build during the Franklin Roosevelt era, was a handsome structure with extensive flagstone patios, a swimming pool, and an artificial pond. Renovated numerous times, Aspen was the size of a large ranch house and currently had a kitchen, a pantry, a living room/dining room, four bedrooms, two baths, a lounge, and five fireplaces. Jon could picture Bob Meredith sitting before the large stone fireplace with the presidential seal, contentedly smoking his Godawful pipe. Yet no amount of rustic comfort could make up for the deep ache that now filled the president's life.

There was no one else in sight, and the roadways were deserted. Saunders pulled to a stop at a guest cabin called Birch. When he got out and unlocked the door, Jon followed him inside, carrying the briefcase.

"Wait here," Dave said, leaving the lights off. "I'll see if I can drag him down here. Just keep the lights off and sit tight."

"Where are the others?"

"Mr. Forbes is at Aspen with the president. The vice president and his wife are in Holly." He watched Jon reach into his pocket. "What the hell are you doing?"

Jon removed his new cell phone. "I want to check on Mireille. It's been a while since I spoke to her."

"Give me that." Dave snatched the phone from Jon's hand. "What're you, nuts? There's some of the world's most sophisticated listening equipment right around the corner, and you're trying to give your location away!"

"I thought that was the reason I bought the new cell," said Jon, confused. "So they wouldn't be able to track me."

"Don't take any chances, okay? Just stay here until I get back."

Saunders walked away, leaving Jon in the dark. When the agent left the cabin, there was a click as the front door was locked. Jon stood there in silence, absorbing his surroundings.

His eyes slowly grew accustomed to the darkness. Outside, a low moan was a windsong that sailed through snow-laden trees. A modest amount of moonlight came through the thin curtains of Birch's ample windows. When Jon's night vision was sufficient, he gingerly walked through the cabin.

He found himself in the center of a large living room with a vaulted ceiling and a huge stone fireplace. He'd heard that the guest cabins had all been rebuilt, and this one was certainly handsome enough. In the midst of these forested mountains, the cabin had a relaxed, lazy informality that could cut through the tension of politics or peace talks. Yet although Jon was calm enough, he was hardly relaxed. What Dave said bothered him.

His friend's words sounded plausible enough, but they didn't ring true. What was wrong with checking on Mireille? Jon was no expert on electronic eavesdropping, but he did know that such surveillance had to be conducted by orbiting satellites, not some parabolic mike a few hundred yards away. Maybe the agent was just overly cautious. And perhaps Jon had misread the furtive look in his friend's eyes when Dave had grabbed the cell phone. Still…unconvinced, Jon crept through the cabin with a growing apprehension.

Birch had two bedrooms and two baths, and the down-to-earth furnishings gave the cabin a warm, lived-in look. By now, Jon thought, Saunders should have reached the president in Aspen. If Bob Meredith was the friend Jon thought he was, he'd free himself up and get down there in a few minutes, if for no other reason than to confront the doctor about what was being said on the news. As the minutes passed, Jon slowly ambled through the darkness, growing more and more apprehensive. Hiding in an unlit building in one of the nation's most secret locations was spooky enough. The fact that there were people out there who wanted him dead added to his misgivings. He fidgeted, drumming his fingers against the walls, unable to keep still. He returned to the living room and paused before the drawn curtains, slowly inching them apart.

Outside, the snow-covered tree limbs swayed in the inconstant moonlight. Beyond the branches, a three-quarters moon played hide and seek behind fast-moving gray clouds.

Sensing movement, Jon looked closer. What he saw left him as pale as the snow.

Beyond the living room was a patio. At its edge, not twenty feet away, was the unmistakable moonlit face of Agent Lewis. Heart pounding, Jon jerked his head back before he could be seen. As his shock wore off, he cautiously looked back.

Jon doubted the man had seen the slight rustling of the curtains. Momentarily bathed in moonlight, Lewis' head was lowered. The agent was putting on a pair of what were unmistakably night vision goggles. He was carrying a weapon that hung from his shoulder by a sling. Most frightening of all, his footprints indicated he was heading right for the cabin.

With his brain on fire, a thousand thoughts raced through Jon's mind. According to Dave Saunders, Lewis wasn't supposed to be anywhere near Camp David. Yet even if he were a rogue agent, Lewis was also Secret Service on the presidential detail, which meant he could probably go anywhere the president went. But that still didn't explain how Lewis knew Jon was at the presidential retreat, much less why he was now approaching Birch. As Jon struggled with the icy touch of betrayal, his foremost concern was what to do now.

Just how high does this conspiracy go? he thought. Certainly, O'Brien and Agent Lewis were part of it, not to mention Johnson and Fitzpatrick. But how many others knew—and were they here, at Camp David? Mitch Forbes had to be involved in some way, and maybe Mrs. Doria. Jon was sickened by his mounting suspicion of his trusted friend Dave Saunders. Yet beyond such matters was the immediate problem of Agent Lewis, who seemed determined to enter the house and kill him.

As he stepped back from the window, Jon's pulse thudded in his temples. He wondered if Lewis had come alone. There might be another shooter out front. As Jon backed up, he frantically looked from side to side, scouring the room for something with which to defend himself. He still had O'Brien's pocket pistol, but if he used it, the noise would bring others running—and he could forget about a private chat with Bob Meredith. He'd save the automatic for a last resort.

The kitchen, he suddenly thought. There had to be knives in the kitchen. Any sort of knife was better than his bare hands. As Jon retreated, he backed into the stone hearth. There, hanging from an iron rack, was an assortment of fireplace instruments. Jon lifted the poker. The cast-iron rod had considerable heft, and he gripped it by the handle with two hands, like a baseball bat. Raising the poker, he stood there motionless, palms moist, shallow breath coming fast in his throat. He cocked his head, straining to pluck sounds from the background wind. For a while he heard nothing. But then, from the back of the house, he heard the muffled scrape of a window being raised.

Bastard's not coming across the patio at all, Jon thought. *Wants to creep up on me from behind, catch me on the sofa.* Heart in his mouth, Jon forced himself flush with the fireplace stone. Back pressed into the wall, he carefully slid sideways toward a corner of the room, where the intersecting hall emerged from the bedroom area. His raised arms were trembling. He clutched the metal rod with such isometric tension that his muscles started to ache.

Outside, the wind kept up its drone, making it hard for him to hear anything but the pounding of his heart. But then, from midway down the corridor, he heard the faint creak of a floorboard. He held his head sideways, eyes riveted on the hall. He felt starved for oxygen. He was now breathing so fast he was afraid Lewis would hear his respirations. And then, ever so slowly, a dark cylinder emerged from the hall.

He recognized the stout silencer. In his years around the president, Jon had seen his share of close-quarters entry weapons. Behind the silencer was the unmistakable outline of a Heckler & Koch MP5SD submachine gun. Lewis' gloved fingers were already inside the trigger guard. Jon tensed. When the agent's night vision goggles came into view, Jon swung the rod with all his might.

The heavy poker smashed into the goggle lenses with a splintering crash. As Lewis' head snapped back, his fingers contracted on the trigger. The silencer rose toward the ceiling, and an abbreviated, muted series of staccato spits sent nine-millimeter bullets roofward. Jon yanked the poker back and leapt into the hall, poised to swing again. As Lewis thudded against the floor headfirst, the H&K slipped from his fingers.

Jon hesitated. His breath came in fiery spasms, and icy beads of sweat dripped down his neck. Beneath him, the agent was motionless.

"Don't move a fucking muscle," Jon said, watching closely. He reached down and snatched the firearm away. "Lewis?"

A rasping rose up, a gurgling sound. Beneath the silencer, a small flashlight was attached to the MP5's frame. Jon switched it on and pointed it at his assailant. What was left of Lewis' goggles still clung to the man's head by straps. The agent's lower jaw was slack, and his breath rattled wetly through his open mouth. Jon slowly knelt and undid the straps. What he saw made him grit his teeth.

The force of the blow had pulverized the facial bones around Lewis' eyes. Blood and gore dripped from the shattered sockets. The eyes themselves were ruptured by shards of fractured goggle material driven back through the agent's retinas. If some of the pieces had penetrated the brain, the wound would be fatal. Jon lifted the agent's sleeve and felt for the pulse. As he did, Lewis' whistling breath slowed.

Jon found the beat, which was very weak. Abruptly, the pulse stopped. Jon checked closely with his fingertips, but it was gone. He slowly sank onto his haunches, taking a deep breath, staring dispassionately at the face of the man who had tried to kill him. Whatever remorse he might once have felt had vanished.

There had been a time, long ago and far away, when he probably should have killed in anger. The fact that he hadn't haunted him for the rest of his life. Yet today, he had killed in fear and anger not once, but twice. He didn't feel as if he had a choice. It was Survival 101, kill or be killed. Yet what Jon found most curious was not what he'd done, but the absence of negative feelings about what he'd done. Perhaps it was a change that came with age or maturity. *Screw it*, he finally thought. *Whatever the reason, the bastards tried to kill me.*

"Lewis, come in," came a faint, tinny voice.

Jon whirled, alert for someone behind him. There was nothing but the shadows dancing in the intermittent moonlight. Looking back down the hall, he saw only darkness. Then the voice spoke again.

"If you're clear, buddy, let's hear from you."

The faint sound came from below him. Shining the light in that direction, Jon spotted the coiled wire and communications earpiece. Since they were dwarfed by the huge goggles, he hadn't noticed them before. And where there was a Secret Service earpiece, he knew there had to be a mike. He searched under the agent's lapel and found the dime-size microphone. Unpinning it, he lifted it to his lips.

"Go on."

"How's it goin' down there? Thought you'd be done by now."

Jon wasn't sure he recognized the voice. "Just finished."

"Okay, we'll be down soon."

In the ensuing silence, Jon untwisted the communications wires from the agent's clothing. Then he put on the earpiece and attached the mike to his pea coat, all the while wondering who "we" was. He certainly wasn't going to hang around to find out. He might have lucked out with one opponent, but he was no match for a tag team. If the president wouldn't come to him, he had no problem with the idea of going to the president. He picked up the submachine gun and went to the living room to retrieve the briefcase.

It was time to do what he had come for.

CHAPTER 25

Keeping the flashlight off, Jon left the cabin by the patio entrance. Outside, the cold wind continued to sing. The presidential cabin wasn't far. Yet walking straight up the cleared roads was not a good idea. Jon preferred the welcome shelter of the woods, where the thick trunks and dark shadows were an ally. Unfortunately, he wasn't wearing snow boots. In places, the drifts were a foot thick, and the going was treacherous. But there was enough moonlight to guide the way. At length, the outline of Aspen came into view, floodlit by security lamps.

The main entrance to the residence was from the northeast. There was always a guard outside, usually a Secret Service agent. Jon didn't think he could get past the man peacefully, and his weapon was a certain invitation to confrontation. He'd have to enter Aspen from another direction. Jon knew that Meredith was a peripatetic politician whose surplus energy left him always on the move. When Jon had last visited Camp David, the president was constantly going in and out of the cabin through various doors. Hopefully, this would still be the case.

Jon skirted the property outside of the lights' glare. He came in from the north. Stealing across the snow-covered golf green, he moved counterclockwise, circumventing the west-side pond. Circling south, he eventually came to the southwestern edge of the large swimming pool built by President Nixon. Lower and upper patios surrounded the pool area, and several cabin doors abutted the patios. Keeping to a crouch, briefcase in one hand and submachine gun in the other, Jon carefully mounted the patio steps. Now illuminated by the security lights, he was just past the guard's peripheral vision.

Beyond the upper patio, the cabin's rooms were dark, and the interior shades were drawn. Jon slid along the wall until he came to a door. He cautiously tried it. To his relief, it was unlocked. He carefully let himself inside and listened. From across the house, he heard faint voices and music. Ever so slowly, he crept in that direction.

He didn't recognize the voices. But as he tiptoed through the lodge, he realized the sounds were coming from the lounge. The Aspen lounge had motion picture capabilities, and current feature films were the usual fare. As he drew nearer, Jon caught his first whiff of lethal presidential tobacco. He nervously approached the lounge door and chanced a look around the doorframe.

The lights were off, and the room's occupants faced away from him, toward the large projection screen. Horizontal layers of tobacco smoke wafted upward in the projector's beam. Jon could make out the president, Mrs. Doria, and Mitchell Forbes, all seated with their backs toward him. He wondered about the others. Ever so slowly, he walked into the lounge.

Intent on their movie, no one saw him enter. The H&K was in Jon's right hand, and his finger rested outside the trigger guard. He walked over to the projector, switched it off, and flipped on the lights.

"What the hell?" said Bob Meredith, with a rising inflection.

The first to turn around was Forbes. When he saw Jon, he blanched, and his voice was a faint drone. "Jesus Christ."

From Amanda Doria, a startled gasp.

The president was the last to spot him. Meredith's expression bespoke confusion. "Godalmighty, son, what are you doing here? And will you put that thing down?"

"I'm sorry, Mr. President, no can do. I need this for my own protection."

"Bullshit," said Forbes, "you came to kill us, didn't you? And what do you think's going to happen then? There's Secret Service all over this place!"

"I'm not here to kill anyone, and you know it. If I was, you'd already be dead."

"He's got a point there, Mitch."

"Mr. President, I was told you knew I was coming up here tonight."

Meredith shook his head. "I'm afraid not."

Jon's feeling of betrayal rose. "I came here to save your life, Bob."

"Oh, please," said Forbes. "Carrying a machine gun with a silencer? What medical school did you learn that in?"

Jon ignored the taunt. "Where's everybody else?"

"Who?" Meredith asked.

Jon turned to Amanda Doria. "Your husband, for one."

"He went for a walk a little while ago."

"By himself?"

"No, with Agent Saunders."

"Really?" said Jon, demoralized. "Then I'd better say what I have to. Take a look at this, Mr. President."

He gently tossed the briefcase underhanded. Meredith's reflexes had deteriorated to the point he couldn't catch it, and the case fell to the floor at his feet. He picked it up and opened the latch. "Exactly what do you want me to look at?"

"There's a manila folder with pictures inside."

Meredith's hand shook, more from his poisoning than the uninvited guest. He removed the folder, placed it on his lap, and opened it to the first photo. He looked at it long and hard, then glanced at Forbes and Amanda. Returning his gaze to the pictures, he slowly studied the next one, then the print beneath it. As he did, a sly grin curled his lips. "I'd heard rumors," he said. "But until now, I never gave it much thought."

"Let me see that," Forbes insisted, reaching out.

Meredith snapped the folder closed. "Keep your pants on," he said sharply. "At least, tonight." To Jon, "Okay, I've looked. We're all adults here, Jon. Things like this happen. Am I supposed to make something out of this?"

"That's what I was hoping you'd tell me, sir. All I know is that it's part of a bigger picture, and I need help in figuring it out."

Forbes rolled his eyes. "This is such monumental crap."

"I'm listening," said Meredith.

"For starters, Mr. President, I didn't shoot your wife, and—"

"He's full of shit, Bob," Forbes interrupted. "We've already gone over this. The evidence is just too solid."

Meredith looked at Jon. "What about that, Doc?"

"I can't say, Mr. President. All I can say is that I didn't do it. But I *can* tell you this: that I have some new information about your medical exam. I didn't give you all the test results, Mitch, because there were one or two tests I overlooked. But the results are in now, Mr. President, and they're a matter of record in the hospital lab."

Meredith's shakes were pronounced. "And?" he asked.

"You have mercury poisoning, sir. The mercury levels in your blood are highly toxic and have been for months."

"Did you say mercury?"

"Yes, sir, I did. Two months ago, your wife came to me. We spoke confidentially about certain symptoms you were having. Things like irritability, memory loss, personality change. I know you, Bob. You're a proud man, and at first I think you didn't want to admit there was a problem."

At the mention of Roxanne, Meredith's eyes clouded over. "Well, maybe I didn't. But she was right." He paused, staring at his shaking hands. "She's always right."

"And she can keep being right," Jon continued. "If you're still open to the idea of something experimental, I think I've found a way to help her. But as far as your health's concerned," Jon went on, "I now know that of your symptoms come from mercury. It's what chronic ingestion of mercury does to the brain. It can make you seem like some doddering old fool who can't get his act together. The sad part is, your wife *knew* there was something wrong. She kept pressing me to look into it. And in the end, her insistence led to her shooting."

"Bob," Amanda said sharply, "this is ridiculous!"

"I thought so too, sir," Jon went on. "In the beginning, I couldn't see any connection. But when I finally did what she wanted and began looking for answers, funny things started happening to me, too. First it was cyanide, then a couple of FBI guys named Johnson and Fitzpatrick. I'm sure you've heard of them by now. They were followed by two other boys with toys, one a Secret Service agent named Lewis." He lifted the H&K.

"This belonged to him."

"Bob," said an exasperated Forbes, "he's delusional. You don't have to keep humoring this idiot."

"For once in your life," Meredith said to his chief of staff, "just shut the hell up!" He turned to Jon. "For Rocky's sake, I hope there's at least some truth in what you're saying. But why would wanting to learn what's wrong with me get make someone want to kill her?"

"That's what we need to figure out. Let's start with *how* you're getting sick. A lot of ordinary people suffer from mercury intoxication, Mr. President. Usually through eating it, or from inhaling fumes in factories. But no one, to my knowledge, has ever gotten it through smoking."

Meredith's eyes narrowed. "What are you saying?"

"Do you remember Mr. Phillips, the old White House usher?" Off the president's nod, Jon continued. "He had exactly the same problem you do. The shakes, memory loss, irritability. Unfortunately, he wasn't in as good a shape as you. He used to roll his own cigarettes, and guess what he smoked? Your pipe tobacco."

Until then, Meredith had been holding his pipe by the bowl. Ever so slowly, he looked at it and placed it in the ashtray. "I gave it to him, you know. He loved the aroma, so I let him have some." He paused. "My God, you're saying he was poisoned, too?"

Jon nodded.

"So, my pipe tobacco..." He didn't finish, instead casting a long look at Amanda Doria.

Forbes got to his feet. "This is such a load of crap! I—"

"Sit down!" Meredith shouted, his anger apparent. He thrust the folder into Forbes' hands. "Maybe this will shut you up a while. So, you're suggesting, Dr. Townsend, that my Virginia hurley's contaminated with mercury?"

"Yes, sir. And when you smoke it, the toxic mercury vapors enter your body through your lungs."

Forbes glanced at the first photo. "Oh, my God," he softly mouthed.

"My memory's not too good any more, but I think you're

also suggesting," the president continued, "that if the mercury got into my humidor intentionally, somebody might be guilty of a federal crime."

"Yes, sir, I am. There's an antidote for your condition, Mr. President. It'll work if given now. But in another year or so, you'd be dead."

"I see." The president arose unsteadily and slowly began to pace, walking as he thought, as was his custom. "So, if Rocky had never turned you on to this, and if you hadn't checked me out—well, that would have been it for me."

"That's how I see it, yes."

"And maybe some old boy might have stood to gain by my death."

"I hadn't gotten that far, sir."

Amanda Doria, who had walked over to look past Forbes' shoulder at the folder, emitted a stifled cry. Then she pivoted and looked away.

"Now, who might that have been?" Meredith continued. "You mentioned the big picture before, Jon, and I'm starting to get a glimmer. Damn, talk about the night they drove Dixie down. Owing to my memory, you don't mind if I talk this out while I think, do you?"

"That was the general idea, sir. I need help with this."

"You see, Jon, until this very second, I never really understood the Arab connection."

"Before you go on," Jon interrupted, "you might want to check out the smaller folder in there."

Meredith reached into the briefcase and removed the Raskin documents, slowly looking them over. "This is the researcher that got killed, that Southern Cross thing. I don't get what this has to do with me."

"That briefcase belonged to a man named Sean O'Brien. He was the Southern Cross leader who took orders from someone very high up, probably in the administration. He tried to kill me today. And unless I've figured everything wrong, he was the one who killed the man who shot your wife. It seems to me that the Southern Cross people were actually behind Mrs. Meredith's assassination attempt."

"You're not denying that the Palestinian shot Rocky, are you?"

"No, I'm not. I'm just saying that it's very complicated, and things aren't what they seem."

"But let's stick with the Arab piece a second," the president slowly said. "Now, this whole Middle East thing—sending our boys in as peacekeepers, for starters—is taking a beating these days. Ever since Rocky was shot, most of our fellow citizens want us out of that area. Give the desert back to the camel jockeys. Down with OPEC. Let 'em keep the damn oil, we'll use our own. You see where I'm going with this?"

Jon wasn't sure. "It's a little confusing, Mr. President."

"All right, then let me clear it up for you. Maybe the Palestinian was set up like you say, but he *did* shoot the first lady. Do the Palestinians want us in the Golan and Gaza as peacekeepers? Hell, no. They'd rather push the Israelis back into the Med. But even someone as cynical as me doesn't think they're crazy enough to send an assassin to Washington."

"What about the other countries in that region?"

"You've always had a quick mind, Jon. I was just getting to that. But whatever those countries might say, the answer to your question is no. They don't want American troops there any more than the Palestinians, because our presence keeps oil prices low. But I seriously doubt any Middle Eastern leader would be so rash as to go after Roxanne and me. The price they'd pay is just too great. So, getting back to what I asked before, if it's not the Arabs, who stands to gain by my death?"

"The same people who hired Mahmoud Al-Abed?"

"You got it," Meredith nodded. "That's where I'd put my money. Maybe it was these Southern Cross boys. But that begs the question."

Jon just stared back in silence.

"Look at it this way. If America retrenches and we pull out of the Middle East, and oil prices rise, what people in this country benefit?'

"Domestic oil producers, I guess."

"That's a given. But who else? No takers?" Meredith's cheeks twitched grotesquely from the mercury. Voice rising, he turned to his side. "Care to venture a guess, Mandy dearest?"

Jon spoke up. "Probably the same people who put the mercury in your tobacco."

"Precisely!" said Meredith, thrusting a shaking finger in the air. "And besides oil men, there are the oil man's enemies. The folks who make fuel cells, hydropower, flywheels. In a word, alternative energy."

Peering at Jon, the president hesitated, letting his words sink in. All at once, the spark of recognition flared in Jon's eyes, and he had a sinking, sickening feeling. He stared at Amanda Doria's turned back. He was so flabbergasted that when he opened his mouth to speak, no words came out. A wry, tortured smile twisted the president's mouth, and he slowly approached the physician.

"You see it now, don't you? How it all comes together so nicely? How the man who has the most to gain—the most influential voice in alternative energy policy in this hemisphere—is also the man who gave me a gift of choice pipe tobacco early last summer?"

Jon's hoarse voice felt stuck in his throat. "Vice President Doria?"

Meredith clapped him on the shoulder. "You got it, son."

"Bob, please!" Forbes cried, getting to his feet once more. "I swear to God, I had no idea!"

"If that's so," Meredith calmly replied, "how come you're messing around with Tony's wife?"

"It's not what you think," Forbes murmured, crestfallen. "Amanda and I, we... There was actually something between us."

"How touching." Meredith turned to Mrs. Doria. "That right, sugar?"

"With that horse's ass?" She sniffed derisively. "What a joke."

Forbes gasped, dumbstruck. Seeing this, Meredith chuckled. "Looks like you've been had, old friend. I'm sure a special prosecutor will be able to straighten this all out. But in the meantime, tell me. I know this couldn't have been a one-way street. Just what did you do for this little lady in exchange for her favors?"

"Not enough, that's obvious," said Mrs. Doria.

"Mr. President," Forbes pleaded, "you've got to believe me! I had no idea it would turn out like this!"

"You don't say? You had nothing to do with Rocky, or with the sweetener in my pipe tobacco?"

"On my mother's grave, I swear it!"

"So, what *did* you tell her?"

"Little things," Forbes said sheepishly. "Schedules, timing. It seemed so inconsequential that…" he gave his head a forlorn shake. "I honestly had no idea."

"The village idiot," Jon said.

But no sooner had Jon uttered the words than the back of his head seemed to explode. Everything went dark. Jon's knees gave way, and he pitched forward onto the floor. Lying there semiconscious, he was unable to move, but he could hear everything being said. Footsteps came up behind him. A hand reached down to retrieve the H&K.

"That's an active mike, Jon," said Dave Saunders from above him. "Guess you didn't know about that, but we could hear everything you said in here."

Jon's head was pounding, and he could feel blood trickling down to his ear. He forced his eyes open and turned his head painfully to one side. Dave was holding a government-issue nine-millimeter Beretta to which a long silencer was attached, a silencer he'd used to club Jon. He pressed the tip of his shoe into Jon's back.

"Sit tight, my friend."

My friend, Jon thought. Despite the throbbing in his head, his mind was completely lucid. Had he ever been Dave Saunders' friend at all? Fishing buddies…pals who shared a laugh and a beer together. If so, the laugh was on him. Was it all a ruse? Had Dave simply been using him as a conduit for information about the president?

Back in college, his fraternity brothers issued an annual "wedge" award for the person considered to be the simplest tool. That's how Jon felt now: used and dirty, like a simple tool. As he lay there, he wondered how long it took to truly get to know someone. To rely on them, to trust them, to know their every thought. As the months and years went by, you grew more and more comfortable in their presence, until finally, at some point, you say, *Yes, I really know this person.* And the hardest part is when you discover that it's all an illusion.

"Christ almighty, it took you long enough," said Amanda. She rushed across the room to her husband, who stood beside Agent Saunders.

"Amanda!" Forbes cried, obviously wounded. "I don't understand. How could you?"

"That's easy," said Tony Doria. "She's a pragmatist, fella. My wife wants to be first lady, and she knows you sometimes have to do distasteful things to get what you want."

"Distasteful?" Hurt and irony twisted Forbes' face. "Good God, you knew we were being photographed?"

"Of course I knew," she casually replied. "Does that hurt your sensibilities, Mitch? What's wrong, never fucked before an audience? I didn't think so. We figured that if you ever found out what was going on, the pictures would convince you to keep your mouth shut."

"A moot point, now," said the vice president.

Stung, Forbes' eyes blazed. His nostrils flared, and the muscles worked in his cheeks. Bursting with anger, he took a menacing step toward Amanda.

Saunders' arm swung up steady as a metronome. When it reached the horizontal, a muted "pffft" came from the Beretta. Forbes' head snapped back, and he collapsed in a lifeless heap. Droplets of blood splattered the president.

Shocked though he was, Meredith struggled to appear unruffled. With jerky movements, he nonchalantly wiped at the crimson spots that dotted his cheek. Despite his neurological symptoms, he looked resolute. "My memory's not what it used to be," he said. "And my moods might have changed. But I'm still pretty good at figuring things out. And I have to tell you, Tony, without what Dr. Townsend told me, I never would've guessed."

"You're not supposed to guess. You're supposed to die. We've been trying to do you in for months now."

"The pipe tobacco?"

"That was one way," Doria said with apparent disinterest. "And you should have died at the Israeli state dinner, if things had worked out right. Your wife was supposed to die too, except the assholes O'Brien hired couldn't get the job done. What a bunch of fuck-ups. Too bad about Sean, though."

"Who was this Sean O'Brien?"

"Sean was an Irish kid who got in way over his head in Boston. After I saved his ass, he'd do anything for me. Townsend was right. O'Brien set up the Southern Cross. It was all misdirection. Why not use the fucking Palestinians? Everyone else does."

"So, it was about me, all along?" said the president. "The Southern Cross, the Palestinians—they were just to throw people off the scent?"

"And to make it easier to get rid of you," said Doria. "But since we can't wait for the mercury to kill you, we'll have to do it the old-fashioned way."

As he lay on the floor, Jon could feel the outline of O'Brien's small automatic in his pants pocket.

"What's going to be your explanation for killing me?"

"That's just it—we're not the ones who are going to kill you. Dr. Townsend here is going to kill you. The poor man just couldn't take the resentment that built up over thirty years. He drove all the way up here to give you a personal New Year's greeting. First, he killed the guard at the main gate—"

God in heaven, thought Jon.

"—and then he caved in Agent Lewis' face on his way up to get you."

"Nobody's going to believe that."

"When all three of us say the same thing?" Doria continued. "That when we went out for a walk, we saw Townsend shoot the cabin guard? That poor Agent Saunders rushed back a fraction late to save you? Come on, they'll believe it just fine."

Jon needed an opening. Lying there, beneath a man holding a submachine gun, he knew he didn't stand a chance. But since they planned to kill him anyway, he was going to seize the slightest opportunity.

"I had no idea how much you hated my guts, Tony."

"I don't hate you, Mr. President. I hate what you're doing to this country. Your stupid softness on abortion. Your bullshit economic globalization. Your troops in the Middle East, gimme a break. The country deserves better."

"Put down the gun, Mr. Saunders!"

Out of the corner of his eye, Jon saw a blur of movement. A Secret Service agent appeared in the doorway, blood streaming down his face from a head wound. If Saunders was surprised, he didn't show it. He whirled and crouched at the same time, firing two quick shots before the weakened agent could return fire.

Jon needed no prompting. He quickly rolled onto his back and reached into his pocket. The president also reacted swiftly, lunging toward Saunders. The fingertips of his outstretched arms nearly reached the agent's neck when Saunders pivoted back again. Before his aim was thrown off, his silenced Beretta fired one more time.

The bullet tore through Meredith's shoulder and spun him around. Momentarily thrown off stride, Saunders was undeterred. He carefully took aim at the center of the president's torso. But before he could deliver the kill shot, Jon freed the automatic and quickly fired upward, without aiming. The bullets ripped upwards through Saunders' neck, into his brain. Jon pulled the trigger over and over, but the gun was now empty.

Agent Saunders toppled backward. He struck the floor with a crash, and the Beretta slid from his hand, skittering across the floor toward Vice President Doria's feet.

By now, Meredith had sunk to one knee. Grimacing in pain, he clutched his shoulder with his other hand. Blood flowed freely through his fingertips.

"Tony!" Amanda cried. "The gun!"

Jon rolled to his knees, head pounding. With the president to his left and the Dorias to his right, he was distracted by the events on either side of him. The president clearly needed medical assistance, but the Dorias were an immediate threat. He tossed away the empty pistol and reached for the H&K.

Tony Doria stared numbly at the Beretta. He seemed

incapable of action, frozen in place. Beside him, his wife gaped at him in disbelief. As Jon glanced their way, the truth about who was ultimately behind the conspiracy became abundantly clear. For all the vice president's political acumen, his wife was the consummate controller.

"God, you're unbelievable," she snapped at her husband, rolling her eyes. "I can't depend on you for a damn thing." She bent over and reached for the Beretta.

Through his pain, the president watched the drama unfold. Looking at his doctor, he saw Townsend's hand grasp the submachine gun. But then, as the H&K's silencer rose toward the threat, it hesitated. The president was incredulous.

"Shoot her!" he cried. "For Christ sake, shoot her!"

From the distant reaches of his memory, Jon recalled a similar order once issued by his commander. A blur of thoughts raced through his mind, not the least of which was that his adversary was a woman. Despite having to defend himself repeatedly that day, at heart he was a healer, not a killer. Yet the foremost thing on his mind, as he knelt there in a rustic cabin on a frigid New Year's Eve, was of holding an M-16 thirty years before, half a world away, on the hillside of a warm but frightening forest. He'd been unable to act, then; and that inability had haunted him for the rest of his life.

Amanda's hand closed around the Beretta. She lifted it toward the president.

Jon pulled the trigger.

EPILOGUE

The Potomac River

As the presidential yacht cruised up the Potomac, returning to its base at Quantico, the afternoon June sun spread its warming rays across the river, anointing each choppy wave with a golden crest. Motoring lazily northwest in mid-channel, the yacht was ferrying its five passengers back to their starting point after an all-day voyage. Basking in the sun, Tommie and Roxanne sat on the bridge in identical wheelchairs, flanked by Jon, Mireille, and the president. Meredith was fully recovered from his gunshot wound. It had been six months since Tommie had been treated by her father, and nearly as long for the first lady. Both patients had done remarkably well since their stem cell treatments.

"They call this 'the nation's river'," Meredith said to Jon. "Sometimes the history's so thick you can feel it. George Washington was born right over there, at Wakefield," he said, pointing with a finger that no longer shook from mercury poisoning.

"I thought he was born at Mount Vernon."

"No, Mount Vernon came later in his life. James Monroe was born nearby, too. Folks from Captain John Smith to Robert E. Lee sailed these waters. The Potomac's always been at the center of our country's past."

Listening to the president speak, Jon had to marvel at the man's articulation of national pride. This was the Bob Meredith he'd always known and respected, free of memory loss, shakes, and irritability. Shortly after the incident at Camp David, the president began taking chelating agents, compounds that physically bound to substances like metallic mercury, removing them from the body. By all estimates, the drugs had been extremely effective.

"You sound more like a historian than a politician."

"Politics and history are bedfellows, Jon. History's alive, and every politician should learn from it. Someone once said a page of history's worth a volume of logic, and I firmly believe that now. In my case, maybe I wasn't paying enough attention when I should've been."

"Come on, Mr. President, you were a victim. What happened wasn't your fault."

"That's baloney. I should've seen it coming. I didn't because I got too distracted from what's most important to me," he said, gesturing toward Roxanne. "But no more."

Looking over at the first lady's sun-softened face, Jon understood. Though she still faced a lengthy rehabilitation, Mrs. Meredith was now alert, active, and speaking. Tommie, similarly, had made dramatic progress and was on the verge of walking.

"So, you've ruled out another term?"

"Yes, I have. Best leave it to someone a little more dedicated than I am. But you and I are lucky men, Jon. We went through some bad times, but in the end, we wound up with what's most precious to us, wouldn't you say?"

Jon simply nodded. *And maybe*, he thought, *learned a little more about ourselves in the process.*

ABOUT THE AUTHOR

David Shobin is an obstetrician/gynecologist who has been an Assistant Clinical Professor at the State University of New York at Stony Brook for over three decades. His first novel, THE UNBORN, was a New York Times bestseller. An author of medical thrillers, he has also written THE SEEDING, THE OBSESSION, THE CENTER, TERMINAL CONDITION, THE PROVIDER, and THE CURE. He is currently in the private practice of OB/GYN, specializing in reproductive health. He lives and works on Long Island.

Curious about other Crossroad Press books?
Stop by our site:
http://www.crossroadpress.com
We offer quality writing
in digital, audio, and print formats.

Made in the USA
Las Vegas, NV
08 March 2021